Written Wings

A Vectra Tillerman Adventure 1

Originally Published September 2024

Sarah Ickes

Greek Mythology | Fantasy Adventure | YA

"*If you find yourself spilling your most darkened secrets and feelings, you might want to lay off of the honesty syrup in your tea.*"

Thank you!

to both Sherrys, who were my guinea pigs with
this story.

A Special Note for the Reader

Many of the references to the historical objects and events in this book, have real research to back them up. If you are interested in taking a peek behind the writer's curtain, to glimpse into the works I used for inspiration, you can check out three bullet points included in the back of this novel, as well as visit my website for a more indepth look.

www.SarahIckesArt.com

Some words in this novel are older, and are not spelling errors. Definitions can be found at my website.

Thank you for trying out my story, and I hope that you enjoy the shared journey with history that Vectra is about to embark on, with you.

and don't miss out on all the action!

<u>Murial Robertson Mysteries</u>
The Serpent's Star
Angled for Revenge
A Counterfeit of Death
An Ancient Poison (2025)

<u>Vectra Tillerman Adventures</u>
Written Wings
The Fall of Time (coming soon)

<u>Vectra and Murial Cross-Over</u>
The Nation's Grief (coming soon)

<u>A Family's Masterpiece Series</u>
A Family's Masterpiece (2025)

<u>Cybil Lawson Mysteries</u>
The Ghost of Christmas Pastel (2024)

Dedicated to the "real" Portobello road, and the treasure of a story it carries.

Characters

Monica Browning	fourteen-year-old teenager, older sister to Dare
Derrick "Dare" Browning	ten-year-old boy, youngest sibling of the Brownings
Trevor Browning	brother, and Legal Guardian of Monica and Dare
Artenian	ancient Greek warrior, visited Monica in a dream
Vectra Tillerman	mysterious woman Monica and Dare are sent to find
Gaither	millionaire, used to employ the Brownings' parents, and Trevor's boss
Weston	works for Gaither
Nicholas	works for Gaither
Tom	works for Gaither
Ergon	works for Gaither
Catriona Locksmith	old tea seller, lives in a run-down house with her brother
Jeffrey Locksmith	old plant hunter, lives in a rundown house with his sister
Servius	curio shop owner, deals in Olde Realm trades

Characters Continued...

Taminus............................ ancient warrior, after Vectra's job for centuries

Gregon.......................... old book seller, a Kurzian, who is friends with Vectra

Rolan Gingerton...................... soldier ghost from the Civil War, is Vectra's roommate

Rae.............................. coyote/fox creature, is Vectra's pet

Gears............................ an Olde Realm inventor

Rudi.............................. Christmas elf, lives in a jolly camper most of the year

Aiden............................ annoying leprechaun, home-sick for Ireland

Ailsing (Astrid)...................... an archer, and Celtic nymph, who is friends with Vectra

Martiban.........who you will have to find out about later!

Along with the other members of this great tale.

Chapter One

Monica gazed up at the street sign with its rectangular green background and sharp white lettering. Its metal surface reflected the sun's light and almost blinded her eyes from where she stood along the sidewalk. Dipping her head to the left, she was finally able to read what the street's name was: Portobello Road. *Finally!* This was supposed to be the place where she could find help in locating her missing older brother. At least, that was what the fourteen-year-old had been told.

Ever since their parents disappeared eight years ago, Trevor stepped up to become a legal guardian at the age of twenty-eight. He worked for a large company that operated from behind a heavily secured fence with a singular name on the front gate, and nothing else. Her brother never discussed his job at dinnertime, but would make a point to keep their parents' adventurous stories alive through made-up tales of treasure hunts. Though the orally shared memories would never be a true replacement for their parents, it was one of the ways the estranged siblings grew closer together. Such an age difference used to bother Trevor, but he gradually warmed up to his younger sister and younger brother over time, even allowing Monica to see some of his journals he kept as a hobby. One afternoon, she captured a glimpse of a sketch lying atop her brother's attaché case and thought it was related to the ancient artifacts he liked to learn about during his time off. From her first glimpse, she could tell that the very old parchment consisted of multiple drawn lines which crisscrossed to create a schematic of a primitive machine. Before she could venture any closer to it, however, Trevor hurriedly stashed it away from her view.

I wonder if that drawing has anything to do with his kidnapping? Standing on the sidewalk, Monica couldn't help but feel a tiny sense of hope take aflame within her heart. Determined to not allow Trevor to vanish like their parents did, never to return home again, she secretly vowed to the smaller boy beside her that she would prevent them from being forced into foster care. Lovingly, Monica gazed upon her younger brother, seeing the studious look he also gave the road sign situated high above them. Though they dressed similarly in casual clothing and black sneakers, they did not share any familial traits to any of the strangers passing by them. *I can't let him go back into the system again. I just can't.*

She resisted the urge to wrap her arm around her brother's shoulders, as her mother would do for her whenever she needed comforting. Instead, Monica fought back the doubts trying to plant themselves inside her brain, and tried not to lose her own courage in the face of the enormous task ahead. "Well, Dare, should we get going?" The girl tapped her fingers on the nine-year-old's head in order to grab his attention. "No use in procrastinating."

"I suppose. But are you going to be alright in that crowd in there?" Dare pointed his short index finger at the packed street with people shoehorned in tighter than sardines in a metal can.

Monica gulped down her anxiety, flashing him a crooked smile in an attempt to convince him that everything would be alright. "I guess I will just have to deal. Come on. It's already twelve o'clock."

Walking in single file, the siblings entered the antique market that took place every Saturday afternoon during the summer months in Pennsylvania. Vendors flanked the street with long chains of carts and awnings in a multitude of shapes, colors, and sizes. Tables were overburdened with a plethora of vintage items ranging from small furniture to jewelry pendants and rings. Wooden cabinets took up a large section of one seller's nine by nine foot space, whilst a neighboring seller was loudly hocking knick-knacks discovered in trash bins from over the mountain. Paintings carelessly hung from thin wire, in a tent further down the line, glistened with fresh paint, as fake jewels dazzled in the shining sunlight from across the street. To their right, a man was demonstrating how good the piano was that he was trying to sell; out-of-tune keys and all. His voice only added to the ear-piercing tragedy, and succeeded at keeping potential buyers moving swiftly by his booth.

"It's just a bunch of junk." Dare flatly stated.

"Remember what Trevor always says."

"What? Don't pee in flower pots?" Dare grinned upward at his sister sarcastically. "Or don't use our shirt sleeves to clean our nose?"

"No. One person's junk is another's treasure."

"I know. I was just trying to get you to smile. A real smile, I mean."

"I'll be smiling when we see Trevor again." Monica grabbed ahold of his hand, ignored her need to vomit within the fray of wandering people, and plunged into the crowded marketplace. Normally, Dare would resist holding hands with his sister, being that he was far too old for that anymore, but this was under unusual circumstances. They had to find their older brother before Gaither decided that he was a liability, and better off being dead than alive.

Monica and Dare still felt that their predicament was as unbelievable as sending people to the planet of Jupiter. It all happened three nights ago, when Trevor was taken from their front porch. He was arriving home, late from his research, when Gaither's men placed a hood over his head and dragged him away into a dark minivan, off the lit sidewalk. The New York license plate, spelling out the words "GthBoys" told them who was to blame for the criminal deed. Since they knew their brother was working for a company called Gaither, it wasn't hard to connect the bread crumbs.

The following night, Monica had a dream of the most bizarre of sorts.

It was daybreak, and the siblings were walking toward an unmarked grave in the woods at the edge of their neighborhood. After many years of weathering, the name was illegible and the dates of the person's lifespan were barely visible themselves. Monica had been trying to make out what the numbers were, when the sound of crunching leaves grabbed her attention. She quickly turned to the left, only to find a gentle stream bubbling along the river rocks and the trees as silent as ever. Hearing the loud footsteps once again, Monica and Dare swung their heads back around to see a huntress standing poised with a cloak draped over her shoulders.

Her left hand pulled down the hood, shrouding her face from their view, revealing two long brown braids cascading in front of her chest. Mindlessly flowing around her body, a cream-col-

ored toga extended to her ankles, where gladiator sandals were wrapped around her feet and shins. A quiver rested against her back as a sterling silver bow was cradled in her right hand. "Do not be scared. I am here to help you save your brother."

"H...o...w do you k...n...o...w him?" Monica positioned herself between Dare and the ancient warrior. Her eyes frantically searched the forest floor for any form of a weapon she could lay her hands on.

"Let us just say that his work has captured a lot of attention, including that of my own." The woman smiled at the two siblings. And for some unknown reason to Monica, she had a strong feeling that they could trust this strange woman. "He was searching for something very powerful, and ancient, when a man by the name of Gaither took him. I fear that he will be forced to help them locate it in exchange for his life. Or perhaps, that of your own."

"Looking for what exactly?" Monica couldn't help but think back to the drawing on the parchment she had briefly seen months earlier. Trevor had acted strangely secretive about it, and nearly pushed her away from his leather case in the process of concealing it under the opened flap.

"A weapon mightier than the sword. If you wish to save your brother, travel to a place called Nectar Hill. Visit Portobello Road and find a unique woman by the name of Vectra Tillerman. She will be able to help you." A slight Greek accent lingered in her words.

"How can we trust what you are telling us?"

"If you do not, the world will be no more as you now know it; but a planet ravaged to ruin by a powerful dictator and no future worth living for."

"No offense, but don't the rich and powerful already ruin things?" Dare sassed. He always did like to crack a joke when feeling pressured. It was seen as a tactless coping mechanism by many, but his sister did not say anything. The ancient woman took a step forward, causing Monica to do likewise in the opposite direction, ensuring the six foot separation between them.

"I can see you are no fool, Monica Browning. You will need your smarts for this task at hand."

"For someone I have never met before, you seem to know a bit about us. I don't care for that." Monica's eyes narrowed and her brows inched downward. "What's your name?"

"Artenian. Time is short, Monica. Visit Portobello Road when the antique market comes alive every Saturday afternoon and find the woman wearing a black fedora. Three playing cards will be atop her hat band. She has an aura about her of an older world long gone, and not of any modern appearance you would be used to."

"Like you?" Monica's spine was becoming prickly with suspicion. Being under trees in the woods was uncomfortable enough without talking to a woman dressed from Ancient Greece. For all she knew, the warrior could be crazy in the head, or an escapee from some psych ward. But her gut was still telling her that she could trust Artenian.

"Her attire would be akin to what your generation calls 'steampunk,' though it is no costume, and she has a mannerism with a life of its own. Tell her that her sister sent you." As Artenian spoke the final word, she disappeared in a flash of green fire in the blink of an eye.

When Dare first heard his sister tell him about her vivid dream, all he could manage was a blank stare at her for an elongated moment, before his lips began to move once more. "Are you sure we did not just have way too much soda for breakfast yesterday?"

"Dare!" Monica's call for him shook his memories away, bringing him back to the present. *I still cannot believe we are doing this!* He wanted to call the police, anonymously, to report her dream to them, and let the officers deal with the possible lead into their brother's disappearance. But that was when Monica warned him about having to go through child services again, if they were to involve the authorities. With no other relatives to mention, this was their only chance to save Trevor, and they were going to have to take it upon themselves to find Vectra Tillerman before it was too late.

Chapter Two

"Monica, we have been looking for an hour and still no sign of this 'Vectra' woman. You think this is all a wild goose chase?" Dare asked just when his eyes fell upon a large man swallowing a whole pastry at once. His mouth watered as the tantalizing smell made its way into his nose. Powdered sugar coated the man's facial hairs, causing him to appear older than he truly was. Seeing the young boy gawking at him, the man huffed, and turned his back as he dove into another of the fluffy fasnachts.

"No. Unless you think my imagination was able to conjure up that woman named 'Artenian' and everything else she told us. And I mean, who vanishes in a blaze of green flame? While that was pretty cool, I have to admit, I do not recall ever dreaming about fire before. How would I even go about creating someone like her anyway?"

"Perhaps you forged her from that magic show you like to binge on the tv?" Dare briefly lost his sister in the moving current of the patrons, catching up to her a heartbeat later. "That show has hosted a lot of magicians, their assistants, and their specialized equipment. It would be fairly easy to think up a trick like that one." He paused to take a breath. "I feel like an idiot." Stopping by a nearby vendor, Dare slowed his pace, picked up a random old book and stroked the worn pages still intact. "I don't know about this, I just…"

Monica abruptly knocked the book from his hands and wildly pointed into the air. Her voice rang out in overjoyed excitement. "I SEE HER! I SEE HER! Over there!"

Seen between the heads of three teenage boys, Monica zoned in on the black fedora with three miniature black and gold playing cards under the band. A cluster of brown feathers rested on the brim and created a flag above the other people, as unruly brown hair fell slightly past her shoulders. When one of the boys moved away from his friends, he allowed Vectra Tillerman to come more into view and the two kids' eyes widened at the sight. She wore a coat vest of brown leather, which cascaded against her legs in a waterfall cut along the back, which only revealed her dark brown boots underneath.

Monica grabbed onto Dare's hand and hastily pulled him through the entanglement of legs. She turned around to check on her brother, nearly running straight into Vectra, and stopped within a hair's length of collision. The woman was standing still in front of a vendor's cart, rummaging through a small box of lockets. Both Brownings watched her in hesitation as she proceeded to move to the side, continuing to search for something small in an eclectic assortment of buttons. They were not sure how to introduce themselves to a person they only knew through a mentioning in a dream. *How do you tell someone without sounding crazy?*

With a cold shoulder shirt of moss green, and black ruffles upon her chest, her black and gray checkered pants did not seem out of place. Around her neck sat a black lace choker with charms dangling from its ends and layered necklaces of different lengths swayed in the sudden gust of wind. Monica took another glance down at their own clothing, feeling underdressed compared to the woman's snappy fashion sense. *She was right however. She would fit in at the next steampunk convention.* A long, thin chain laid across Vectra's torso, ending in a bulging pocket on her left. *Is that a pocket watch?*

Her mind instantly drifted into a long-lost memory of a pocket watch she had seen the day after they called the police about their parents' disappearance. She saw it for a second at most, as the officers bustled around the house in search of any clues as to where Mr. and Mrs. Browning had ventured off too. The brass watch shined like a bright new penny, and had caught young Monica's attention because it did not belong to her family. When the seven-year-old did manage to return to the side table to inspect it further, the piece had vanished. All she could see was the back of a person strutting along the side of the house with a cloak hiding all of their features. No footprints were discovered, nor any evidence that she had even seen the person to begin with.

"Monica, she's getting away! We're losing her." Dare regained his sister's attention by yanking on her arm as the woman fled up the street. "We better do something, and fast." He went to lead his sister in pursuit and ended up walking straight into the back of a gentleman instead. The man turned around, not seeing anyone at his eye's level, and returned to the painting he had been staring at.

"And you are sure that Rembrandt painted this one?" A skeptical woman inquired of the vendor who blurted out his annoyance at her insult. Voices from sellers and customers alike, filled the crisp air as prices were being dickered down and money fanned out from people's wallets. It was a scene Monica and Dare had never witnessed before, and reminded them of their old school's cafeteria.

"Come on." Monica weaved their way through the mayhem of faked guarantees and unreal "bargains." While she assumed that some of the peddlers were of good standing, many flaunted their fakes with gusto, and warded off any children from getting their grubby hands on the merchandise. Trying to keep up with the woman's fast pace, Monica and Dare would no sooner catch up to Vectra, then she would slip from their sight once again. "Miss! Miss! Wait up!"

"Were you looking for me?" An older lady bent over from her table, approximately four feet to their right. Her knitted shawl held numerous tints and shades of purple and laid over a light blue dress complementing her eyes. Despite having glasses on the bridge of her nose, the older lady could not see very well and squinted through her rounded spectacles. "Francesca? My, you have gotten younger since we last saw one another. Please lend me whatever you take for that. I fear more wrinkles have dawned my cheeks since last winter." The woman's aged skin was fair in complexion, matching that of Monica's tone, and a shade lighter than that of Dare's.

"I'm sorry Ma'am. My name isn't Francesca and we are looking for someone else." Monica politely corrected the lady. A slight tinge of lavender perfume blossomed around her tables, providing a comforting feel one would expect to find at their grandmother's house. Part of the scent leaked from the wonderful samples of tea primed for tasting nearby, and the rest came from the potpourri left to air from inside opened mason jars. Overall, it was a very inviting booth filled with a wide assortment of teas from different sources.

"Oh, well. That's alright deary. Since my birthday five years ago, my sight has dwindled and my hearing has begun to fail me as well."

"How old are you?" Dare asked. Monica pinched her brother to reprimand him for such an offensive question. "Owww." He stared at his sister while the older lady chuckled.

"Oh, I don't mind. Young Man, I turned 145 last month and I am still going strong."

Monica and Dare were not sure if they had heard the lady quite right. They guessed their faces expressed their disbelief, because the woman gladly restated her age for them. "But, that's impossible," the teenager stated. She was starting to think this elderly lady didn't have all her marbles.

"On the contrary, my dear, I am quite young for my family. I'll have you know that my father lived to be 351 when he passed. Outlasting my grandmother by five WHOLE years to claim the record. That was his goal." She held her index finger up in the air as though she was teaching a class something important for a future test. "My poor mother did not make it past the age of 256, you see. She became rather ill and could not recover. That is what motivated my father to outlast his mother-in-law. Could not stand the sight of her. Wanted to best her at what she treasured the most, living the longest of our family."

"Wow. That is a great accomplishment." Monica tried to keep the sound of sarcasm low in her voice. "Well, thanks for the introduction, and the history lesson, but we really must be off now. We're meeting up with someone and don't wish to be late." She was about to be dragged into the sea of shoppers once more by her brother, when the older lady asked them who they were looking for.

Glancing down to see Dare's shaking head, Monica was

not sure what to do. They had lost sight of Vectra, and any help in locating her would be appreciated. However, they did not know this lady and asking for her assistance might be more dangerous than that of searching alone. She saw the grave stare in her brother's eyes, disapproving even the notion of sharing information with the delusional seller. *It is not like we exactly know this Vectra woman either. What harm could be done by asking?*

Against her brother's wishes, Monica described Vectra to the older lady, and asked if she knew anything about the steampunk-dressed woman. Suddenly, the tea seller's eyes cleared until they glistened in the sunlight, and her vision became sharper than that of a hawk's. "You children best be on your way and forget about that one. Turn back now while you still can."

"Why?" The abrupt change in the lady's demeanor was puzzling enough for Monica. However, the way she warned them, scared her to the bone. With words coated in caution, a serious weight of uncertainty planted itself in the teenager's mind. "What do you mean?"

"Never mind why. Just get away and go home. You should never have come here in the first place. I would have thought that…" Shaking away the remaining part of her statement, the older lady scolded herself. "Now I am feeling old, for not having noticed your aroma sooner. Your eyes tell enough as it is." Turning her back sharply at them, the older lady rose from her seat and positioned herself behind another table offering bags of tea leaves. She fiddled with an arrangement that appeared perfect to both Monica and Dare, and restocked a few open holes on the far side of her tables.

Dare looked up at his sister in confusion. "What was she talking about?"

"Search me. I don't have the foggiest clue and now we lost Vectra for sure." Monica frowned out of disappointment. If the tea seller wouldn't have stopped them, then they would still be on the trail of the woman with the fedora hat. *What did she mean by her warning? But more importantly, what other choice do we have but to find Vectra?* She shared a worried look with her brother. Things were getting weirder by the minute and who knew what more was to follow.

"Are we certain we WANT to find Vectra?" He asked her.

"We have to, Dare. We have to."

Chapter Three

"There! I see her." Dare called out to Monica, who was briefly checking out a small pendant dangling by a thin chain at the next vendor. "By that vase with the cherry blossoms painted on the side." They watched with curiosity as the woman focused on the seller whilst her hands played with the mostly white vase. At first, it seemed like a normal thing to be doing before purchasing an item for sale; inspecting the inside and out for any cracks, or deformities within the piece. But their faces soon showed their vexation as a playing card materialized in Vectra's left hand. She stuck it to the genuine antique as though it were magnetized and switched her focus onto the other potential customers. "What is she doing?"

Determined not to allow the woman to vanish again, Monica cleared her throat and politely said "Hi." Vectra nearly jumped out of her skin, and gave a slight yelp that caused people to look over, perplexed. She smiled at the passing crowd and then stared down at the children who had blown her discrete cover.

"Did you not see that I was doing something *very* important?" She fumed. "Thanks to you, Taminus will most likely pick up on the fact that I am on to him. And this time, I finally had an upper hand." Her cold, green eyes harbored daggers in their deep irises.

"Are you Vectra Tillerman?" Monica studied the woman's face.

"Who's asking?" Her brows inched over the bridge of her nose, trying to deduce how they knew her name and if she had ever seen them before.

"My name is Monica and this is my younger brother, Derrick. 'Dare' for short. We were sent to find you."

"I highly doubt that." Vectra chuckled at the silly idea, as she rejoined the wave of customers, purposefully not looking back at the children following her. "No one wants to find me." Sass painted her voice, making the older lady's warning seem friendly.

"It's the truth. Elsewise, how would we have known where to find you? Let alone know your name." Monica almost ran into the back of Vectra when the woman suddenly stopped. Spinning around on the heels of her boots, she peered down at the two children with her fingers playing in the air.

"And if I were to believe that, then who, might I ask, sent you?"

Monica gulped and squeezed her brother's hand for support. "Your sister."

A sound, resembling a snort, came from Vectra, quickly turning about-face to continue walking through the crowd with considerable ease. "I don't have a sister." She shouted over her shoulder.

Monica's frustration was beginning to mount. They had already lost almost two hours trying to find the elusive woman, and the fair would only be open until four. "She said she was your sister!" She yelled over the loud noise of the people suffocating the street. Her throat suddenly started closing up after handling the crowds for longer than her claustrophobia usually allotted. The teen's breathing rapidly increased as two women bumped into her, spiking her level of desperation to leave the confined space, in order to seek clear air from behind a seller's booth. Against her own desires, however, she pushed down her rising anxiety, and pressed on instead. *I am not going to fail Trevor!*

"Then she was lying." Vectra replied with a short look backwards.

Monica's face gained a slight shade of red as her hands balled into fists. Letting go of her brother's hand, she stomped her way up to the strange woman. Keeping pace with Vectra's longer strides, however, Monica inadvertently lost track of her brother as a large family group tried to weave their way to the other side of the street. "You might want to hold onto your brother." Vectra's voice rang out.

Monica's eyes widened at her commanding statement. *Of course I know where my brother is!* She stopped herself, and expectantly glanced behind to prove to the woman that Dare was still with her. *DARE!* Her heart raced even faster as panic consumed her mind and she called out his name in the ever-changing flow of people. All of a sudden, a hand grabbed ahold of her arm and yanked her to the edge of the street. "Hey, let me go!" Overhearing her cries for help, a few men noticed her being restrained by Vectra, and ventured over to ensure that everything was alright.

"My niece and nephew. They don't listen to me very well." Vectra put on a faked smile. "That is what you get when parents no longer spank their kids." The men shrugged at her statement, with two of the group agreeing with what she said, and made their way to a vendor promising that his gun-shot tin cans were used by the famous Buffalo Bill for target practice.

"I said let me go!" Monica jerked herself free of the woman's grasp. Her eyes immediately lit up in relief when she saw her brother standing next to her and instinctively hugged him. "Thank goodness you are alright."

"I told you to hold onto him. This is a pretty large crowd this weekend, and small ones can become easily lost."

Monica's eyes blistered with anger. "Well, if you would just take a moment to hear us out, instead of making us chase you through a crowded street, this wouldn't have happened!"

"Don't be mad at her, Monica. We are the ones that busted in on her life." Dare slipped a piece of gum into his mouth from his pocket. "Besides, she was the one who found me."

"Very sensible young man. Now, I must be off. Why don't you find your parents and do some shopping? Word to the wise, stay away from the vendors along the south side. They like to preach as though their items are made from gold, though tin would be an improvement." Vectra tipped her hat to them and began to leave when Monica stepped in her way.

"Just wait a second! We need your help."

"My help? No one needs my help. And if they did, they would be fools to accept such services. My price does not come cheap."

"We do need your help. Our older brother was kidnapped and we need to save him."

"How does that involve me?"

"He works for a man named Gaither, and while I do not know what all he does for the man, I do know that he was kidnapped by two men hired by him." Vectra's eyes glazed over upon the mentioning of Gaither's name. Not sure what to make of the strange woman's reaction, Monica continued her plea. "Please...we need your help in finding Trevor. He is all we have left and..." She slowly stopped speaking when it dawned on her that Vectra was staring at something far above her head, appearing to be in a sort of trance. Dare also opened his mouth to talk, but was not able to utter a single letter before Vectra quietly instructed them to get behind her.

Obeying her words, the siblings followed her as she led them to a vendor's booth three spots down. Vectra slipped them under the tarp sides of a blue canopy, appearing beside them after surveying their surroundings and deeming that she had a few minutes to spare before chaos was to break out.

Dare had to blink his eyes to make sure he was seeing the seller correctly; who was holding two very worn, leather books and held a surprised look plastered on his face. The man was older than he was, yet shorter in height. His hands were slightly too large for his body; however, his ears were a touch too small. He was well-dressed like a business owner from the 1930s, and sported a small black bowler hat atop his head.

"He's a dwarf." Dare murmured in his sister's ear, who only nodded her head in acknowledgement as they waited for Vectra's next move.

"Vectra?" His voice was tinted by a Norwegian accent and his expression was now vexed at seeing the siblings with his old friend. "Good to see you as always. But...what are those doing here?"

"Come on, Gregon. Don't tell me you have not seen children before?" She purposefully deflected his question.

"I know children." He sniffed the air. "But they are..."

"In danger. I need you to..."

"Ah hah! Asking for my help after you firmly, and dare I say adamantly, told me that you would not ask me for help ever again." Gregon smirked as Vectra's eyes rolled. "Should I say those magically annoying four words now or later?"

"You can tell me 'I told you so' at another time. Right now, we are in a bit of a rush."

Gregon waved a book in the air at her. "Sorry, I cannot help you today. The crowds have been sifting through my books like kids in sand, so my booth is wrecked. And I cannot have it this way when the mayor comes by. You know that I actually sold her on the 1938 edition of…"

"You don't have a choice in the matter, Gregon. Taminus is here. He has seen me, or sensed me, because of these two breaking my…forget it. The point is, you have to hide them until the coast is clear." Vectra turned her back to a passing customer, shuffling Monica and Dare in front of her in order to shield them from view of the street.

"Fine, fine. Here." Gregon sighed, picking up the end of a tablecloth draped over one of his book-filled tables and ushered the siblings underneath the fabric. "Stay there and do not make a sound."

"Do you have your normal security measures activated?" Vectra peered around the corner of the tarp walls in search of the man she knew to be following her.

"Yes, yes. Now go and deal with him so these "things" can leave my shop. They are hotter than a blacksmith's fire and you brought them to me. ME, mind you. After you promised…"

"You are a saint, Gregon." Vectra flashed him a half-hearted grin just as she vanished into the crowd.

"Yeah, so she says. But she forgets I don't care for saints much." Gregon mumbled, pausing to secretly smile at the ground. "Perhaps she is not so hardened beyond help yet."

His neck quivered with the feeling of eyes staring at him, and glanced over to where Monica had been peeking out from under the cloth. "Will she face her mistake, though? One does not speculate." Grumbling at the state of one of the books in his hands, Gregon went about his job at mending a rip in its cover, and acted as though nothing happened.

Chapter Four

People milled about like cattle, looking for an extraordinary find that would make them rich enough to lose their day job. Watching the highly-intrigued customers very closely, Vectra scanned their faces in search of the man that had been after her job for as long as she could remember. His tell-tale jet-black hair and pointed chin was hard to miss. He always held his nose upward, believing himself to be better than the mere peasants walking along the streets, and went to great lengths to ensure that his short, boxed beard was kept at a specific measurement all the way around. Goggles adorned his forehead like a headband, which was hardly a disguise, considering he was wearing the same blue, pinstriped suit he liked to sport, while being seen in public.

It didn't take long for Vectra to locate him. His eyes locked onto her own and he grinned when he saw her tip her hat in his direction. Anyone who knew Vectra, or had merely heard of her within their world, was told about the signal she used when readied for battle. A simple gesture, one born out of chivalry and respect, was her trademark tell. Taminus pulled his collar upward and closer to his cheeks. No wind was blowing, nor any small breezes, but no one asked why he hid the sides of his face as he straightened out his tie. "Why can't we just enjoy a nice antique fair together, like old times? Must we always end up fighting one another? It is such a lovely day out and these folks are enjoying themselves, I dare say."

"Since when did you care about anyone other than yourself, Taminus?" Vectra motioned for him to join her on the sidewalk and away from the crowd. "Well, I guess I can say that you have cared for your father. However, even that relationship is most likely due to what he did for you, only, and not for any cherished love between a father and son." Her eyes glinted mischievously. "How is your father doing, by the way? Have not seen him since before…"

"Before this bloody country prohibited liquor; if memory serves me right." Taminus shuttered at the mentioning of the Great Prohibition years of the 1920s and early 1930s. "But you probably know more about his welfare than that of myself. Seeing as how you were the last to speak to him." Standing taller than Vectra by over four inches, he stared down at her with snarling contempt. "That is about to change, dear Vectra. And there is nothing you can do to stop it from happening." She studied his face, wanting to be able to believe that what he was saying was not the truth. He saw it in her expression, smugly smiling like the snake he was. "You know that I do not lie, Vectra Tillerman."

"You misunderstand, Taminus. I was thinking that you should leave the cane for your father. It suits him more than it does you." Gesturing toward the stained-wood and hand-sculpted stick, she did not stop there. "Makes you look older than what you are." Vectra blinked her eyes and flashed him a curled grin. "How old are you, Taminus?" She watched his eyes narrow in on her, and his mouth became a thin line under this nose. Swiftly, he reached into the right breast pocket of his jacket to produce an old-fashioned monocle he placed in front of his pupil on the same side.

"The time for small talk has ended." He gripped onto the end of his cane in the manner one would hold a sword. "Let us see if you are in a chipper mood when I am done with you."

Vectra eyed the cane suspiciously, figuring that he was going to be a little more unpredictable than usual this time around. *Nothing I cannot handle, that I am sure of.* Cards flew from her hands piling up on either side in two large mounds. People continued to move around them as though they did not exist, oblivious to what was about to happen. Reaching into his left side pocket, Taminus pulled out a river rock and waited for her move.

Raising the first two fingers on her right hand, Vectra moved her index finger back and a two of hearts appeared within the gap. Like a fourth of July sparkler, tiny white lines of energy ignited on the card as she flung it upward. Whilst in the air, the sparkling small rectangular paper split into two and landed on both piles. Controlled columns of fire were born from the stacks, creating a fiery gateway any flame swallower would have envied. Vectra unsheathed the short sword hanging from the belt under her brown vest. "You will not be victorious Taminus. Not today."

"Spoken like the liar and thief that you still are." Taminus pursed his lips and blew across the top of the river rock to launch a small wave of water at her. The charging wave caught Vectra off guard for a moment, but she instantly flicked a six of hearts in front of the attack. In a flash of blue and orange, a hot wall of protection evaporated the water in a matter of seconds, giving her barely enough time to comprehend what was happening.

"How is this possible?" Vectra muttered to herself. "For him to have the power of water, would mean…" She stared at him with unblinking eyes once the water had vanished into air. Upon his pinky finger, sat the semi-clear, blue gem that used to sit on the hand of another. "You killed Bregit?!"

"It was no easy fete, that I can dutifully announce." Taminus sneered. "The recluse was hiding out in an old monastery, well supplied with many protections that I had a little help at disarming." He tossed the rock at her, watching it skip along the sidewalk like on the top of a lake. Vectra readied herself with two more cards in her left hand, holding her knife in her right palm. She positioned herself to strike it away, but on the last bounce in front of her, the rock landed with the force of a massive boulder onto the ground.

With the power of a small earthquake, the land under her feet buckled and imploded upward. Crashing back down, Vectra managed to keep herself upright and flew three cards marked five of hearts in his direction. Back and forth, they sparred with their powers, each deflecting the other's until they paused to catch their breaths. Vectra stared down at her hands, seeing her skin growing slightly charred. "I am guessing that we are going to have to create a spectacle of ourselves." She glanced over to see the short nod of his head in agreement.

Pushing herself up from the ground, hovering about two feet in the air, fire spewed out from the bottom of her heels where she had tacked on a seven of hearts under both boots. Readjusting her grip on the ancient hilt, Vectra began to run straight through the air at him as the blade slowly glowed orange from being heated up in-between her fingers. Taminus drew his own weapon as well, with a matching wooden grip and bronze cross-hilts; its blade crafted from obsidian rock, like her own. He stomped the ground in her direction, preparing for the ultimate collision.

Their blades clashed as they tried slashing one another. The sound of razor-sharp rock grinding against itself, easily overcame the loud commotion of the street fair. As the battle continued, Monica and Dare watched from the safety of Gregon's booth. Looking up at his sister, Dare's widened eyes spoke for the both of them. "What is happening?"

"Taminus and Vectra are dueling it out like they have countless times before." Gregon nonchalantly stated. "Have so for eons. He being the one who wants her job. For his own greedy self, no doubt." Kindly shuffling books around on the tables, the shorter man ignored the noisy battle. "A nuisance is what it is. Taminus never wins. But that does not stop him from trying."

"Wait." Monica watched the chaotic scene unfolding across the street. "So…Vectra is fighting with fire, but the other guy is fighting with stone and water?"

"What?!" Gregon immediately swung around to see what she was talking about. "That cannot be." He pulled an odd set of bifocals out from a case wrapped around his wrist. "Bless us, St. Thomas Aquinas. The only way for him to have acquired strength in water was to kill Bregit. If that has happened, we may be in serious trouble."

Two more clicks of their blades soon caused a noise loud enough to capture the crowd's attention. Energy pulsated out from the polished stone, creating engraved symbols within the top layer of their purple surface. Illuminated by the mounting energy, Vectra's eyes widened at Taminus's snickering stare. She could feel her power being drained and quickly willed the burning stacks of playing cards to reach over like hands in her defense. Blinded by the intensity of the blaze, Taminus bent down and summoned a wall of rocks up from the ground to shield his eyes.

Chants for both sides rose into the air and money exchanged hands in bets on who was going to be left standing. Monica was appalled by their behavior. "What do they think this is? Some sort of entertainment sideshow? It looks too real to be projections and virtual reality."

"Best they believe that than what the truth is." Gregon motioned for them to push further back under the cloth again. "Taminus cannot find you. If he does, you will wish you were dead."

Dare latched onto his sister. "Monica, maybe we should just go home."

"I am afraid we are too late to be thinking about doing that." Monica didn't understand how they got themselves mixed up in this bizarre street fight, let alone not knowing what was actually going down. However, she had a gut feeling that they were not going to be able to call it a day and head back home like her brother wanted.

"I have a bad feeling about this." Dare's voice quivered as he gulped. "What was Trevor doing at his job? How is he involved in all of this? Whatever 'this' is."

Vectra flicked a nine of hearts from her wrist, smashing through the rocky barrier with the sword's hilt. She wasted no time in stabbing Taminus in the chest with the card, after it folded itself into an origami blade. An electric shock raced through his body. But, to Vectra's disappointment, he remained standing with no more than smoke rising out of his ears. Countering her attack with a stab through her right boot with his blade, Taminus's action sent a searing burst of pain up her leg.

Vectra punched him in the chin with an upper cut and drove her elbow into his ribs, shouting out in aggravation of the tightening sensation behind her knee. She went to step away, but was denied to move from the petrifying ink now swimming in her veins. Taminus choked out the air in his lungs, whispering to the sentimentary rocks near his feet in a weakened voice. Two rocks obeyed the command and jumped into his hands. Crushing them with an easy flex of his fingers, Taminus threw the dust into Vectra's face.

Not being able to see, she closed her eyelids and listened to Taminus still recovering from her elbow hit. The sound of his labored breathing made it easier to distinguish him from the rest of the noise roaring around the fight. Vectra summoned two more cards in her hands and threw them at the ground. The cards spun around her in a complete circle, laser cutting the sidewalk with great ease. She fell through the hole that opened under her feet. Once she surpassed the surface level, the pavement closed up the hole behind her, giving the appearance that the Earth swallowed her whole. Silence fell over the crowd, not sure what to do or where she had gone.

Then, suddenly, a slicing sound erupted from over their heads and Vectra came down on top of Taminus with her sword at the ready. He moved out from underneath her, just in time, and Vectra landed on the ground with a loud thud. The fighting ensued for five more minutes until a police siren was growing louder in the distance. Men and women scattered in all directions to make sure they were far away by the time the police had arrived at Portobello Road. Vectra glared at Taminus, continuing to fight him until the red and blue flashing lights showed up at both ends of the road.

As a cop ran toward the commotion, Taminus looked back to see who it was and Vectra took the opportunity to stab him in the heart. Instantly, Taminus's face froze, his body becoming a statue before dissolving into the soil below. Vectra picked her blade up from the ground when a group of five cops surrounded her with their guns drawn.

"Vectra, put the sword down." The chief demanded in an authoritative and booming voice. Monica peeked out from under the table, still not believing what she was witnessing.

"Honestly, Raymond." Vectra tilted her head to one side. "It's only me. Are the guns really necessary?"

"That's Chief Warren to you, Ms. Tillerman." His nose twitched, aching to be scratched as he held his weapon. "Drop the sword." Vectra proceeded to do what the chief had ordered. The bronze metal clinked against the torn-up sidewalk, ending in a dulled thud just before a cracked chip fell off the blade. A peek at the inner forged metal revealed a pulsating light of its own making as the pile of Taminus's dust began drifting away on the breeze. "Search her, Robert."

A man with gray-tipped hair walked toward Vectra and patted her down. Her eyes stayed focused on the blade that was being carried along with the dust. Every muscle in her body wanted to reach down and snatch it up from the ashy remains, but she forced herself not to make any abrupt movement. Vectra could feel her blood boiling hot as the sword inched further and further away while the Chief responded to a call on his radio. The other cops' attentions were steadfastly trained on her, with only one of them acknowledging the moving weapon by a tipping of his head.

"All good, Chief." The man named Robert moved swiftly back to his post as his boss finished up on the radio.

"Ms. Tillerman, how many times do we have to talk to you about this?"

"He attacked me, Chief Warren. It was self-defense."

"That's right Chief." Gregon piped up from his booth.

"Why am I not surprised to find you mixed up in this?" Chief Warren pointed at the dwarf, balancing four large dictionaries in his hands. "Two peas in a pod you two are. I should have you arrested for disturbing the peace and being an endangerment to society, at the very least."

"But you are a good man, Raymond, and there is no need for all the paperwork." Vectra smiled and batted her eyelashes as the chief narrowed his gaze in on her façade of sweet mannerism.

"Watch yourself, Ms. Tillerman. You may be friends with the judge, but the old guy won't last forever." Chief Warren put his gun back in its holster and ordered his men to return to their vehicles. Vectra smiled and waved a sassy farewell to the men in blue, clutching onto one of her necklaces with the other hand as they departed.

Monica and Dare unearthed themselves from underneath the table when they heard Gregon informing them that everything was alright. "Why did the cops not arrest her?" Dare stood a foot's distance behind his sister.

"Well, not sure how she was able to get the judge in such good graces with her. Nothing scandalous though, that I can attest to. But I have a pretty good idea when I see him walking down the streets with his childhood dog panting along. Loves that dog like a son."

"Childhood dog? How old is the judge?" Monica brushed off her brother's clothes after noticing some dirt on his knee.

"Fifty-five." Gregon remarked. He zipped his lip shut as Vectra walked over to the book-scattered booth, her sides still heaving from the fight.

"Well, that was fun."

"What happened?" Monica asked, gazing around at the antique fair that was now in shambles. "Who, or what, is Taminus? And…" She gestured to the sidewalk ruins, the vendors beginning to clean up their booths, and the few remaining customers gossiping about the showdown. "What is going on?"

"Taminus is a man who has been after my job for years. Too many to count, in point of fact. Now, time for you two to run along and go find your parents." Vectra glanced down at the necklace she had been holding. "I wondered." She muttered, examining the broken chain barely clinging together. "That will have to be taken care of immediately."

"Ah, Vectra…" Gregon was interrupted by a very irritated teen.

"Our parents are dead." Monica crossed her chest with her arms. "And our older brother, who is our legal guardian, has been kidnapped. That's who you are going to help us search for."

"While I am quite sorry to hear about your parents, that is none of my affair. Call the police and take it up with them. They have teams who specialize in kidnappings."

"Vectra…" Gregon tried again, and was interrupted once more.

"We were told to find you."

"By who, exactly? Everyone I know of no longer speaks to me. That is, except for Gregon."

"She said her name was Artenian." Monica took a rigid stance in an attempt to make herself sound determined. *Hopefully she cannot see my fear.*

Vectra's eyes darkened and a snarl formed on her lips. "She is not my sister."

Chapter Five

Vectra fiddled with the pendant dangling from the eighteen-inch bronze chain in need of repair. It consisted of twisted wires and curled small springs encasing a green stone cut in a teardrop shape. She pulled a Jack of Hearts from underneath her leather armband, crunched it around the busted chain as best she could, and snapped her fingers. A small tunnel of green fire soldered the chain whole again and it fell into place around her neck unblemished. "That would imply that we are either born from the same mother or possess a kinship through being close friends. Neither, of which, is the case."

"Then how would you describe it?" Monica asked.

She took a pause to think before answering. "More of a mutual dislike."

"If she didn't like you, why would she send us to find you?" Dare inquired.

Gregon stepped forth from behind a table of books he had started to reorganize. "You know what they are, Vectra. A simple whiff would have told you."

"Yes, I know." Her voice was annoyed and she dismissed his statement with a passive brushing of the air with her hand. "I just didn't want to believe it."

"You have to…"

"Shut up, Gregon!" Vectra snapped her fingers and a black playing card materialized out of nowhere. She practiced her sleight of hand while thinking over the situation. Monica wasn't sure what was going on and turned to the dwarf for answers.

"Gregon, what is happening? What has my brother gotten himself into?"

"Something above his head. I think that would be quite obvious." Vectra did not give Gregon a chance to respond. "Most likely an artifact from an older world that is highly sought after by other people."

"I think he was after a press. An old-fashioned printing press. I saw a sketch of it once, before Trevor put it away. He wasn't allowed to discuss his work with us."

"Ugh! That cursed Artenian." Despite the fact that she had mumbled it under her breath, Monica could still make out what the woman had said.

"Look, I don't know why, nor care, what this 'Artenian' person did to you. What I do care about is finding my brother and getting him back…alive." Monica felt that last word get stuck in her throat and was surprised that it made it out at all. The idea that her brother might already be dead was an all too real possibility. Her head shook the notion away as Gregon stepped forward.

"Vectra…" He paused upon seeing Vectra's hardened stare bearing down onto his gentler expression. "You have too. You can't skip out again. If you deny them help this time…"

"Why do you care?" She snapped. "What does it matter to you what happens to me?"

"Because you are my friend."

Vectra snorted at his comment. "Friend? I am your friend? Were you not the one who told me you cared for no other than yourself?" She slipped the playing card under the leather cuff over her left arm. Squatting next to Gregon, visibly wounded by her words, Vectra's balance did not falter while she spoke. "Do not lie, my friend. It is not very becoming of you. Remember, you are not a thief, like I."

"People can change." The dwarf retreated to the back table in his booth and began to clean up his books.

"Why are you so mean?" Monica walked right up to Vectra. "You seem to be the one who doesn't care about anyone but yourself."

Vectra stood up straight. She leaned her face until she came within mere millimeters with the young girl's stare. Their eyes matched in intensity. "It's best that way. If you knew what was good for you, you would go home and forget you ever saw me. Your brother is most likely dead, or will be soon."

"Don't say that!" Dare shouted. His anger filled the air and caused what few people were left to turn their heads toward his outburst. "Trevor is not dead!"

Vectra grabbed a hold of Dare's arm and motioned Monica to shush when she noticed the teen's mouth open in protest. "Listen to me, and hear me well. If you want to live, I suggest you leave at once. There is no place for you here."

"Vectra, you have to do this." Gregon nearly begged.

"Stop it!" Vectra released Dare, raising her hands in the air, and causing all of the seller's books to scatter onto the ground. Her nose flared and eyes flamed with outrage. "Do not interfere with problems not of your own doing." Nothing more was uttered as she briskly spun on the heels of her boots and whisked away down the street. She soon vanished into the retreating shoppers and left the two siblings wondering what to do next.

Chapter Six

"That went over well." Monica's sarcasm dripped from her lips.

"She certainly is strange." Dare remarked with a passive shrug, giving his sister a worried expression.

They both shifted their focus back onto Gregon's booth and the mess Vectra left behind for him to clean up. Books of any and all subject matters were strewn across the ground like tossed playing cards, with some flipped open to random pages of text. Monica took note of how their respective covers and spines were characters within themselves; battle wounds and repair jobs showed scars of past lives in varying degrees of severity. The spine of one such book, her brother observed, had been repaired by three different people and still contained pages falling loose at the binding.

"There was no call for her doing this." Monica's hands cradled a book detailing a collection of folklore tales from Germany, in handwritten words. "She has no respect for you, does she?" Her gaze transfixed on a page partially torn by the forceful throw it endured.

"Vectra has her reasons for what she does."

"You two must have been through a lot together for you

to keep defending her as you do." Dare handed over two leather-bound books on sailing in the Mediterranean. His foot brushed against a copy of Spanish law from 1794, and quickly picked it up from the ground as well.

"She is the closest thing to a relative I have anymore." Gregon whispered into the stillness surrounding them. "I would do anything for her."

"Sounds like you are more committed than she is."

Gregon flashed around to see Monica's outstretched hand giving him another book; this one with gold-tipped pages. "You do not understand. But then again, how could you?" He flipped over the front cover and placed his fingers over the top of the previous owner's initials: VT. "When she sees you, she sees one of the worst mistakes of her life."

Dare blinked at his sister, clearly vexed by what the dwarf said. He did not wish to sound stupid, but he was feeling more and more as though there was something he missed. "Ah…was that supposed to clear anything up for us?"

"Not necessarily. But it is not my place to tell you. That burden is for her to carry, as she frequently reminds us."

"Us?" Monica was questioning whether or not she was awake, or in the middle of a warped dream. Nothing was making sense, so it stood to reason that she had conjured up the entire madness. As though he could hear her thoughts, however, Gregon denied her theory.

"You are in no dream, Brownings. This is real and is truly happening. Unfortunately, Vectra does not want to be a part of it anymore." His voice quieted down before he spoke again. "Or does not wish to face it."

"She's done it again, hasn't she?" A faint cracking in the voice over Dare's shoulder told them who was approaching. Monica turned to see the older tea seller standing with her hands on wide hips. "Gregon, I told you she would not set things right. It is not in her nature."

"Ms. Locksmith, I think you are being unfair."

"UNFAIR? UNFAIR?! Am I being unfair? Vectra is neglecting her job, yet again, and you think I am the one being unfair?" Ms. Locksmith gestured toward the siblings. "She has a duty to uphold. And this time, she NEEDS to oblige."

"You and I both know that she wants them to stay out of it for their own protection. Their brother should never have continued their parents' work."

Monica suddenly wanted to bust in on the conversation upon hearing Gregon talk about their parents. Against her desire to jump in, however, she struggled to keep her mouth shut and decided it was better to keep on listening in order to see what else might be divulged.

"If she was actually protecting these kids, she would lead them to their brother and put a stop to the whole ordeal. But NO! She won't do it because of the past. I tried to warn her."

"Pointing blame is not going to help matters, Ms. Locksmith." Gregon gave the kids a sideways glance as he continued. "There is no guarantee that they would survive and you know that perfectly well. If they turn back now, they get a chance to live out their lives."

Ms. Locksmith's eyes faded into red balls of frustration, and Monica took a step back in case she exploded. It wouldn't have been the weirdest thing to happen that day. "You are a dwarf, so you don't understand what it is like to have someone you love being stolen from you. But I do. These two have a right to get their brother back. They deserve that much after what they have been through." Ms. Locksmith pointed a mostly bony finger at Monica and Dare. "I say they have courage to even come here in the first place. Most normal people would not have done what a strange woman said to do in a dream."

"I do know what it is like, for YOUR information, and I understand both sides to the argument. Now, if you would let me get back to tearing down my booth, I suggest you do the same, Gloria." Gregon stared her down, a hard feat to do at just over four feet tall. With a short twist of her waist, Ms. Locksmith proceeded back the way she came. Monica's mouth hung lower than a submarine.

"Gregon, how does she know that I heard a woman tell me in a dream to find Vectra?"

The dwarf slowed his movements, shielding his face from the two kids as best he could while still cleaning up his booth. However, Monica was not so easily deterred. "GREGON?!"

"It was a wild guess she happened to have right. Things like that do occur, you know."

"Yes, I would be one of the first people to admit that coincidences do happen. BUT…" Monica jumped in Gregon's path, making sure that he had to look her in the face. "That was an awful lucky guess. Most normal people would not have come to that conclusion."

"See? You answered your own question. You said 'most normal people,' and Gloria is NOT a normal person; by any means of the word. That must explain it." Gregon gave her a faked smile and moved around her with considerable ease. Dare stepped in, coming in a little more at eye level with the dwarf.

"You need to tell us, Gregon. What is Vectra protecting us from? What does our brother, and parents, have to do with any of this?"

A heavy sigh escaped Gregon's mouth, sinking his chin into his chest. "I am allowed to tell you some of the story, at least. For I do not know it all." He popped open one of his trunks and whispered some words that caused the books to levitate down into the trunks. Monica took a moment to watch the marvelous spectacle with less surprise after seeing the street fight. "Your parents were in search of an old artifact, much like a treasure hunt. They managed to piece together a majority of the path that lead to an old device with immense power. That was their job for their boss, Gaither. When they realized the full scope of his greed, they came here in search of Vectra's help. I don't know how they knew to find her, nor her name, but they asked and she refused. She went against her job, her sworn duty, and it cost her dearly."

"What job does Vectra have, anyway?" Monica ventured, not wanting him to stop talking.

"She is known in our world as 'The Protector of Thirteen.' Simply put, she guards thirteen objects left behind from the ancient world of Greece when it's culture fell to the Roman Empire, and everyone fled to Harpeon."

"Harpeon?" Dare thought it sounded like a land from a video game on his phone.

"The cultural land that survives in the shadows, between the light and the dark. It is where the ancient world still resides. There, a band of warriors, Celestial Warriors, are led by the same woman that sent you to find Vectra."

"Artenian?"

"Yes. She and Vectra…" Gregon stopped himself. "Have a shared past. I dare tell no more on the matter."

"So, where does our brother fit into all of this?" Dare inquired. "Ms. Locksmith said about him continuing our parents' work."

"It's a press." Monica blurted out; her mind spinning around in her own memories. "A press. An old-fashioned newspaper press." She looked over to find Gregon's face frozen in shock.

"How do you know that?"

"Our brother would keep papers in his attaché case at home. I caught a glimpse at a schematic sketch, in mother's hand, just as he put it away and told me to keep my nose out of it."

"And he should have obeyed his own warning." Gregon yanked the rectangular cloths from the tables and watched them fold themselves into neat piles. "Your brother was kidnapped, you said?"

"Yes. Right off our front porch." Dare's hushed voice came out rather sheepishly. "We watched from the window like cowards." He shoved his right hand into a back pants pocket, and stared at the ground until Gregon walked into his view.

"As hard as it must have been to see your brother being taken away, it was the best thing for you to do." A snap of his fingers, and trunks were latched shut without a single touch on any of them.

"What do you mean?" Dare hid his intrigue over the magic on display.

"If something would have happened to you also, there would be no one to search for your brother." Gregon gave Dare a small smile, trying to cheer the boy up from his depressing thoughts. "All three of you might have been dead by now."

"Gregon, what does the press do? Why is it so important for Gaither's men to be after it? For them to go to all this trouble?" Monica picked the last book up from the debris coated macadam and placed it on top of the largest trunk; which proceeded to eat the book after she left.

"It can rewrite history."

Chapter Seven

"He said right at the tree with the red vines, or was it left?" Dare had taken charge of locating Vectra's camp from the directions Gregon gave them; and against his sister's better judgement. So far, he had successfully turned them around three times in the midst of a patch of overgrown vegetation, stepped into a gopher hole near an abandoned kiddie pool, and was nearly bitten by a guard dog on someone's private property. Their new acquaintance had only verbally given them the way to reach the river's edge, a task more suited for his older sister who excelled in lecture-style classrooms.

"Left. Can't you hear the water?" Monica joshed her brother. The gurgling of the river sounded from behind a line of bushes up ahead. With a simple push of the palm of her hand, Monica opened up a hole in the mountain laurel to show Dare the tranquil water flowing over rocks and fallen tree limbs. Sunlight danced across its rippled surface as the sun began its descent in the sky.

"Right. I knew left was right." Dare gave himself a bewildered look. "That sounded better in my head." Rolling her eyes, Monica retook the lead. They carefully walked down the sloped embankment to where a purple-striped tent stood out from the surrounding green and brown plant life. Nestled between brambles and trees, the cozy campsite gave off a century old circus vibe in the small corner of land. A well-used metal pot, suspended above the dirty fire pit, swung in the light breeze gently pushing the tide toward shore. Monica took note of the singular camping chair, with its back to the east. *Someone likes to watch the sunsets in the west*, she thought to herself.

"Vectra?" Monica hesitantly called out; figuring it was best not to surprise the woman again, considering the earlier entanglement.

"Go away!" The guardian's voice bellowed from behind the flapped-over entrance to the tent.

"We can't. We are not leaving until you help us find our brother."

"Good luck in the rain tonight, then. Hope you don't catch pneumonia. Or worse."

"We know about the Thirteen Objects you protect. And the press my brother is trying to locate." Monica stopped herself before saying anything more. She wasn't sure how much she should state aloud in the quiet air of the public embankment. There was no telling what prying eyes and nosy ears could be trained in on them at that very moment.

To the siblings' mutual disappointment, Vectra did not respond. Monica looked down at her brother, seeing his saddened face. "We are not giving up." She reassured him. Glancing at the fire pit's ring, it puzzled Monica why the metal was so shiny at the base where the ground touched the orange tinted metal.

"That's odd. The pit is made from bronze." Dare watched his sister, matching his gaze with hers.

A sudden smile formed on the young girl's mouth as an

idea struck her. *I don't think she would like us talking about everything out in the open either.* "Well, Dare, I guess we are just going to have to find Trevor on our own. Hopefully we won't end up like Mom and Dad. You know, I wonder why we remind Vectra of the worst mistake of her life?" Her brother's eyes widened in surprise at her abrupt change in tone, hastily tapping her arm and gesturing at the tent confusedly.

Vectra whipped the flap back and stepped out in view. Her stance rigid as she squinted against the strong sunbeams drenching the shore in a golden hue. A sense of inner pride started sprouting inside Monica's mind, now that Vectra's attention was captured. "Gregon, I presume." The guardian did not try to hide her displeasure, spitting as she talked. "That Kurzian!"

"Don't blame him. He was only trying to help."

"Help? The last time he tried to help…"

"He saved us." Dare interjected. Vectra studied the siblings carefully, scoffing at the notion.

"My first impression is that you would be daft enough to repeat your parents' mistake. Very well. Come inside." She motioned for them to follow her into the canvas covered shelter.

Monica stepped forward first, and was taken aback to see that the interior was really just as small as the exterior showed it to be. "Wow. I was expecting the inside to be much larger." She proceeded to sit down on a large pillow while her brother did likewise to her right. *It is as though she was expecting us.*

"What? You thought it would be some grand hotel suite disguised as a small tent from the outside? Sorry to disappoint you." Vectra rummaged around in a large-sized duffle bag, in search of food. "Clearly someone has been reading too many wizardly books. Although, that one series was a pretty good read. There were a few parts the author got right." Turning around with four shrink-wrapped meat sticks in her hand, Vectra offered them to her "unexpected" guests. "Venison, beef, gator, or crocodile?"

"Crocodile?" Monica shared a bizarre look with her brother.

"And clearly you have not visited the south."

"I'll try the venison. Thanks." Dare pulled out the one closest to him. "Seeing all those fluffy pastries at the farmer's market made my stomach hungry." He tore into his stick without much hesitation. Monica eyed the remaining options suspiciously, before picking out the one marked "beef" in permanent marker.

"So, you want to find your brother?" Vectra returned the gator meat stick to the bag whilst opening the crocodile-labeled stick for herself.

"For the fifteenth time today, YES." Monica was not known for being a problem child, nor wished to be. However, time was ticking and she was beginning to feel like a broken record. Trevor was gone and Vectra was the only one who could help. If it took a firmer approach to obtain the woman's assistance, then that was what she was going to have to do.

"I just want to make sure you know what you are getting yourself into, is all. Because once we begin, there is no going back."

Monica's mouth dropped. She was becoming increasingly frustrated telling Ms. Tillerman the same thing over and over again. "Why else would we be here, in the first place? We came here to get my brother back and that is exactly what we are going to do."

"Besides," Dare took a pause from chewing, "he is our

home-school teacher. You wouldn't want to be the reason that two kids fell behind in their schoolwork, now would you?"

Vectra bore her eyes through the young boy's, making him feel uncomfortable. He shyly shifted his butt in the pillow, wishing for her to stop glaring at him. "Sass will not earn you any points with me, young one. And it would do you no good to think me dumber than you look either. Just because I choose to live my life not as modern as others, does not mean I do not know about online schooling."

"My brother isn't dumb." Monica objected. "And how did you know that we attend online schooling?"

"One would be blind not to see the computer glasses stowed away in his pants pocket. The bulge on the thigh is not concealed too well." Vectra gracefully crisscrossed her legs as she sat down across from them while chomping down on her meat stick. Her expression turned perplexing, and she gazed down at the food out of curiosity. One quick sniff of the end she bit off, explained the problem, and disgust became written on her face as her nose squinched up in revolt. "Varmit. I should have known that little rascal would have given me a dud."

Monica gulped, giving her own meat stick a cautionary look, studying the wobbly, handwritten label with doubt.

"You should be in the clear, Kid. Yankis only gives me one dud each lot." Vectra tossed her meat stick out of the tent, making sure to have peeled the plastic wrapper entirely off before discarding. "At least it makes for a good fire starter."

"Do you like sitting on the floor?" Dare pointed to the pillows and the lack of any chairs within the tent. "Is this what the Japanese sit on during a tea?"

"In Japan, they sit on what is called a zabuton. These

are just large pillows I sewed with a few yards of fabric. There are a number of differences, beginning with the fact that these do not have tassels on their corners. But that is another day's talk." Vectra leaned toward Monica and Dare, clasping her hands together. "What you witnessed today was only the start of what is to come, if you choose to embark on this journey." She took a breath. "Do you still want to do this?"

Monica nodded in unison with her younger brother, who was in the midst of shoving the last of his meat stick into his mouth. "We do."

"I do not know whether you are brave or foolish."

"We have no choice in the matter. Trevor is our legal guardian. Without him…" Monica paused. "our future is the children's home."

"You have no other relatives?"

"Not that we know of." Dare answered.

"Very well." With a smirk on her face, and her right hand spinning a two of hearts, Vectra suddenly blew on the card and it dissolved into a fine mist in the air between them. Slowly, the mist floated toward the two kids and coated them from head to toe in daintily small sparkles. Monica sneezed as it tickled her nose hairs, while Dare watched the dazzling mist disappear upon coming in contact with his skin.

"What was that?" He looked at Vectra in wonder. "I have never seen glitter that vanished. Normally, you can't even look at the stuff without it sticking to you."

Vectra's back straightened like a board, her face gravely serious in its nature. "I abhor glitter. You will NEVER EVER find me using that monstrous embellishment."

"Duly noted." Monica checked her clothing for any trace of the disappearing substance she watched touch her shirt. "But, then…what is it?"

"A concealing powder. To keep the others from tracking you. We wouldn't want you to die before we have completed our task, now would we?"

"Come again?" Dare poked his sister in the shoulder.

"This isn't some video game. I hope you realize this. Gaither's men kidnapped your brother. Most likely because he found Clio's Press, one of the Thirteen Objects I was so fortunate to inherit." Vectra's voice grew sarcastic on the last note before reverting back to all seriousness. "Or came very close to doing so, at least." She shook her head. "I thought I took care of hiding it exceedingly well last time."

"Gregon says that it has the power to literally rewrite history. Is that true?" Monica risked her meat choice, and chewed, satisfied at the normal flavor.

"Gregon has an oversized mouth for such a little man." Vectra shifted on top of her pillow. "But, yes, it is true. Clio is the Greek goddess of history and poetry. She created a press that made it easier for her to record dates and times, as well as stories."

"Don't you mean 'was' the goddess of history and poetry?" Dare crumbled the plastic wrap up in his hands before stuffing it into his free pants pocket. "That was back in ancient times."

"I can see that you have a lot to learn, my dear boy." Vectra pulled out a metal thermos from the duffle bag. Though the stainless-steel body was common in appearance, the lid was modified in a unique way. "When the Greek world was crumbling to the rule of the Romans, all the gods and goddesses fled to Harpeon. It is the land between the light and the dark, living in-between the shadows of time. During their escape, not all of their items were able to come with them, hence the reasoning behind the need for my job.

One of the objects I guard is her press. Whoever uses it, can rewrite history anyway they wish. It will change the world you know in a blink of an eye and erase the past as if it never even happened. No one will remember how it was, except for the person controlling the press."

"Why are objects like that still on Earth? Why are they not in that land…Harpeon…by now?" Monica's head moved to the side in fascination of the horizontal gear spokes protruding from where the spill-proof seal should have been. With a twist to the right, Vectra dialed it to match the top drink icon she wished for. A flattened red light blinked on and the softened sound of a motor hummed.

"Do I look like a goddess?" Vectra swept a few hairs from her eyes.

"I don't know. What does a goddess look like?" Dare ventured, equally intrigued by the portable drink maker.

"Fair point. But the answer is, I am not sure. I am only the one assigned to protect them, not the one hired to move them to Harpeon. Although, it would be nice if they were."

"Wait," Dare broke his concentration on the steaming cylinder. The light clicked to green and flashed twice. "The Romans adopted the gods and goddesses, so why did they flee? Or for that matter, how could they?"

"Objects representing their Greek forms were sent to Harpeon in order to preserve parts of the culture they could, before they were changed into their Roman forms. See, not only their names and some symbols are different, but their powers changed as well. As Rome gave way, they fled to Harpeon themselves, this time for good."

"Okay. So where do we need to go first?" Monica tucked her meat stick under her leg. There was no telling when they were going to be able to eat again, and she wanted to save it for later.

"We will need to visit Martiban. He is the one with the key." Vectra popped the gear lid open and sipped on the hot liquid.

"Great. How do we get to him?"

"Not so fast, Monica Browning. First, we will need to retrieve the…map…from Gregon."

"He didn't tell us anything about a map." Dare hungrily looked at the duffel bag for the last stick of meat.

"That is because he does not know he has it." Vectra reached in and gave the boy what he craved. "It is hidden in a book he is sworn to keep for me."

"Why do you not keep it yourself?" Monica asked.

"Just in case of people wanting to get to the press like you two do. I would fail at my job if I had it served on a silver platter for anyone who strolled on by." Vectra pulled the pillow out from underneath her. "You ask a lot of questions."

"I like to know things."

"Sometimes, it is better not to know." Vectra gently placed the hot bottle on the ground and folded the pillow in half to find an oversized blanket hidden within. She took her hat off, laid it next to her and flicked out the blanket to full length. "We will start out at first light. Gregon does not leave to return home until the following day, so we will be able to catch up to him tomorrow."

"Night is coming on fast. Where are we going to sleep?" Dare looked to his older sister for an answer, shivering as the grip of night seeped in through the crack in the tent flap. "We don't have much money. And our jackets are…"

"Best you two stay here with Taminus lurking about."

"Taminus? I thought you killed him at the market today?" Monica felt the grumbles in her stomach and gave in their call. She ripped off another chuck of meat, plunking it gratefully into her mouth.

"That will be the day. He isn't dead. Just dormant, or sleeping. I merely knocked him out for a while." Vectra went to wriggle herself under the blanket when she winced in pain from the stabbing wound in her boot. The temporary medicine she gave herself earlier was fading in its potency, causing her leg to slowly swell back up again.

"Are you alright?" Dare crunched up the other plastic wrapper and shoved it into his pants pocket to join with the first.

"I will be. There is another stop I must attend to before we meet up with Gregon. I may…need some help getting there." Vectra painfully turned her back, brought the blanket's edge to her chin, and stared at the barren tent wall. "You will find blankets in your pillows as well."

"So cool." Dare whispered to his sister. Monica shrugged her shoulders as they followed suit and prepped for bed.

"And we are going to need to get you two thicker coats if you are to go with me. Those thin, jersey knit outer jackets don't even break the wind."

"I hate waking up early." Monica muttered under her breath whilst trying to get comfortable on the hardened floor. She was not a morning person and was always the last one running down the drive for the school bus in the morning for elementary school. A memory of her racing out the door, her mouth filled with a whole piece of toast, and literal bread crumbs falling in her wake, surfaced. The nostalgic sound of her mother calling out to her, telling her to slow down, brought a bittersweet grin to her face. *We will find Trevor, alive. I promise you that Mother. I promise.*

Chapter Eight

Morning streamed into the tent, through the opening slit, and landed between the two siblings on the floor. Monica's eyes felt weary when she opened them and rubbed the sleep dirt from their corners with her hand. Out of habit, Dare reached over with his arm, to hit the snooze button on his alarm clock, and ended up poking his sister in the eye instead.

"Owww! Wake up Derrick!" Monica wished she had a pillow to throw at his head. *Wait a second!* She looked down at the ground where the absence of last night's pillow was, causing her to search for the blanket that appeared missing as well. *I could have sworn that part was not a dream.* Her neck was cramped and sore, causing her to massage near the base of her head and bringing her fingers to glide over the faint birthmark underneath her hair.

"What? Sorry." Dare apologized. His arms reached to the sky as his back flexed in a massive morning stretch. "I thought I had heard my alarm go off. Must have been dreaming we were back home."

"Yeah, and my eyeball is proof of that." Her right eye remained nearly squinched closed. "Where's Vectra?"

Monica looked over at where they had last seen Ms. Tillerman sleeping before they succumbed to fatigue. Her pillow and blanket were layered on top of one another, poised for travel.

"Morning Sleepyheads." Vectra poked her head inside the tent's flap and showed them a morning sausage sizzling in a metal skillet. "Breakfast is ready before you two are." Dare and Monica straightened out their clothes before exiting the tent. The intense sunlight blinded them for a moment, catching them off guard.

"I forgot to pack my sunglasses." Dare instantly held his hands up as a shield and stumbled his way over to the fire pit. "But it does smell delicious."

"Do we need to stop by Brockston's B and B, or any of the hotels by the interstate, to gather your things? I noticed the lack of a backpack on either of you yesterday." Vectra picked out the sausage from the hot pan, and transferred them onto metal camping plates.

"No. We came by bus. Besides, we are too young to check into hotels without an adult being present." Once Monica's eyesight returned, she was immediately transfixed by the morning light dancing across the river. It mesmerized her into a trace and a longing to watch it for the rest of the day while her brother went straight for the food.

"I find it difficult to believe you didn't bring any packs, at all. Seems to me that two kids, who consistently inform me they are not stupid, would have brought along provisions. Especially considering the fact they know not of what the day shall bring."

"Oh, yeah, we did. We stored them at the…" Dare stopped talking when he noticed his sister vehemently shaking her head at him to keep quiet.

"Where did you store them?"

"It's safe. That's all that matters. Can we go now?" Monica picked up a piece of the bacon cut sausage. "This is really good."

"You might want to try it first before declaring your opinion."

"But Dare has and he likes it." Monica quickly responded, cracking her stoic expression into a cover-up smile.

"You aren't a vegetarian, are you? Because I do not do special orders." Vectra pulled the skillet from the flames. Dumping it in a half-filled galvanized tub, she picked a washcloth up from the soapy water and proceeded to clean the pan. "If you don't eat what I make, you might as well starve now, because if it is not on clearance at the grocery store, it stays on the shelf. Unless it is that fake meat crap. I only do the real stuff."

"No, I'm not. Just waiting for the sausage to cool down, is all."

"We will not be coming this way again, so I suggest you pick up your backpacks before we head out." Vectra used a quilted hot pad, covered in cats, in order to grab a flame-scarred teapot from above the fire pit. Carefully, she aimed the spout at a small, matching teacup perched on a collapsible side table. Monica noticed the paper tip of a tea bag resting on the outside of the cup. "Anyone else care for some tea? European blend."

"No thanks." Monica tore a piece of the sausage bacon off with her teeth. She was surprised to find that it tasted rather to her liking, and her stomach rumbled for more. "Is there by chance any more sausage?"

"Here ya go, Sis." Dare handed her another one of the strips, leaving him with five still greasing up his palms.

"Wash your hands off in the river when you are finished. First task of the day is to see a man in town. Then we will pick up your belongings, wherever you stashed them."

"Thanks for the breakfast." Dare eagerly chomped down on the rest of the hot meat whilst walking down to the water's edge. The refreshing feeling of the river was enough to wake anyone up from lingering tiredness. "Whoa, it's cold!"

By the time Monica joined him in washing her hands, she grew horrified at her messy hair in the water's reflection. What used to be neatly brushed black locks of semi-curly hair had become an entangled nest engulfing her head. The sun's light made her pale skin glisten and forced her brown eyes to blink a few more times. "Oh my gosh!" Her fingers flew into action as she tried combing the frizzy explosion with water and saliva. "I have a wild lion's mane on my head."

"I thought you were just going for a new look." Her brother teased, receiving an elbow jab in the ribs for his joke.

"Time to go." Vectra called out. "Come inside and help me collapse the tent." She limped her way into the canvas structure, followed by the siblings. "Fold up the floor covering and shove everything into my duffel bag, Monica. Dare, here are the keys for the padlocks on the outer ties. Unlock them, place them in the bag as well, and remove the looped strings. Let me know when you are done."

They carried out her instructions, and within five minutes, all tasks had been completed. Vectra reached up to where a gearbox was attached to the middle pole and gave a short hand crank two turns. Letting the machine do the rest, all three of them watched the pole spring up four inches from the ground. The corner poles shot straight out, folded into themselves at the halfway mark, and folded again into a large inside-out umbrella. In a total of sixty seconds, the entire tent fitted into the middle pole before Vectra snapped it in half and latched the two ends together with a metal piece on the hand crank.

Monica and Dare turned around to find themselves speechless at the campsite that was no more. Only the remnants of the fire ring and a large-sized duffel bag were left. "Did you invent that contraption?" Dare stood wide-eyed.

"No. Now, we are going to see Servius." Vectra limped her way over to the bag and shoved the pole inside. She zipped it shut and tossed it beside the fire pit. "I would take the vehicle; however, my driving foot is the one that was damaged. So we are going to walk."

"I could drive." Offered the eager boy.

"While that is a kind gesture, I do not wish to attract more unwanted attention from the police with an underage driver at the helm."

"Who is Servius?" Monica stepped to the right of Vectra and helped her up the embankment.

"An old…collector of oddities." Vectra tried moving as fast as she could. "Best we not dawdle while in this area. Once we reach the woods, there will be better protection there."

Turning down Portobello Road, it looked like any lazy town in America on Sunday. There was no evidence of the previous day's events and it was eerily quiet. Monica's neck tingled. She felt as if someone was watching them, but each time she scanned up and down the road, there was no one to be found.

Two right turns and one left turn later, Vectra paused outside of a curio shop's worn entrance. Despite the age of the brick-constructed building, the tired wooden frames around the bay windows and door were more artistically distressed than ancient looking. One could tell that the wood had been painted originally a dark blue at one point because of the paint's intense coloring behind a park bench to their right. Vectra attempted to twist the 18th century knob, but it was locked.

"I don't see any lights on inside." Monica raised herself another inch by standing on the tips of her toes. Her hands were cupped around her eyes as her nose almost made contact with the dusty window. "I don't even see any movement." Vectra ignored her observations and quickly produced an oxidized key from the 'stay away' door mat underneath her feet.

"Be on your best manners in here. Do not touch anything."

"Doesn't he know that is the oldest trick in the book? Putting a key under the door mat. Highly unsafe." Dare studied the skeleton key discolored from the natural elements.

"You would be right, if it were not for one thing. Only certain people, such as myself, can access the key. For it appears for the ones living in my realm, and no others."

"What is your realm, exactly?" Monica heard the lock open as Vectra turned the key.

"When you figure that out, you can let me know. We just call it the Olde Realm."

Chapter Nine

The place was stocked with antiques all over. Shelves were littered with knick-knacks from closed-up dime stores and gas stations long since considered bygones. The floor creaked in protest as Dare stepped gingerly over to a wall plastered with license plates from each of the fifty states. His interest was piqued at the bullet holes in the one from Illinois. "Probably from Chicago." He whispered to his sister, who had her eyes set on the small selection of leather books in need of a good dusting.

"Would you look at that!" Monica stopped herself short of touching the first edition of Mark Twain's Huckleberry Finn. *Vectra said no touching,* she scolded herself. "Com'on Dare. Let's stay close to Vectra." She grabbed hold of her brother's shoulder and guided him up to the counter. "Are those pennies?"

"Yep. 882 of them to be exact." Vectra gazed down at the resin poured countertop with all of the pennies shining bright in their clear prison. She tapped the bell to the side of a sign stating 'please ring for service.' Shortly thereafter, a man in a dark leather apron, a light blue peasant shirt, green khakis and comfy shoes strode out from a back room.

He peered over small specks resting on the large bridge of his nose. Through a lack of wrinkles and deep lines, in and around his face, Monica wagered the owner to be in his late forties. Premature grey hair poked out from above and below a green dealer's visor.

"Vectra…" He smiled with crooked teeth, "what brings you here on my day off?"

"Do I need a reason to visit you Servius? Perhaps it was just to give you a break from online gambling. What is it today? Trying your luck at the wheel or at the poker games?"

"Neither. Slots, if you are so interested in knowing." He smacked a wad of pink gum against his left cheek while clicking on a pocket-sized dice randomizer. "Now, what do you need?" Servius laid the clicker down, where it continued to self-generate various combinations, and placed his hands on top of the counter defensively.

"No cause for dramatics, Servius. I am not here as a spy for your wife. Although, why she still puts up with you is beyond me. After a century or two, you would think she would have grown fed up with your gambling habits."

Servius shrugged. "Why should she complain after all I have given her?"

Monica and Dare stared at the man who could have been a cartoon drawing in an old animated film. He smelled of tobacco and peppermint, an odd combination in Dare's mind. The man's eyes were mischievous in nature, giving the pair a mixed feeling about the owner of the curio shop.

"A few drops of nectar, if possible." Vectra leaned over the counter and lowered her voice to keep the others from eavesdropping. "I need some of your traditional honesty as well." Servius cast a look over at Monica and Dare. His eyes squinted studiously at the two, giving Monica the creeps. Without a word, Servius left the counter. Shuffling into the back room, he reappeared a moment later with a small package cradled in his palm. It was wrapped in plain kraft paper and tied with a twine bow, as if it were illegal alcohol in miniature form.

"You have the goods?" Servius maintained a three foot distance from the counter until Vectra nodded.

"Not too shabby, this one." She gently placed a flat European button, made from tombac, in front of him. "Comes from the Gallegos de Argañán region. Late 18th century."

"That will do for the nectar." Servius eyed the button with fascination. "But not for the other request. It is getting harder to make the brew, and…"

"How come every time I come in here, your price goes higher?!" Vectra hit the counter and winced in pain. A burning sensation was consuming her leg, making it difficult to stand. "Taminus, curse you!" She mumbled.

"So he finally wounded you." Servius smirked. "Appears you are not as invincible as you thought you were."

"If you don't want your wife to know where you sneak off to on Tuesday nights, then I suggest you keep your mouth shut. I do not believe that Bruno and his friends would like the police raiding his midnight poker."

Servius stepped back from the counter, quickly picking up the flat button and stashing it in a pouch strapped to his waist before Vectra changed her mind. "No, he wouldn't. But you still have to trade for the…"

"Fine." Vectra muttered. She reached into a small pocket on her vest to produce a hand painted, enamel button from the 19th century with a girl in a pink dress standing against a chipper blue sky. "That should be enough payment. Since you have been after it for years."

The man happily tossed the package to Vectra, jumping in gitty glee over having finally obtained his long sought after prize. "At last!" He held it up in the air, and brought a magnifying glass out to examine the piece. "Just confirming that it is the genuine article. No offense, Vectra."

"Servius, I would be offended if you did not check it." Vectra grinned and reached over for Monica to assist her to the door.

"Wow." Dare gazed at the case full of buttons to the left of the counter. Servius flipped a switch and the entire case lit up with LED bulbs.

"Want to take a closer peek at my collection?" The man's sleaziness oozed in the air.

"Dare." Monica softly called for her brother, who followed them out of the strange shop without another word.

Chapter Ten

Dare continued to stuff his face with an extra-large candy bar, in his new dark blue jacket, while his sister dragged him away from the sidewalk. "Why did you tell Vectra about the backpacks?" She cast a weary glance at the Guardian, sitting on a bench and waiting for her portable drink maker to craft another hot beverage. "Did you forget that the whole reason for us to keep the backpacks hidden is so that it wouldn't fall into the wrong hands?"

"But won't it be safer around Vectra, than sitting in a bus locker?" Dare objected. "You saw how she took care of that Taminus guy." His sister remained silent, knowing that her brother was actually right and not wanting to give him the satisfaction of agreeing. "Besides, she gave you four dollars for a candy bar. Go in and spend it while you can." He pointed to Georgina's Candiporium behind him. "They have a great selection of gummi candies."

Monica's mouth watered. "I hate you." She whispered to Dare as she went into the shop. Her brother chuckled, knowing his sister's weakness and watched her through the glass in a cream-colored winter coat. It was nice to see her smiling again, purchasing a small bag of gummi sharks from the older cashier. He hadn't seen joy on her face since the night they fought with Trevor about him wanting to leave on a business trip. That night really shook Monica to the core. Memories of their parents' final goodbyes hit like a brick wall, and she did not hold anything back during the argument.

"I am surprised you haven't finished your chocolate by now." Monica spooked her brother back to the present. "You alright?"

"Fine. Just thinking." Dare smiled to give his sister reassurance. "Let's go check in on Vectra." They walked side by side over to where the Guardian was finishing her drink.

"Feel better?" Monica asked, still intrigued with the abnormal thermos container.

"Better. But I think I will rest here while you two grab your pack from wherever you hid it."

"What about Taminus?"

"I will keep an eye out for him." Vectra glanced down at her pocket watch. "The time is 9:47 am. Can you get to the location and back within thirty minutes from here?" Monica nodded. "Good. If you don't return in precisely thirty minutes, I will come in search of you two. I should be back to being myself by then. In case he does happen to find you," she handed them each a matchstick, "strike this and blow the flame into the air. It will create a beacon and I will come find you."

"You shouldn't be giving kids matches!" The older cashier from the candy shop scolded from the doorway. "Who do you think you are?!" She stormed up to them, readjusted her glasses, and took a step back. "Vectra, I am terribly sorry. Mistook you for a tourist."

"That is quite alright Ms. Weinstock. Hope your brother is faring well after his fall."

"The big oaf is becoming antsy from lying in bed all day and night. I try to give him small projects to keep him busy, but you know how he is. Still sharp as a fiddle. Or is it fit as a tack." Ms. Weinstock shook her head. "Must be getting back to my shop. See you another time, Vectra."

"That woman is a little messed up in the head." Dare stated as he threw his trash in a waste can next to the bench.

"Don't allow her words to fool you. She may be bad at metaphors, but she can balance her shop's books down to the penny." Vectra smiled. "It is good to see her shop survive the test of time. When internet orders were becoming more and more popular, Ms. Weinstock feared that her shop would have to close down. Luckily, I knew someone who owed me a favor. Got her a website that works great and a few of the school students come to volunteer their time to help her ship out orders until her brother is up and moving around again."

"I can't believe you actually smiled."

Vectra looked over to see Monica watching her. "You should be moving along. Remember, thirty minutes and no more."

Chapter Eleven

Dare hastily followed his sister up Main Street, onto Norton Hollow, and down past the park to where the bus station was located. All the shops lining the streets were closed, including the station itself. "Oh no." Monica went for the door, seeing if it was locked, and to their surprise, it wasn't. "What if he is waiting for us inside?"

"How would he know where we stashed them?" Dare pulled the key from his pocket and held it in the air. "One way to find out."

Reluctantly, Monica led the way to where the lockers were kept and stood watch as her brother opened up locker thirty-four. The worn, blue door creaked open to reveal a tiny space jammed full with their black and grey backpacks. Dare struggled to free them and asked his sister for some help, moaning about one of the straps getting caught on the hinge. "How did we get this in here?" With a few more tugs, the backpacks were yanked out and Dare slammed the door shut.

"Nice job." Taminus stepped out from the shadows and peered down at the two Brownings. "They was pretty wedged in there." Dare took a step backwards from him, holding onto his sister with one hand. "Vectra was smart to cloak your aroma. But, unfortunately for you, I already caught onto your scent during yesterday's dual." Now that Monica could see him up close, and not through a tablecloth, she looked over his appearance.

The hazy blue tailored suit fit comfortably on Taminus's lean build. His trimmed goatee helped to define his already strong chin and jawline while a monocle sat in front of his left eye. Hazelnut hair curled slightly out from underneath a matching blue top hat with goggles resting along the ribbon line. A high white collar was held closed by a dark chocolate-colored tie, coordinating with the leather strap securing his shoulder armor in place. Small grommets and metal adornments added to the flare of it all.

"She may have knocked you out yesterday, but she will finish you off today!" Monica stood as tall as possible with her chest puffed out. *These people sure do like their steampunk looks,* she told herself.

"Did she tell you that?" Taminus asked in skepticism. "Hard to believe she would have lied about a fact like that. However, she is a thief and is known for twisting truths." Waving his right hand around his head, a lava rock appeared as if in a magic show. "My dear girl, Vectra and I cannot kill one another." He toyed with the rock in his hand.

Monica's brows bent inward. "Why are you after Vectra's job?" She asked, counting the minutes in her head. *If I keep him talking long enough, perhaps Vectra will come searching for us.*

"Do you think me stupid, child? I knew you were with Gregon. And knowing how much that dwarf likes to talk about his precious Vectra, you should already know that little tidbit." Taminus came down to their eye level. "He did tell you, didn't he?" Monica and Dare shook their heads in unison. "Don't lie to me."

"We aren't. Gregon didn't mention why."

Taminus stroke his short beard, assessing their expressions. "Well, I'll be." He pulled the top hat from his head, popped it down flat as a pancake with a simple tap, and tossed it into the air. It sprang back open and he used his cane to catch it again. "So, he didn't tell you."

"Seems to me like you would not want to be bothered with the ancient relics Vectra protects."

"Ancient relics, you say? My, how little you truly do know. I find it almost amusing." Taminus repositioned the monocle, whose glass was tinted blue. "To find out where they are hidden of course. Simple greed is my motive. Oldest in the book, but still as viable as ever." He held the lava rock up to the light coming in from a singular window. "Remarkable things about lava rocks…they can manufacture the heat from their previous environment." His fingers held the rock close to Monica's face. Her skin could feel the heat pulsating from the porous surface and she tried to move away from the increasing warmth.

"Closest thing I have to feeling the power of fire in my veins. It won't be like that for much longer. Vectra's time will come."

Dare grabbed ahold of his sister's arm and dragged her out of the locker room, past Taminus. "What is the matter with you?!" He shouted at her without looking behind, racing at his top speed to get away from the man. "You don't just stand there! You run!"

"We shouldn't…" Monica didn't get to finish her statement before they both went catapulting through the air and right out the door of the bus station. Falling toward the ground, Monica tried preparing herself for the hard collision that might mean her death. She closed her eyes, only to find herself in a net hovering above the ground. Though it kept them from being smashed onto the pavement, the sudden stop knocked the breath from her lungs. Vectra's netting slowly disintegrated and eased the two kids down as Monica's breathing began to recover, "…turn our backs to him."

Chapter Twelve

"Taminus, let the children go. They know nothing about any of this." Vectra placed herself in front of Monica and Dare. She eyed the backpacks by his feet, wondering what might be in them that would make the Brownings so desperate to keep hidden. *Most likely, Taminus should not get his hands on them either.*

"You know I can't, Vectra. Not after I had a whiff of their aroma. They're Brownings. They reek of it."

"That may be true, but like I said, they know nothing about the press. It is their brother, Trevor, you should be looking for." A realization dawned on her. "But that probably is what brought you to me in the first place." Vectra whipped an eight of hearts at Taminus. He side stepped it with ease, laughing at the feeble attempt of an attack.

"Have you been weakened so much already by the tiny drop of petrifying ink I dipped my blade in? It wasn't even a millimeter's worth." Taminus laughed until he noticed the horrified expressions on the kids' faces. He turned around to see the enormous, fire-fueled black widow spider looming about five feet away.

Taminus pulled some sedimentary rocks from his pockets and threw them into the air, knocking his hat off balance atop his head. He was about to clap his hands when Vectra whipped more cards out from her own palms. Their razor-sharp edges sliced the rocks in half. But instead of thwarting Taminus's plans, his face bore a grin right before he double clapped. The broken pieces, now multiplied, grew ten times their original sizes and rained upon the spider. Thrusting his hands upward, the rocks defied gravity by heading into the sky, and prepared another blow to snuff out her fire beast. Vectra pulled her blade out like the previous day and raced toward Taminus, his attention focused in on the rock attack.

He erupted in a whaling cry as she stabbed him in the back while the pummeling rocks finished off her spider's last breath. "Do you remember what this feels like? To be stabbed in the back?!" Vectra suddenly heard a whistling sound and looked to her right as a large boulder slammed into her side. She struck the ground with the heel of her boot and used it to pivot out from under the rock's momen-tum. Her body swung around and she took a second to catch her breath.

As Vectra balled her hands into fists, Dare and Monica watched the boulder continue its way across the park and crash into the pharmacy building's brick wall. "You didn't even give me a chance to say hello." Taminus kissed the stolen ring on his pinky finger. "Such rude manners."

"If you were half the fighter Bregit was, you would have already mastered the water skill enough to call it when none can be found." Vectra brought her fists together and twisted them in opposite directions. Separating her hands again, a string of black and gold playing cards spanned her reach. Though they were individually hard and unbending, the invisible bond holding them together moved fluidly. She released one end, keeping the other hand attached to the line of killer cards.

Wielding the magical rope with great care and purpose, Vectra swung it over her head in a large circular pattern before taking direct aim at Taminus. The ending cards sparked off from the rope and launched themselves as missiles. Dare leaned over to his sister while the battle commenced. "Should we try to get our backpacks?"

"No. We would only be in the way." Monica observed the sparring match-up between the two warriors and how Taminus always remained within two feet of their packs. "He isn't moving far enough away from them for us to get a clear shot at taking them back. And I do not want to accidently get hit by one of those cards."

Vectra shouted out into the heavens above, and the magical rope enlarged into a lasso. Casting the loop at Taminus, who was preoccupied with fending off a fire snake, she roped him like a steer. "You shall not win." Her heels dug deep into the pavement, causing the ground to crumble under her feet.

Taminus strained under the power of the rope, his arms attempting to push the tightening grip away. In his eyes' reflection, a golden circle of light began to race around him, draining his energy and transferring it back to Vectra. "I will not go down so easily this time." He snarled at her, the glass in his monocle cracking from his anger and remaining strength bulging his cheeks. He instinctively reached down for one of the backpacks as the earth was beginning to fall underneath his feet. Monica knew she had to think fast when she saw him grabbing onto hers.

"Take mine, but not Dare's. Don't take the other one." She shouted.

Taminus immediately went for her brother's and disap-

peared into the ground. Nothing more than a dust mound
was left.

Chapter Thirteen

"Come on." Vectra did not waste any time in her footsteps. She sped down Main Street and took a back alleyway with the two kids in tow. "We must hurry and leave to catch up to Gregon."

Monica clutched tightly onto the backpack straps wrapped over her shoulders. She could not believe that it worked; saving the right pack by asking him not to take the wrong one. "Wait a second! I want to make sure that all my things are still in this bag."

Vectra flung around so quickly, Dare thought his eyes were spinning. "No, you wait a second. Taminus is highly drained of power, for the moment. But if you want to end up back in his hands, by all means…wait a second and let him catch up to you." She caught sight of the wave of fear filling Monica's eyes. "Good. Then I suggest you keep up. We have already lost precious time and have a far distance to go by nightfall."

The trash littering the back alleyway didn't seem to bother Vectra as much as it did Monica and Dare. Large cardboard boxes, and trash bags spilling their contents onto the cobblestone footpaths, were strewn all over the place.

Monica had to keep moving trash out of their way in order to follow the Guardian. "How is it that you can walk so nimbly around everything?" Her voice choked out as the smell of freshly cut onions reached her nose.

Vectra snapped her fingers and the trash was incinerated within the blink of an eye. Dare couldn't keep his mouth shut any longer after seeing all of the recently impossible things that had been happening. "How is it that you can do all of this?" He nearly tripped over a tree root pushing its way up from under the cobblestones when Monica caught him.

"Keep moving." Vectra ordered. "We need to get back to the campsite."

"I thought you said something about having a vehicle?"

"You shall see." Vectra led them down dirt paths long forgotten by the people of the town and brought them out to the embankment where they first started out three hours ago. "Stand back now. I am going to start the fire."

"What?" Monica did not see the point to starting a fire now, but she dare not challenge Vectra's command. Holding her brother back with an outstretched arm, the teenage girl watched in disbelief at the sight before them. Vectra flicked a card into the charred logs of the fire pit and a green flame ignited. Soon, rounded headlights appeared on either side of the pit and wheels protruded from newly expanding fissures in the ground. Slowly making its way up from the earthly crypt it had lived in for a month, a maroon painted 1911 Delaunay-Belleville Landaulette emerged as if brand new.

"Monica, are we in a dream?" Dare whispered to his sister; his eyes widened to their limit. "Because it feels like we walked into a movie of sorts."

"Get in!" Vectra jumped into the driver's side and waited

for the two kids to pile into the singular long bench seat in the back. She quickly pulled the lever towards her body and revved up the engine. "Dare, grab my duffle."

"This can go faster than ten miles per hour, right?" Monica's voice was drenched in doubt.

"But of course. Gears modified this specially for me. He is the inventor of pretty much all of my equipment." Vectra pressed a brassy button on a wooden panel built into the bench seat she was occupying. "And off we go." She stepped on the gas pedal and drove the car on the main roads at a leisurely pace.

"Aren't you going to drive a little faster?" Monica asked, while studying the hard top enclosure that felt more akin to a see-through cage.

"I am blending in. If we rush through town, we are bound to be caught by Chief Warren's men."

"What does everyone else see?" Dare pondered. "Do they see the same car we do?"

"They see what they want to see. For some, it is a four door sedan. To others, it is an SUV with a windshield wiper on the back." Vectra smiled at a passing stranger, waving at them like childhood friends. "And you can always tell when someone envisions one of the sporty muscle cars. They usually have a gaping mouth and a drop of drool dripping down their chin."

Dare glanced over on the left side to witness a young boy pulling wildly on his mother's arm and pointing madly at the old car. Just as Vectra had described, his mouth was wide open and a bead of saliva ran down his chin. "Mommy, look!"

"I see the van dear. It looks a lot like our's, you're right." His mother returned back to the conversation with the other woman about the upcoming bake sale and missed her son's confused expression.

"So, are you a magician?" Monica ventured a guess.

"No, I am not. But perhaps we should keep our eyes peeled for Gregon. He will most likely be in a pick-up truck. It is a beat-up green mess of machinery, but he cherishes it like nothing else." Vectra picked up the pace a little, having reached the outskirts of town where the speed limit was forty-five.

"There." Dare tried to point at the truck pulled off the road about half a mile away. Instead, his finger ended up colliding into the clear glass separating the driver's seat from the back. "Ow."

"Nice catch, Dare." Vectra sped up even faster.

Chapter Fourteen

Coming in behind Gregon's overheating truck, Vectra parked off the road and immediately got out to see her friend. Monica and Dare rapidly climbed down to join her and the dwarf at the propped-up hood, not wishing to be left out of anything. "Vectra, what brings you out this way?" The dwarf peered over his large hands, atop his step ladder, to see the two Brownings staring up at him. "Ah, I see you have decided to help them." His face broke into a joyous grin, curling up into his cheeks with glee. "I am pleased you are setting things right."

"Thanks Gregon, but we are here to borrow the book I gave you for safe keeping." Vectra informed him. "Time is of the essence. Taminus knows who they are."

"Oh my! St. Thomas Aquinas help us." Gregon quickly descended back to the ground and folded the step ladder into the grill of his truck. "I must really have Gears check into the engine. This is the fourth time in the past eight weeks it has overheated."

I wonder if it seems weird to anyone else about Gregon asking for help from saints he does not care for, Monica pondered.

"Did you try using more olive oil?" Vectra glanced over the gears seemingly placed haphazardly in the compartment. "You have had issues with the one piston in the past."

"Yes, I tried six different olive oils from Greece, and none of them have helped. Anyway, you are here for the book. It is in my largest trunk. You know the way. I should keep watch for Taminus."

Vectra spoke her thanks and hurried the kids to the back of the wooden bed frame. Unlatching the tailgate, she lifted both Monica and Dare into the flatbed before hauling herself up. "Open the largest one, Monica."

"It's locked."

"Gregon. The key." Vectra held her hand through the wooden slats of the bed frame and clasped tightly onto the tiny metal object.

"Sorry. I tend to forget about that." Gregon gave a short chuckle as Monica inserted the key. A simple twist moved the interior mechanisms so that the lid could be lifted and she stared into the darkened void that greeted her.

"See the stairs?" Vectra struck a match and dropped it into the deep and darkened hole. Descending past the flight of two hundred steps, Monica and Dare wondered if there even was a bottom to the cavern-like room.

"I thought this was going to be like your tent."

"I did say that the author got some things right." Vectra swung her legs over the trunk's side and began the trek to the bottom. "It does not take as long going down as you may think. It is going up that is the problem."

A gulp sounded out from Dare's throat. He went in after Vectra, keeping an eye on his sister coming down behind him. "Um…" Monica gripped onto her brother's hand.

"It is alright. I am right here. You are not going to fall, Dare. You are going to be alright." Her voice was softer and more tranquil. "We can do this."

"Is he afraid of heights or something?" Vectra paused at the midpoint.

"Yes, he is." Monica called back.

"You two better keep moving." Gregon warned. "Traffic is getting heavier along the road and we don't need more eyes around."

Dare used the wall for balance and a sense of security. "You go on ahead without me. Help Vectra find the book." He wheezed out, his brain spinning from seeing the distance downward yet to be traveled.

"Alright. I will be back for you. I promise." Monica placed her brother's other hand onto the wall as well and left him behind. "I'm coming." She used Vectra's newly created torch as her target in the otherwise dimly lit area.

"The book should be on a shelf marked 'Reserved.' It will be leather-bound, sporting a red band near the top and bottom of the spine, and will be marked with my initials on the top right-hand corner of the first interior page."

"What is the title?"

"How to Survive the End of the World." Vectra flashed the torch over to see Monica's look. "It is just a title. The actual content inside is far more important." They walked over to the section labeled "Reserve" and perused the authors sorted alphabetically by last name. "Here." Under the letter "T," sat one book with no stripes along the spine. "What the…?"

Beside the lonely volume, where another book should have been, a small wooden handled awl rested in the middle of the dusty outline. "AIDAN!" Vectra's voice bellowed into the still air, reverberating off the walls and shaking the cavern from her anger. "That blazen little patty wagon, sheepherder, and all around miserable, insufferable…"

"Vectra, what is the matter?" Gregon called from above.

"Your security has been a little lax, Gregon." Vectra stormed up the steps, leaving Monica in the dust. "Aidan has stolen my book."

A shameful blush appeared on his face. "That must have happened when I got drunk for my birthday and turned the alarm off by mistake."

"Gregon…" Vectra briefly closed her eyes and then reopened them in flames. "That was SEVENTY YEARS AGO!" She climbed out of the trunk and waited for Monica and Dare to do likewise. "That freaking turd of a leprechaun enjoys getting back at me for stealing his favorite pair of shoes."

"Are you talking about a real leprechaun?" Monica relocked the trunk and handed the key back to Gregon. "I thought they were gold miners. Not shoemakers."

"Traditionally speaking, they are shoemakers." Gregon ushered them off his truck. "You have places to go, as do I. So off with the lot of you. If Aidan is getting his tiny hands mixed up in this mess, count me out. That trickster and I do not get on."

"No one likes Aidan, Gregon. That is a fact of life itself." Vectra glared at her friend.

"Be that as it may, I hear my engine purring again and I have to go when the iron is hot. Good luck." Gregon waved them good-bye and jumped into the cab within a minute's time.

"I haven't seen him so quick to move in eons." Vectra squinted at the truck speeding away. "Odd that he should not be searching his inventory for any other books absent from their rightful shelf as soon as I discovered the breach. Unless, he already knew about the missing books."

Chapter Fifteen

"You had to tell Taminus not to grab my bag." Dare rolled his eyes in frustration at his sister.

"For the fifth, and LAST time, I am truly sorry about that. I did tell you not to pack your limited-edition action figure when we left the house." Monica sat the backpack upon her lap and wrapped her arms protectively around it. She rested her chin on the top fabric handle.

"Hey, we didn't know what was going to happen to us. So I wanted to be sure to have my favorite action figure along, in case we didn't make it back home." Dare shoved his hands under his legs. "You know." His head dipped toward his chest as he stared at the floorboard to Vectra's car.

"It's alright, Derrick." Monica reassured him that they would get another action figure when their mission was over. "Trevor will owe us more than just one figurine after we are done saving his butt."

"Why don't you two pick a record to listen to while I am driving?" Vectra offered through the clear wall.

"A record? Like a vinyl record?" Monica saw a drop-down bin pop out of the front wall for them to select one of the many thin black discs in sleeves. "Where is the player?"

"Right behind me, in front of where your brother is sitting."

Dare's head moved to the side at the sight of a yellow button he did not realize was there before. Pressing it in with his thumb, a panel slid left to reveal a vertically installed turntable. "No way." He scooched closer to his sister, looking over the options. "Which one do you want, Monica?"

"How about you pick. After all, you did make a pretty expensive sacrifice back there."

Dare pulled a few of the records out, reading over the titles hand written on their white protective sleeves. Monica expected to find the entire collection to be comprised of classical music scores recorded from great orchestras both past and present. Instead, she was pleasantly surprised to find a variety of songs and singers spanning over all genres. There was country music from the 70s, classic rock from the 80s, pop music from the 90s and early 2000s, and doo wap songs from the 50s. Celtic and Scottish folk songs were listed on one slightly beat up disc, and a brand-new record was recently labeled a "Collection of Harp Masters."

"You have a wide span of musical interest." Monica commented. "I see everything here but rap."

"Let's choose this one." Dare picked up the 50s record. "Seems fitting. Don't you agree?" Monica nodded and went to place it on the turntable. She had seen them back in fashion at the retail stores and recognized the iconic player instantly, but she never heard one being played before; nor seen one with extra attachments such as Vectra's.

"See the extra arms in the large Y shape over the slip mat? It's the circular area where the record goes." Vectra called over her shoulder.

"Yeah."

"Unlatch the feet to the Y arms, and place the record's

middle hole on the center spindle. Then, re-latch the Y; you will find that the underside is felt-covered, and drop the needle onto the outer lines of the disc. It should already be set at 33 rpm, so you don't have to adjust the knob. Nothing else to it, because it automatically plays." Vectra smiled with a tinge of pride on her lips. It was her idea to have Gears install the record player and asked him to make it vertical in order to save on space. He answered the problematic issue of it falling off the spindle with the extra arms to hold it in place, without damaging the surface.

Monica gently put the needle down like she was told, and watched the record spin round and round. Music filled the space with a sound cleaner and more alive than any streaming service or downloaded MP3 could match. "Did you ever think this possible?" Dare looked to his sister. "I don't want to ever wake up if this is a dream."

"Where are we going now?" Monica re-gripped onto her backpack like it was about to fly away. She heard the volume of the music being turned down from Vectra's con-trols at the steering wheel.

"We are headed into the woods by the river. Since the book has been taken by Aidan, there is something I need to fetch from where I live. He will not be giving us my property back without a trade."

"I thought your tent was where you lived." Dare bounced a little up and down to test out the seats.

"In a shipwreck." The way Vectra stated the fact so non-chalantly, Monica assumed that she meant the way it was kept.

"We don't mind. I'm not the best housekeeper either. My room is a wreck on most days."

Vectra shifted the gears and stomped her foot on the gas to begin the climb up a twenty-four-degree graded hill.

"No, no. You misunderstand. I really live in a ship's wreck."

Dare's eyes lit up. "What is the ship?"

"A large boat."

"No, the name of the ship. What is its name?" Dare insisted. "I have been reading about old battleships for one of my class projects. And have come to find that the ships' names were as important as the ships themselves. Care is given in selecting a name for each destroyer, sub, and carrier."

"Does it matter when the ship no longer functions as such?" Vectra tried deflecting the question altogether. "I mean, once you have seen one, you have seen them all." Being in the back, Monica and Dare could not see the look of worry brewing in her eyes.

"That's not true!" Dare argued. He was not going to let it go as easily as she had hoped. "Each ship has their own spirit about them and each one is unique, just like people are."

With a sigh, Vectra decided it was best to tell the boy. *There is no reason he should recognize the name of it. That generation is long gone.* "It was the U.S.S. Chrysaor in a former life." Vectra held her breath for a moment. Even revealing that little detail about her personal life, was beyond her normal standards; especially when talking with strangers she met not twenty-four hours before.

"That name rings a bell." Dare whispered to Monica. "Though, I don't know why."

Vectra breached the hill's top and shifted the gears for the descent. She dreaded what the day would bring, more so than being alone on the river banks with her resident ghost for conversation and her fellow protector for companionship. *The more they know about me, the closer they will be to finding out the truth. And the more who will know my secret. I can't allow that to happen.* If there was one thing she knew about children, it was that they were endlessly curious, and it was going to be an all-consuming effort to keep her past her own.

But then another thought surfaced in her mind; one that shuddered her feelings into a jumbled heap. It wasn't her job to protect them, only the press. *It would have been better, all the way around, if they would have just gone home.*

Chapter Sixteen

The maroon and golden car would have been considered disproportionate by today's standards. Two enlarged headlights sat on either side of the rounded grill; which was a complete opposite to the rectangular hard top covering over both rows of passenger seating. Wooden beams connected the top to the body's frame, matching the darkened color of the large steering wheel between Vectra's hands. In front of the passenger door, to the side of the windshield, was a movable spotlight blazing green instead of the white-yellowish light of the headlights.

"Is your spot light supposed to be green?" Monica asked. She watched the ghoulish light blink on, and follow the passing car until it was out of sight, and the light dimmed once more. "Did it just watch that blue car?"

"Of course. It detects and scans the surrounding area for any possible threats. Blue vehicles always throw it off for some reason. I will have to remember to ask Gears about it the next time I see him."

Dare quizzically stared at the black and white wooden sign hanging along the side of the road. For the past two hours, he had been imagining what Vectra's shipwreck would look like and what lavishly re-modeled interior it would hold; like out of a spy movie. But seeing the state park sign dashed his grand dreams. "I was not expecting a state park. I thought we were going to a marina or some harbor. A state park?"

Vectra turned the vehicle into the main entrance to Leonard Brimy State Park and proceeded pass the ranger station. Two hikers paused at the beginning of the single car bridge, waved to the kids, and continued their walk once the car reached the other side. The large parking lot on the left was half full of mini vans and SUVs, while their families splashed, tossed Frisbees, and played in the leaves. Near the second set of bathrooms, a middle-aged man and his dog were enjoying an easy walk in the woods as they were returning to their car.

Monica gulped down her anxiety after Vectra changed course off the main road and onto a service entrance meant for rangers only. "I don't believe we are allowed to go down this lane." Without a word, Vectra hopped out of her seat, opened the lock with a key, and swung the gate open. She then returned to where she parked, jumped into her one-of-a-kind car, and drove through.

"Monica, can you and your brother re-close the gate please?" Vectra watched them in the side mirrors as they exited the back row.

"Man, my legs are stiff." Dare stretched out his back, legs, and arms. A massive yawn pushed his mouth wide enough that a leaf almost blew onto his tongue. "Yuck, bleah!" He spit out the fowl tasting piece of nature. "That's gross!" His sister laughed at his face of disgust and quickly re-locked the long, yellow swing gate back into place.

"Come on you two. Night will be falling soon and it gets darker rather quickly in the woods." Vectra motioned with her hand for the two kids to hurry up.

"Whoa." Monica's butt sunk into the plush seats again. She still found it remarkable that the black leather appeared new, except for some minor tearing on the corners. It was an experience she could not have dreamt possible; sitting in a fully operational car from the early 1900s, in immaculate condition, and modified to search for monsters living in a fantasy world of old. "How do you happen to have the key?"

"I knew the founding father of the park. His family used to own the iron furnace that was in production from the late 1830s until halfway through the Civil War. The confederates burned down the furnace, though a few remnants of the stone and brick structure still stands a little ways past the main entrance. There is a trail you can take from the Uphill Campground, that gives you a wonderful view of where it would have been."

"You knew the owner of the land?" Dare stared at the back of Vectra's head. "What was the furnace like?"

"It destroyed a large part of the original forest. The process of operating an iron furnace takes a large amount of trees in order for the fire to burn continuously and…"

"Wait, if the owner had this land in the 1830s, that would mean that you are over…" Monica calculated the years in her head.

"You are just now figuring that out, Kid?" Vectra glanced at them through the glass separator. "Anyways, when he donated it to the state to become a park, it was put into writing that I would have access to the park at all times."

"Yeah right." Monica crossed her arms over her chest, leaving her backpack balancing on her knees. "Wouldn't someone have noticed that you are still around? Longer than a human's life span should be?"

"Well, the wording did declare that any of my relatives

and/or descendants would inherit my right for total access to the park. So, I occasionally come up with different names to use." Vectra smirked into the trees. "And before your inquisitive minds ask, it was because I saved his daughter from imminent death when she was twelve years old."

Monica remained silent. She wanted to catch the look on Dare's face, an expression she would have loved to try describing in words. But guilt kept her staring down at the backpack now back in her hands. The blackened cloth was rough to the skin and the zippers took on a whole new meaning for her. It locked in the item that not even her brother knew about. An item whose weight pulled on her mind, and its purpose was one of great mystery to her. *Why did mother and father burden me with this?*

"Here we are." Vectra's sudden announcement jolted Monica awake. She expected to find the ship with the name that Dare had pestered about, and not the trees and more dense landscape that greeted them instead.

"I thought you said it was a shipwreck? Is it buried?" Dare offered the interesting theory. "Kind of like a buried treasure chest?"

"That is an idea worth pondering." Vectra opened their passenger door, waiting for them to disembark. "However, we must walk from here on out."

"And the car?" Monica swung her backpack back over her shoulders and protectively held the straps with her hands.

"Blaze will be fine. Won't you my precious?" Vectra patted the top hood, near the front grill, and started walking down a path barely visible between all of the low ferns. Monica and Dare could feel the ground vibrating under their feet and quickly fell in step behind the Guardian not a moment too soon. Taking a backwards look, Dare witnessed the ground swing down like a trap door while the remaining top edges closed in over the hole to meet the car's front. Staring at the sight, anyone passing by would assume it was a random fire pit left there from an old camp spot.

"Are you going to be alright?" Dare asked his older sister. He saw her face darting frantically around at every noise that reached their ears.

"I am going to try my best." Monica's panic subsided a bit when they stepped onto a wooden beam extending over a trickling stream of mountain water. The calmness of the tiny waves, the way it reflected the light and spun the shadows in a mesmerizing art form of its own, helped to sooth the worry consuming her mind.

"Is something wrong back there?" Vectra called out whilst readjusting the canvas strap of the duffel bag in her hand.

"My sister doesn't like the woods." Dare answered, seeing Monica's evil glare in return.

"Doesn't like them?"

"I will be alright." Monica tried to gather her courage as leaves fell down upon their group. "I just had a bad experience when I was six years old, that's all."

For the next fifteen minutes of trotting along easy paths, no one said a word. The peaceful crunching of the fall foliage painted the silent air in unique sounds, and it wasn't until they made it to the water's edge, that Monica's fear retreated a bit.

"There it is." Vectra pointed off from the river's shoreline, at a clump of trees seemingly floating atop the water. From their angle on the short upward slope, Monica didn't see anything that looked like a ship, and neither did her brother.

"I just see trees." She squinted her eyes whilst approaching the shoreline. "Are those trees…floating?" Leading the kids down the steep, three foot descent, Vectra uttered no explanation for the bizarre looking ship. Rather, she kept rotating her gaze around the area with a perplexed look on her face. "What's wrong?"

"Nothing." Vectra muttered unconvincingly.

"Monica, look!" Dare tugged on his sister's shirt and gasped as the rest of the ship came into focus. With no more natural obstacles to block their view, the Brownings observed the deteriorating leftovers of a ship's hull at the base of the floating island. "No way! There are trees growing inside the wreckage." He pointed to the far side of the historical marvel. "Whoa! You can see more of the ship's side down this way."

The *Proteus*-class collier stood lonely against the wooded landscape, incapable of sailing on its own for quite some time. Only 175 feet survived of the nearly 542 it was supposed to be. Much of the original steel exterior was rusted at the waterline, leaving little for the still attached barnacles to cling to. It would take a great deal of imagination to see her restored into the glorious cargo ship she had once been. Where the coal used to be stored, during her final active days of the First World War, was now a vacant hole, capable of holding air alone. A shell remained of the fine steam engine that once propelled it through eight years of service for the American Navy. "Ghostly" was a mild word to describe the way the trees grew atop its deck like forest soil, and appeared unfazed to be floating above the water below.

Dare closed his eyes, trying to envision the first day the ship was launched into duty in 1910 and soaked up the excitement of it all. As his eyes reopened, he suddenly realized that his sister was no longer by his side and had, in fact, abandoned him in favor of joining Vectra by a gang-plank. Racing along the rocky shoreline, Dare jumped in line behind his sister just as they were about to board.

Vectra abruptly spun around to face them without any warning, catching them off guard and giving the siblings a little scare. "Night is quickly encroaching. You two should begin building a fire to keep the cold at bay, whilst I search for the item I need." She glanced up at the massive sky, studying the incoming clouds coming across the mountains. "The temperature will be dropping to almost freezing tonight. I can feel it in the air. Besides, we could all do with some nourishment."

"We can start by gathering the twigs and branches." Monica nodded and flashed a smile at the Guardian. She hurriedly latched onto her brother's arm and pulled him back down the wooden walk. As they soon ventured out of ear-shot, Monica slowed her pace and released Dare from her hard grip.

"Ow! What was that all about?" Dare massaged the soreness aching above his elbow from her harsh yanking and gave her a squinting look of curiosity. "You know I have never started a fire before, so you are going to have to do it."

"Dare, I have a feeling that we shouldn't trust her more than we can throw her."

"I can't even throw a paper airplane more than five feet."

"Exactly what I mean. Ever since we have met this woman, strange and unnatural things have been occurring. Who is to say that she doesn't know more information about Mom's and Dad's disappearance?"

"Well…" The boy placed a finger to his lips in deep concentration. "I guess no one. But Monica, what other choice do we have? She hasn't done anything to us in a harmful way."

"Not yet." Monica's skepticism drenched her words. "That could change the closer we get to locating Trevor. All I am saying is that we should watch what we say around her. To not give out any unwarranted details."

"What kind of details?"

"Never mind. Just, don't speak that much. Alright?" His sister rolled her eyes and readjusted the backpack's straps over the top of her shoulders. The bag felt surprisingly heavier than it had a moment ago and her stomach growled unhappily. "Let's go and gather up the wood. She was right about one thing. We could really do with some food."

Chapter Seventeen

"All set." Monica shouted at the top of the gangplank. She looked around in the impending darkness and cautiously stepped onto the poop deck one foot at a time. Her eyes searched for Vectra until she noticed a flickering warm glow coming from the old captain's quarters under the After Bridge. Vines coated three vents protruding up from the deck, making them appear like evil gremlins standing their posts as she slowly made her way over to the light and tried to ignore the creepy sensation tingling her spine. "Vectra?"

She peered into the blowtorch-crafted entrance from around the corner, making sure to keep her hands inside her pockets, and refusing to touch the walls. Monica did not want to risk having to get another tetanus shot earlier than planned. "Vectra? Are you in here?" Her voice lowered to merely a whisper, afraid of who or what might answer back. *I really don't need another freaky thing to happen to me today, not on a spooky ship that makes a house of toothpicks look safer to walk on.*

Inside the cabin, Monica noted that the space looked fit for a steampunk convention. The walls were painted in moss green with an inventive coat rack hanging between an antique desk, along the far inner wall, and a bed messily covered in blankets. The door nearest the bed was left partially ajar, though it led only to a closed-in bathroom and closet. Monica wasn't sure what to make of it all. *It appears to be getting weirder the longer we stay in her presence.*

"Vectra?" Monica hesitantly asked the empty space. It was clearly obvious that the woman was nowhere to be found within its confines. But the lit lantern suggested that she had been in there recently. Staring at its decorative mount, Monica's ears picked up on the sound of faint voices coming from further inside the ship. *Ah man! Come on.* The tingling sensation climbed higher up her back as the voices grew a shade louder, and a small reflection in the lantern's glass showed the way to a hidden door behind the hangers.

Creeping across the floorboards, Monica's foot touched down on a spot that groaned under her weight. She swung her head around in frightful anticipation of seeing Vectra standing there, accusing her of sneaking aboard in order to steal something of value. But she didn't. No one entered, and soon, Monica reached the other side of the room undetected. Peeking her head past the clicking gears of the mechanical hanger, she gazed into the larger space which resembled a conference room. Softness bathed the area in the setting sun's pink and purple tones from the busted skylight above the long table and chairs. Various rooms branched off through passageways welded shut, except for one on the western side and two to the south. Containers of flour, sugar, and other baking ingredients were lined up in an organized row, as different tools hung by hooks over a short prep table next to the open door.

"I know it must be here." Vectra's frustrated words echoed two openings down from Monica's. The sound of breaking glass split the air as the woman was moving glass bottles around too hastily, and cursed in a language the teen didn't recognize.

"You used it all up. Or do you not remember?"

Monica's eyes widened at the sound of a hollowed male's voice. It held a low, patient tone, akin to her fourth grade math teacher's; though she hazarded a guess that it wasn't him based on the southern accent this one contained.

"Ugh. That means I have to steal some more. There is absolutely no realm in which Jeffrey would hand me over his last specimen of that particular plant. Not for all the money in the world, and not for all the gold on Mount Olympus."

"Should not be a problem for the *Great Vectra Tiller-man.*"

"Stop the mockery. It does not suit you." Vectra heaved a sigh. "Alas, I have not taken anything worth more than $1,500 in so long. There is a chance I may not be able to pull it off any more."

Monica inched her way across the aging threshold and toward the voices, taking a short look back the way she came before continuing on. That was when the journal she didn't notice before, caught her attention. Her hand brushed against its real leather spine hanging over the edge of the desk. It was stained dark brown and she could feel the initials MR engraved on the front cover. Curiously, Monica flipped the journal open to where a folded paper bookmarked a specific location. A woman's handwritten notes were arranged around the sketch of a sword, with lines drawn to various points coating both pages. She could barely read any of the wordage due to being so far away from the indoor lanterns, and was about to open the folded paper when the male voice stopped her.

"You could just use the light to search. Instead of the

candle. I know you have your peculiarities, but refusing to utilize better lighting is not amongst them."

"This is not a place for those kids outside. I do not want them knowing where I am."

A small pause in the air sent a bad shiver through Monica as Vectra kept her mouth suspiciously silent. Not a fly moved during the still minute. Utter quietness filled the broken ship to such a degree a cemetery would have envied. Monica's heartbeat began to race at the man's next statement.

"I sense that there is another on this ship." His voice spoke without any worry. "It appears as though you were unsuccessful at hiding. One of the kids is aboard as we speak."

Quickly trying to stuff the paper back into the journal, Monica's hand fumbled and the paper opened up on the floor instead, in-between her feet. A drawing of two women on a train was revealed with the fold line split right down the middle. Their dresses, well-detailed by the artist's hand, resembled a late 1800s order catalogue and she instantly recognized Vectra's facial features on the woman to the left. She hurriedly picked the drawing up and shoved it into the journal, slamming the book shut, and briskly walked in the direction of the exit to the deck.

"WHAT ARE YOU DOING?" Vectra shouted. She stared at the teen's back with her nose flared and hands on her hips. It was the kind of commanding tone that would have demanded the attention of every living thing on the ship, if it were not just Monica shaking in the room. "WELL?"

Monica reluctantly turned around to face Vectra, who switched her gaze onto the journal no longer sitting precariously over the desk's edge. "I don't believe you would care for me to go poking and prodding into that darling backpack of yours. So why do you feel inclined to do so with my belongings?"

"I…I…I was simply looking for you." An itch suddenly festered in the back of her throat, causing her to cough a little. "We have the wood ready and I came up here to tell you. But…"

"There you are." Dare easily stepped into the room where the other two were having their standoff, briefly easing the lingering tension. "Neat place you have here."

Vectra dismissed the siblings with her hand. "If the wood is ready, start the fire then. I shall be along shortly."

"We haven't started a fire on our own before." The boy answered sheepishly. He placed his hands in his pockets and swayed his body from the embarrassment of seeing Vectra's expression of disbelief. "And kids should not handle matches without an adult present." Dare did his best interpretation of a teacher giving a valuable lesson to his students.

"I suppose someone should demonstrate the proper way to go about it. We would not want to have a forest fire due to incompetence." Vectra marched to the plank and walked down to where the pile of fire wood was waiting to be used. She maintained a watchful eye on Monica as she trailed behind, glancing backwards every few steps, while the solar lights came to life along the entire length of the board. The Guardian did not know what to say to the teenager, nor did she know how to approach asking her what their real motive was for seeking her help. *Could it be that they have come to get revenge for what has happened? For that to be true, however, that would mean that they already know. And that is not possible.*

"What in the name of Hades is this?" Vectra scoffed.

Within a minute, she had the ring of rocks structurally sound and a fire roaring by a flick of a single playing card. Then the Brownings watched her leave for the ship again after excusing herself in order to grab the food for their dinner.

"What happened up there?" Dare asked his sister. "You were gone for so long, and then I overheard Vectra barking those orders at you. I wasn't sure what to do."

"I peeked at a journal lying on her desk in the captain's quarters."

"Monica! For crying out loud, why? You didn't *think* she was going to catch you?" He scolded, giving her a doubtful glare.

"I was trying to find her, and I saw the journal, and…"

"Went prying into her things like a nosy busybody."

Monica was trying not to get frustrated with her brother, though he was making it quite difficult. "Okay, yes, it was wrong of me to go poking into her things. But I saw a sketch of a sword and a whole bunch of writing all around with descriptions and arrows pointing to other key notes. It looked a lot like the sword from Camelot and King Arthur."

"Yeah…"

"There were initials engraved on the front cover of the journal. They were…"

"Monica, what has any of this got to do with finding Trevor?" Dare saw his sister smacking her hands together like she often did whenever she was keeping her temper in check, and wasn't sure why she was so flustered when he was only telling her what she would have told him, if he had been the one snooping.

"Derrick, knock it off and listen to me. The initials were MR. Just like Mom's before she married; Mable Roader. Camelot was her favorite myth. And that's not all. There was a man's voice in the ship. I heard…"

"Here you go." Vectra silently approached to hand them each an elongated metal fork with a hot dog stabbed through the prongs. "These are not going to cook themselves. I presume you two know how to cook a hot dog?"

"Of course." Monica held the wooden handle between both hands, slowly turning it over the flames like in a movie she once saw a few years back. Dare watched her, matching her movements, and placed his meat into the fire as well.

"Good. I will be back with the drinks shortly. I am afraid that I have some bad news for us." Vectra dashed off to where a piece of rope was tied around a sturdy tree stump by the water's edge. As she pulled the rope up, a hard-sided cooler emerged from the river and Vectra pulled three glass bottles of brownish liquid from underneath the insulated lid.

"What does the journal mean?" Dare whispered, turning his hot dog around too fast in the higher flames to really cook any side well. "You think it is one of Mom's journals? And that Vectra killed her and Dad?"

Monica leaned his way and stopped his shaking hands, forcing him to turn at a slower pace. "I'm not sure. I couldn't get a good enough look at the handwriting to see if it was hers. Just act like we don't know for now."

Vectra offered them each one of the bottles. "Apple cider. Chilled the best way nature intended."

"You keep your drinks cold in the river?" Monica eyed the bottle suspiciously. *It is made from apples, and look what happened to Snow White.*

"Everything tastes better when it is naturally chilled. By that, I mean not kept cold through artificial ways such as refrigerators and freezers."

Both Brownings uncapped their drinks with intrigue at

what a 'naturally chilled' beverage was like, waiting to see Vectra drink hers first. They sipped down the pasteurized liquid and their parched throats were very grateful for the hydration. Dare licked his lips as a dog would, and eagerly drank up some more. "This is delicious! Tastes fresher than what we have at home."

"And that is the same stuff you will find at a local grocery store. Nothing different. 'Cept for the fact that I used nature to chill it down, and poured it into these glass bottles since it conducts cold better. And it can't freeze in glass either. No room for it to expand as it would in a plastic bottle."

"So cool. Wish we had a stream or pond or anything like that back home. Then we could do the same thing with our milk, water, everything." Dare chugged the rest of his drink so fast that he forgot all about his hotdog on the fork and nearly burnt a side of his dinner into a piece of charcoal. Monica saved his food and helped him fix the mess as Vectra shook her head.

"No river is required. Just keep a glass soda bottle in a mound of fresh snow in the winter, by your house overnight, and enjoy it the next day." Vectra finished hers in one dragged out swig, refusing to come up for air until it was all gone. She rested the bottle on the ground and leaned back on her hands planted firmly on top the damp soil. "Unfortunately, I am out of the buns for your hot dogs. So you are going to have to eat them like that."

"Is that the bad news you were going to tell us about?" Monica pulled her fork from the flames and inspected the bubbles beginning to form on the reddening skin.

Vectra shook her head again. "No. The bad news is that I do not have any more of the flower Aidan will want in exchange for my book. The only other person to have a living specimen is Jeffrey, Catriona Locksmith's brother. So it will be another early morning tomorrow."

Silence fell over the campfire for the next three minutes until Dare decided to break the ice. He didn't care for the eerie feeling consuming the wooden landscape and needed something to occupy his wandering mind. "Don't people usually tell ghost stories around a fire?"

"I don't know any good ones." Monica looked over at Vectra, unsure as to what the Guardian was going to say. She had an inclination that any scary story the woman had to share was one she didn't wish to hear. There was no telling how long she had lived, and the tales would most likely be true and more horrifying in that sense. "We don't have to share any stories."

"What about any old legends and myths? Like King Arthur? Or any folk songs that are based in reality?" The ten-year-old pleaded from their hostess. "Please! It's not every day that we get to go camping."

Vectra arched her brow at him.

Chapter Eighteen

"You were really there when the Wright brothers flew for the first time?" Dare nearly jumped out of his seat at the idea of witnessing such a milestone day in the history books. "Wicked!" He had been thoroughly enjoying Vectra's tales of African lions, speaking with British code breakers during the First World War, and being in the same theater as President Lincoln on that fatal night.

"You certainly have been all over, haven't you?" Monica chomped down on the end of her hot dog. She had to admit that cooking it over a fire pit did taste better than nuking it in the microwave. *Now I understand part of the lure of camping.*

"I have simply gone wherever my job demanded of me." Vectra brushed minor particles of dust from her pant legs. She figured that by telling the kids stories of her duller missions, it would help to keep their inquisitive nature at bay. However, she was not accustomed to dealing with children.

"Tell us more. Where else have you been and what else have you seen?" The boy's eyes glinted in the fire's yellow-orange glow. "Did you see the Battle of Gettysburg? Have you seen the Statue of Lady Liberty before she turned green? Did you survive the Titanic?" He almost leaned too close to the heat, out of pure excitement, catching Vectra off guard at seeing him so enthusiastic over her past adventures. Monica even thought she saw a tiny smile form on her lips.

Suddenly, the fire's flames began pulsating with images of people and places long since gone. They were brief glimpses into scenes of Vectra's memories, much like a movie trailer being played twice as fast. Monica watched them rotate between medieval knights to theatrical performances from the 1980s to train rides through the Old West and dinner in 15th century Romania. As soon as Vectra noticed them on public display, she shot up from the ground and stepped away from the fire. *No, no, no!* Her heart pounded inside her chest from the fear of her emotions breaking down the walls she fought so hard to cement. "The less you know about me, the better it is for the both of you. And vice versa."

Monica flashed a glance up at Vectra and then back down at the flames. The images were rapidly fading from view, but they still changed every three seconds or so. When two recognizable faces appeared just above the burning logs, Monica's face froze and her body went cold. They were one of the last few people projected in the fire before it returned to normal. "I will be right back." Vectra left them alone along the shoreline again, walking toward the ship's deck and the captain's quarters she called home for the last seven years.

Dare poked at a bubble on his fourth hot dog as his sister grabbed ahold of his empty fork and placed it on the ground next to hers. She blinked into the flames once more, wondering if what she saw for a split second had been real or imaginary. "Dare, did you see what I saw?"

"I don't know. Tell me what you saw and then I can tell you whether I saw it or not."

"Did you happen to see people's faces in the campfire just as Vectra was stepping away?"

"No. But I was focused on my tasty dinner." Dare bit down on the toasted meat with a wide grin. "I love hot dogs."

"I could have sworn that Mom and Dad were one of the last two people in that fire." Monica shook her head to clear her mind. *I must be losing it.*

"Perhaps you are just tired? We have had a long day and you saw that journal. Maybe it's your imagination running wild."

"Let me remind you, Dear Brother, that you were also concerned about what the journal might mean. Or has the smoke screen of free hot dogs cured you of worrying?"

"Monica, I find it a little odd, I admit. But as the cop shows would say, there is no hard proof. You have a theory and nothing else." Monica shushed her brother from talking any more on the subject as Vectra came down the gang-plank.

"Sorry I did not have much in the way of food for this evening." She stopped before their cozy camping spot with her hands hidden behind her back.

"Are you kidding?" Dare gave her a toothy grin with a piece of hot dog stuck in-between two teeth. "These hot dogs are the best I ever had."

"I am delighted to hear that." Vectra smiled, bringing her hands around to the front to show them her portable hot drink maker, and three metal camping cups woven in her fingers. "I did not anticipate having to bring guests out here, so these will have to do in lieu of finer drinkware." She handed a cup to each of the kids and dialed her drink first into the inventive contraption. "I figured you two might like to have some hot chocolate to warm your insides against this night air."

"That would be great!" Dare elbowed his sister, who was still staring at the fire in a vain attempt to see any more people's faces within its blaze.

"What? Oh, yeah, thank you." Monica tried using the odd-looking thermos after Vectra was done pouring steaming hot cocoa from the spout. She let the woman reset the drink maker in order to show her how to dial it to the right settings, using the bronze gear and the painted icons.

"Twist the gear until that dot is pointing to the chocolate icon. Now switch the smaller gear to hot. Press down on the top middle button, and it will be ready in two minutes."

Monica looked up at the clear sky dazzling above their heads as she waited for her drink to be ready. Far from the light pollution of the modern world, the farthest reaches of the Milky Way Galaxy speckled the black void of space. Her eyes lit up as a white streak raced across the heavens and vanished in a snap of fire. "Isn't it amazing to see a shooting star just vanish as quickly as it appears?" She asked the air, feeling a sense of sudden calmness sweeping over her.

Vectra scoffed.

"What? Is it so bad to find comfort in the stars?"

"All I see are heartless, cold, and hypocritical dots judging us without mercy or a single ounce of kindness." The Guardian fiddled with her necklaces, as she sat back on the opposite side of the campfire like before. She cradled the smaller pendent in her hands, leaving an elaborate cross and her lacy choke collar to dangle freely against her skin. Carefully wrapped into a metal prison of miniature springs and spun wire, a green stone glowed inside the homemade charm attached to a tiny chain. It was the same necklace that Taminus had been trying to cut loose from her neck that day in Nectar Hill.

"I imagine there must be a reason you are so cynical."

"If imagination gives you wings, my cynical nature is not where you want to fly."

"Taminus said that you two cannot kill one another. Is this true?" Monica studied Vectra's body language, trying to determine if the Guardian was going to tell the truth or not.

"It is far more complicated than you know." Vectra was about to turn her back to them, when the sound of rustling in the bushes caught her attention.

"Wait, so can he die?" Dare, apparently oblivious to the noise, picked up where his sister left the conversation.

"Yes, he can die, just like you and me." Squinting her eyes at the shivering mountain laurel behind the siblings, Vectra instinctively reached for her knife that was frightfully absent. "He has my blade." She muttered in worry. Then suddenly, an animal busted through the branches and leaped over the fire, causing the two kids to quickly lean out of the way.

"What the…?" Dare and Monica were speechless. At first sight, the four-legged creature appeared to be a coyote, but the color of its fur was not right and the shape of its ears were slightly off too. Whatever the thing was, their hostess was certainly not afraid of it any longer.

"There you are, my friend." Vectra hugged and petted the animal acting like a dog and licking her chin with affection. "I was wondering where you had gotten too."

"Is that a coyote?" Dare asked, watching the color of the animal's pelt change in the waning glow. "Or is that a fox?"

"Both, I think." Monica replied.

"His name is Rae." Vectra kissed the coyote fox on the top of his furry head. "Rae, you did not have to scare our guests like that." The creature gave her a sad look in turn.

"I understand. You don't get to play that much anymore."

"What's up with his right eye?" Dare gawked. Instead of having the normal distinction separating the pupil from the iris, there was only one large, rust orange colored circle in the center of Rae's eye. A sliver of silver-tinged light illuminated the left side of the enlarged pupil, causing it to appear strangely like a full moon.

"It's called an Eclipse Eye. Only those born on the same night of a certain eclipse have it." Vectra nodded her head to Rae, giving her permission to smell out the Brownings.

"Which eclipse?" Dare was becoming even more curious by the strange anomaly while he petted the coyote fox and scratched under his muzzle.

"One that occurs about once every six hundred years. It is a partial lunar eclipse that happens when the moon is full in the fall, also known as the Beaver Moon by the current world. The color of the moon changes to the color you see in Rae's eye as it passes through Earth's shadow."

"So, you answer his question but you evade mine?" Monica crossed her arms in front of her chest again, pressing her lips together in annoyance.

"I like him better. He doesn't ask so many questions." Vectra smirked as the teenager fumed and huffed into the cold night air.

"If there was an eclipse this year like that, then that would mean that the last eclipse was…" Dare made a quick calculation in his head. He stared at Rae in shock, the gentle animal's tongue hanging out the side of his smiling mouth. "In the 1400s?" A loud gulp came from the boy's throat as he gazed down at Rae. "How old are you?"

"Older than either of us cares to admit. He watches this place when I am away. Does a pretty good job of it too. Huh, boy?" Vectra waited for Rae to bounce back into her arms and share the same patch of leaves she was on. The coyote fox curled up in her lap, extending himself out like an oversized body pillow across her legs. His eyes closed in contentment and his breathing slowed as he began to fall asleep in his comfortable state. "Alright. I think it is a good time for all of us to head to bed. We have a busy day ahead of us tomorrow as we go to visit Ms. Locksmith and her brother."

Rae reluctantly clambered off of Vectra, and followed her up the walk. Monica opened her mouth to ask about the fire when the Guardian snapped her fingers, instantly extinguishing the flames and causing the two kids to race up the plank. "Where are we going to sleep?" Dare asked.

"Monica can take my bed, and Dare, I will have another one made up for you in a flash." As instructed, the siblings waited outside the doorway until the other cot was ready inside the captain's quarters.

Three plush blankets, and two animal-shaped pillows, had been tidied up for Monica on the larger bed. She took note of the out-of-place bright colors that added a sense of cheerfulness to the drab surroundings and vintage interior. Her brother's cot was furbished in blue and green blankets with a dinosaur pillow aching to be hugged. *Huh. I would not have expected her to...what am I saying? Why am I still surprised at this rate?*

"But you need to get some sleep too." Dare objected. He refused to go to sleep before finding out where Vectra planned on going to bed. "I can sleep in a chair if you would like to have the cot."

"How very gentlemanly of you. However, I will be fine with the futon in the executive officer's room."

She moved swiftly over to the closet and swung the door out wider. Inside, the ship's wheel had become Vectra's coat and hat hanger, displaying varying shades of green, black, and brown clothing. She spun the wheel around from the ceiling in order for the proper empty spot to come her way. "I don't understand. You have a coat hanger on the wall." Monica pointed to the mechanicalized rack.

"Do not be daft." Vectra pulled on the rod closest to her and waited for the wall to flip over, revealing a welded-on counter with pieces of radar equipment from last century also fastened on with bolts. Above the setup, a brown satchel, a rolled-up piece of leather, and other odd looking items sat poised at the ready for whenever their owner would call upon them. They were strapped onto a metal grid, except for one that popped loose and it rolled on the floor in Monica's direction. She watched it stop halfway on the weary boards, due to its pentagon-shaped sides, each containing circular holes of different diameters. "I would not touch that."

Monica retracted her hand from the strange object. Its bronze exterior glinted in the light of the room as Vectra scooped it up to re-strap it in more securely. "Are you a kind of spy?" Dare unzipped his coat and gratefully slid under the warm blankets. "Like covert ops or a secret agent?"

Vectra untied small strings holding rolled animal hides above the doorway, releasing deer and bear pelts over the openings. "If secret agents have special powers and are trapped under the control of their employers, then sure." She clipped the hides at four locations on either side of the entrance to keep the colder temperatures from coming in. "And before you two say anything, the entire animal was used when they were captured by Martiban. He is a stickler for wasting as little as possible." The lights dimmed at the wave of her hand, and she made for the conference room, leaving Monica and Dare to themselves. "Good night."

"Ah, Vectra?" Monica called. "What about Taminus? Shouldn't one of us be a lookout down along the shoreline?"

"Do not worry about him. I can handle Taminus, if he so chooses to venture this far into the woods. Like you, they are not his particular cup of tea." Vectra poked her head back into the room, checking in on Rae getting his bed under the desk ready. He walked in a circle three times, just the right number, and settled down on top his favorite, plushy stripped pillow. The Guardian snatched the journal up from the desk and dived back into the darkened hole. "Go to sleep. You are going to need your mind sharp when we visit Catriona and her brother.

Chapter Nineteen

Monica tossed and turned under the layers of blankets she never wanted to leave. Though she was certainly cozy and plenty warm, she could not manage to fall asleep. Glancing over at her younger brother, she soon realized what he was doing. With his body facing the other way, a faint whitish-blue hue emanated from something in his hands, in front of his face. "Dare!" Her voice rang out in an angry whisper. "Get off your phone. We have to save the batteries for emergencies only."

"I'm only on to check a few things out." He retorted. "I wanted to find out more about this ship. I will turn it off in five minutes."

"Fine. But don't come crying to me when the battery goes dead and we have no way of charging it." Monica stared into the empty ceiling, debating on whether she should rip the phone from his hands right then and there. She had to admit that, unlike other kids her age who were attached to their phones, she never really had that problem. It had been fairly easy for her to leave it in her backpack. But in Dare's case, it worked out in their favor that he had kept it in his pocket after what happened back in town.

"Monica."

"What?"

"I found out something you are going to want to hear about this ship."

"Not interested, Dare." Monica turned to face the wall. She was already maxed-out out on strange things happening for one day. "Tell me tomorrow."

"This ship had three sisters."

"Not interested. I already can't sleep from being creeped out by staying in an abandoned, rotting ship, floating on a river in the middle of the woods. I do not need anything else to freak me out any more." She rolled her eyes as her brother ignored her pleads.

"One was sunk in WWII while transporting soldiers to Asia. Japanese planes had dropped bombs on it and the ship ended up getting the final blow by our own destroyers after the ship was scuttled."

"Still not interested, Derrick!" She shoved a cat pillow over her ears.

"The other two were sold to the Canadian government in 1941 with less than a month separating the sales."

Monica huffed as she swung back around to face her brother, who was now staring at her. The cellphone's light illuminated his chin like a horror film. "Is there a point to you telling me all of this? And ignoring the fact that I don't want to hear it?"

"Both of those ships disappeared that same year with less than a month between their vanishings." Monica's eyes grew wide as her brother scrolled down the screen with his thumb. "Both were carrying bauxite ore when it happened."

"And this ship, what was it carrying when it went missing?" She hesitantly asked, afraid to hear the answer.

"Manganese ore. Bauxite ore is used for making aluminum and manganese ore is used for making steel." Dare took a pause to relish the fact that he had his sister's undying attention, a feat hard to accomplish. "All of them were named after Greek gods and goddesses. It's just a bit strange, if you ask me. And…that's not all."

"Of course it isn't."

"Each of the remaining three, that survived WWII, disappeared in the Bermuda Triangle."

"Stop it! Now I am too freaked out to even entertain merely the idea of sleeping." She returned her gaze onto the moss painted wall against the side of the bed. How did the ship end up here? *No, never mind. Who cares? We are here to locate Trevor and all of this will be over. We can go home and forget this ever happened.*

Chapter Twenty

Time ticked by at the speed of stagnant water. Dare had since turned his phone off, and lightly snored next to Monica's restless form. Her mind would not shut down, rolling through the events of the day on a non-stop cycle and the mysterious truths behind the ship they were staying the night in. She tried counting sheep, thinking of ocean waves and sea breezes, and even forced herself to stare at a single point on the ceiling for over twenty minutes. Nothing was helping to calm her nerves and, eventually, she flicked the blankets off to find where Vectra was.

Monica picked up an unlit lantern from atop the antique desk and struck a match lying next to it. *What am I doing?* She quickly snuffed it out by waving the small stick in the air. *I don't know how to light a lantern like this. With my luck, I'll probably burn something up and make more of a mess of things.* Her feet inched their way across the room from her fuzzy memory, and she held her hands outward like a zombie. *Good thing it is almost pitch black in here. I feel ridiculous.*

Within another three feet, the teen felt the threshold against her fingers and slowly dipped her head into the darkened room. The moon was rising in the sky, sending moonbeams through the skylight positioned over the table. It was a ghostly sight to see the rays of grey-white light hit the chairs as though spirits were sitting there. *Knock it off. You are scaring yourself silly. That's right. Just scaring yourself silly. Keep moving.* In the same room, Monica had heard Vectra searching earlier in the evening, came a warm light stronger than before. As quiet as she could muster, Monica tiptoed her way over to the lit entrance and dared a peek inside.

Sitting at another desk, arm rested upon its well-cared for surface and propping her head up with her right hand, Vectra stared at the journal Monica had mentioned to her brother. Rae softly approached from behind the Guardian's tall chair and bumped her left hand with his muzzle. His simple gesture prodded her away from the inner depths of the past, and like an orchestrated song, she gently stroked Rae's head in rhythmic harmony.

Monica silently looked on. She had failed to notice that Rae had not been in his bed back in the Captain's Quarters as she had walked by. *That creature can sure move without making a sound.* The scene she was witnessing, a special bond between human and animal, was unlike anything she could have comprehended. This duo had more in tune with one another than any pairing she saw on tv, in their neighborhood, or in the park. *It is as though they are a part of each other.* Her eyes continued to stare out of sheer fascination, squinting in order to see a faint tear roll down Vectra's cheek.

The Guardian's eyes were glazed in sorrow, as if an invisible pain had suddenly taken ahold of her soul. Monica could gather that Rae was thoroughly enjoying all of the attention, particularly with a spot behind his left ear. But

Vectra seemed unfazed by what was transpiring in the current time. Although there was no physical evidence to suggest it, Monica got the feeling that she was reliving the past, and most undoubtedly, the same one shared with MR's journal.

Just then, Vectra's face smiled with a bittersweet expression painted on her lips. Lowering herself down to the coyote fox's level, she whispered in his ear. "Don't you ever leave me. You hear? I forbid it." Monica still stood awkwardly at the cusp of the room; swaying back and forth in indecision, not sure on what to do. Going to bed was a waste of energy, since she didn't feel the least bit tired, and she had no idea what the next day was going to bring. On the other hand, part of her was suspicious of the odd woman. Unpredictable events had occurred once they met her at the antique fair, and there was the matter of how much Vectra knew about their parents' disappearance. But Dare was right. They had to trust her, for now at least.

"I'm sorry about looking through your belongings. I had no right to do that." Her voice almost squeaked out as she spoke, barely recognizable as her own. Instantly, Vectra's eyes cleared and she looked at the young teen with a half-smug smile. It sent a fright straight through Monica's chest at her immediate change in attitude.

"That is okay, Kid. Because I also had no right to take this." Vectra stopped petting Rae and raised her fingers up to reveal a flower bracelet. The peridot gems were fashionably set in antique, gold-plated sterling silver and were linked together like a chain. Shocked, Monica hastily went for the bracelet she expected to be around her wrist, only to find nothing there. She rushed into the room to retrieve the piece of jewelry her mother had given her, on her seventh birthday. "Peridot. Must be that your birthday is in August."

Monica dangled the bracelet over her left arm and went to re-fasten it without saying a word.

"Am I to assume that it is on the tenth of August, then? Considering there are ten flowers." Vectra erased her smugness into an emotionless fine line. "Now we are even."

"I guess we are." Monica finished re-snapping the clasp. "For someone who doesn't want us to know anything about her own life, you certainly like to pry into mine."

"You need to double-check a dictionary before you go accusing people of shoving their nose where it does not belong."

"Seems like I used the right word. You stole from me in order to find out information." Monica glanced down at the inscription on the inside of the bracelet. Though the lettering was small, the date of her birthday could easily be read.

"And you looked into this journal trying to unearth more of my past."

"I recognized the initials, that's all. Who is MR?"

"An old friend. Long gone by now." Vectra placed a gentle hand over the two letters carved into the worn, leather cover.

"Would I have heard of them before? Whoever MR is?"

"Doubtful." Vectra flashed her gaze onto the teenager again. "What are you doing up anyway?"

"Can't sleep. Not tired enough to settle down." Monica watched her move to the opposite side of the room and riffle through a number of blue bottles stored above a filing cabinet. Vectra tossed her a smaller one that clinked with pills inside.

"Take one and leave the bottle on my desk."

"And these are…"

"They will help you sleep. No need to worry about the ingredients inside. I made them myself out of a secret mixture of plants and herbs. Nothing habit forming, so there is no concern."

"Uh…thanks?" Monica twisted the cap open to find a dozen or so faintly yellow capsules. She picked one up, returned the bottle and shuffled her way back to bed in the other room. Dare was already snoring away in his cot, his phone screen black beside him as she crawled under the blankets and hid the pill in her pocket. There was no way she was going to take unidentified medicine from a person she met less than forty-eight hours ago.

Monica wrapped her hand around the bracelet, not certain as to why she was even wearing it in the first place. She supposed that the piece of jewelry carried sentimental value, in some odd way to her; but whenever she looked upon it, anger bubbled up much more than any source of happiness ever did. Still, after Trevor was taken, the bracelet seemed like a necessity for a trip into the unknown. And before long, she drifted asleep to the memory of a trip to the zoo and a lion playing with a large watermelon.

Chapter Twenty-One

An hour after Monica left the room with one of the sleeping pills, Vectra got up from her desk and walked over to the Captain's Quarters. She watched Monica by the doorway, observing how the teen's breathing grew increasingly shallower as she slipped into a deep slumber, while the boy, Dare, wriggled around as if a snake was coming after him in his dreams. *What I am doing? Does this not look as though I am stalking these children?* Her mind wished to return to the other room, but an undeniable pull refused to let her leave where she stood. "Are you going to tell them?" The hollowed male voice reverberated off the mostly barren walls.

"Now you decide to venture forth for a proper visit?" Vectra did not turn to see the ghostly form materializing behind her. The blurry figure began to come into focus enough for his grey Civil War uniform to be displayed in meticulous order. His brown hair was kept in the same condition, minus the matted section of blood near the base of his skull. Deep blue eyes watched the kids curiously, trying to take in the scene of modern-day clothing.

"Did not want to cause them a scare their first night

aboard."

"This being their *only* night aboard." She clarified. "Tomorrow, we are leaving."

"You know the time will come." The spirit moved effortlessly around Vectra, nearly going straight through her shoulder as she blocked the entire doorway. "Why do you torture yourself by bottling the truth up? Tell the girl and her brother what happened. They deserve to know."

"It can wait. Perhaps they already know. Or maybe they do not care at all. Seven years is long enough to change a person."

"Those are kids sleeping there, Vectra. Kids who long for their parents to hug them one more time. I do admit that their clothing is very different than that of my own childhood, but they have the same feelings. Have you extinguished all of yours?" He walked in front of her view, as though his transparent body kept her from seeing the siblings, and tried to get her undivided attention. "I, of all people, have an idea of the oppression caged truth places upon someone. You know I wait until my family comes to terms with ours. These kids do not have to bear their doubts and worries any longer if you would only *tell them.*"

"You do not see." Vectra's eyes hardened into daggers. "If I were to explain what happened now, both of their fates are signed and sealed without a glimmer of hope in sight. Regardless of how much, or little, she understands of this realm, Monica would push on for the press without me. And her younger brother would follow her into Hades and back if he had too. No, Rolan. There is too much of her parents in her."

"And she will not trust your word, once all is revealed?" The spirit placed his ghostly hand on the corner of the antique desk. "Perhaps she possesses more brains than you believe."

"And what would you know? I have been around her longer than you. Yet, here we are…with you lecturing me on what I do or do not see in her." Vectra pointed at Monica's sleeping form. Her hand began to tremble in the air as her thoughts drifted back to the afternoon Mr. and Mrs. Browning died. Their voices taking one final stand before… "She has her mother's hair and face, and her father's eyes."

"For someone who glimpsed their faces but once, you remember them extremely well." Rolan squinted at her, searching for the secret she refused to share. "I have always suspected that you saw them more times than what you confessed to me. You have cut everyone off from you, isolated yourself in this ship for most of the past several years, and when your chance to change the outcome finally comes along, you hide from it."

"I have handled my burdens for many centuries before you came strolling down this shoreline. I do not require your help now." Vectra abruptly turned to leave.

"That may be. But you are scared, Vectra Tillerman. Scared for when the day comes and she finds out what truly happened to her parents."

Vectra looked back at him, her eyes failing to conceal the sadness and fear contained within.

Chapter Twenty-Two

"Breakfast is served!" Monica woke up to the sound of Vectra's voice calling from the prep station inside the conference-like room. Groggily, she pulled herself up from the bed and stumbled over to the table where her brother was already seated. His gums smacked together in anticipation of the sweet-smelling food being cooked over a portable burner. At the sight of his bedhead hair, Monica couldn't hold back a chuckle at how deranged he looked in the old ship.

"What's so funny?" Dare eyed his sister suspiciously.

"Your hair needs a good brushing."

"Oh, *yeah*?" He grinned. "Well, you don't look like a supermodel either. And a good morning to you too, A." Dare smirked, figuring that she would clam up after he used her private nickname in front of another. Monica's face tightened up, confirming his theory.

"Who is 'A'?" Vectra stirred the speckled pot above the hot coils with a ladle she took from a hook on the wall, dished out two spoonfuls into a ceramic bowl and passed it to the boy.

"No one." Monica quickly answered, shooting her

brother a killer look. "Isn't that right, Derrick?" Her stomach growled at the sight of steam rising from its hot contents.

"I have been meaning to ask, why are you called 'Dare?' Is it primarily just short for Derrick, or is there another reason behind the nickname?" Vectra continued to fill another two bowls before coming over to join them at the table.

"Don't we need a spoon or something to eat this with?" Dare licked his lips. He might not have known what the brown and chunky mashed fruit was in front of him, but it didn't matter to his starving stomach.

"For someone so young, your eyesight is very poor. What is that, then, beside your left hand?"

The boy looked surprisingly down to see a metal spoon on top of a white napkin. "I'm pretty sure that wasn't there before." He eagerly picked up the eating utensil and dug into the mixture. "It is short for Derrick, but I'm also known for taking on any kind of dare. You know, when a friend says 'I dare you to do…whatever' and then you either have to do it or be called a chicken for the rest of your life."

"My, that sounds extreme." Vectra blew on her spoon, pushing the steam away from the mouth-watering gloop.

Monica sat down next to her brother and curiously studied an 18oz bottle of rich, molasses-colored liquid that was on the table. "What is this?" A white label had been slightly worn off at the top where a few English letters remained. Written down in vertical lines, black Japanese characters stood out in stark contrast to the plain background.

"Aged soy sauce made by the traditional methods in Japan."

"You import your soy sauce?" Dare leaned toward his sister and stole the bottle from her hand in order to see it for himself. "Awesome!"

"Be careful with that. It is rather expensive and I do not particularly feel like ordering another one so soon." Vectra put her hat gently down to her right and fluffed her curls. "It goes through a process of aging for four years in large wooden barrels, called Kioke barrels, that will outlast your lifespan. It is all hand-made and does not contain any commercial additives."

"What do you use it on?" Monica was waiting to hear about some centuries old Japanese recipe that involved a hard to acquire fish or duck; most likely to be prepared in an ancient pot that she had never heard of before.

"On the local Chinese takeout food." Vectra's passive answer just about stole the wind from Monica and her brother.

"Isn't that like sacrilegious? Using highly crafted sauce on lowly take-out grub?" Dare held his head high in the air, acting like a judge on a baking show. He gestured to the bottle with the flare of a tv show girl. "Having traveled all the way here from Japan, and having waited four long years in a vat of wood, this soy sauce has battered the waves of the ocean and long nights at sea, so that it can be consumed on $4.35 worth of battered chicken chunks."

"It is the sauce that makes or breaks a meal you know." Vectra defended her choice. She held her hand up to stop the boy from another dramatic impersonation and produced a small salt shaker from one of her pockets. "See this? I order this salt in special, from the Philippines. It is coconut based and…"

Monica blinked her eyes. "You carry around a salt shaker filled with salt from the Philippines, you import hand-crafted soy sauce from Japan and you live in an old shipwreck that has been transformed into a floating island.

Is there anything about you that is normal?"

"Define *normal*? For a long time in the Netherlands, it was *normal* for people to wear wooden Klompen made by their local clog maker. Now, there are so few artisans left that still craft them by hand, and fewer pairs that are actually worn instead of becoming souvenirs." Vectra tilted her head. "Besides, why would you want to be considered *normal*?"

Monica cast her eyes upon the pea-sized soft chunks scattered around in the mush of the breakfast and took note of the cinnamon flecks, which helped to make the pleasant aroma. The soft scent of vanilla hit her nose and added a comforting feel to the bowl. *It does look delicious...and smells like applesauce. Apples again!* She poked at the food cautiously.

"Were you never taught not to pick at your food? Or is that considered to be an old-fashioned idea nowadays?" Vectra eyed the girl curiously. "I do not mingle with many from your world on a daily basis, so perhaps it is."

"I just want to make sure that you're not going to poison us." She half-heartedly joked. *Though it is a little late to be thinking about that now.* Monica watched her brother eat without coming up for air.

Vectra chuckled. "If I wanted to do that, there would be far easier ways to accomplish such a task. Besides, this recipe takes a long time to make, and it would be a shame to waste it by making it deadly." She kept eye contact with Monica as she swallowed another spoonful herself.

"It tastes great, Sis. And it's your favorite..." Dare joshed her. Monica took a risk and tried the freshly-made applesauce. Her mouth sung when the cinnamon struck her taste buds and the apple chunks slid against her tongue. She hadn't realized how empty her stomach truly was until it hurt after tasting one bite of the food and immediately craved for more. It was the best applesauce she had ever experienced, and that was saying something since apples were her favorite fruit.

"Where did you find such tasty apples?" She inquired in between swallows.

"There's an orchard on the other side of the mountain."

"A wild orchard?"

"No. I tend to borrow some when the season is right."

"Steal them, you mean?" Monica almost felt sick now. "I just ate stolen food."

"I prefer to think of it as borrowing without returning." Vectra finished her portion of the meal and walked back for seconds.

"A pig dressed up as anything else, is still a pig." Monica fought with her conscious; on one side, she was far too hungry to argue, and the on the other side, she didn't care for the idea of eating food that had not been paid for.

Vectra's eyes widened in bafflement for a moment, then broke out into sparkling amusement at the young girl's statement. "I have been compared to many things in my life. But never a pig. I must admit that to be a first. Which is very hard to do after all I have seen and heard." Walking over to the pot, Vectra offered them both another helping. Dare didn't hesitate to take her up on it, and Monica reluctantly joined him. Her head moved to the left, trying to better see the collection of oddly shaped bottles arranged by the burner. *I hope that this doesn't turn out to be like in a fairytale. Though I see no motive for her to do that.*

"What is in this? I can only identify apples and cinnamon. Although, I did smell a hint of vanilla."

"An old recipe I have sworn to keep secret until the ends of time itself." The Guardian smiled. "Ms. Locksmith's words of course, she being the one who taught me her mother's special touch. Catriona used to sneak into this ship to steal things from me. That way, I was forced to visit her. She gets lonely, you see, and I like to think that she enjoyed my company from time to time." Her eyes lit up with a genuine fondness for their shared memories and her smile widened until her cheeks hurt. "One day, I witnessed her mixing up a batch of Huckleberry Muffins and asked her to show me what makes them so addictive. After that, she gave me a few more of her inherited recipes in confidence and this so happens to be one of them."

"She didn't talk so kindly about you at the antique fair," Monica slurped the delectable applesauce into her mouth. "Seemed rather hostile when she talked to Gregon about what happened before."

Vectra recomposed herself and began clearing up the kitchen by stashing the odd bottles into the drawers of the prep station. She grabbed hold of the large pot, gave it a good hand washing and waited for the burner to cool down. All of a sudden, the green long-necked glass container of dried lucky clovers felt differently in her hand. Past joys of Locksmith's baking and cooking classes stung the hard-to-see wounds, only opening deeper with each recollection. "Time goes by, and people change because of their decisions in life."

"That sounds like a fortune cookie saying." Dare added for a laugh, "Lucky Numbers are…33 45 78 and…" He gave a drumroll with his fingers on the tabletop for the big reveal of the last number. "19!"

"I must say, Dare, you have a certain style of humor that is a welcomed change to my usual company." Vectra shared a small chuckle with the kids whilst giving a sideways glance toward the room she kept the medicine in.

"I saw that." The hollowed male voice announced out of nowhere.

"Who was that?" Both kids flashed their heads around, trying to find the person belonging to the voice. Much to their confusion, all they saw was Rae still fast asleep in his bed. A food dish had been filled beside him, with his name lovingly painted in red on the outside of the white bowl.

"That was a mean trick, Rolan. The Brownings are not used to dealing with your kind." Vectra paid no attention to the disembodied voice. Instead, she went about her business putting the last of the ingredients away and wiped down her makeshift kitchen. "Now you will have to show yourself to them. Be careful to keep your battle wound hidden from their view. I do not want to have my applesauce being thrown up on the floor."

"Well, *pardon me* for wanting to meet some new people after having an audience of one for so long." A ghostly figure materialized before their eyes. Dare's mouth dropped like a drawbridge, and Monica grabbed ahold of the table.

"A ghost? That is what we heard? A ghost?" Her eyes remained open, frozen in shock.

The ghost stood proud and strong in his Confederate uniform with mud smeared hands and face. He gave the siblings a courteous bow and introduced himself as Captain Rolan Gingerton of the 15th South Carolina Infantry Regiment. "It is a pleasure to meet such fine young people as yourselves. Not to mention, ones interested in history that a few of us still live in."

"You're a…a…" Dare's face went white, "a floating, dead being."

"One could describe my current predicament as that, yes. I have an abnormal situation upon my shoulders, and have been marooned here ever since I switched to the other side. Death being the other side, that is."

"Rolan, they are not here to listen to your long and dismal story. We are about to leave." Vectra cast him a glare. "A fact you perfectly well knew about."

"But, the little boy, Dare…I think he is called…he knows of this ship. He searched it up on that glowing rectangle of his. He might hold an answer for me."

Vectra's eyes went straight for Monica's brother. At first, a horrified look flashed on her face. "I am quite sure that he will not have that piece of information." Her lips flattened into a thin line. "We have to go. Now. Rolan, you can say a short good-bye, but then you need to vanish."

"You do not command me, Vectra Tillerman." Captain Rolan took a stance in his waving form. "We are both residents here. Equally inhabiting this space. And I was here before you stepped foot on deck."

"By three whole seconds."

"If the glowing rectangle can find out about this ship, then it might be able to do a lot more."

"Rolan, do not get your hopes up. *He does not know.*"

"I will ask the question if I wish." The ghost turned to Dare. "Tell me, do you know who my relatives are? My father is…"

"Wait just a moment." Monica put a protective arm out in front of her brother. "He doesn't have to help you at all. Especially since you fought for the Confederates. How could…"

Vectra stopped her before she started to call the dead man names. "That is enough, Monica Browning. The Civil War was personal on many different levels that those of today do not fully understand. It was not just personal for the country, but it was an individual battle as well. You may not agree with his view points, but you do need to show him a little respect for having the courage to die for his beliefs. How many of your modern 'so-called influencers' would do that?"

Monica quieted down as Dare removed her arm. "Ah… Captain Rolan, Sir…" He eased into what he was going to say next. "My glowing rectangle ran out of battery. Out of charge. Out of life, you might say."

"Oh." The Captain's mood fell to a state of disappointment. "That happens. We all need a good rest once and again."

"Rolan…" Vectra took a step forward, but was halted from coming any closer by his raised hand.

"You may fear the future, Vectra. Me, I want it so badly it hurts my very soul. I will never apologize, nor regret, any bit of hope I find." With his final statement lingering in the air, his ghostly spirit evaporated until not a trace remained.

Vectra shook her head out of frustration. "I try to warn him every time. And he still insists on not listening to me." She motioned for the Brownings to pack up their belongings, tiding up the place along the way. "We need to leave while we can."

"Is he a mean ghost?" Monica shoved her arms through the holes in her jacket and latched onto her backpack with a grip of steel. She wasn't sure what all the rush was about.

"No. Just embittered by his life. He is stuck here until his family makes things right; his estranged family that is. We don't know who any of his relatives are."

"Where did he die?"

"Just up the shoreline. He got lonely and became my roommate." Vectra gave Rae a kiss on the head in farewell and dashed off the ship, armed with a satchel and rolled wrap strapped around her waist. Dare brought up the rear of the line as he carried the duffel bag containing the tent down the gangplank after his sister. "He will be fine, so do not dwell on his troubles. We have enough of our own to worry about."

"Are we going to be able to get *into* the Locksmith's house? You're not exactly on good speaking terms with Catriona right now." Monica kept an eye on her brother as they walked over a dry bed of rocks.

"I need no reminders of that." Vectra pushed a branch out of the way and dove to the left to avoid a medium-sized spider web. "We should still be able to go in. Curiosity is one of her weaknesses, and it will intrigue her brain cells to see me on her porch."

As they continued along their path, Monica looked up to find an opening in the tree canopy, vaguely in the shape of a bear. Sunlight poured onto the faintly outlined trail they were using to re-locate Vectra's car, and she couldn't ignore the beautiful morning surrounding them on all fronts. It was as though nature was handing them an invitation to stay forever within the fold of its natural serenity, and her mind reluctantly drifted back to their present task. "Is her house anything like her booth at the antique fair? It smelled lovely with lavenders and tea."

"You will find out soon enough."

Chapter Twenty-Three

"Don't you think you should change into an outfit that doesn't attract so much attention? At the antique fair, you fit right in. But not on an uneventful, normal Monday, in this sleepy town." Monica gestured toward Vectra's cosplay-like attire.

Two hours had already been claimed by the clock and their vehicle just arrived in the picturesque town of Herbio. All the residents were dressed in casual clothes, milling up and down the sidewalks for lunchtime. Coats of many colors made them easy to spot against the historical buildings of red brick, yellow ochre, and eggshell white. Vectra parked the car in a lot facing the town square, where they had a clear view of the tall statue standing in the middle of a roundabout and the small landscaped area surrounding its sculpted base. Monica was right. This was not the city, where she could easily be mistaken for someone who has gone looney.

"Alright, Smarty Pants. Just because I do not associate myself with your generation regularly, does not mean that I am completely ignorant either." Closing her eyes, Vectra flicked out a deuce of hearts from in-between her fingers, and waved the card counter-clockwise around her head, without saying a word. A second later, her outfit morphed into a pink heather V-neck shirt over green capris. The brown leather jacket vest was replaced by a maroon utility jacket and black walking sneakers adorned her feet, rather than the calf-high brown boots she was accustomed to wearing. Upon her head, the fedora hat changed into a pair of blue tinted aviator sunglasses with three gemstones laid into both lens.

"I wish changing my clothes could be that easy." Dare let out a short huff as an idea popped into his head. "Oooh! Do you have to do laundry or can you just wave one of those magical cards over your clothes to have it all cleaned for you? That would be an extremely useful way to apply your powers. In my opinion."

Monica glared at him. "You simply want to get out from having to do your own chores at home." She was already irritated with her brother for allowing his phone battery to die, and held in the scolding she wanted to give for the past few hours because Vectra was along. That would have to wait until they were alone, and Monica had a whole speech prepared for that moment. There was no telling where their argument might lead and the less spilled to the Guardian, the better for the time being.

Dare shrugged his shoulders. "Can you blame a kid for trying?"

"It was a nice try, Dare. However, I still have to do most chores myself. Time to go everyone. And do not forget to bring the duffel bag along." Vectra locked up her vehicle and tapped on the middle of the bronze grill's top rim with a single finger. A glowing circle remained visible for a total of three seconds after she lifted her finger from the warm metal. Then it completely vanished like a mood ring. "If we need to dash back to Blaze in case of an emergency, you must NOT touch any part of this car before I do. Is that clear?"

"Yes, Ma'am." Both Monica and Dare answered in unison. They followed Vectra away from the local pharmacy's parking lot at a brisk pace, joining a large family group on their way to Pop's Grill and Seafood.

"Today is going to be on the warmer side." One of the older people stated aloud. "I heard on the TV that it is supposed to be nearing 65 degrees come four o'clock this afternoon." Dare tended to agree with the man's prediction as sweat began to fall down on the back of his neck in the winter coat he was sporting.

"Here. I can try to stick your jacket in my backpack." Monica offered, after she noticed her brother feeling uncomfortable. She pulled the bag off and whipped it around to open the zipper. "Or maybe not." Her eyes surveyed all of the items shoved into every pocket and divided section available.

"If you are too hot in those jackets, put them in the duffel bag." Vectra suggested in front of them. She kept her focus pinned to the patrons walking across the streets and those waiting for the 'walk' symbol to flash. Whoever she was searching for, Monica figured that the person must be very important as the Guardian's gaze studied the people's faces and body postures. Clearly, they were okay for the time being.

Dare thanked Vectra for the reminder and gladly stuffed the bag with both coats. "Now watch tomorrow be colder than anything. The weather can be truly freaky this time of year."

"And at the most inconvenient of times, if you ask me, at any point of the year." Monica commented as a flashback of finding Easter eggs in the snow came into her head.

"No one asked you. But that didn't stop you from putting your two cents into the ring." Dare stuck his tongue out at his sister.

"You two need to behave and stay close to me. Keep your eyes peeled for anyone acting suspicious or anyone who seems out of place. If you do, speak up and say something. I have a feeling that we might have been followed." Vectra walked due south on Main Street with the siblings right behind.

"But we checked out the back of the car every ten minutes on the way over here. How could someone have followed us?" Monica helped her brother up from tripping over a raised brick in the sidewalk as they pressed onward.

"We are out of the forest now and Taminus has his ways. Better to stay alert than to get caught off guard and dead."

At the end of Main Street, about half a mile back an overgrown gravel drive, sat an old house that had been built during the American Revolution. Its sharply angled roof did not create a sense of a cozy English cottage, but rather that of a creepy witch house with busted shutters and wooden sidings in desperate need of repair. Vines coated a majority of the second level, except for a few windows peeking through their curtain, and the chipping paint almost made the building appear pixelated. Rotten floorboards littered the porch where termites had enjoyed a buffet of wooden delights, and the remains of weather-beaten statues helped to complete the abandoned feel of the property.

Monica found it hard to believe that the sweet, elderly woman from the street fair did not maintain her house in better shape. "That old lady lives here?"

"Catriona would not allow it to be seen in any other condition." Vectra forged down a forgotten path through the overreaching weeds, threatening to snag onto any trespassers. "They would kill you if you tried to recreate its heyday by sprucing it up. It does extremely well at deterring any unwanted attention and possible salesmen from darkening their door." She glanced over at an empty hitching post near the house. "Jeffrey's bicycle is gone. That gives us a fairly good chance at coming through this alive."

"Are they hiding Bigfoot in there?" Monica joked with her brother and bumped him with her elbow. "Maybe they have Giants and magical gnomes too."

"They got rid of their last gnome two years back. He was an absolute troublemaker. Insisted on a tidy garden and the Locksmiths could not have any of that." Vectra leaned down to Dare's level. "I think they were trying to find another Harold. He was certainly precious to them and would join in on their afternoon tea and all. But you cannot replace them. No matter how hard you try, each one is as unique as a snowflake."

"A gnome? Named Harold?" Dare looked at Monica in puzzlement. *Surely a gnome could not have had tea with real humans.*

Vectra nodded her head with the most serious of expressions.

"Did Harold die?" Monica asked, now curious about the surprise twist of reality her joke took.

"In the line of duty. A bunch of schoolboys decided it would be fun to dare their friend into going up to the 'haunted house,' and Harold went to defend his home." Vectra pulled back a section of bush to reveal a short gravestone dedicated to the late garden ornament. "His so-called 'friends' nicknamed him 'Smasher' after that night. But at least they don't call him a chicken anymore." Dare remained silent as he stared at the crumbling marker.

"Are you being serious with us?" The story sounded pretty made-up to Monica. "A gnome that died from school pranks?"

"I can joke about many things, Ms. Browning, but not about gnomes in general. And I would not kid about Harold at all. Especially, not here. Catriona and Jeffrey are still quite sore regarding the cruel tragedy of what transpired. It would be in your best interests to not bring it up in conversation, nor to ask when you see his picture on the wall in the kitchen." Vectra's stoic facial expression quashed all doubts in the teen's mind.

As Monica went to back up from the grave, she instinctively pulled her hand away from a plant she swore had not been there a second before. "Ah, Vectra? Is it possible that the plants are moving?"

"Quite possible. Keep in step and do not dilly dally. I do not have the time to fight off a Rose Fly bush today. They are very grouchy and like to shred clothing. Cotton-based fabric is their favorite." Vectra motioned in the direction of the front porch with her right hand. "A Rose Fly is a combination of a rose bush and a Venus fly trap. Such nasty tempers they have. I don't recall ever meeting one that was nice in any remote sense of the word." She paused upon making it to the foot of the stairs leading up to the rickety porch. "Now, if I remember this correctly…"

Both kids watched the Guardian place her feet to the left side of the first step, hopped to the right side of the second, and then proceeded up the rest of the stairs in an almost fluid dance style. Once at the top, Vectra turned around and told the siblings to copy exactly what she had done. "If not, well…let us not go there. Don't step anywhere that I did not and everything will be fine."

"You could just go on without us and return when you

find the plant you need." Monica suggested. Fear riddled the teen's mind. She wasn't certain she could remember where Vectra walked to avoid the traps they might trigger along any of the seventeen steps. Dare shared her concerns and shuffled his feet backward until the heel of his sneaker hit a Rose Fly bush coming for him. He raced onto the stairs as his sister also took note of the traveling bush targeting them. Dirt flew at the kids from the plant's roots kicking up the ground as they increased their speed, spraying up unsuspecting worms along with bits of stone.

"Monica, are you coming?" Vectra pulled her pocket watch up to her face. "Time is ticking."

"Okay! Okay!" Monica slowly placed her foot on the left side of the first step and gripped onto the splintering handrail to steady both her balance and her nerves. *Was it left or right next?* Her right foot went straight up, to the left of the next step and almost touched it when Vectra's voice shouted at her to halt immediately.

"No. The right side. Then the left. Left again." Together, they listened to Vectra's instructions in order to join her on the porch unscathed.

"See, you two did a marvelous job. Nothing to it, right?" Vectra smiled at their panicked faces. "It was not *that* bad." She handed Monica a damp cloth from her satchel. "Almost forgot. Wipe your arm with this. It will clean off those specs of dirt you got from that unruly vegetation. And make sure to keep Catriona distracted once we are in."

"Don't I get a cloth too?" Dare inquired, gazing at the soil on his shirt.

The sound of footsteps approaching from inside the house, reached their ears, and caused the group to go silent. A moment later, Catriona Locksmith appeared when she opened the antique white door to greet her guests. Between two wrinkled cheeks, spread a wide smile that beamed like the sun, and raised her pencil thin eyebrows up in joy.

"Vectra! How nice of you to be stopping by without an invite. I was growing tiresome of sending out proper invitations, embossed and given the royal treatment, mind you, and to not hear so much as a peep back in response. We haven't had tea together in so long…" Ms. Locksmith cut her words short when she noticed the two Browning kids also on the porch. She moved her glasses closer to her eyes and squinted through the thin lenses. A twinkle appeared in her irises at seeing them. "I am so proud of you, my dear Vectra. You have decided to right a wrong and help these children out."

"Unfortunately." Vectra pointed at Monica, who's look of puzzlement was returning. The way the older woman phrased why Vectra was helping them did not escape the teen's attention. She found it odd how Catriona restated the line in the same manner on Saturday, and a seed of suspicion planted itself in the midst of her present thoughts. *I wonder what all Vectra knows about our parents' disappearance? And how deep does her involvement go?* Her brain was racking through an entire line of new questions until she realized that Vectra was talking about her. "This one came into contact with poison ivy in the woods and is need of a little relief."

Monica suddenly felt an extreme itchiness on her arm and peered down to see a rash had formed where she recently used the dampened cloth on her skin. Anger began boiling in her blood from the deception. *I knew she was not to be trusted.*

"Say no more. Say no more. Come inside for me to take a gander at that poor arm." Ms. Locksmith held the door open for them to walk through the hallway filled to the brim with teapots galore. She led them down the corridor and toward the kitchen where the small passageway emptied into. "I have the perfect remedy to fix that right up, Young Lady. It will be healed in practically no time whatsoever."

Monica and Dare could not believe their eyes, again. The overabundance of teapots were not confined to the hall, but consumed the house on overstuffed shelves bursting full of every variety imaginable. Even the nooks and crevices were incapable of holding anything more. Long wooden shelves, held up by many cast iron brackets, lined the vintage wallpaper and supported at least fifty teapots each. All sizes, designs, materials, and colors were stacked and displayed like a crazy quilt surrounding them. Especially the sideboard, whose too short countertop was covered with a much longer board, and hosted a cluttered arrangement of pots and their lids. Books were stacked on either side of the sideboard, matching the height of the old furniture to hold up more teapots along the right hallway wall.

"Wow! This is one MASSIVE collection." Monica stated, observing a smaller teapot from Indonesia.

"Thank you. It has taken countless years to procure all you see before you. I have a passion for tea, you see. As if you could not tell." Catriona laughed to herself. "My brother tells me that I need to stop collecting so many of them. But when that happens, I simply remind him about his collection, and that shuts him up for a spell."

"I wonder what he collects?" Dare whispered to Monica as he stepped into the kitchen. Surprisingly, it was the total opposite than the rest of the house. The very minimalist design, and lack of any objects, led the boy to dread what lurked behind the cupboard doors. *I have a feeling it is going to be like a jack-in-the-box.*

"Ah, it should be here somewhere." Ms. Locksmith

headed straight for the door that was to the left of the kitchen sink, two over. Dare stepped backward in anticipation for the cupboard to explode and accidentally bumped into a rack system bolted onto the wall. He glanced upward at the multitudes of corkscrews in just as many varieties as there were teapots.

"Are you also into wine as well?" He swallowed hard when he saw the length and sharpness of the worm on a particularly large corkscrew from France. It was a collapsible compound-lever model, circa 1900s, that was extended to its full height of 10 inches. Rivets held the unit together; which in Dare's opinion, helped it look like an item from the black and white horror films of the past.

"That would be my brother's collection. Or one of them, in point of fact. You should see the wine cellar if you think my tea collection is large." Ms. Locksmith searched through the jars labeled by a sharpie marker on tape, "Rattlesnake scales. Butterfly juice. Hemlock. Ahh..." She yanked out her prize from the back of the lowest shelf and sat it on the dining table where the light was strongest. "Made this myself not long ago. Should work wonders. Though, it will be a little potent in the smell, considering how fresh it will be."

"If it was not that long ago, then shouldn't it be to the front of the cupboard?" Monica eyed the jar skeptically. She studied the white goo inside the clear glass, thinking it was probably just whipped cream the old lady mislabeled.

"Time is rather a relative thing, is it not?" Ms. Locksmith's eyes smiled with a glimmer. "Now, where did you say the poison was?" Monica rolled up her sleeve and showed the woman her sudden red rash and festering itch. "Oh, my. I bet that is itching like it is on fire."

"That's a way of putting it."

"Well, Catriona, I am going to use the bathroom while we are here. If you would like to brew up a fresh batch of tea, I am sure that the kids would enjoy partaking in some." Vectra made her way down the hall and quickened her pace once she was out of sight.

"I sure would." Dare faked a toothy grin. "Say, what kind do you have?"

The elderly woman chuckled. "I do not believe that you have *that* much time to spare."

"You have that many?" Monica felt the cool relief of the homemade cream touching her skin. When the lady was done lathering it on, she thanked her for the help and slightly cursed Vectra in her head. "Sorry we barged in on you like this."

"No problem, Deary. My pleasure, in fact. Apart from my booth at the local farmer's markets, I do not get to chat with others as much as I used too. We did have a tea house in town where I seemed to fit right in with the owner and I enjoyed our talks. However, she had to close down after Covid hit, and moved closer to her other family members in Ohio." Ms. Locksmith turned her back to the kids and replaced the jar.

"I'm sorry to hear that."

"That is quite alright. We must do what we must for family, even when it comes at a sacrifice at times." Catriona washed her hands at the sink as Dare looked at the ceiling and Monica stared out the kitchen window overlooking the backyard.

"Is your tea grown out there?" She pointed at the large greenhouse setup that was stationed on the sloping hillside running into the house.

"Some of my mixtures are grown locally, while I have to specially order in others. And then there are the plants I have yet to experiment with because they are locked away in my brother's Wardian cases. I suppose you do not know what those are?" She sighed, witnessing Dare's blinking eyes and Monica's blank face. "Back in the 1800s, a man by the name of Nathaniel Bagshaw Ward made a discovery that literally changed the planet. He observed that a plant, completely sealed in a bottle…and given the appropriate amount of sunlight, could survive for years without being given any water."

"Because of the water cycle and photosynthesis?" The boy asked.

"Precisely. It revolutionized the way that plants were transported from country to country and across oceans in a time period when travel took months and not hours. Before Wardian cases, many plant specimens died during the voyages and so botanists would have to study the dead samples." Her eyes lit up like a Christmas tree. "This invention altered everything. Now, plants could be transplanted from gardens in China to the rolling hills of the Himalayans. Flowers could be kept safe aboard a ship heading home to England from Jamaica." Ms. Locksmith swung open a set of pantry doors extending from the floor to the ceiling. A cavern of tea options, in every possible combination imaginable, was revealed as sensored lights flashed on above. Endless rows of bags containing dried tea leaves had been carefully placed in organized fashion, by their corresponding names scribbled in marker on the front, in a system only she knew. "You won't find anything but loose leaf tea in my house."

"Holy macaronis!" Dare exclaimed, trying to take it all in. "There is more to choose from in there, than in the entire country of China!"

"Thank you, that means so much to me." Ms. Locksmith

smiled from ear to ear again, beaming in pride. "However, I do believe that they have a bit more than I do. Now then, have you two ever had tea before?" She waited for their response, which was unanimously "no," and happily slapped her hands together. "Alright. I would suggest a green or dark tea to start with."

"What's the difference?" Dare wanted so badly to step into the cavern of tea wonders, but resisted the urge to dive into the awe-inspiring selections.

Catriona's eyes rolled in their sockets. "What is the difference? My goodness, dear boy, there is very much so a difference indeed. Not only in flavors, but in the quality of pick and the season from which it is harvested." Their host handed them each one of the pamphlets she included in every new customer's first purchase from her booth. "This is only a generalization, mind you. The world of tea is so vast, that my brother has at least two wide bookshelves dedicated to that very plant in his study."

Dare flipped the three-folded brochure open and saw an extensive ancestral tree diagram listing out various sub-species of the camellia-sinensis, also known as the tea plant. Six main categories were listed beside one another, such as green, white, oolong, and dark tea. From there, the lines branched out into a web of confusion for the young boy. "And this is supposed to make sense?"

Catriona looked him up and down in an assessment, studying him with her glasses as she had done before. "I think a green would be the right choice for you." Her finger tapped on the furthest listing to the left. "Peruse the options above and let me know which one you think sounds tempting to try."

Dare scanned over options like Dàfāng, qí qiāng, and Dragonwell. "How about Dragonwell? The name sounds

intriguing, and it's also one of the only names I can pro-
nounce."

After a small chuckle, Catriona nodded in agreement.
"That would be a lovely selection indeed." Her hand perked
up in the air as a thought came into her mind. "I do believe
I have one bag left of my finest grade. Being as how this will
be your first tasting, it should be of the upmost robust in its
flavor." She immediately went for a narrow rack attached to
the back of the door, counting in a whisper until she saw the
one she was looking for. "A first grade pan-fired Dragonwell
tea, hand-picked from the West Lake region in China."

"What does *that* mean?" Dare pointed to the words
"Pingyang Tezao" printed on the bag's front label.

"Pingyang Tezao means that it is from an early harvest.
The first of the year, in fact. Right after the snow melts is the
optimal time to pick the buds from the plant. And it also
signifies that the price will be much higher than that of the
summer and fall picks."

Dare glanced over at his sister. "Well, what do you think,
A? Are you good with it?"

"Sure." Monica shrugged her shoulders as she bent over
to unzip her backpack. Her hand reached in and felt around
as a way of comforting herself that everything was still there:
a blanket, cell phone, charging cord, journal, hairbrush,
toothbrush, an emergency credit card, cookies and water,
among other things. Dare didn't know about the credit card
and she wanted to keep it that way. It was for emergencies
only and had been used once a month for a drink in order
to keep the account open, by Trevor. She re-hid the card
behind a flap and continued to go over the contents until
her finger brushed a kraft paper wrapped package. *I had the
blanket wrapped around that. How'd it come off?*

Chapter Twenty-Four

Hastily, Monica re-fixed the blanket and shot up to see if the others had seen it. She sighed out of relief when she saw Ms. Locksmith fiddling with bags of tea whilst Dare ogled the odd mixes of dried plants, both none the wiser. She quietly pulled her journal out of the bag with ease and clicked open a pen concealed in the metal spiral binding. *I need to keep that hidden. Who knows who I can trust with it?* "Ms. Locksmith, where is your brother? Jeffrey?"

"Oh, he is off on another one of his world-wind adventures." Ms. Locksmith began to boil water on the stove with a more modern kettle. "Nowadays, that only means a trip to the grocery store. And please, call me Catriona." She shuffled her way over to the cupboard and grabbed ahold of four teacups in matching paisley designs. "If I may be so bold, why did you call your sister 'A' a moment ago?" The whisper was low enough for only Dare to hear.

"Oh, it's just a nickname our parents gave her when she was younger. She was always writing words and phrases down on paper; whether or not they made sense. They used to joke about how she was going to grow up to be an author someday. 'A' for author. At least, that is what Trevor told me."

Dare stood on the tips of his toes in order to look above the countertops. "But the truth is that she is not very good when it comes to grammar."

"I heard that." Monica balled up a piece of paper and threw it at her brother. "You are not the best speller either. And yet, you want to enter into the local spelling bee. I still say you won't make it past the first round."

"A spelling bee? I haven't been to one of those in ages." Catriona's stare grew distant. "Last one was when…" The sound of the oven dinging brought Ms. Locksmith up short from reminiscing into the past. "Good heavens! I forgot about the scones I was baking."

"Scones?" Dare's tongue smacked against the inside of his mouth. "I thought that wonderful smell was just a candle. I could go for a few of those." Monica rolled her eyes and worked on her day's entry while Catriona pulled a piping hot pan of fresh blueberry scones from the oven. "Smells delicious."

"I should say that they do." The older lady sat the pan down on two large hot pads she sewed a century before. "It's a new recipe I have been tinkering on for many a moon now. Even handpicked the blueberries myself from the garden earlier this year." A sudden thought dawned in her mind. "Where *is* Jeffrey?" She looked around the room as if expecting to find him lurking in the shadows too small for a mouse to find safety in. "He should be home by now. I remember I made sure to have timed it precisely so that the scones would be out just as soon as he returned."

A shared look of panic was felt between the Brownings. "I'm sure he will be along any minute now." Monica forced a smile onto her face. *Vectra had better hurry up.* To settle her worries, the teen read through what she had already written on the page and found the day's events to sound crazier and more farfetched then she thought they would. *If I were to read this, not knowing what all I know, I would have thought I was a nutjob. This reads more like a fantasy novel than it does my own life.* She shook her head and offered a hopeful explanation for Jeffrey's tardiness. "Perhaps it took him a little longer due to an interesting plant he noticed along the way?"

"Perhaps. Still…though. It is highly unusual for him to be late from the store."

"Ms. Locksmith…" Dare quietly spoke in a childish manner. He wasn't convinced that asking her was a good idea, but there would not be a better time like the present. "Catriona…did you know our parents?" His eyes looked nervously at her, almost scared to hear the answer. But like Monica, the boy was beginning to have doubts about Vectra and wanted another's viewpoint.

Catriona removed the green oven mitts from her hands and wringed them out for no particular reason. A saddened expression took hold of her face, knitting her brows together and deepening the bags under her eyes. "Not like you two did. I met them once, at the same antique fair that you showed up at, actually. They were looking for Vectra, and I pointed her out to them. I saw them talking to her in a mad rush. Kept glancing back as if someone was following their footsteps, and I managed to overhear part of their conversation."

"Do you remember what they talked about?" Monica immediately stopped writing and flipped her journal closed.

The elderly woman thought to herself a brief moment, pausing her words before continuing on. "Yes. They told her about a man named Gaither and that he was close to finding the press. They wanted her to help them in stopping him, and she refused. Gregon and I tried our best at persuading her to change her mind, given her charged duty as the Guardian. But alas, we were not successful."

"Do you know if they continued on their own or..." Monica used her foot to bring the backpack in closer to her body. She was finally one step closer to finding out what happened, and she suddenly found herself unsure if she wanted to know at all. Mixed feelings stirred up in her stomach: anger, pain, confusion, sadness and hatred, all spun around like a washing machine inside. For the longest time after their disappearance, she wondered if they were still alive somewhere, waiting to be rescued, or never coming back for personal reasons. As the days blended into months and years, their deaths became a necessary explanation for her to try to move on from the hurt.

"As I packed up my booth that afternoon, your parents were already bound and determined to make it there themselves. How? I could not possibly imagine. Vectra does not simply guard ancient artifacts, but she hides them in crafty and clever ways. She is no fool and takes precautionary measures to ensure their safety. Without her, the task is too foolhardy a venture."

"Did you see them leave?"

"They left down Roger's Ave. I assumed it was to stay out of sight of whoever was coming after them." Catriona saw the kids' depressed faces and zoned in on Dare first. "You were what...a toddler when they left?"

"I was three years old. Monica was seven."

"Do not be blaming yourself for their decisions in life. Leaving you two by yourselves was irresponsible in anyone's book. Naturally you want answers, and that is only human. But..."

"What is Vectra's charged duty Catriona? I mean, we know that she protects thirteen old world artifacts, but what does that exactly *mean*?" Monica huffed into her hand. She wanted nothing more than to change the subject and stifle the raw emotions resurfacing. "I feel like a broken record by constantly asking…"

"Do not be sorry for asking. You are in this as deep as any of us now, though you might not realize how much so. It means that her sworn duty is to protect those artifacts and nothing more. But when your parents came to warn her, and she outright ignored them, the Greek gods saw that as a negligence of her job. And she was already on thin ice after what happened before in…"

"I SMELL SCONES!" A male voiced crackled in the hallway as the door creaked shut. "Catriona, are those blueberry?" The thinner gentleman, unmistakably aged past seventy-five, cantered into the kitchen with two brown paper bags filled with groceries. "Oh, my!" His narrow eyebrows arched at the sight of Monica and Dare staring back at his hazel eyes, sunken cheeks, and rounded chin.

"Jeffrey, our guests are Monica and Dare, respectably." Catriona picked up five small plates from one of the many antique white cupboards and dropped them on the table. "They were about to join me in some afternoon tea."

"Splendid. Splendid." Jeffrey stated with suspicion caking his words. "So, how did you get past the front steps?"

"Vectra showed them." His sister nonchalantly answered for the Brownings. "It is great to have her in the house once again."

"VECTRA?!" Jeffrey threw the bags of food onto the counter by the deep farm-style sink and scoffed into the delicious aroma of the fresh pastries. "What is she doing here?"

"They are the kids of…the ones who went missing." Catriona's eyes signaled to her brother, who immediately got the message. "She is using the restroom."

"Ah. That would explain as such." He yanked down his blue polo shirt to cover his belt and grabbed a tissue from a nearby box at the end of the counter. "Hamish was at the grocery store today." Jeffrey blew his nose like a trumpet blast.

"Really? Is that why you were late getting back?"

"No." His voice shifted to being filled with anger. "I happened to chance upon an opuntia humifusa on the way back and stopped to admire it for a time." Jeffrey disposed of the tissue in the short black garbage can to his left, not noticing Monica's smirk behind his back. "He told me something disturbingly awful, Cat."

"The plant talked to you?"

"Hamish did, Sis. You know that plants do not talk. What a silly notion." Jeffrey was fuming at Catriona's sarcasm. "That the farm off Dairy Road is going to be sold to a developer who has plans to create four hundred townhomes. FOUR HUNDRED!" His worn fingers rubbed the temples on his head as his eyes closed from the strain of reality. "I could not believe it. I just could not BELIEVE it. That farm is as old as us and it has a large patch of box huckleberry living in the back field. A patch going on 1200 years old come next year." He had to stop himself from continuing onward as his sister stomped her foot on the linoleum flooring.

"They make me so mad. Then we will just have to fight against it."

"But they already sold the land."

"I am pretty certain that area is still marked for rural. Has it been zoned residential yet?" She studied her brother's face as he thought to himself, eyes remaining closed, and his hand scratching his chin.

"No. Not that I recall."

"Then, it is settled. Tuesday night is the next board meeting and we will be in attendance to make sure nothing happens until the zoning is discussed, and then we will work on making sure that it doesn't get changed." Catriona gazed up at the wooden analog clock on the wall behind Monica, flanked by two pictures of their beloved gnome. "Now, you better get down into the cellar for your three o'clock drink." She took an iron key ring from a hook under the kitchen counter, expertly tossing it to her brother. "You know how long it takes for you to get ready." Dare looked at the clock to find that it was only 2:10 pm and shook his head.

"But I mustn't go without my corkscrew." Jeffrey surveyed the array of options littering the display rack and studied them with a collector's eye. "I shall be drinking a French wine this fine afternoon, so I must take a French corkscrew to complete the experience." He pointed at the young boy. "You there!"

"Dare."

"Dare. Fetch me a French corkscrew."

"Which one is that?" Dare's nervous eyes scanned the wall three times, feeling overwhelmed by the endless possibilities. He made sure to stay away from the one he noticed earlier, and asked Mr. Locksmith about an iridescent-painted alligator handle marked as number 234. "Will this one do?"

"Nah. That was made in Germany. See the stamp near the footed lever and the clover logo on the other side? Give me…the one to the right of your hand. It is the wine bottle made from bone and steel." Jeffrey thanked the boy after Dare pried it off of the wall and handed it to him.

"Were you prepping for a tornado? That was really stuck

on that rack."

"Can't be too careful, Sonny. Have to make sure that all the tools are neatly organized and are not to be lost. The one you handed me is over a century old." Jeffrey leaned down to meet Dare on the boy's level. "A scientist is always exact and careful in his measurements and details. Without such a method of collecting and experimenting, no botanist would be worth a seedling."

"Yes, Sir." Dare stepped back from the strange man, not caring for anyone he did not personally know to be so close to his face.

"You are all set now, Jeffrey. So have a lovely chat with Robert and I will see you later."

"My scone?" Catriona's brother patiently waited for his sister to deliver a hot scone into his free hand before making a beeline for the living room, calling over his shoulder as he left the kitchen. "I bet you that these children have not heard of Mr. Fortune."

"And I bet that you are right. Now, have a wonderful time and I will talk to you again at dinner." Catriona hurried him on his way to the wine cellar, returning in haste as the kettle whistled for her.

"Is there someone actually in the cellar?" Monica was horrified. "You are keeping a real person locked down there?!"

"Of course not. At the same time every day, my brother fancies himself a drink of wine and a friendly chat with a portrait of Robert Fortune that hangs on the wall. He was my brother's mentor in plant hunting, and Jeffrey likes to tell him about his daily excursions, like they used to talk in the olden days." Catriona's eyes suddenly squinted at Monica's arm. A tinge of red on her skin slowly faded from view, but not before the woman realized what it meant. "I wonder what could be keeping Vectra so long in the bathroom? I hope that the toilet has not stuffed up again." Dare and Monica noticed the undertone of curiosity in their hostess's voice. "I shan't be long."

Monica looked frantically over at her brother. Vectra had not shown up yet and they weren't sure what to do. Time had run out and it would be up to them to keep the ruse going. "But, what about the tea?"

"It can hold a moment longer." Catriona sped walked down a windy hall ending at a double-door entrance crafted from mahogany. Before the kids could prevent her from throwing the doors wide open, Catriona did exactly that and found Vectra in mid-steal. Her head shook disappointedly. "Really, my dear, I thought you would be better than that."

"That makes two of us." Vectra rolled her leather stealing kit back up and buckled the straps to keep it from reopening. "Either I am sadly out of practice or you elevated your security measures. By my calculations, both would be correct." Her curly brown hair spread wildly across the back of her neck as she placed her hands on her hips. "Well, what now? I heard your brother came home."

"What do you mean?" Catriona moved through the immense room lined with floor to ceiling bookshelves that gave Jeffrey's study a classic and timeless feel. She placed a bony hand on her old friend's shoulder, both of them now standing beside the large, oak desk. "I have an inkling that since you did not simply ask me for the plant you are undoubtedly looking for, that it would be one of my brother's more…uniquely acquired specimens?"

"Silphium, to be precise." Vectra appeared to shrink in size in the midst of Catriona's confrontation, much to the surprise of Monica and Dare. The way the Guardian held her confidence gave Monica the impression that nothing would cause her to display her shame. And here, she had been proven wrong.

"You just had to get that troublesome leprechaun onto that ancient herb, didn't you?" Catriona scolded.

"I did not give it willingly. The little bas…" Vectra stopped herself as she glanced over at Monica and Dare. "Fiend. He was the one who stole it from me. It was all I had that year, the rascal, and he has been hooked on its flavor ever since."

"Quit your mumblings, they will do you no good in this house." Catriona's face grew a mischievous smile as an idea came to her. "Come with me." She motioned for them to join her in the kitchen where she continued to finish prepping the tea. Allowing the water to be steeped properly, Catriona placed a little frog tea pet on the tray she organized and began teaching the Brownings the basics, paying Vectra no mind. "It is tradition not to drink the first cup that is poured from the teapot. You will come to find that its taste is weaker than the second and its coloring not as rich."

"I see you have changed your tea pet." Vectra observed the small clay frog grinning at her from his crocheted lily pad. "Did your cat run away?"

"I see things have not changed much." Catriona's eyes stared into the Guardian's with an unspoken message. "Frances has been retired. So Miles has taken up the role." She poured the tea from the pot's spout into one cup, as they watched the tinted water steam from the porcelain in curly-cue wisps. Gently picking the cup up, the older woman poured its contents over the frog in silence, before proceeding to fill the rest of their cups.

"What is in this?" Monica's index finger pointed at the transparent yellow-green liquid.

"It is tea, my dear. Give it a sip and try it." Catriona watched in anticipation at the faces of the two kids seated beside one another. As soon as the sweet liquid reached their tongues, their expressions displayed how wonderful the flavors melted together for them. "I thought you would like it. Most do. It is the best seller at my stand whenever I am at market."

Vectra cradled the teacup in her palms, swirling the tea around and not tasting a sip. She was more partial to rooibos lately. "Are you going to tell your brother?"

"No." Catriona continued to stare into the bottom of her cup. "In fact, I'd rather you take the specimen with you when you leave."

"What?" Shock was written all over Vectra's wide-eyed face.

"Well, I say you can have it. Jeffrey would not be so kind on the other hand. Ever since he turned two hundred years old, and retired, I have been going simply mad in this trap with him." She dealt each of them a scone from the pan on the counter after drizzling a thin line of glaze on top. "I mean, he is my brother, so I love him beyond reason, but he is driving me over the edge with his insistence on neat and orderly things. Organization is his style, but it is certainly not my forte. It will give him a new adventure, as he will see to it to replace the lost plant." Her voice lowered. "Give me a little 'me' time again amongst my teapots."

"Excuse me, did you say two hundred years old?" Dare picked apart his scone with his fingers. "As in two centuries?"

"Yes, my child. You heard me right." Ms. Locksmith pumped up the loose curls on her head. "I, as a matter of fact, just turned 150 last July."

"I thought you said 145 on Saturday?" Monica repacked

her journal.

"And you tell me that nothing has changed?" Vectra devoured the scone in a minute flat. "This is fabulous by the way." Catriona lifted her chin slightly into the air from the praise. "But seriously? Why would you think that anyone would believe that you are younger than Jeffrey for starters, and you seem to have a new answer each time someone asks you your age."

"Well, perhaps I am just a tad older than the impression I first gave off." Catriona shifted in the 19th century chair imported from England whilst sipping on her tea. A quiet hush fell upon the table, allowing them to enjoy their tea in peace until Vectra noticed the time on the wall clock.

"Does Jeffrey still have his daily chat with Robert Fortune?"

"Oh my yes."

"It is a little bit odd." Dare picked himself up from his chair to grab himself a second helping of the delectable pastries.

"We are all peculiar to one person or another. So why worry about what other people think?" Catriona gave Miles a few pats on the head just as the pocket watch in Vectra's vest pocket vibrated.

"Time to be going. We have to keep moving if we are to find your brother." She instantly raised herself up from the table, leaving her tea untouched. "Where is my kettle?"

"Over in the living room. Between the Cadogan teapot and the wine ewer from Nepal." Catriona looked at the kids. "Fascinating pieces those two are. Both were created to have tea poured into the bottom of the pot, rather than from the top as a regular teapot would. So there is no lid, just one solid pot with a spout. Makes it easier with my clumsiness." She smiled. "Now, please be careful with my cups when you go to wash and dry them by the sink."

Monica and Dare went about cleaning up from their tea as the older woman trailed into the eclectic living room after Vectra. She watched her longtime friend gracefully pluck out the cast iron relic from the topmost shelf above the fireplace. Its blackened exterior was no worse for wear, having looked the same since the day it had been entrusted to Catriona many moons ago. It was unusual, in the sense that it contained two handles; the largest one looped far above the lid-covered opening, twisted by hand in the same devotion and care that each dot had been individually placed on its sides. The smallest loop resembled a modern day teapot style and contained two whistle-like holes on the top of the handle. "When has that wretched pot ever been used for something good? Except for Alexander the Great's mysterious demise, that is."

"You think me fooled? Your memory is far sharper than that, Catriona. It was with a tea bowl back then, and I have not steeped ambrosia for quite a few centuries now." A smirk appeared on Vectra's lips before disappearing into a tight line once again. It felt good to rub her fingers over the Arare design, and to have the surge of its history through her veins as the past crashed upon her.

"I know well enough when teapots came about, Vectra Tillerman. But I also have not forgotten what those shards of worthless clay used to be, before being transformed into those dangling charms, attached to that handle."

"Here." Vectra reached for the rusty shears hanging just below the right side of the mantel shelf. Used for snipping the Locksmiths' firewood bundles free of their twine wrappings, the blades easily sliced through the woven threads tied to the clay pieces. "Is this what you wanted?" She held the cut strings in her fist, offering them up to Catriona before madly chucking them into the fireplace.

"Why do you purposefully do this to yourself?" The older woman asked as she gestured toward the kettle.

"We have been over this already, Catriona. I erased Bregit's memory for a reason. It protected him from anyone searching for that horrid device. If you wish to talk of objects not doing anyone any good, that press would be on the top of my list." Vectra stood steadfast in front of the brick fireplace situated in the middle of the room's innermost wall. Her fingers continued to stroke the teapot fondly in the awkward silence that followed.

"Vectra," Catriona stared into the empty and dirty firebox, whose ashes from the previous night had filled under the grate. "I do not know the full scope of what is going on here, but I worry for you. Thus far, I have not asked any questions into…"

"Then let us keep it that way and we will be off. No questions asked," her eyes hardened on her old friend, "nor NEEDED."

"I just do not wish to see you dig yourself into a deeper hole then you are already in, my friend. Artenian stuck her neck out for you before, but…"

"She is the reason I am in this to begin with, so it only seemed fitting for her to have 'stuck her neck out for me,' as you say. Besides, I can't go down much farther, now can I?" Vectra's face cracked a small smile of sadness, changing her temper in the blink of an eye; though Catriona was not as easily convinced with the poor attempt at humor.

"You and I both know exactly how far down this path leads you, and what awaits you there; should you ever reach it. Now, I am telling you as one of your closest friends, that you have to succeed this time around. For I fear this will be the last meeting we shall ever have together." She paused, keeping back a pang of sorrow threatening to show on her face. "You know I will not be able to visit you there."

"Nor would I ever want you too." Vectra dropped the teapot into her satchel and gave the older woman a European kiss on the cheek. "Thanks for the tea. It was great, like always." She headed back toward the kitchen to check in on the Brownings just as Catriona stopped her in her tracks, right at the threshold, with another question.

"Where does Gregon fit into all of this?"

Vectra's lips barely moved, though her mounting irritation drenched her words. "He doesn't."

"He pledged his life to defending you at all costs. Perhaps he could be of service in this instance." Catriona pleaded, taking a step back at the anger now flaming up in Vectra's eyes at her.

"I will not ask him, and neither will you. THAT is an order!"

Chapter Twenty-Five

A knock at the door made everyone jump inside the Locksmith's house. Catriona tip-toed her way up to the front and peeked through the peephole Gears recently installed the previous summer. The tinted glass revealed a poor beggar, hunched over a cane with his shaky build. She pressed a small button to the right of the hole, and an x-ray image alerted her to the present danger of another Olde Realm figure: Taminus. "Go away."

"But ma'am. I only humbly ask of a small donation for a poor soul left behind by this cruel world." A deep voice responded. The old man continued to shield his eyes from the door through the use of a top hat and pulled his wrinkled collar up to his stubbled chin.

"I am not feeling charitable today, so move along." Catriona touched a knot in the door and a bronze-colored panel slid open. "I said GO!"

"Please…don't deny me a single penny." His voice drew out a long foreboding sigh. "You would not wish to push me away without a single coin for comfort surely. From one old person to another?"

"I said 'beat it,' Taminus! Or I will unleash our security defenses against you; and boy, have I been aching to try them out." Catriona poised her index finger over a red button marked with an 'x' on top.

Vectra grabbed onto Monica and Dare, pushing them toward the long hallway leading into the study. "Hurry. Catriona can take care of herself, but we have to evacuate. It is safer for everyone that way."

"But I didn't get a chance to grab the duffel bag." Dare warned.

"Leave it. We are out of time." She took them back into the same room she had been caught sneaking into earlier and went straight for the third shelf from the bottom, on the bookcase behind Jeffrey's desk. Pulling out a book on plants in the Yucatan Peninsula, a short click was heard as a series of gears and cranks moved into position to pop open the escape doorway. They dashed inside before it automatically closed and looked at the spiral staircase taking them below ground level.

"Shouldn't we have put the book back?" Monica held on tight to her backpack straps, thankful to still have her bag along.

"No need to. See that stack of books there…like balls in a pinball machine?" Vectra gestured to the thirty-eight novels neatly arranged behind a Plexiglas wall as a mechanical arm reached for the top book. A suction cup adhered itself to the front cover and picked the book up to fill the gap on the library shelf. "The door is designed to replace the book each time it is opened. That way it disguises where we went while still keeping us safe. All you do is pick the right location, instead of the same title."

"They should put that into a movie." Dare noted, whilst racing down the stairs to keep up with the other two. They soon reached the bottom step and found themselves entering a brick-enclosed tunnel that ended at the greenhouse. Lights came on automatically, due to sensors, and illuminated the well maintained passageway any janitor would have been proud to claim their own.

"Lucky for us that Jeffrey had this put in to keep himself from getting wet." Vectra continued up the slight incline taking them up to a fortified metal door. A simple turn of the knob flew the mechanism open and she ushered them into the warm tropics.

"This feels great in here." Dare glanced over all of the plants growing at their own pace, in a very haphazardly arranged garden. Some flowers were blooming in bold colors as others were beginning to bud and the rest were past their season. Greenery in all tints, tones and shades decorated the greenhouse in a beautiful array that was both pleasing to the eye and carefully designed. "I thought he said that he keeps his stuff tidy?"

"Don't be fooled by the random appearance. Each plant is tagged and identified with their scientific name, year first discovered and by whom, the place of origin, the year Jeffrey found his specimen, and their watering schedule. To him, it's organized, and he keeps it like this as a failsafe for any burglary attempts."

"He must have some pretty rare plants hidden in this mess to have gone to all these lengths of security." Monica saw a tag dangling from the plant beside her. She read over the handwritten information for the Bottlebrush, native to Australia, and noticed the year dated on the tag as to when Jeffrey obtained the sample. "This plant is nearly 150 years old!"

"That is one of Jeffrey's first plants. He was into them as a young child, and his father purchased that one for him to begin his collection. But unlike that plant, which was fairly easy to obtain after being brought to England in the 18th century, the flower we are looking for is far, far older. And much more rare."

Suddenly, a red light whirled to life inside the greenhouse and drowned the area in a tinted hue of imminent danger. A buzzer sound filled the air, alerting them to the intruder and matched the loudness of their panicked heartbeats. "Taminus broke through the barriers." Vectra quickened her pace. "We must find the plant before he reaches us. Derek, take the furthest lane. Monica, you take the middle. We cannot leave here without that plant."

"It would help if I knew what I was looking for!" Derek tried calling out above the overbearing sound. He threw his hands up in defeat as Vectra was already out of hearing range and started flipping tags over when the red light flashed back to white. "Is that good or bad?"

Monica rushed down the middle lane, whipping her head back and forth in a rapid search for a flower she knew nothing about. *This is hopeless! How are we supposed to find the flower that...* Her eyes stopped at the sight of yellow blooms resembling dandelions, branching off a thick central stem with leaves akin to celery. "VECTRA! I found it."

"Great!" Vectra looked for Monica and joined her in a matter of seconds. She used a pair of razor sharp scissors to cut a chunk of the plant off and shoved it into a leather pouch she had in her satchel.

"He's coming!" Dare pointed to Taminus, no longer in his beggar's disguise, strolling across the Locksmith's backyard.

"We need to go. Head to the back of the greenhouse, but do not open the door. Keep your feet on the doormat and I will be with you momentarily." Vectra handed her bag to the boy for safe keeping.

"Alright." Monica led her brother across the vast greenhouse as massive boulders fell from the sky to smash the structure into particles of dust. Shards of glass fell all around the Brownings as they made a mad dash to get to the door, and dirt began flying in the air like confetti as plant specimens were crushed under the weight of the heavy rocks. The buzzer's loud sound returned, prompting metal bars to shoot up from the ground on all sides of the greenhouse to secure what was left intact from the bombardment.

Vectra elbowed the lower corner of a large, central panel of the glass wall, creating an opening she could use to target Taminus directly. She whipped out an eight of hearts, cupped it in the palm of her hand and blew on the card. Smoke rolled down the exterior wall, seeped onto the ground and coated the land in a thick layer that only grew in size and strength. Before long, Taminus was enveloped in the stifling fog, along with two figures standing in the shadows of the house. Their voices shouted into the congested air as she quickly joined the kids on the mat just as rain started to pelt upon them from Taminus's attempt to clear the dramatic smokescreen.

Jumping onto the natural fiber mat, Vectra issued a final warning to the siblings. "Make sure your feet are firmly planted on the doormat. Your entire body please." Monica and Dare looked down to ensure that they were squarely standing over top the chestnut brown mat. Underneath their shoes, Monica was able to read 'Give me tea, or give me death' printed in black. She exchanged a worried look with her brother. "Here we go. Hold onto me now." Vectra produced a drachma from her pants pocket whilst Dare latched onto her left leg and his sister grabbed onto the Guardian's arm. They watched her feed the old coin into a vertical slot in the padlock near the door's handle. A brightly lit button popped open above the slot in the shape of a pentagon, complete with a skull and crossbones outlined in white.

"No need to fret. Nothing poisonous or deadly. Just a bit of decoration." Vectra pressed in the button, closed her eyes, and listened for the tell-tale release sound of the trap door. Anxiously, Monica and Dare waited for whatever was supposed to happen next. They squeezed their eyes shut as well, and shifted their bodies to ensure they were indeed all on the mat. When nothing happened, the group shared a mutual feeling of confusion.

Vectra cautiously reopened her left eye, and then her right. "I thought Gears…" CLINK! The noise of a turning gear lurched below the ground, followed by the sound of grinding and metal scraping against one another. "There we go." She smiled as the mat began to descend below the dirt floor like an underground elevator.

Monica could feel her heart pounding with a sense of increasing fear. She gazed upward at the clouded sky as the hole closed up, and the terrors of her past experience in the woods bubbled to the surface. Without realizing it, the teen's grip immediately tightened on Vectra's arm in a desperate look for security in the pitch black darkness of the subterranean shaft.

"Monica. Monica." Vectra waited for the warehouse grade light that served as the benchmark for passing a hundred feet. The elevator was briefly lit up, and she could see the horror flashing in the teen's face. "You are going to make it of out here alive. Do you hear me?" She could not see Monica's head moving up and down slowly, so Vectra repeated her question until the girl gave a mouse squeak of a verbal reply.

Ten seconds later, after they dropped past another light

marked for two hundred feet, their underground elevator gently landed to reveal an illuminated tunnel with no end in sight. Torches were stationed at intervals of fifteen feet on both sides, sporting green flames that billowed no smoke and gave off an eerie glow. "Greek fire. It burns eternal and is the hottest fire you will ever see. Do not go near its flames. There is ancient power held within its alluring flickers and unless respected, it will devour you without hesitation." Vectra took the lead down the tunnel. "We need to press onward to find Aidan. That means taking the Gopher Express to keep us on schedule."

Monica and Dare walked in single file behind the Guardian, too scared to say much or argue with any decision. "Do you think that Catriona and her brother are alright?" The teen's voice half-frightened herself as it strangely echoed off the soil packed walls.

"I hope so." Vectra hid her uncertain look from the two kids. The Locksmiths were a tough sister-brother combo, but not invincible. No one was invincible. And after they stopped taking their anti-aging remedies, they were not as nimble and prepared as they could have been. *Then again, they did not know there was a need to be prepared for. Although, they did have Gears update their security measures, so maybe trouble had been lurking after them as of late?*

Dare curiously watched the walls of the tunnel and the small movements he caught in the light every so often. He stared at the little worms crawling in all directions and the blackened bugs scurrying around in all varieties and sorts. "I don't believe the exterminator has been here in some time."

Suddenly, Monica stopped cold in her tracks, her face frozen in disgust, as she felt something fall on her head and move about wildly. "Ewww! Ewww! Just, ewww!" She hastily brushed her fingers through her hair, trying to get the non-insect out of her locks.

"What's the matter?" Vectra spun on her heels. She glared at the teen doing a crazy sort of dance whilst removing the scared little worm.

"A worm landed in my hair!"

"Be happy it wasn't a cockroach or a bedbug." An amused grin spread on Vectra's face, much to the displeasure of Monica. "Come on. We have another half of a mile until we reach the Express."

Chapter Twenty-Six

"Are we there soon?" Dare could have sworn that half a mile had expired three hundred feet ago. "My feet are sore and I need some nourishment."

"You just had a few of Catriona's scones." Monica rolled her eyes. Her brother was the classic growing boy who seemed to be hungry every waking minute of his life.

"So?"

"We are almost there. See the sign up ahead?" Vectra pointed to a flashing neon board in the distance. "That is where we get on." Her boots began to click on the tunnel's floor as they reached the cobblestone paving that widened out into a miniature train platform. "Oh, Monica, I wanted to ask you one thing. How were you able to spot the Silphium in the greenhouse?"

Monica placed her focus on the ground as they walked through a turnstile that had seen better days.

"Yeah, sis. How did you pick it out?"

"Saw it somewhere, I guess." She nervously fiddled with the nail on her index finger, passively glancing down to see the tracks. "Lucky catch."

"Uh-huh." Vectra was unconvinced, but decided to drop

the matter for the time being. "Back away from the edge. The express likes to run at a fast pace." She stepped up to a short, rectangular box atop a long post. A lever, rusty from the moist conditions of residing underground, sat at the ready to be pulled once another slot was filled. One more drachma made its way from Vectra's pockets as she plunked it through the narrow hole. Leaning forward to listen for the whirling sound of the incoming transportation, Vectra hastily brought her head back. "Ah, here we are."

Dare nearly jumped up and down at sheer delight when he saw a long roller coaster train speeding their way. "You mean, I get to ride in this? I'm not too short or anything?"

"No, Dare. You are just the right height." Vectra instructed them to climb into the seats, pull the safety bar down over their legs and to press the green button whenever they were ready. Monica stashed her bag between her legs, keeping it tightly contained in case of any inversions as her brother handed the satchel back to its owner.

"Are we all set?" Vectra waited for both kids to nod in agreement before pressing her green button last. The ride automatically lowered the rest of the safety bars, and an engine roared to life behind the gopher head decorating the front car. "Hold on!"

"Where to?" An enchanting voice played over a speaker in the cars.

"Clover Land." Vectra picked her sunglasses from atop her head and slid them into a secured pocket.

"Very well." The voice replied. "Next stop, Clover Land."

The wheels began spinning under the coaster, without it moving at all, until it suddenly launched itself like a pinball machine. Dare yelled at the top of his lungs in joy, keeping his hands up in the air as they whipped around wicked corners at 124 miles an hour. His teeth felt the wind rushing into his wide open mouth, while his sister managed to find some enjoyment in the thrill ride as well. Torches illuminated the tracks at even spaces, highlighting the dirt compacted walls and the spiders which called it home. Monica tried not to look at the multitude of insects as they passed by, keeping her focus on the tracks in front and not losing her backpack while the coaster continued to speed up.

In what felt more like fifteen minutes, the Gopher Express had covered 150 miles underneath the great state of Pennsylvania. The enchanting voice announced the arrival of their destination at the same moment that sunlight could be spotted in the far off distance. Brake squeals split the air as the coaster prepared to surface onto the abandoned tracks of a roller coaster from the 90s. Monica and Dare held on as best they could to the safety bar, keeping them in their seats just as the express hit a hard bump in transition. Once above ground, a rundown platform came into view, marking the end of their ride and the beginning of their next segment of the journey.

Both Brownings were ejected from their seats as the safety bar automatically lifted up. The spring loaded cushions pushed them onto the exit platform to their right, and barely waited for their feet to touch the wood before it charged its way back into the tunnel. Their eyes blinked as the ground swallowed up after the coaster disappeared, sealing up the hole as though nothing ever happened. Only the remaining dirt swirling in the breeze was any evidence of their bizarre trip.

Vectra strolled up to the kids, expertly dusting the soil off her clothes as they coughed their lungs out from the pollution. "I must say that was the fastest it ever made me disembark. Someone else must have called for it."

"Where are we?" Dare managed to ask between coughs.

His hair was wildly spiked in all directions and he sported the wind-blown look very well.

"The place where Irish creatures are banished when they have done crimes against their country."

"A jail for convicts?" Monica tried suppressing another wave of fear. "Great."

"They have the freedom to move about on their own accord, no daily schedule or anything." Vectra explained as they walked down the long ramp leading to the over-grown ground. With the cloud of dirt no longer in their faces, Monica and Dare looked around at the deteriorating remains of an abandoned amusement park.

Buildings, large and small, sat devoid of life with sagging overhangs and side murals faded beyond recognition. An old concession stand still held ten year old prices listed on plastic slot signs above a weather-beaten counter. It was one of the more astonishing sights the kids had seen during the whole adventure. "$2.00 for a cheeseburger? $1.50 for fries? $0.50 for a can of soda?" Monica elbowed her brother. "You would have been able to eat like a king on your allowance back then."

Large, green, open patches of ground laid dotted amongst the forgotten landscaping where diseased trees had been cleared many moons ago. "Most of the rides are here yet." Monica stared at the decaying metal rotting away from decades of neglect and northern weather. She suddenly felt very alone in the empty vastness of the wooded cemetery of fun.

"Yes. When an amusement park closes its doors for the final time, they tend to auction off the rides to other parks so they can be rehomed. This park, however, was not able to do that due to the poor conditions the rides were already in. Maintenance was severely lacking, and the park closed for financial reasons. It's been rusting away ever since." Vectra walked briskly by the arcade building, whose crooked doors creaked on busted hinges in the wind.

"So where do we find Aidan?"

"In the funhouse, of course. He likes jokes and making faces at the wavy mirrors."

"This certainly is a strange place." Dare kicked an old soda can toward a trashcan sitting next to a park bench. "And an even weirder place to keep exiled creatures."

"Not at all. The park's original owners immigrated to the United States from Ireland in 1879, hence the name Clover Land, and started the park in 1893 to be a center of amusement for the surrounding area. For over a century, this place was popular with locals and tourists alike, until attendance began dropping and a flood nailed the coffin on the park. So when there became a need to send the traitors somewhere, this place came up as a possible location." Vectra abruptly stopped and turned to face the kids with a dead serious look. "Do not step foot in the Tunnel of Love."

"Why would I?" Dare made a disgusted face, sticking out his tongue and pretended to barf.

"Alright, Mr. Laughs. But you will not be in such a joyous mood when you meet the banshees."

"Anyone else reside here? Except for the banshees and Aidan." The place's entire atmosphere was creeping up Monica's spine and causing shivers to race in the opposite direction. "Could they be watching us this very minute? Because I have a feeling…"

"Sure. They could be watching, and most likely are." Vectra stiffened her back when she realized the time of day and charged across an open plot of land in determination. "We have no time to worry about the others right now." She turned to see if the siblings were still behind her and stopped at the sight of the approaching thunderstorm looming on the horizon.

"What is it Vectra?" Dare almost ran into her by accident.

"We better set up camp. Aidan is impossible during the day and worse at night."

"It's 4:30 in the afternoon."

"It will be dark when that storm passes. By the height of those clouds, I would say that it is going to be a strong one coming through the area. Besides, my tent is in the duffle bag in Herbio. So we will need to find a small building to use for shelter this evening." A menacing sound coming from behind the bushes, to their left, set the group on high alert. Monica and Dare slowly stepped backward while Vectra flicked two playing cards from her fingers, poised at the ready. Nothing came out from the shadow of the branches, nor did it continue the low growl they all heard. Eerie silence fell upon them in the encroaching night as faint thunder boomed in the sky. "Move to the picnic area where the sunlight is the strongest. And hurry."

Chapter Twenty-Seven

"Looking at all of those wonderful foods is making me sooooo hungry!" Dare whined. For the last twenty minutes, he had been staring at the old menu consisting of every fair food imaginable: hot dogs, cotton candy, funnel cakes, onion rings, bacon cheeseburgers, slushies, milkshakes, and more.

"If you would stop looking at the list, then you might forget about how hungry you are." Monica leaned up against the counter with her head, her eyes wishing to close and fall asleep under the stars peeking around the clouds. The cold shivered her muscles without the coats they ended up leaving behind at the Locksmith's house. Despite using the blanket she had stowed away in her backpack, the teen shook uncontrollably and wondered how well her brother was managing beside her. Half of the dark blue fabric was wrapped around his body in an effort to conserve warmth as well. "I cannot believe that it is only eight o'clock." She checked Dare's phone again, wishing for it to be morning and not only the three hours they had been sitting in front of the concession stand. The talk she had out with him, about his phone usage, ended up being very light once

Vectra walked off to gather firewood. Instead of the ring dinger of a speech she was aching to tell him earlier in the day, her body was too exhausted to care now.

It had taken nearly thirty minutes to pick out what Vectra believed to be the best location for staying the night; due to its view of the park and the ability to jump inside if necessary. The back door was no longer attached on its hinges, so their escape would be unimpeded if an attack would occur at a moment's notice.

Those wonderful words of encouragement did not help to put any of Monica's worries to rest though. She had little knowledge in the way of Irish tales and was not planning on attending a crash course that evening. Still, it was better than trying to sleep out in the open where they were completely vulnerable and the wet grass would soak them to the bone. Better yet, that they had an escape route detailed in advance instead of being cornered in the woods at the edges of the park. Vines, hidden roots, and night prowlers would have made an escape rather difficult and Monica was glad to be safer than sorrier for a little extra false sense of security. "You better turn your phone off, Dare. It is just depressing me and you need to save the battery." It did make her feel better that her brother had lied to the ghost soldier in the ship when he said his battery was dead. Having two phones to call out was better than one, but there was no need to waste any of the phone's power at all.

"I will. Once I look into this park a little more." Her brother scrolled down an internet search of the park located near Rabortsville and Mechanicsburg. Various news articles, videos, and blog posts of people's childhood memories were listed on the screen. From what he could tell, the park was well beloved by the locals and brought tears to their eyes when it closed. "Look here, Monica." Dare showed her a picture of the Tunnel of Love painted up and shining in the sunlight of a bright Tuesday afternoon. "I guess that is what it looked like before the banshees took it over, huh?"

Simultaneously, the Brownings looked across the way in the darkness to where Vectra told them it was located. "Couldn't say, Dare. Nothing but black out there tonight."

"Here we go." Vectra strode up to the fire with more logs in her hands. "I hope you two have not been napping whilst I was gone. You cannot leave the flames unattended and our guard down."

"No. We haven't." *Though I wish I was*, Monica muttered in her head. She hugged herself even harder, trying to squeeze all the cold out from her being.

"Good."

The overhang at the concession stand still did a decent job at keeping the water off the kids below, however, the fire needed to have a clearing for the smoke to exit. Three holed canopies made up the rest of their overhead "shelter" and allowed half of the rain to hit right around them. Damp and cold, the boy's fingers were growing numb. "Dare, what are you doing on your phone?" Vectra peered down at his lit touchscreen while raindrops began splattering the ground for the second time that night. "Doing a bit of research on the park, are ye?"

"Thought I better do some homework on the place." Dare's face grew a smirk. "Speaking of homework, our online teacher will have a load for us to catch up on when we get home, eh, Monica?" He poked his sister in the side and mimicked Ms. Grateson's voice when she tried to give constructive criticism on a student's work over the video chat. "No, that is not the way we use the word 'astronomical.' It is meant to be used in reference to the sky above, as in astronomy and not as a description of how large a person's butt is." His voice raised an octave higher, tilted his head upward to appear more regal, and pretended to tap an invisible screen out of annoyance. "Class, are you paying attention? Verity, you turned your video off. You better not be sleeping over the keyboard again!"

Both Vectra and Monica found themselves laughing at the boy's mockery. His small nose held higher than his eyebrows was a sight to see in itself. "Is your teacher really that odd?" The Guardian tossed two branches onto the fire to keep it from dying too low.

"You think she is odd?" Dare replied. "I guess she is, if you view your world as being normal."

"Do you play that candy game that is so popular on the television?" Vectra rummaged in her satchel in the search for a bit of food she thought was stored in her reserve compartment.

"I used to until I hit level 849. It was getting too hard and I don't spend money in the games like others do. Don't have a credit card." He picked at his shirt, trying to remove a thorn from one of the bushes he walked into by accident on their way to the stand. The blue shirt was one of his favorites and he wouldn't have left for the moon without it. "I am surprised that you know about phone games and apps."

"I am not ignorant of your technology. I just have little use for it. We do things a little differently in the Olde Realm, but we are able to do the same tasks. For instance, you surf the web for answers to questions while we utilize the bronze circuit. It taps into your world's networking for certain requirements though, depending on what we are searching for. And we even have a social platform that is much like yours. We call it Greek To Meet You. Sirens are forbidden from the site however, so they fashioned their own."

"That is a terrible pun." Monica shook her head. "With

all the bronze your realm has, why wasn't it named 'the New Bronze Age?'"

"Oh, that had been debated upon. However, none of us were around for the first Bronze Age, so we thought best not to rehash ancient history." Vectra's eyes lit up when her fingers brushed against the last of her meat sticks. "I have found food!"

"Wait, I forgot that I have a bag of cookies in my backpack." Monica unzipped the bag and handed the cookies over to her brother.

"You don't want any?" Dare feigned a look of utter shock. "But they are chocolate chip! You LOVE chocolate chip cookies."

"Actually, the meat sticks grew on me a tad." The teen plucked one from Vectra's outstretched hand. "You can enjoy the junk food."

"Like yours is any healthier." Dare snickered, chomping down on the cookies without any hesitation.

"Must be an important object you have wrapped up in your bag." Vectra noted, motioning to the kraft paper item with the dip of her head "Family memento?"

"Sort of." Monica quickly re-closed the backpack, clearly uncomfortable with another's eyes prying into her business. "I am not exactly sure what it is."

"Interesting. Considering you decided to bring along an object you have no idea about."

"Well, people do weird things."

"No argument there." Vectra got up from her spot and held her hands past the deep overhangs. "Rain appears to be staying the night. I am going to collect a few more branches before they are all swept away by the water." Without another word, she disappeared in the darkness and blended into the shadows.

"Do you feel like we are sitting ducks?" Dare pulled his phone out again. "That reminds me, I need to keep my score up this week for my team."

"Dare," his sister sighed, "if Mom and Dad would have told you to keep a secret no matter what happened to them, you would keep it, right?"

"Yeah." The boy shrugged his shoulders. "I would certainly fulfill my promise. Why?"

"Nothing. No reason." The teen brought the pack closer to her chest, cradling it in her arms and resting her chin on the top of its handle. "What if it went against what you thought was right? Or that it…"

"Monica, I am just ten years old." Dare stared into his big sister's worried eyes. "Not a kung-fu master from another planet. Speaking out random pieces of wisdom is not my style."

"You're right. Sorry." She gave a small chuckle in an attempt to cover up her frazzled nerves. Monica could sense Vectra's suspicion, and the Guardian had good reason to be skeptical about her. Especially after she recognized the plant in the green house out of the thousands there were to choose from. In the pit of her stomach, an uneasiness rooted itself and started to take hold from within.

She had seen that flower before, in color and in great detail. It was not on some internet search, nor on any advertisement people casually strolled past on social media. The image had not been in an old farming magazine, nor in the archives of dusty books in the back corner of a library. Monica could not claim that it had been on a billboard, the side of a bus, or anything else for that matter either. Any of those options would have been easily explainable, and would have made her so much happier to have been true. Much worse, was the real truth behind how she knew what the flower looked like, and she was scared to see if her underlying theory was correct.

With Dare preoccupied on making another score record for his team on a word game, Monica used the chance to sneak a peek at the spine of the book hidden under the plain wrapping. Her hands pulled the object out and she laid it in the middle of her crisscrossed legs. She dreaded to see the top, hoping that with every ounce of her being she was wrong. Reluctantly, Monica ripped the wrapper just enough to see the three inches down from the top and felt her heart sink to a newly found low when she saw VT painted on the spine.

"Cell reception is getting really funky with the storms. I think another one is coming in." Dare put his phone on sleep mode and turned his head to look at his sister. Monica's chest pumped faster as she quickly shoved the book back into the bag upside down. "Have us in the number two position. Maybe our team will actually win some coins this time around."

"Maybe." Monica bore a nervous smile. She wasn't sure what to do. Here the book was, the item they had been after this entire time, in her backpack all along. One would think she'd be delighted to have found it, but it was quite the opposite. Her stomach rumbled from a lack of food and misery, and churned over from the stress of having to decide on what to do next. *Vectra is sure to be angry that I had the book this whole time, and undoubtedly won't trust me after this. She might not help us locate Trevor anymore if I show it to her. On the other hand, she is going to meet up with Aidan tomorrow and find out anyway. Maybe I should just confess to it. I really didn't know what all it truly was. That is the honest truth of it. But she is not going to believe that. I could explain why I have it and who gave it to me. That might clear it up.*

However, that was what bothered Monica even more than having it in her backpack in the first place. Her mother was the one who had given her the book right before she left to find the press. "If anything should happen to us, keep this book safe with you and don't leave it where others can find it. It will tell you all you need to know. Do not tell anyone of its existence. Including your brothers. Do you understand?" Monica's head became filled with her mother's words in her sweet voice that almost made her tear up from the nostalgic memory. The only page she had read over was the one bookmarked to the hand-drawn illustration of the flower Vectra was searching for. There were various sticky notes in her parents' scribblings of jotted down questions, ideas, and comments. She figured it was one of their antiquity books they liked to collect.

But when they went missing, Monica could not bear to see the book and wrapped it up in brown paper in an attempt to stop the visions of her parents. It angered her that they would leave her and Dare behind, with little guidance in the form of their estranged older brother. Then anger changed to worry and worry morphed to pure sadness. So many unanswered questions rolled around inside her mind for so long, that she had forgotten about the book for a while. It wasn't until Artenian visited her in the dream, that she picked up the wrapped package, remembering her mother's last message, and brought it along in the search for Trevor. *Vectra will see that I am not at fault here, right? But how did my parents get ahold of Vectra's journal to begin with? Surely they did not know about Gregon. Or did they? Wait...*Monica thought about what the Kurzian had said when they visited his enormous trunk. *The break in happened when he was drunk for his birthday, which Vectra* *stated as having been seventy years ago. My parents hadn't been the ones to take the book. They couldn't have. But that doesn't mean that Vectra won't be mad at my family for having this in our possession. She may call off the whole search for Trevor because of it. It is not as though she is the most trustworthy. Then am I…if I keep this secret?*

Monica sighed at the start of a headache beginning to take over. There was no cut-and-dry answer she could see. Rather, the waters appeared to become even muddier no matter which angle she used to look at the problem. *What am I going to do?*

A small wave of relief fell upon her shoulders that her parents could not have been the original thieves. However, they were still accessories to whoever stole it. *And then there is Catriona's odd saying about Vectra righting a wrong. If she feels that the journal being returned already rights whatever happened, then we are out of our only hope at locating our brother.* The weight of the burdened decision felt suffocating and Monica decided that it was perhaps a good idea to share it with Dare. While he was no older than ten, he was the closest friend she had in any realm and the decision would ultimately affect him as well. "Dare…"

"That should be enough for us this evening." Vectra materialized to their right with more branches from fallen trees. The wood hit the ground with a soft thud from being soaked by the thunderstorms, and cut Monica off from being able to talk to her brother.

"How are rain-soaked branches going to burn?" Dare realized the obvious answer when Vectra held up her hand. "Never mind." He shuffled his butt up against the back of the counter, leaned his head against the wooden side, and turned his feet in and out, back and forth, as the fire crackled into the night. "Is it lonely? Being the Guardian of Thirteen?"

"I have had acquaintances over the years, and there are far more in my realm than the few you have seen so far. Way more than you realize. But I keep mainly to myself these days."

"You are good at dodging answers to questions. Aren't you?"

"Comes with great practice." Vectra used a four of hearts in both hands, closed them over with her fingers, and blew through the hole near her thumb. When her fingers reopened, hand warmers pulsated like the fire. "Here. Use these to keep you warm tonight."

"What about you?" Dare asked.

Vectra blinked. "I already have some in my pockets." Even though the boy had taken her into account back at the shipwreck, his interest in her well-being this time hit her surprisingly hard. She had become so accustomed to living within the shadows of the modern world, that witnessing a young boy care for someone who was mostly a stranger to him, felt like an illuminating light of its own.

"Have you had any really good friends, besides Catriona?" Monica reflected on her own life and her lack of a large circle of friends. Being in home school, she didn't tend to have many friends and her parents moved a few times, so it was hard to be excited at starting up any new friendships. There was one girl she kept in touch with though, from her time spent in Maryland before moving back to Pennsylvania. It brought a smile to her face whenever she saw a text message from her, or a letter in the mailbox. Even if the other kids in her virtual class thought it strange that they still wrote "old fashioned letters."

"I used to. Not many though. One in particular betrayed me so much so that I nearly died."

"What happened?" Dare inquired as his sister bumped him in the arm. "What?"

"I took a bullet for her." Vectra stared into the flames, seeing the images of her past dance in the flickering light. "And she ended up being the one who pulled the trigger." As if to prove that she was not speaking metaphorically, Vectra peeled up her pant leg and showed them the scar over the area where her main artery had been struck. "We used to steal together. Best friends, non-blood sisters, the whole deal."

"What is it like? Being betrayed by someone so close to you?" Shame cast Monica's head low into her chest, staring at her fingers intently through the loops of her bag.

"Like a large boulder being strapped to your heart, and it plummeting into unfathomable depths. As though, you could reach deep into your chest to find nothing but an empty pit consumed by darkness. And you cannot curl into a ball tight enough to escape the tears of pain streaming down your cheeks." Vectra's eyes glazed over with memories she believed to have been lost to time itself. "It is soul wrenching." She absently grabbed onto the green stone necklace perched overtop of her jacket. Her hand covered the stone, cradling its handcrafted prison. "It is something I hope you never have to endure."

The orange blaze of the fire struck out boldly into the blackness of the night surrounding them while Monica's mind spun in an endless cycle. *Now what?* Catriona's words filled her thoughts. *Vectra's only duty is to protect the artifacts, regardless. That is what the tea lady said.*

"Are you okay?" Dare looked over at his big sister in concern, his brows pinched inward as he leaned over the gap between them.

Monica instantly forced another smile on her lips and

straightened her back. "Of course. Don't be so ridiculous." She tried brushing the troublesome feeling aside by telling herself it would all be over soon when they found the Leprechaun. *He is a deceptive creature. Is he not? I can just blame everything on his twisted lies if things should go sour. Why would Vectra believe him over me?*

Chapter Twenty-Eight

Morning swept in like the tide as the stars melted into sunshine saturating the landscape in utter beauty. What was once a scary and frightening nightmare of a park, morphed into a sad and desolate place. Monica blinked her eyes open, still weary and drained from a night of barely any sleep. Her exhausted body begged for rest throughout the night, but her mind refused to quiet down. Too much uncertainty weighed on her conscious with the inevitable reality of what was to happen in just a few hours.

"Good Morning." Vectra removed a twisted up spider web from her hair. "Ready to meet a leprechaun?"

"As ready as I'll ever be." Dare loudly declared, hands on hips and chest puffed out in a superhero pose. He was grateful for the hand warmer to still be activated in his pants pocket in the crisp chill of morning. *At least my leg is warm,* he told himself. "How about you, Sis?"

"Right behind ya." Monica spoke in the middle of yawning herself awake. "No time like the present."

"After we get my book back from Aidan, we will be able to stop to collect more food for the rest of the trip. Stay close to me as we walk across the green." Vectra quickly made her way over the empty park, determined to end her search for the journal, and to discover an answer she wanted to desperately find within its pages.

Monica fell instep behind her brother as they approached the old funhouse. The paintings on the outside were peeling off in chunks and she couldn't determine on whether the barred up windows were part of the original decor from the 70s or were an "after the park closed" addition. Smells of mildew wafted in from the threshold, crying out in need of being replaced. "Is it safe in there for us to enter?"

"We are not going into the ride. That part is most *definitely* unsafe. No, we are going into the side entrance through the ride." Vectra stepped passed the doorway, and through the western-style saloon doors still whipping around on hinges newer than the rest of the park. Monica pushed her brother in front of her, willingly taking the rear in case the worst should happen. *She did say that she preferred Dare over me*, Monica told herself.

The first stage of the funhouse consisted of a mirror maze with half of its fogged surfaces lying on the floor. Vectra stopped in front of the farthest one to the left and pressed in on the panel. It slid to one side, allowing them to enter into a cavern of sorts. "No 'open sesame?'" Dare's disappointment was felt in his words. "That's too easy, just pushing the panel open."

With a roll of her eyes, Monica walked into the war room of Ireland. Posters, maps, and CDs of popular bands strewn the shelves of the bookcases fashioned from disregarded parts of the park. Postcards dug out of trash bins from Ireland were pinned to the walls and woolen blankets ordered online were neatly arranged by color. Monica could not get the feeling of *Alice in Wonderland,* out of her mind.

If one of the characters was a sneaky leprechaun missing his home in an obsessive way, she would have guessed she walked into the book.

A refrigerator from the 50s lined one side of a larger cavern, complete with a full kitchen and toaster that likely would outlive Monica. Taped onto the above cupboards were old pictures of Celtic singers from bygone eras while strings of green Christmas lights added a nice homey touch to the otherwise dimly lit place. "Leave your shoes on the mat." An amused voice said.

Vectra glanced down to see a "Go Celts or Go Home to Ireland" saying painted over a clearanced St. Patrick's Day welcome mat. "I was wondering when you would arrive." The voice announced again. "Been ages since we've seen one another."

"Where is the voice coming from?" Dare searched the room with his eyes, only to find objects resting peacefully in their places and no leprechaun to be found. An empty arm-chair was positioned in front of a television with a rabbit antenna set up and a multitude of wires dripping down the wall to meet the back of the unit. At first, he thought he might have witnessed the movement of a large bug dashing up the cobblestone fireplace, but he rejected the idea when no other sound was present.

"Do as he says." Vectra urged. All three of them removed their shoes and waited for the next set of instructions from the disembodied host.

"So, it took you seventy years to grace my doorway. Either your treasures are fading into myth, forgotten by the people now roaming this Earth, or you…nope, that is my best guess. Because the other option would be that you have gotten better at your job, and that is not possible. Not in any realm."

"I am here to retrieve what is mine, Aidan. You want to make a trade?" Vectra had to muster every ounce of her being to keep her temper in check. Since being banished from his home in the early 1700s, he had been a thorn in her side and never took a rest from being obnoxious. His speech may have changed, along with his taste in music, but his antics were still the same.

"Trade in what? Only thing I'd consider trading for is that RARE item that no longer exists. You know that and I know that. Despite," the voice paused to chew on his lip, "some others having claimed that they discovered its return under that other name, *Ferula Drudeana*, no true Silphium remains."

"And yet, you seem to be in better spirits than I would expect. Is it because you think you have the upper hand on me?" Vectra walked up to the empty armchair rather cautiously. Her eyes peered around the room, watching the air very closely to find where the leprechaun was hiding out.

"Not at all. Quite simpler in point of fact, and much more pleasing." The voice teased, and then gave a cackling laugh that bordered on being almost sinister.

"Alright, you tricky little devil, show your face! I know you are in here."

"But that is half the fun."

"It won't be when I ignite this place with a flick of my hand."

"Okay, okay already." Dare's large bug whistled a tune he did not recognize and grew to being two feet tall, and just about that wide. "You are so testy."

"I do not relish wasting my time by being forced into playing one of your so-called games." Vectra reached into her satchel and showed him the Silphium she stole from the Locksmith's greenhouse. She waved the plant just outside

Aidan's arm length and shoved it back into her bag as his hands ached to grasp its leaves. "Think of all the wonderful tea you can make from it. Now, WHERE IS MY BOOK?!"

"I already gave it to someone else." His tiny beard waved as he walked along the edge of the beat-up coffee table in the middle of the cavern. "You are far too late, you see. Gave it away seven years ago."

"To who?!" Vectra's eyes blazed red hot. "To who, Aidan?!"

"A woman like you, but not the same of course. A woman from Harpeon. No name, as I recall. Only traded for the book and spoke very little."

"Artenian!" Vectra's words seethed in anger and were marked in vengeance. "That good for nothing…"

"Red hair she had. Yep." Aidan interjected. He touched the tips of his shoes whilst sitting atop the short table. "Locks of deep fire twisted in a single braid extending past her chest."

"Wait, red hair?"

"Yes, not brown, nor black, nor golden, nor paled, but red." In the blink of an eye, Aidan had moved over to the kitchen and was standing on the counter by the sink. His finger pressed on his bottom lip in thought, recalling the other woman as he stepped around an opened peanut butter jar without missing a beat. "That was she. I know it was. Yep, she asked me for it. Said she knew I was the one who stole it from the Kurzian. Offered me a bag of Silphium in exchange for the book. That was the good stuff." Aidan licked his lips in mouthwatering remembrance and slumped to the counter from weak knees. "That tea was amazing."

"And she was not Irish?"

Aidan suddenly stopped his childish manner and took

on a serious tone that scared the Brownings. "I would recognize me kin, and mention such a feature as in-mistakable as that. You have stated an insult I do not take kindly of."

Vectra made her apologies in Gaelic and continued on with her questions. "So this red-haired person, a female from Harpeon, has my book?"

The little leprechaun shrugged as he jumped up from the counter effortlessly. "Could not say. Could be anywhere, your book. I only know I gave it to her. After that, it is a mystery." His eyes picked up on Monica's backpack, and they lit up with fireworks of intrigue at its sight. "As mysterious as this bag…and what is inside it." He moved with quick speed, and before either of them knew it, Aidan was picking at the zipper and running in place out of sheer excitement.

"What could be inside this wondrous bag? Could be great treasure or nothing at all. I must have a look-see, must take a glimpse to find out."

Monica's fear billowed into anger. "Excuse me!" She twisted around to see him starting to pull the pack open. "Get off my bag!"

"No!" Aidan shouted back, tightening his grip on the zipper pull, and threateningly opened the main pocket a shade more. "I want to see."

"Get off of my bag!" Monica repeated, and went to remove the strap from her right shoulder in order to rip it from his hands. She ended up whipping the bag around with Aidan's added weight and the leprechaun used the wall to catch himself, punching upward at the bottom of the bag. He laughed in glee as the contents spilled onto the floor. The horror of being helpless to stop it was shown in Monica's eyes as the wrapped book leaped into the air. It landed on the ground with a dooming thud, along with her journal, a few pens, and a purple wallet.

Dare began to pick the items up when Monica frantically snatched the book from his hands, but it was already too late. Vectra narrowed in on her painted initials at the spine's top where the wrapper had been ripped off. Her eyes moved up from the worn binding to see Monica squinching down to the height of a worm. The look of ultimate shame could be seen on the teenager's face, making her cheeks blush and her bottom lip quiver, as the cavern was left in an awkward silence.

"HA!" Aidan jumped up and down, pointing at the book in jubilation. "See! See! I told you, did I not? I told you. The book could be anywhere, and in fact, the book was here!"

Monica wished for Vectra to say something…anything, other than being subjected to the wordless stare she found herself trapped within. Guilt weighed her down, shifting Monica's face to the floor while her brother finally realized what the book was and pleadingly looked up to her for an answer. "Sis?"

"Oooooh! You are going to be in trouble." Aidan mocked with pouting lips in a low voice. He enjoyed rubbing salt into the fresh wounds and delighted in seeing Vectra so hurt, since she was one of the ones who caught him.

"Shut up Aidan!" Vectra held her hand up, rubbing two playing cards together with her fingers at the jolly green joker.

"Tell me you had no idea what this book was." Dare begged. He wanted to believe that his sister had innocently packed it in her bag by mistake, unbeknownst to its real identity. Unfortunately, he recognized the expression as plain as daylight on her face. It was the same look that saved him from being grounded over a three day weekend after a picture frame was broken in the living room. The only picture they still had up of their parents, and one that all three of them cherished as a golden treasure, had laid strewn on the hall floor from a misaimed basketball they were tossing about the house. Trevor was ready to ream Dare out, having been caught holding the ball when he arrived home, but his sister confessed the truth and received the punishment instead. That face could only mean one thing, and he desperately wished for the reality to be different.

"I…I…" Monica's throat closed up. She felt a universal blockade keeping her from revealing anything more. Her lips froze at the sight of Vectra's pain-filled eyes glassed over in scorn and frustration at herself.

"It is quite obvious that she knew about the significance of this book, Dare. For she would not have wrapped it up and hid it from everyone's view if she hadn't. Including from you."

"Monica, tell me that this isn't true." Dare ripped the rest of the plain brown paper from the book and let it drop on the dirty old carpet in need of a deep clean. "Please." He latched onto his sister's arm and begged some more. "Please tell me that we did not waste THREE DAYS searching for the book you had in your backpack this entire time."

"Yes, Monica." Vectra's ice cold words chilled the air down at least twenty degrees. "Do enlighten us."

Chapter Twenty-Nine

"Well," Monica's mouth could not move fast enough once the wall of silence was broken. "I had no idea that it was your book, Vectra. Not until I tore off the wrapping just last night and saw your initials on the spine and…"

Suddenly, the earsplitting sound of rock scraping against itself interrupted her confession. The deafening vibrations of the grinding worried everyone inside, including Aidan, and they all ventured up to the funhouse entrance to find it closed over by an enormous boulder. "Taminus!" Vectra stomped her foot into the ground. "How did he know where to find us?"

"Having a laugh with the old funhouse elf?" Taminus's voice echoed through the chimney flue. "How is that jelly bean doing these days?"

"Was having a grand old time until a rockhead trapped me in my own house!" Aidan called back. "Not very inventive, are we Taminus? You merely imitate. Never the clever one. Never the original thinker."

A loud snort filtered down the flue. "If it were my way, I would drown you all in that disgraceful hobble of a home. However, I need you alive. So you are going to come quietly with us as soon as that boulder is removed from the entrance way. Got it?"

"And of course we are going to just fall right in with your demands." Vectra sassily replied. "Very good thinking, Taminus."

"DO NOT PUSH MY BUTTONS!" Water began to fall from the sooty flue, mixing into a dirty black liquid that was slowly rolling over the rocky surface of the floor. "YOU HAVE TO BE ALIVE, BUT IT WAS NOT SPECIFIED IN WHAT CONDITION."

"Listen to me." Vectra huddled Monica and Dare together, instructing them to put their shoes on while she talked. "Follow my lead. And do exactly as I say. Do you understand?" The kids nodded their heads in unison and watched Vectra make her way over to the entrance after retrieving her boots. "Keep the book safe in your bag." She whispered over her right shoulder.

Dare rushed to scoop it up right before the water hit it and zipped the book up in his sister's pack. Once it was safe, he nodded to the Guardian.

"NO NEED FOR THE DRAMATICS TAMINUS." Vectra called out. "WE WON'T GIVE YOU A FIGHT OVER THE DOOR. JUST LET US OUT."

Taminus's voice boomed overhead, ordering the men who were guarding the boulder to release them and the unbearable sound of scraping rock once again pierced the air. Two men flanked the entrance and waited for their prisoners to join them outside. Without a word, the small group obeyed their commands and were taken to the sunlit field where Monica and Dare had their first good look at the crew working for Taminus.

Monica's face nearly fell off when she noticed the same tattoo on the taller one's neck from when Trevor had been kidnapped. *These men must work for Gaither. That means... that Taminus is helping them.* Her mind was blown trying to decipher what this all meant as the man with the tattoo pushed her to go faster down the short ramp. "Easy. I'm going."

"Vectra…" Taminus clicked his tongue against his teeth. "The great Vectra Tillerman has finally been captured! I must say that it was rather easier than I first believed it would be." He gave her attire a study from the bottom up. "And in a new wardrobe as well, I see. Tell me, did you have it tailor-made or was it from the rack?"

"What I see is that you have stooped to a new low, even for you. Having hired help now, are we Taminus?" Vectra's head tipped in the direction of the two burly men in front and the additional three in the back. "I should have figured it out back at the Locksmiths' house, when there were multiple voices coughing in my smokescreen. But, then I thought to myself and said, 'no, Taminus works alone. He refuses help. I had to have been mistaken.'"

Taminus's top lip slightly wavered. "Not my idea. But, you know, the boss has orders."

"Boss?"

"Vectra, dear Vectra. Surely you have put the pieces together *by now*. You may be a sneaky little thief, and a traitor, but you are not THAT stupid." Taminus inched forward and pulled a short sword from each hip. "By the way, I found a new home for your blade. I tend to like how it makes things even and balanced around my waist."

"Do not get used to it. Because I will get it back." Vectra placed her hands behind her back, flinging four playing cards into her palm at the ready. She kept her eyes like stone as Taminus closely studied her lack of any expression and the guards at the back prepped their guns.

"My, my! You really did not have it all worked out, did you?"

"This conversation is boring me. So move out of my way!" Vectra slipped the cards atop one another and closed her fists. Instantly, a fiery sword grew out of each hand, and she expertly wielded them to the front. "Do I have to repeat myself?"

The guards aimed their weapons at the kids and Aidan, but backed down when Taminus held his hand up. "I would expect nothing less from you." He waved his hand over the grass and called all the recent rains up from the ground to surround them in watery walls, topping eleven feet in height. Vectra tried piercing the shifting liquid with her fiery blades, only for their heated blaze to be doused and reduced into ashes of smoking card remains. "Now, you will surrender to me."

"Never." Vectra dipped her head, closed her eyes, and then reopened them for Taminus to see burning balls of fire within her eyelids. Instead of producing any more cards from her hands, the guardian's body ignited into a walking pillar of living flame. With a simple gesture toward the walls, blazes extended outward and merged into the water. Smoke quickly transformed from the elemental clash and Vectra walked right through, returning to herself on the other side with Monica and Dare in tow. Her outfit reverted back to the steampunk style she was known for, with three playing cards in her hat's band and a smirk on her face.

The Brownings raced after her, leaving Aidan behind in their wake, and made a beeline to where the bumper cars were. In the daylight, the trio could see the old pieces of equipment more clearly and how they had been placed on top of kiddie cars in some mad mechanic's experiment. "Hurry." Vectra warned as Taminus and his crew were bearing down. "I can't stall them for long. Get to the main road and find the path leading away between two maple trees. Keep driving until you reach the short fern-like plants. Find the triple evergreen and look up to find safety." She veered off, and braced her stance to shield their exit, forging more cards together and ran straight at Taminus.

Once the kids reached the dilapidated ride, Monica's hopes dashed at the sight of the worn down vehicles. "How are we supposed to escape on these?" She took note of the foam barren steering wheels and the yellow metal now left exposed. Blue lightning streaks were peeling along the sides of the white-painted car bodies and the interior seats were half-eaten through by bugs and extreme weathering. "They probably ran on electric. In a ride."

"Look." Dare showed her where the missing gas tank cover used to be. "We just need to find some gas that still works."

His sister gazed skeptically inside the plastic opening. "This tank has been exposed to the rain for years."

A loud crash came from behind the kids, and they turned to watch Vectra get pushed backward by a wave of water, sliding her heels in the ground to create two long tracks carved out of the soil.

"Look for a filled gas can." Monica pointed to an area by a broken workbench to their left for her brother to search as she went to the right. Hastily, they dove through garbage piles, old cans, and under discarded equipment until Gaither's men appeared about fifty feet from the ride.

"Monica!" Dare jumped into the bumper car. "We need to go." He reached into his pockets for a last ditch effort at coming up with a miracle.

"How?" His sister hurried over to him. "We don't have any of Gear's inventions, nor Vectra's powers." She matched eyes with Dare for a split moment as he pulled out the match Vectra had given him on Saturday.

"No, but we do have this." Dare struck it along the side of the bumper car and threw the lit match into the empty gas tank. "Get in!" Monica leaped into the other side of the seat just in time for green sparks to ping-pong around inside the tank, generating the power needed for the machine to roar to life. The car picked up momentum and went zinging through the ride's ancient netting and posts, before Dare turned the wheel in the direction of the main road. "Hang on tight!"

"You don't know how to drive."

"And neither do you!" Dare called out at Monica, who was glancing backwards to see if Vectra was still keeping Taminus at bay. "How is the fight going?"

"Can't tell." She weaved her head around her brother's, trying to see the guardian in the midst of an elemental battle that dulled the best fireworks shows in comparison. Then her eyes widened at the sight pursuing them. "We have company!" Monica tapped on her brother's shoulder and he turned to see Gaither's men driving their own strange bumper cars right after them.

"How did they manage that one?"

Monica shrugged, watching the taller man have a hard hit on a pothole and a gallon of water spilled out of the back. "Hydro-power. Taminus probably gave them some help like Vectra did for us."

"Great!" Dare suddenly gave the wheel a sharp and violent twist, madly changing their direction away from exiting the abandoned amusement park.

"What are you doing? Vectra said to reach the main road and…"

"And we will be dead out there. No protection or coverage. I always end up losing on Road Racer 5 when I go for the path out in the open."

"This isn't a video game!" Monica bent down at the first sound of a gunshot being fired at them.

"I realize that. But…you have to trust me!" Dare drove straight toward the Tunnel of Love, his face more determined than his sister had ever seen. "Brace yourself." He pressed the small metal pedal to the ground and gripped onto the steering wheel so tight his knuckles were turning white. Monica held onto an old safety bar on the dash, scared to the bone as the dark tunnel loomed closer and closer.

SPLASH! The scum-coated water sprung upward as their car collided into the old river. Fortunately, the water's depth was a mere twelve inches, and Dare slowed the vehicle's speed to a crawl after the crash. "Dare," Monica whispered, "I don't care for this. Do you even know what a banshee is?" Darkness was all either one of them could see in the deserted ride, giving the teenager's spine a constant tingling. There was no controlling her fear now. Devoid of any light, drips from the ceiling sounded like footsteps and a wind coming around the corner whistled an eerie tune. Haunted was an understatement in Monica's opinion. It seemed that in any instant, ghosts and ghouls would rise from every nook and cranny, in search of their next unwitting victims.

"Where'd they go?" Called out the husky voice of the taller man from the two chasing them. "Gerald, you see them?" His vehicle hummed inside the tunnel, which grew louder as his partner arrived soon after.

"No. You Ozzie? I can't even see ya, Mate." Replied the shorter of the pair, with a British accent originating from the west country of England.

"All we have to do is find a banshee." Dare tried peering into the blackened sheet of the tunnel as the soft sound of sobbing echoed all around.

"There." Monica pointed in the direction of a pale light slowly materializing behind a section of the fabricated interior. "I see one. At least, I think I see one."

The ghostly figure, graceful in appearance, was draped in mourning garbs and sat with her knees to her chin. Tears gently ran down her nearly transparent cheeks and right through the rest of her body, ending on the rocks in a stream of sorrow. Reddened eyes, puffy from the constant state of crying, were bleakly fixated to a place beyond the ground as her hands combed through her long hair.

The boy steered their car in the direction of the glow. "Excuse, me. Miss?"

"Dare?" Monica stared into the ghostly face of an unaged woman of twenty-three. "You better know what you're doing."

"Miss? We could use a little help." Dare tried to position the vehicle closer to where she sat, but ended up slamming the car's body into a barrier of real rocks. She glanced at him with curious eyes, wondering who he was and why these strangers would be disrupting her sadness. "Oops." He placed his hand onto the cold boulders in an effort to find the outline of land. "There are other men in this tunnel after us, and they killed our parents. Could you help us lose them?"

The woman's eyes shifted upward, taking a look back the way they came, and then returned her gaze upon the two kids once again. Her staring made Monica feel extremely awkward as the lone bystander to the silent conversation passing between the banshee and her brother. As the voices of Gaither's men grew closer to their branch of the tunnel, the banshee nodded at Dare. She floated over the water and waited by the edge of a jutting beam for the men to make the turn. "You might want to cover your ears." Dare told his sister before cupping his hands over his own.

"I see a light up ahead." Ozzie shouted back to his partner, Gerald, just as the banshee sweetly stepped in front of their bumper cars. "What the…"

The ghostly figure opened her mouth and wailed so loud it made the entire structure begin to shake. Rocks and rusted metal fell down from the ceiling above, trapping Gaither's men under the weight of the heavy materials. Monica and Dare waited to remove their hands until the banshee looked at them, nodding that the deed was done.

"Wow." Monica gave her brother a proud smile. "Nice job, little bro."

"Thanks. When I was looking up about the park on my phone, I did a little research into banshees. Grief and the loss of family members is something they most relate to. Like a universal language in a sense."

"Ohh…" A voice flowed with the water's pace, coming from underneath its disturbed slumber. "Do I smell fresh blood lurking within this tunnel?" One by one, more banshees rose from the depths of the neglected river, piqued by the interesting action happening above the surface. "What is this?"

"Uh oh!" Monica rapidly patted her brother on the arm. "We might want to get the car started…right now!"

"But you have just arrived to our home. And we have been so lonely this past century." A higher pitched banshee chimed in, joining in with her sister ghostly figures. "Time for some tea, do you not agree Caoimhe?" The older woman teased another, who's cloak was grey with a green trim. "It would be pleasant to have some fresh, new additions to our small community here."

"Dare!" Monica frantically looked in either direction of the tunnel they were now trapped within. "Have a plan?"

"Working on it." The boy's scared face said it all in the glow of a banshee sitting on the hood of the running bumper car. "Um…" His eyes surveyed the area in search of any kind of a clue as to a way out of the mess he put them in. "Yay…"

"I see light!" His sister pulled her own match from her pants pocket and told him to make for the pinhole of daylight streaming in from the other end of the ride. "Punch it."

Dare hit the pedal to the metal, flinging the banshee off the hood and driving the vehicle straight at a collapsed opening. "Monica, it's a dead end!" He started to slow down, when his sister insisted that he keep increasing their speed.

"Keep going. Don't slow up for any reason."

"Okay." Dare's voice quivered.

"I hope this works." Monica struck her match off the side of the car body and held the green flame up. Counting to three, she inhaled as much air as her lungs could muster and blew the fire at the collapsed ride. A green spark sailed through the pinhole, rising into the sky, and ignited into a rescue signal for Vectra to see. The next thing both Brownings knew was an enormous mallet pounding the collapsed equipment to pieces. "Now!"

Dare braced for impact as the vehicle bolted up and off the rubble constructed ramp, flying in the air briefly before coming to land on the grass again. Their screams could be heard all along the nearby mountain range as their wheels regained traction on the ground. Without hesitation, Dare took a sharp turn toward the main road and joined the rest of afternoon traffic. Two cars passed them in the opposite direction across the median, drivers mesmerized by the strange automobile going down the road.

"Hi." Dare waved to the little kid in the back seat of the vehicle in front of them, her face plastered to the glass out of shock.

"Focus on the driving." Monica flashed the kid a toothy smile. "The sooner we get to the two maple trees, the better."

"Okay, okay. No argument there." Dare kept his eyes peeled for the side road forking off, like Vectra had mentioned. Monica was about to say something when a vibration from Dare's phone clicked an answer into place to a question they all had. She felt the ding through the pocket of his pants, against her side, and felt like an idiot.

"Derrick Browning! You didn't turn your phone off!"

"Oops, sorry. I must have put it into silent mode by mistake."

"Give me that phone right now!" Monica tried sticking her hand into his pocket, looking for the smooth surface of his smartphone.

"No! What are you going to do with it?! You are not going to throw it out of this bumper car are you?"

"You're darn right I am." She yanked it out and was about to toss it off the road as Dare grabbed onto the device in the nick of time, swerving the vehicle hard to the right.

"The battery is not THAT important when you still have yours."

"You don't understand. They tracked us by your phone's location."

"WHAT? That's impossible. My location tracker isn't on."

Monica shook her head. "Never mind. I'll turn it off and explain later. Keep your eyes on the road and for that path we need."

Within three minutes, the dirt lane came into view and

Dare moved the steering wheel to the right. All of a sudden, the wheel popped off in his hands, and the bumper car was driving itself down the dirt lane. Monica and her brother hugged one another, hoping for the best since the wheel did not want to go back on without a fight.

The car sped down the lane until traction began slowing its pace and progression with every foot it traveled. Eventually, the car glided into a tree trunk, which stopped it altogether, and the Brownings heaved a sigh of relief. "At least we made it to the fern-like plants." Dare gestured to the covered forest floor on his left. As he climbed out of the car, the boy felt his sister poking him in the side, and looked up to see her staring back the lane.

"You cannot escape. No matter what that silly and naive woman has told you." Taminus shouted at them from the entrance off the main road.

"Oh, come on!" Dare saw two of Gaither's crew on either side of the well-dressed man and pushed his legs to go faster into the woods. He followed Monica over entangled roots, leaf-covered rocks and moss-sided tree trunks as they raced to find the triple evergreen.

"Where is that tree?" Monica growled at herself in frustration. The further they ran down the path, the more unlikely it appeared for them to find the elusive marker before Taminus caught up to them.

Rocks began shifting from underneath their feet, being pulled back by Taminus's outstretched arms. Monica pulled her brother off a flat stone just in time, as the rock reacted like a magnet to the powerful man. Water from the stream bubbled beside them and crept up the embankment straight for the kids. It was not long until they were both soaked from the water, madly wiping their eyes clean so they could see the path ahead. "You won't escape me!"

Dare's lungs were growing tired of the cold air and he could feel his muscles being drained from the shivering chills of his damp skin. Monica was fading fast as well, silently crying out for Vectra, who was missing in action. Rounding a corner of the trail, the Brownings had to skid to a halt when they came face to face with a rising rock wall. "Trapped." Was all Dare could muster with his heaving chest.

"VECTRA!" Monica desperately called out. "VECTRA!"

"No one is going to save you this time." Taminus jeered, coming around the bend with an evil grin. "You are mine now."

"RUN!" Vectra's voice echoed off the wall as she torpedoed her way through it. Dare and Monica lowered their heads as they raced into the opening, waiting for debris to begin dropping on them. But there was no debris as most of the shards of rock instantly incinerated, and any residual matter turned to ash before touching the ground.

They continued on their way, quickly relocating the path and remained silent as the battle raged behind. "I don't see it yet." Monica gazed up at the maple leaves adorning the branches over their heads.

"There!" Dare took the lead and showed his sister the evergreen patch he saw in the near distance. To their delight, a trunk with three main sprouts shot into the sky next to two scraggy pine trees. "Look up she said." The kids glanced upward at the canopy, seeing nothing there. "What? I don't understand. Something has to be here."

"Maybe we should just forget about it and find another tree. This could be the wrong one." Monica suggested.

"No. This is the right one. See the symbol?" Dare pointed to the initials carved in the middle of a set of five, on a smooth section of the bark. "VT" was clearly legible, making the mystery even more perplexing. "We just aren't seeing it right or doing something right, or I don't know." Then the boy moved his head to the side, glimpsing deeper into the woods, when he suddenly caught sight of a hidden ladder grown in the side of one of the trunks. He rechecked the space in-between the triple spokes and smiled in victory. "Wild."

Monica watched her brother clamber up what appeared invisible at her angle and immediately moved over to see what Dare did. "Whoa." She followed him into a square hole that floated in the middle of the canopy and ultimately found herself inside a treehouse-like structure. "Close the door."

Dare locked it shut and joined his sister on the floor against the southern wall. "How is this possible? It's like a crazy, camouflaged, hunter's perch."

"Shhh." Monica cautioned as the sound of crunching leaves reached their ears.

"Where'd they go?" A deep tone penetrated the peaceful woods. "I don't see them."

"They were just here." Another responded.

"The boss isn't going to like us losing them again."

"You don't think I know that? My ears are still ringing from the last scolding he gave us." The man urged his partner to be quiet, listened to the trees, and shook his head in defeat. "Let's go in further. But we turn back if we can't find them in the next ten minutes."

As the men's voices and footsteps faded away, Monica placed an arm over her brother, and mouthed for him to remain perfectly still. There was always the possibility that the men were lying in wait below the tree, hoping for the kids to feel a false sense of security and accidently give away their hide out. She had seen it done in the movies before, and knew full well about tracks on the ground. *They might have seen our footprints outside in the areas not covered by rocks. So we should stay here and wait for Vectra, if she hasn't been caught already.*

Chapter Thirty

Dare still sat in utter silence while Monica tried controlling her breathing to a regular pace as best she could. Their ears were vigilant for any sounds coming in their direction, as they refused to look out the one-way windows as a precaution. Minutes passed rather painstakingly slow as nothing could be heard for what seemed like an hour or more; until leaves crunching under a person's foot disturbed the quiet once more. The kids gulped down their panic, trying to suppress the overwhelming desire to pop the hatch and flee. It didn't seem like a good idea to be cornered in a tree house with no other means of escape.

Their heartbeats quickened at the noise of someone making their way up the ladder, and their hearts nearly burst when a knock struck on the outside of the hatch. "It's me, Vectra." A weakened sound softly penetrated through the disguised structure.

Monica gratefully let the air out of her lungs as she unlocked the latch for the familiar voice. "We are sure glad to see you." Her face took on a worried expression the instant she saw Vectra's limp body requiring help to finish the climb inside. "Are you alright?"

"Does she look alright?" Dare cast his sister a "get-real" look, and aided Vectra in sitting down near the far wall alongside them. She leaned heavily against its painted surface, heaving from the toll of the fight and the pain of various cuts she had up and down her arms.

"Thank you." The words barely made it out of her lips before she coughed up a few pieces of smoldering ashes. "They're gone."

"At what cost?" Monica's hands waved all around at Vectra's current state. "You look close to death. We would rather have been captured than have you killed."

"Must…get…to…Rudi." Vectra managed to squeak the message out as she slumped further down the wall.

"We can go anywhere you need to, but tomorrow." Monica picked up a blanket from a short, square organizer in a well-supplied corner of the treehouse. "There is no way you are going to be able to travel like this. Besides, if those guys come back, we won't stand a ghost of a chance."

"Yeah, and we have no powers to defend ourselves against Taminus." Dare added, reminding himself about the question his sister failed to answer while they were on the main road. He turned his attention away from the Guardian. "I think now would be a good time to explain to me how my phone gave away our location, Monica."

The teenager picked up on Vectra's widened eyes from her peripheral, and dreaded having to explain yet another detail that she hid from the woman. "Remember that Thursday night, two years ago, when you headed over to Ethan's house without telling Trevor or myself?"

"Yeah. Trevor gave me a right ol' yelling for that one." Dare's mind churned in thought. "Oh no."

"Trevor asked me to help him ensure that it didn't happen again. So, he distracted you after dinner the following evening, while I went into the settings of your phone, and turned the tracker on." Monica was so embarrassed as she said it aloud. "It was for your safety, Dare. You scared him, and me, that night. You know that you need to let another person know where you are going before heading anywhere."

"I forgot that evening. I was going to text you two, but we got wrapped up in this video game and…that's when I found out that Ethan is a jerk anyhow." Dare look sheepishly at Vectra. "I'm so sorry. I didn't realize she had it changed."

"They must be using Trevor's phone in order to track us. Dare, that means you can't use your phone at all. Not even to alter the settings. Because my tracking is not hooked up, we can use it for emergencies ONLY." Monica crossed her arms in front of her chest, shaking her head. "Taminus must be working for Gaither. And yet, Taminus is so much more powerful than he is. So what would he have to gain from joining forces?"

"Gaither must have something over Taminus. Maybe blackmail…or a deal of some kind?" Dare offered. "Your guess is as good as mine on that one. But it would have to be something of true value for Taminus to bring himself to work under Gaither. He obviously despises the idea of not being his own boss."

"Whatever it is, maybe we can use it in our favor."

"Great. But first we should probably figure out what 'it' is before we go all double-agent on them." Dare's tongue happily licked his lips when he located two cans of beans, still within expiration date, on a shelf above the blankets. "Found some food."

Monica ignored her brother's joyous statement and continued thinking aloud. "Even with Taminus having the power of two elements, he is allowing Gaither to give him orders." She turned her back to Dare as he struggled with a manual can opener. "It could be a mystical object? Or maybe it is a map to a hidden location? Heck, it could be a simple piece of information for all we know."

"What difference does it make? Oww!" Dare stuck his index finger in his mouth, sucking the droplets of blood from his broken skin.

"It makes all the difference, Dare."

"Look, Monica, I understand that we have been through a lot of pretty unreal things lately, but take a step back from this one. Whatever Gaither has with Taminus…be it a deal, trade or whatever…he is going to have it double secured. Might even have it triple secured. So maybe we should stick to the plan we have and leave it be."

The teen spun around to face him, grabbing the first aid kit from a nearby shelf to put a band aid over his cut. "Because we could get ahold of the object and use it against him ourselves. With Taminus working on our side, we would have the power of three elements versus Gaither."

"Yeah, and it always works out in the end for the person who befriends the devil." Her brother rolled his eyes. "Face it, Monica. Gaither has signed his own death warrant whenever Taminus gets his end of the bargain. If Gaither keeps his word, that is."

"Rest." Vectra gave Monica a 'come hither' wave with her hand. "Rest. We will talk in the morning." Dare helped his sister get the Guardian comfortable. They draped her in one of the blankets, placed crackers by her hand, and moved to the other side of the treehouse in order to give her space.

As Monica placed her backpack on the floor, its softened thud sounded louder in the back of her mind. The weight of deception still lingered on her shoulders from the book being carried within. "Oh, Trevor, where are you?"

She whispered.

Dare reached over to give his sister a comforting squeeze. "Everything is going to be alright."

Monica smiled, though tears welled up in her eyes. "I thought I was supposed to be the one looking after you."

"Eh. It is more of a mutual thing."

Chapter Thirty-One

An eastern window gave a perfect view of the rising sun that following morning. Monica stretched her arms toward the ceiling, feeling a good pull in her muscles to help wake herself up from the best sleep she had had in months. *I guess that's what happens after running for your life*, she noted.

"Breakfast is served." Dare pleasantly announced with a large grin on his face. He handed her a can of apple pie filling, already opened, and stabbed a fork straight down the middle. "Here ya go!"

"Looks like you are now a pro at using the manual can opener."

"Nah. Vectra took pity on me." He shrugged and walked back to the empty spot on the floor where the Guardian had slept. No trace of her remained, as though she was nothing more than a memory or a ghostly being.

"Is she…mad at me?" Monica glanced about the tree-house to see if Vectra was within hearing distance, and was surprised to find her missing completely from the small space. Dare was the only other person in the room with her.

He hesitantly replied. "I don't think so. Just irritated, annoyed, and disgruntled." He thought about it, with a finger at his chin. "Oh, and betrayed. Yep, I believe that's all she mumbled under her breath."

"Oh, boy." Monica's hand slapped her forehead. "I should have said something the night before we reached Aidan's."

"Maybe you should have told us from the get-go. You know, tried being up front with us so we wouldn't have wasted all this time in search for the book you already packed for the trip."

"I already explained all of that to you yesterday."

"But you knew what the plant looked like." Dare sat down, scraping the sides of his tin can with a spoon. The last of the apple filling dripped from the end as he played with the extra sauce pooling in the bottom. "Vectra told me this morning that the flower has been extinct and the only image to have survived, in our world, is carved on Greek coins. The only way you would have seen it, would have been within the pages of her journal. Because the Greek coins lack any color."

"You're right. Okay? You want me to tell you all over again? I did open the pages to where a sticky note had bookmarked an illustration of the flower. Mom and Dad had written notes on more stickies around the image, but I had no idea of what it was until we were in the green-house and I recognized it." Monica's stomach was not even hungry at this point. Weighed down by the guilt she could not unearth herself from, the teen placed her can on the floor, and retrieved the journal from her backpack. She had wanted to go through its contents yesterday, while Vectra slept, but felt it wasn't right to pry after what she had done. "Before our parents left, Mom handed me this book and made me promise not to tell another soul, you and Trevor included. She told me to keep it by my side at all times, and to ensure that it didn't end up in the wrong hands."

"So, she was the one who wrapped it?"

"Did you not hear anything of what I told you yesterday? After they disappeared, I was so angry with them. I opened the journal up, thinking that it might give us a clue as to where they went. But I only saw these two pages before slamming it shut." Monica opened up to the bookmark, putting the pages and handwritten notes on display for Dare to read. "I couldn't stand to look at it, being reminded of what it meant. So I wrapped it up in that brown paper and tried forgetting all about it." She studied her brother skeptically as he asked another repeat question from the day before. "Dare, what is going on?"

"What do you mean?"

"Your memory isn't that short term. Where is Vectra? Just what is going on here?"

Dare sighed and knocked on the hatch. "Are you convinced already?"

"Dare?" Monica wasn't sure if she was still asleep or whether she was awake in the middle of a nightmare. "Please tell me that you are my brother and I didn't just jeopardize the mission."

"Yes, I'm your brother. Did you think I was some shape-shifting alien or something?" Dare plunked himself down atop a bean bag chair Monica didn't notice before.

"You can never be too careful." Vectra popped up through the hatch.

"I think she actually cracked a joke in front of us. Perhaps she is human after all." Dare laughed. "See? I told you she was telling me the truth."

"You put him up to this?" Monica asked the Guardian before switching her attention back onto her younger brother. "And you went along with it? Interrogating me with all those questions like we never talked about it yesterday?"

"I had to do something to convince her to still help us after…you know…" Dare didn't have to finish the statement.

"I'm sorry. What more do you want from me?"

"I want the truth!" Vectra demanded, inches away from Monica's face. "I want to know the real reason why you two came to find me in Nectar Hill."

"To save our brother from Gaither. Trevor. He was kidnapped. That is the truth!" Monica nearly shouted, using the last ounce of self-control she had left to keep the fight from leveling up. "We need your help in bringing him home."

"Sure is a nice story."

"It's no story. It really happened! I honestly did not know anything about what the book was, nor who owned it or anything like that. That night, at the concession stand, I was going to tell you, I really was, but…"

"But WHAT?!" Vectra's hardened stare watched the teen sink her chin into her chest.

"Catriona told us that your duty is only to the press. To keep it safe at all costs, no matter what. Same for the all of the other artifacts. If I gave you the book before, you might have left without helping us after the wrong was righted." Monica braved the waters by glancing up to see the woman's reaction. She wasn't sure what to expect anymore.

Vectra closed her eyes and took a deep breath. "It is not your fault that you did not know what Catriona was talking about, nor should she have opened her big mouth to either of you. But I will tell you this: we may not be able to foresee the future, but if you had given the book to me as soon as you realized what it was, we would not still be here today. Taminus would not have caught up to us like he did and I would not have…"

"Been injured if I had spoken up." Monica interjected.

She played with the bracelet around her wrist, rubbing the flower gems like she did whenever the stress was getting to her. "Vectra, Trevor is all we have left of our family. Is he perfect? No. No one is. But I would do anything to get him back."

"I believe you." Vectra crossed her arms, giving the teen a stern look. "You are a smart girl, Monica, there is no denying that. But you do not understand the full scope of what my job entails and the risk I take every time I have to battle one of my enemies. With Taminus in possession of two elemental powers, his strength is stronger than that of my own now. This is not your world we are dealing with here."

"Yeah. So we've noticed." Dare's spoon clinked in the metal can.

"Does this mean…"

"Yes. I am still going to help you two rescue your brother. Under one condition. That you stop keeping secrets from me regarding the press. Deal?"

"Deal." The siblings replied in unison.

Monica pulled the journal from her bag and offered it to Vectra. "It belongs to you."

"No." The Guardian refused by waving her hands and warding off the girl's gesture. After waiting this long, a few more hours wouldn't make much difference in finding out an answer to a lingering question in her mind. She had grappled with taking a look for years, just a quick peak at a few pages for a number of years. And now that the book was in her possession, she suddenly didn't want to know. *Perhaps the lost memory is a mercy.* "You take it. It is far better being stowed away from me. That is why I gave it to Gregon to begin with. Besides, I think you have proven a certain amount of respect for it when you asked Taminus not to take your brother's pack instead of your own. Clever thinking, and quick too."

"What is she talking about?" Dare's face begged for an explanation.

"If a teacher tells you not to touch something, doesn't that make you want to touch it?" Monica watched her brother nod in agreement. "That is why I told Taminus not to take your bag at the bus station. Faking that your bag was more important than my own, caused him to believe that your bag held more value in what it was carrying. Hence why, he took yours and left mine."

"Are you telling me that I sacrificed my favorite action figure to save this journal?" Dare studied his sister's expression in turn. "Okay…maybe I can forgive for that…three years in the future."

"You two can discuss your bargaining chips on the way to Rudi's. Time to go." Vectra instructed them to clean up the treehouse as she descended the ladder and waited for the kids to join her. Monica was the last to leave, and was about to close the hatch when the Guardian stopped her.

"Leave it open. There is an invisible barrier that allows whoever I deem to pass. And if you close it, it will be very hard to see where the entrance is; should I have to send anyone else this way."

"How is it camouflaged so well?" Dare eagerly asked.

"Oh, that? It is done through the use of well positioned mirrors. Although, there is a reflective film placed over them so that the birds can see them. That is actually an invention from your world and not of mine. Pretty ingenious, I think." Vectra gave a small wave to the crafty marvel as they began their walk back to the main road. Every third step caused the Guardian a stronger pang of pain she tried to disguise as best she could, though Monica noticed.

"So, are we going to ride on the Gopher Express again?"

Dare skipped out of pure happiness.

"Sorry to burst your bubble Dare, but Rudi is not near one of the stops. We are going to take the regular bus. There is a bus station about a mile from the entrance to this lane. I already have our tickets and called in for a pick-up."

"The regular bus?" The boy's eyebrows bounced up and down. "Right…"

"No, seriously. It is a regular bus. The bus driver lives in our realm but works for the company part-time. His shift is in the morning, so I placed a call and he should be here…" Vectra checked the time on her pocket watch. "…in fifteen minutes. We better get a move on. Take this." She flicked six playing cards out from her fingers. "Stick these to the bottom of your heels. Do not worry. They are self-adhesive." Monica put two seven of hearts under her shoes as Dare did the same on his. "Good. Now place these two under my boots. I am afraid that I am having a little issue with bending backwards at the moment."

"All done." Monica announced after they had one on each of Vectra's heels.

"Great. That will make our travel a little easier, and faster."

"Are we going to fly? Like from jet propulsion?" Dare clapped his hands in excitement as Vectra smiled.

Chapter Thirty-Two

The uneventful bus ride was rather dull in comparison to the last couple of days and Monica was alright with that. It was pleasant not to have someone chasing her through a greenhouse or into amusement rides for a change, and it was comforting to have her backpack nestled safe on her lap once again. While their journey, thus far, certainly would fill the pages of her journal with fantastical scenes of adventure, Monica wondered if she should put all of the past events down on paper. She suddenly worried that if someone were to see it in the future, they would deem her a lunatic and lock her away in a psych ward with a white jacket wrapped around her body. Look at the mess Vectra's journal has gotten us into. Oh well, perhaps all of my worrying is just a phase.

Still, the looming silence shared between the trio was no passing phase in its own right. Vectra had barely spoken to her since they used her fire power to propel them to the bus shelter; and the minutes ticking by were dragging into hours in the teen's mind. As passengers boarded, and disembarked, Monica just leaned her head against the cold window with sleepiness creeping into her eyes. The soft motor of the bus engine was a lulling lullaby that paired nicely with the tranquil woods coating the landscape all around them. Pretty soon, the lure of sleep was too inviting, and her eyelids happily closed themselves in exchange for a visit down memory lane.

It was close to Halloween time when Monica was going on seven years old, and her mother was getting her costume ready for trick-or-treating in their neighborhood. Her pick of the year was the ever capable treasure hunter whilst her mother decided to dress as a cowgirl for the night. The clock bonged at 5:30 pm, as her father held Dare in his arms in front of the television. "Have a great time!" He shouted over the loud sounds of the wrestling match coming through the speakers. She remembered how he loved to watch his favorite wrestlers battle it out in the ring, despite believing that most of it was faked. The showmanship was what interested him, as he would constantly say.

The doorbell rang just as her mother's hand gripped the knob. A simple turn revealed the outline of a female in the backlighting of a car's headlights. They talked for a little while, a whole thirty seconds, much to the annoyance of the little girl ready to join the other kids in asking for candy. Seven-year-old Monica fiddled with her outfit, which drew a number of criticisms from her mother for not being able to stand still. Finally, the woman turned to leave, and her red hair fell behind her back as she walked to the driveway. Monica stared after the woman, hearing her mother dash into the living room with something in her hands and eagerly discuss a book with her father. As the strange visitor continued past the driveway, walking over the rocks in the landscaping, the little girl watched her ultimately disappear in the bushes without a trace.

"Monica, Monica." Dare pushed his sister's arm harder

and harder until she bolted awake. "Sorry to startle you, but we are here. It's our stop." He pulled the frazzled teen up from her seat and made sure she had her backpack in her hands before stepping down the stairs behind her. "Are you alright?"

"I'm not sure." Monica swept her hair back from falling into her eyes. "I dreamt while I was sleeping, or no…no… it was a memory of someone from the past."

"What happened in this memory?" Vectra looked at the girl tentatively, her own interest piqued.

"I was getting ready to go trick-or-treating down our street with Mom, when a woman showed up at the door and gave her a book…your book, Vectra. When Mom went to tell Dad, I watched the stranger vanish into thin air in the bushes by our driveway. And I think she had red hair."

"It could have been your mind playing tricks on you. Perhaps it mixed reality with a few spoken suggestions from Aidan's description." Vectra guessed. "Either way, if you didn't see the face, then it doesn't do me any good with finding out her identity."

"Surely you already have a strong candidate based on what Aidan said." Monica's brain was beginning to clear up from her grogginess.

"If it is the one I am thinking of, then she would have had to have broken her word in order to do such a thing."

"Hey!" A man in a grizzly-looking beard and mustache called out from the driver side of his pick-up truck. "Are you three going to yap all dadgum day or are you going to take yer conversation over to the grass along the side? I need to haul this here beast up the hill and I don't want to hit y'all. You ain't exactly made of deer meat."

"Oops. Sorry." Dare and Monica hustled over to join Vectra on the grass. They watched the man take a wide turn on the corner so as to not jackknife his camper on the hitch. The mammoth of a mobile home set-up, second only to the fifth wheel deluxe models of campers, made its way up the hill at a fair clip and revealed a large sign it had been blocking. "Welcome to Crater Lake Campsites?"

"Rudi just loves this area at this time of year." Vectra inhaled a deep breath, enjoying the fresh air filling her lungs just as a sharp twinge of pain stabbed through her gut, mirroring a large muscle spasm she felt in her leg. "We better start the climb ourselves."

"But your leg…" Monica's voice faded out.

"I can make it. Let's go." Vectra spearheaded the hike until they reached the halfway mark. Her leg began cramping with every step, causing more shooting pain to race up her nerves and into the base of her spine. She tried to move her foot forward and nearly fell down with a short yelp escaping her lips.

"This is pointless. Dare and I can go on ahead to find Rudi and ask him for help in getting you up the hill." Monica watched the Guardian think the concept over. "Look, we are not going to leave you here, if that is what you're considering."

"It is not that. I just don't know how Rudi will be with a pair of strangers showing up at his door. He gets a little funny around people he has not met before."

Monica cast a frustrated look at the macadam, more with herself for getting Vectra injured than for anything else. "Is there anyone in your world who doesn't have some sort of peculiar thing about them? Except for you…who appears to be the most normal one we have encountered so far." She popped her hand up in the air to stop Vectra from responding. "Never mind. What does he look like?"

"He is an elf."

"A real elf?" Dare's face illuminated with glee.

"His camper will have a green wreath on the front with a red bow pinned at the top."

"An elf named Rudi, living in a camper with a Christmas wreath tagged on the front before Halloween." Monica's bottom lip jutted out. "Alrighty then. Come on Dare." She picked up the pace, forcing her brother to jog up the rest of the way to catch up.

"This is soooo cool. You think he knows Santa and all? Maybe we could get a few extra presents this year."

"Don't be drinking the hot cocoa yet, bro. We need to find him and get back to Vectra first." Monica reached the crest of the hill, where the campsite's bathroom and showers marked the area for the dump station and, oddly enough, the kids playground. To the left, a loop of campsites was worked into the natural slope of the hill with the last site being numbered fifty-seven, where a tree's strong limbs almost blocked the post. Ten campers were scattered amongst the unoccupied spots, facing different directions to match their fire rings and electric plug-ins. "Do you see a green wreath on any of them?"

"No. But that row in the back is well hidden by those large pine trees." Dare pointed to a trio of campers parked at the farthest end from where they stood. "The one on the far left looks pretty fancy." The boy squinted his eyes, trying to get a better glimpse of the fifth wheel, double-axel camper through the branches. He could just make out the black and white walls, and a small decal that was beginning to peel off. "Monica, I think the decal says something about the North."

"That seems as good a place as any to start with." She motioned Dare to follow her across the top of the loop and down until they reached the luxury unit. Just as Vectra had stated, above the locked hitch, rested a wreath on the front end of the camper. The unit was sitting behind a barbershop pole coming up from the ground, with red and white curving lines spinning around in mesmerizing fashion. Monica looked over at the decal her brother mentioned and praised him for his keen eyes. "You were right, Dare. It says North Winds."

They stepped noisily over the graveled site number thirteen and saw the door shut with a "Do Not Disturb – Hard at Work" sign hanging from the metal knob. A faint touch of golden glitter was added to the Old English font someone painted on a red piece of wood. The picnic table had been decorated in an evergreen colored tablecloth with a singular candle in the center. Holly berries adorned the candle ring the vanilla cylinder sat within, adding a tasteful dash of Christmas to the woodsy setting. To their dismay, the site was missing a vehicle of any sort.

"Who wants to knock?" Dare gave his sister a pleading look. "He still might be home."

"Flip a coin?" Monica pulled a quarter from her wallet, and allowed Dare to make his choice. She flicked it into the air, rapidly moving away to not impede it from falling to the ground. "Heads, you win." Her hand slapped the back of her brother's head to wipe the smirk from his mouth.

"After you." He jokingly smiled, watching her nervously walk up to the door and knock upon the metal. They waited a heartbeat, wondering if they were about to be blasted with a glitter gun or dropped in a vat of hot chocolate by a secret trap door. Instead, the inner door slowly opened with a curious elf staring at them through the outer screen door.

"Yes…" The elf hesitantly stated. His beard was snow white in coloring, matching his eyebrows and the pompom on the tip of his red hat. Green triangles fashioned its trim and continued onto the bottom hem of his pants, while each horizontal red and green stripe on his shirt, lined up with the small antique gold bells on his suspenders. Monica and Dare found it hard to suppress their laughter when looking at his holiday attire.

"Are you Rudi?" The teen's voice was tinged by the smile she was trying to hide.

"Maybe, and maybe not. Who be ask'n?"

"We are friends of Vectra Tillerman and she could use a little help getting up the hill. She is injured and we came up here to borrow your vehicle."

"The camp host, Warren, took my pick-up truck to run some errands. Mainly for parts for that worthless piece of crap he calls a truck. But, I rest my case." His left eye nearly closed at suspicion of the two kids. "Curious that Vectra would be paying me a visit. Must mean she needs to use my equipment."

"She is actually hurt…and in a lot of pain. Most likely she is coming here to get better." Monica retorted in the woman's defense.

"Nice try, Kid. But that Vectra of yours isn't known for visiting others just for a chit chat. Not anymore, anyways." Rudi was about to say something else when a high-pitched voice came shouting over a speaker from within the camper.

"Xavier Jingle Bell, you better not be neglecting your job again!"

Rudi rolled his eyes impatiently. "Excuse me for a moment." He retreated behind the door and answered the voice with a strong response of his own. "No, boss. A few campers need a little help. Be back in a few marshmallows." Before his boss could reply, Rudi pressed a red button on his dashboard to shut the whole system down. "Ugh. New boss. First Christmas and all. So she DOES NOT want anything going wrong for the Big Guy."

"Wait, I'm confused. So your name is Xavier and not Rudi?" Dare moved away from the stairs to make room for the elf to land on the ground.

"One time. ONE TIME my nose gets redder than an ambulance light and I get the nickname Rudi after that TV star of a reindeer. His story becomes legend and I get banished from the North Pole from September 15th to January 1st every year."

"Banished from the North Pole?" Monica thought she heard him wrong. "Santa banishes you during the busiest time of year?"

"I happen to be the only elf allergic to peppermint. You can imagine how bad that is during the holiday craze. Peppermint is in literally everything up there until things settle a bit after the big day. And I mean EVERYTHING! Hot chocolate, cookies, cakes, milk, ice cream, the eggnog, oh, and in the eggs for breakfast too."

"Yuck! Gross." Dare pretended to vomit.

"Yeah, well, I had the misfortune of shadowing the candymakers one afternoon when they were mixing the peppermint for the candy canes. The smell overwhelmed my nose and it glowed hot red from the reaction with the sensory overload. I sneezed up and down the halls, which then needed to be cleaned by many unhappy elves. However, the worst part was when I entered the glitter supply room by mistake and…"

"Oh no!" Monica had a feeling she knew what he was going to say.

"Yep. Blew four whole shelves of the stuff all over the place. Took the crafting elves months to clean it all up." Rudi put a red hoodie over his outfit and replaced his pointed shoes with everyday black sneakers. "That is when they decided I was more of a liability than a help during the busy season. So I help from my mobile station, here, and head home for the off-season once January 2nd rolls around. Peppermint is what helps us do what we do so fast, being on a constant sugar high I guess. Our metabolisms are built differently from you humans. Other than me, that is. I prefer the coffee variant due to my allergy."

"Wow! I am truly glad that my brother is not on a constant sugar high. Huh, Dare?" Monica looked over to see him beaming from ear to ear, lost in the possibilities of being a Christmas elf. "Anyway, how are we going to get Vectra without a vehicle?"

Rudi's small mustache gave way to a mischievous grin underneath the wispy hairs. His hand rose up with a key-ring dangling from his thumb. "The golf cart."

Chapter Thirty-Three

Vectra heard the wanna-be honk of the camp host's golf cart coming down the hill. She glanced up to see Rudi's beard flying over his shoulder and practically into Monica's face in the back seat. "Do you like the upgrade?" He flashed her a toothy half-smile and moved his eyebrows up and down at her sitting atop a large boulder.

"Nice training wheels. What happened to your half ton pick-up?"

"Loaned it to a friend. Found a few of yours here apparently." Rudi hit the brakes on the mini 'Green Machine' and pulled it alongside the road.

"After meeting you, they probably won't speak to me again." Vectra joked as Monica helped her into the back seat. "Thanks." They braced for the uphill climb, having first gone back down to the campground entrance due to the road being too small for the unskilled driver to make a U-turn.

"Nothing like a midafternoon road trip to get the blood pumping again." Rudi laughed to himself. "Of course, it could be the caramel latte I just had before you two kids knocked on my door."

"I see your caffeine addiction has not lessened any."

"Vectra, you stopped by my stoop in October. What did you expect?" Rudi pressed the gas pedal to the floor, roaring the engine to life to whip around the corner of the loop at blazing speed. Monica closed her eyes and held on fast to the bars in the back. She did not want to see the pavement in case the cart toppled over. "Wahoo! I loooove doing that."

"Rudi, you are such a five year old." Vectra hollered, despite showing some enjoyment on her face as well.

"You are so right! And loving every minute of it." The North Pole elf brought the cart to a halt by his camper. "Vectra, you know the mint score. Get yourself comfortable and I'll be right back." He sped off toward the camp host's spot where his pick-up was finally returning from town.

The camper smelled of freshly baked gingerbread, provided by a potent candle burning in the kitchen area. Green pillows accented a deep red couch and matched the color of the drapes, towels, and seat cushions. A snow globe village consumed an end table where faint holiday music was being played through a hidden Bluetooth speaker. Next to the microwave sat an overflowing candy jar in the shape of an old-fashioned milk carton, as vintage postcards dangled nearby, attached to a string of sparkling lights by white clothespins. The entire space screamed of holiday cheer; except for a fake tabletop tree, spray-painted black, and decorated in the festive nature of Halloween.

"Words fail me." Dare said as he looked over a multi-functional desk area that looked like a mobile command center. Three monitors were lined up in a semicircle with a gamer keyboard and a low-tech mouse resting on an "elf of the month" pad. A long scroll of ticker tape spewed out from a small slit in the table, curling up beside a drink and a half-eaten sugar cookie.

"Who are you?" A female elf asked on a dash-cam setup above the screen to the farthest right. "And where is Rudi?"

"Ah, he went out to put the golf cart away." Dare replied, casting a glance at Vectra standing outside. "He helped us out and will be right back." The Guardian quickly tapped on the shutdown button before her face came into view.

"I am not particularly liked by certain elves." Vectra grimaced while making her last effort to enter the camper.

"I'm pretty sure your elf friend turned his computer off before we came to pick you up." Monica told the Guardian about how the machine made the same sound when Rudi pressed the red button earlier.

"Must be up to his old dodging habits if they stuck a M.E. on him. That stands for Monitoring Elf." Vectra explained. "That only happens when an elf isn't doing their job correctly. And it includes complete access to overriding your computer system so they can check in on your activities."

"Can an elf be fired?" Monica turned the chair around to make it easier for the injured woman to sit.

"In a way. First, you're demoted to stall duty in the reindeer barn. Below that, you have to work in the fertilizer plant where they turn all the reindeer feces into Christmas presents for all current and future gardeners of the world. And if you manage to screw up there, then it is off to the Christmas Dump. That is where all the lost, broken, and worn out decorations go. It is the most miserable assignment they have and a very depressing one at that. I had to visit it once." Vectra shuddered. "Like walking onto a horror movie set filled with one-eyed statues, headless lawn ornaments, and miles of busted strings of lights."

"All is well in the world again." Rudi casually strolled into the camper with a different set of keys swinging in his hands. He shut the door behind him and tossed them onto a shallow ceramic bowl. "Got my Berry back in her rightful spot and Warren is delighted to have his golf cart again."

"Rudi, I need to use your I.L.S." Vectra stared at the metal slot in the elf's desk. It was longer than the ticker tape dispenser, and a lot quieter.

"Vectra, you know I can't use that for personal reasons. Strictly business. Since the Yellowhammer Strike of '97, it costs forty-five snickerdoodles a letter. And they have been chewing at the fowl steward's head for another raise this past year."

"I can pay the fee, Rudi, but I need to get a message to Gears."

"I suppose. This better not be like last time though. I nearly lost my camper because of your request." The elf pointed his finger like a disciplinary teacher, staring up at Vectra already pulling a paper and pen from a desk drawer.

"Thanks. You are a sugar plum."

"I'm not that sweet." Rudi gruffed, turning his way to the kitchen for a savory snack of pepperoni and cheese wrapped in crescent rolls.

"What is an I.L.S.?" Dare read the engraved initials, illuminated in a red glow, on the narrow metal rim surrounding the slot.

"It stands for Instant Letter Service. Yellowhammers deliver the letter instantly to the North Pole, or anywhere else in the world for that matter, and you get a reply just as fast." She explained whilst writing down a message for the Olde Realm Inventor.

"Wouldn't an email be cheaper to send?"

"For starters, they can be hacked into, and Gears checks his inbox once a week." Vectra went about drafting up the letter as Dare sniffed the air, picking up on the smell wafting from the elf's snack.

"They smell delicious. Do you happen to have any more?" He stared at the steam coming off the food.

"Ah, so there was another reason for you dropping in. Not only did you want to use my equipment, but you also brought along a pair of hungry kids. How considerate." Rudi cast a glare at Vectra before opening the fridge to pull out a food container filled with the pepperoni delight.

"I will buy you a box of your favorite hot chocolate, Rudi." Vectra finished writing her letter, folded it into an envelope specially stamped "Air Mail" and dropped it into the slot. A heartbeat later, a response popped out from the same narrow opening where Vectra caught it just as it went sailing pass her head. She flipped it over to see a golden wax seal with the image of two gears pressed into it and did not hesitate to yank the message out. The letter was written in a cursive font Monica had trouble deciphering over the Guardian's shoulder, so she took her word as to what it said. "Both good and bad news. He can ship a few of the items we need. But he is mostly out of weapons due to another turf battle. Apparently, he is out of his electrio blades too." Her eyes continued to scan through the message. "Correction, he has only one left. So it will have to do."

Vectra dropped both the letter and the envelope into the shredder and watched them get chopped into tiny pieces. "An electrio blade harnesses the power of lightning by trapping it within a specialized battery pack built into the handle. There is a small gear just under the bolster, where the handler clicks clockwise to adjust how many blades they wish to use: one, two, or three. This doesn't maximize the power concealed within, rather it distributes it in each direction." Vectra explained. "Think of a taser with a serious upgrade in electric voltage with the ability to stab people. Unfortunately, he says that it is not charged, so we will have to do that part ourselves."

"There are no clouds in the sky, let alone a thunderstorm in the area." Monica gazed out a window as she scarfed down three pepperoni rolls at once. She hadn't even noticed the touchscreen radar system behind the keyboard until Vectra used it to fast forward the prediction by a number of hours.

"A storm is brewing in the south and will follow the low pressure system moving into the northeast. Should bring about another storm system in two days. We can put the lightning rod up then and capture us a few lightning strikes. Three strong hits should fill the battery to capacity."

"When does the stuff arrive?" Dare handed his sister another roll. Their empty stomachs were extremely grateful for the nourishment, and they thanked Rudi four times for the much needed food.

Suddenly a knock was heard at the door and everyone turned their heads. "There it is." Vectra rolled over in the desk chair and opened the front door to sign a clipboard like any regular delivery; if the delivery man happened to be a griffin dressed in a milkman cap and a bowtie, that is. "Thanks George." A screech from the griffin filled the air as he flew out of sight.

"At least you picked a smaller order than that tank he almost dropped on top of my camper in '95." Rudi poked his head out the door to see three bicycles with their kickstands keeping them in place. Each one had a bag hanging from the handlebar and a mobile drink maker in their respective cup holders.

"My balance sucks." Dare poked his sister in the side. "And you can't ride one of those either."

"That's alright. Because they are technically not bicycles. That is their disguise around other people." Vectra went to get up from the chair and instantly fell back into the seat again, her body still weakened from the prior day's fight. Rudi gave her a concerned look and ordered the kids to grab the granola bars from the cookie jar marked with the medical cross symbol. They rushed over to the kitchen as the elf helped her to the couch opposite his command desk, letting her use his head to keep from falling down.

"Vectra, I'm truly worried for you. I have never seen you so worn and physically defeated before." Rudi took the bars from the kids and offered one to the Guardian. "What happened to you? You're normally fine after a few hours."

"Taminus has acquired the power of water and is stronger than ever now."

"Then you need to be more careful. Stop trying to run at the danger and lay low until the opportune moment."

"I did not have a choice in the matter, Rudi." Vectra refused to look at Monica, but the teen could sense the tension lingering between them. "He had the drop on us." Rudi cast his eyes back and forth between his friend and the two kids, with the silent understanding that there was more to the story.

"Regardless, you need to rest." The elf glanced at his polar bear wristwatch, telling him it was 4:15 pm. "I have to get back to work until 6:00, and then I will get some dinner ready for everyone."

"Thanks, Rudi." Vectra's eyes drooped as the crushed sleeping tablets in the granola bars began to work. "I owe you for this."

Chapter Thirty-Four

Night fell over the wooded landscape fairly quickly, drenching the friendly campground in utter darkness. Rudi tied the bikes to his camper with the use of some chains and locks left behind by a family of four the past month. He told Monica and Dare about the surprising items people forgot about when they packed up to leave after their vacation was over. "You would not believe how many people bring an entire house load of belongings with them for merely two days in the woods, and then don't take it all back with them."

"I can imagine." Monica stoked the fire with a metal poker and listened to the sounds of the mostly full sites. She heard the laughs of happy campers talking with friends about shared tall tales from high school days and past trips. During the evening, a recent addition of a tent city had been built in a matter of minutes and the tired workers enjoyed cooking their hot dogs and mountain pie sandwiches over a fire of their own. Everyone seemed content in the woods. That was, except for Monica. Trevor had not wavered from her mind and she wondered if he was still alright. *He's fine. We are going to find him and return home before we know it*, she told herself.

She suddenly jumped in the camping chair from the hooting of an owl and tried calming herself down by humming a tune in her head. They were in the woods yet again, testing her will power and determination against the childhood fears she never discussed. And neither did anyone else in the family, for that matter. Dare wasn't a part of their lives yet and Trevor always sidestepped the question whenever her brother asked why she was so unsettled by the woods. "The woods!" A lightbulb dinged on. "The woods! Taminus attacked us when we were in a wooded area, when Vectra said that he isn't fond of them either."

"Ah, there were a lot of clear open spaces at the amusement park. He attacked us there, remember?" Dare kicked a stone with his foot. "He followed us into the woods after that, but that was because he ultimately had too."

"Right. Sorry. Thought I had something there."

"Ah, Rudi…" Dare shyly approached the picnic table where the elf was adding snowflake sprinkles to the whipped cream on a reindeer mug. The amazing scent of the chocolate made his mouth water, even after eating three cheeseburgers and two helpings of waffle fries.

"Yes?"

"My real name is Derrick Browning and I was wondering if you could put in a good word for me because…"

"I know all about you Dare." Rudi's right eye winked at the boy. "And you have been on the bubble between both lists all this year. I cannot meddle in the affairs so closely drawn as yours I'm afraid."

"Oh, okay." Dare masked his disappointment as best he could. "I will endo…enda…endeavor to do better." He picked up a camping life mug topped with chunks of toffee and muttered his thanks as he made his way to a camping chair beside the fire pit.

"And I also know about you, Monica Browning." Rudi handed her the mug he finished adorning as she rose up from her seat for her scrumptious drink. "Your wish is something no one can fulfill. I do admire the true feeling and passion it comes from though."

"That doesn't keep me from trying." Monica glanced at her bracelet in the faint light. "It gives me a certain peace of mind, I suppose. Ensures their memory lasts a little longer and provides me a safe space of comfort."

"Just remember to focus on what you have in front of you, too. Because the past is not for changing, but for learning, teaching, and adapting." Rudi filled another mug with the piping hot drink, this time a Christmas flamingo in a Santa's hat. Grasping onto the pink neck fashioned into the handle, Rudi decorated his with mint and a hint of almond extract. "Would you mind fetching me the mace seasoning from the cupboard?"

Chapter Thirty-Five

Monica pulled the gnome holiday blanket up to her chin, squinching her body further underneath its Sherpa lining. She felt the piercing night chill slowly seep into her clothing, despite the new jacket Gears had sent along, as it tried latching onto her skin. Pressing her knees together, she dreaded the notion of having to leave the snug seat next to the roaring fire. Five minutes later, she surrendered and couldn't hold it any longer. "Where are the closest bathrooms? I only remember the one at the top of the hill." *I understand each person has their quirks, but to not allow ANYONE else to use his bathroom is a little absurd.*

"Four sites up, and then down the small path between the pine trees. Can't miss the side lights peeking through the branches." Dare smiled as he swallowed half a pineapple and ham sandwich. "Want me to walk with you?" He placed a reassuring hand upon his sister's buried arm and stared into her scared eyes. It may have been his brotherly duty to pick on her whenever possible, but there were certain lines he did not cross.

"No. No." Monica's voice cracked as she tried sounding confident and brave. "I can find it." She forced a strained grin across her lips, adding to the transparent façade and quickly unearthed herself from the thick blanket. "You enjoy the sandwich. Really. I'll be fine. Besides, you might end up joining me up there after your eating catches up to your stomach."

"Ha-ha."

Without another word, Monica regrettably left her warm cocoon and headed into the darkening night. A flashlight lit the way before her feet, keeping the blackened shadows at bay as her heart begin to race. She slowed her breathing a little bit, telling herself that everything was going to be okay and that there was no reason to fret as the gravel crunched under her shoes. Her mind fought away the flashbacks threatening to make the situation worse and Monica gathered her courage to press on.

Laughter drifted to her ears from the nearby campfires as she walked past, her dot of light barely shining two feet in front of her. The wind came and went at its whim; and rustled the leaves turning to burnt orange and corn yellow. Her heart pounded as her breathing labored out of heightened concern for the darkness she could not see through, when all of a sudden, a noise thudded from behind. It struck the ground softly, but with force, stopping Monica in her tracks where she was too scared to move. She scolded herself for acting childish and turned around as her imagination spun all sorts of speculations as to what it could be. *I am not sure I want to look. It's going to be okay. It's going to be alright, just breathe...*

The teenager was surprised to find no one there. She looked up and down, side to side, and stepped up to a black walnut still shaking from the dramatic fall it recently took. Her instinct was to pick the large nut off the ground and examine it for a possible time bomb or for a small camera built into a false pit. Since there was no apparent ticking or drilled-in hole, Monica decided it was best to leave the wild nut on the ground where it landed and continued onto the bathrooms.

A motion-activated light snapped on with a soft "click" and a daylight bulb illuminated the protected entrance to the ladies side of the restrooms. Monica swung open the heavy door and immediately noticed that it was warmer inside than it was out. A delighted smile appeared on her face. *These bathrooms are heated!* She slid into the second stall of the white and grey tiled room right before another camper also walked inside to use the facilities. The teen stared oddly at the recycled plastic walls of the stall, as the lady went into the one on her left while talking on the phone.

"No, no. He made a whole thing of chicken noodle soup that you can have. Don't touch that one in the fridge, in the blue container. It probably has too much salt in it for you. The tournament? It is going fine. We have another game tomorrow, and the boys are really pumped up over the win today. I tried telling them to remain focused, but you know…Sis, Sis…I told you not the blue container. Go for the teal set, on the bottom shelf. There ya go!"

The woman's voice raised an octave higher as she told her sister that she was tired of hearing about their grand-mother's veggie soup being superior to everyone else's in the family and that there was going to be a voting contest at their next family get-together. "Of course they are going to vote for her, being the most senior member and all. Talk about a rigged election. Hey, did I not tell you about the weird thing we saw on the road coming into the camp-ground? It was really strange. Two kids driving what looked to be a bumper car with extra wheels underneath its body.

They sprang onto the road…where? Oh back by the old amusement park that shut down years ago. Yeah…this was yesterday. Anyway, hang on." She left the stall and made her way to the counter to wash her hands. "Then, as quick as they flashed onto the road, they shot off on some dirt side lane."

Water running from the spigot over the white sinks blurred out a few of her following lines. Monica desperately leaned closer to the door, extending her head as far as it could go in the hopes of gleaning any more information from the woman. "I know! The police thought Henry was crazy when he called. He even told them about the three men chasing after them. They thought he was going insane until his description of the kids sounded a lot like those two who went missing from…" The woman swung open the door and left the bathroom before completing her statement.

Monica hurriedly washed her hands and dashed outside. She held the flashlight shakily in front of her, afraid to show her face to anyone who passed by. Though the darkness hid everything in disguise, she did not want to risk the other campers identifying her. Rudi's campsite came up sooner than the teen expected as her brother gave her a friendly wave. "You made it! Congrats."

"For now. But you are never going to believe what I just overheard in the bathroom."

"What?" Dare shared a curious look with Rudi.

"The police are looking for us."

"The cops?" Monica's brother cast a look in all directions as if they might pop out of the bushes right then and there. "Why are the cops after us?"

"Because one of your neighbors reported you two as missing." Vectra stepped down the aluminum ladder extending from the door to the ground of the camper. "Apparently, a boy by the name of Ethan, told his mother that you two planned to meet up two days ago, and never responded to numerous phone calls and text messages. Then he watched your house to make sure that everything was alright. Only to have found…" She winced while placing her foot on the gravel, "the house deserted. His mother contacted the police when a secretary from Trevor's job confirmed that your brother has not been at work. And the fact that your mailbox has not been emptied since you two left."

Monica slapped her forehead. "I forgot to have the mail stopped online, and Trevor always has her keep an eye on the house if we go away. We should have let her know so she wouldn't become suspicious. She has a key and probably walked right inside."

"Wait, I had my phone on, remember? That is how Taminus tracked us down. Ethan didn't call or text me." The boy shook his head. "That stinking Ethan. He really is no good. I bet you he is enjoying all of the attention from this."

"I found out from a camper in the bathroom. How did you hear about it?" Monica set up another chair for the woman.

"Listened to it on the radio when I woke up." A blanket draped over Vectra's shoulders, mimicking the cloak of plushy fabric Monica had regrettably left earlier. "A man called it in when you two drove on the main road to the tree house."

Monica nodded. "She said the police thought Henry to be crazy until he described us to them. What are we going to do?"

"Nothing."

"Nothing?" The siblings asked, stunned, and in unison.

"Precisely." Vectra inched her way down and into the chair beside Rudi. "If they get to you two before we reach the press and your brother, then it is game over. We need to maintain a low profile for a while. Blend in with the crowd and keep your faces hidden."

But what happens when we go home? Monica looked at Dare with worry painted in her gaze. The police were now involved, and that meant that child services would not be far behind once they were discovered. *Trevor will be in a mess of trouble, and we will have a lot to explain. No one would ever take our true accounts seriously!* Without a word, Monica retook her seat between Rudi and her brother. *There is no reason for me to upset Dare with this. I should remain quiet.*

"I have a phone call to make." Rudi removed himself from the fire pit to head into the camper. As he shut the door, Monica couldn't help but consider another possible outcome and voiced the option aloud.

"What if we never went back?"

"Back to your home?" Vectra popped the top of a portable drink maker and clicked the dial to milk for the cookies she had stashed in her pocket. Neither one of the kids had seen her take the small machine from one of the bags on the bikes, but they didn't care.

"Yeah. People go missing and never come back for all kinds of reasons. And you have the ability to make us disappear, like in the witness protection program."

"Monica, I'm not liking this." Dare sat straight up in his chair. "The plan was to find our brother and then go back home. Not to run off like fugitives."

"But what if we didn't go back? You said so yourself, Dare. You think the Olde Realm is really neat. We could stay here; living in a camper like Rudi, traveling from place to place across the country. Think of all the sights we could see and the adventures we would have exploring the different parks, beaches, and towns."

"Monica, you do not want to do that. Running from your problems is no way to live."

"Look who's talking." The teen stared at Vectra.

"And I am telling you from someone experienced at doing just that. If you leave your world, it will haunt you for the rest of your life. It will be a ghost that never goes away."

"You don't understand." The teen pleaded. "At least the newspaper reporters will love the headlines the story would make. Kids Follow in Parent's Footsteps. Whole Family Goes the Way of the Dodo. Vanished – A Mystery for the Ages."

Dare stood up. "But Monica, Mom and Dad…"

"Are not here. And we are. We need to decide what is best for us, since they can't. It is not as though they were the best decision makers when it came to responsible choices either."

"Monica, do not borrow worry from the police. If you run, it will only make things worse. You will be marked as a kidnapped victim and your picture will be plastered all over the place." Vectra dunked a cookie into the milk and snapped the star shape in half with her teeth.

"So what?!" Monica threw her hands in the air. "It would eventually die down and Dare, Trevor, and I would still be together. Do you know what will happen to us when we return? Huh?!"

"She means child services." Dare explained to Vectra. "They try their best, they really do, but they are not going to understand any of this. No sane person would."

"Ah." Vectra enveloped herself further into the folds of the blanket. "We might be able to take care of that. For now, just sit back and enjoy the fire. I will have regained my strength by tomorrow, so we will be on the move again to Martiban's for a key."

"How can I 'enjoy the fire,' when it seems as though we haven't gotten anywhere and now our light at the end of the tunnel is diminishing?" Monica sat down angrily. "Why would I expect a loner like you to understand what I am talking about anyways."

"At least, your family still cares for you." Vectra hunched forward and looked into the flames. Her hands enjoyed the heat on her palms, allowing the sensation to gradually warm its way into her soul. She looked to the leaves coating the forest floor as a stubborn, and almost forgotten voice, came into her mind. "Taminus is my cousin." Both Monica and Dare gave her blank stares, frozen in shock. "That is why we cannot kill one another. Family members can only wound, but never strike anything fatal against their own blood. I do not use my higher numbered playing cards for that reason. It would be a waste of my energy as each card takes a certain amount of strength, like a constant subtraction problem. Think of it like a never-ending game of chess."

"Some family." Dare sarcastically remarked. "Yours puts reality TV to shame."

"We all got our powers from my uncle, Leander. My father's death hit him extremely hard when it happened. He was my uncle's youngest brother, and my father almost worshiped the ground he walked. After the burial, my aunt also passed away from a plague that struck their town, and Taminus's brother died from being killed in battle. My uncle decided that he didn't want any more deaths in our family and visited Circe to ask for help. She denied him. But my uncle was persistent and ended up stealing her most powerful potion right out from underneath her nose. Each of us drank from it; My Uncle Leander, Taminus, Bregit, and myself. Bregit was an old family friend, a mentor in the ways of stealing. He taught us, and my father, the best ways to sneak into the temples, to swipe coins from the spectators during the Olympic Games and…well, you have the idea."

Monica did a little math of her own, putting the pieces of the puzzle together. "That is how Taminus was able to defeat Bregit. He was not a blood relative. And his powers were transferred to Taminus when he died."

Vectra nodded. "Each of us were given powers aligned with the four elements. Taminus has Earth, Bregit…had Water, I have Fire, and my Uncle has.."

"Air." Dare answered.

"That's correct. But they did not come without consequences. Bregit could not swim and was afraid of the ocean after almost drowning when he was merely a boy. Leander had always had a thing about the wind because of an accident that occurred during an experiment he was conducting for Archytas. He was the first mathematician to research into how birds fly, and my uncle used to be an apprentice with the group he was a part of, called the Pythagoreans. As for Taminus, he loved the ocean and open sea. He dreamt of becoming a sailor and exploring different ports all over the world."

"So each one of you obtained a power that directly aligned with your fears?" Monica was beginning to see a portion of the bigger picture and decided to venture forth on a more personal question of her own. "Why did you get fire?"

Vectra looked up at the sky far above their heads. "It is getting late and we should go to bed. I will make sure that the fire is extinguished before heading in." The teen understood the unspoken message and bid her farewells for the evening. She went inside the camper, peering back at her brother still holding the empty mug in his hands in the camping chair.

"Vectra, may I ask you a question?" Dare stared at the leftover chocolate residue in the bottom of his mug.

"You just did." Her sarcastic remark brought a smile to both their faces.

"What were my parents like? That day when they came to see you, how were they?"

"What do you mean?" Vectra was caught off guard by the boy's question. She was not quite sure what he was driving at, nor trying to learn by asking, and her stomach knotted up in fear.

"I was three when they disappeared. Monica remembers them a lot more than I do because she was older. I mainly remember Trevor raising me and I was just wondering how they seemed to you. My sister means well, but her memories are not…what is the word…objective."

Once again, Vectra churned with a guilt heavier than the Rocky Mountains. *I thought I was over this by now*, she muttered in her head. *Why does this bother me so much? It was one mistake and one that was not entirely my fault.* "They were kind. Catriona had tripped on the sidewalk that day, behind her booth, and your mother caught her before she face planted into the ground. Your father had a keen eye for an antique and almost planted himself into a fistfight with Mr. Malescho over the authenticity of a silver spittoon. Supposedly, it was from a hotel in Tombstone, of all places." Vectra chuckled. Then she did something she thought she would never do.

Leaning over to get closer to the boy, Vectra let him in on a little secret. Perhaps it was to make her feel better that a piece of the burden would be finally released, or maybe it was so he would be a tiny bit prepared for what he was bound to find out later on. She wasn't exactly sure why she felt compelled to tell him. "And I am going to let you in on a secret I have not told anyone else, Dare. Your parents managed to do something to me that not many have been able to do."

"What was that?" He asked, hesitantly curious.

"Scare me." She looked straight at the boy's tentative eyes. "They told me things about myself that no one should have known. That is when I discovered there had to be a traitor who was close to me, and I cut myself off from every-one."

Chapter Thirty-Six

The sun's unobstructed, and intense rays of light, bathed the landscape in a pure golden hue that made the orange changed leaves appear dipped in honey. Long shadows merged into one another over the grass, painted in yellow, upon the morning's canvas. Monica had never seen a sunrise so illuminating before as its arms extended far beyond the mountain ranges on either side of a massive tree, shielding her from becoming doused as well. "It's gorgeous." But even those two words seemed rather insufficient to describe the surrounding beauty. "The sunlight is so strongly rich, it's like a kiss from the heavens."

"You know, Monica…I have seen countless sunsets and sunrises. And the remarkable thing about them is that they are not ever the same. I am always impressed with their constant ability to take my breath away." Vectra finished off the eggs and bacon Rudi had cooked up for them as a rustling sound snapped her attention to where three maple trees stretched into the deep blue sky. Five deer slowly emerged from the woods to their left, slicing the light beams with their silhouettes and creating a dramatic entrance no one could script-write. "Nature is truly remarkable."

"And the campground is certainly filling up."

"Unfortunately." Vectra looked at the nearly full sites from people who trickled in over the night. Campers of all sizes, and age, populated the grounds with bouncy balls and Frisbees being tossed around in the joy of being outside. A kettle cooked popcorn pull-behind went by them, attached to a blue four-wheel drive pick-up truck. "Don't tell me it's that week!"

"It's what week?"

"The week for the Apple Festival." Rudi popped out of the door to hand an elf cookie to both of them. "It is the year's big event for this area. Vendors come in from neighboring towns for the weekend and camp here. The festival is held in the actual park across the main road."

Monica stepped into one of the few remaining unoccupied sites, number fifteen, in order to get a better view of the park through the branches. She could see where the cars were being directed onto a grassy field, and the two volunteers who were helping to direct the incoming traffic. "Wow. I can see a good portion of the land over there from here. How come so many of the trees are already losing their leaves?"

"It has been rather dry this year." Rudi explained before being summoned back to his desk by an irritated boss.

"Hey, guess what everyone!" Dare approached them in high spirits, a piece of paper crumpled in his hand. His hair was freshly washed from a shower and his skin felt pleasantly clean. "There is a festival going on this weekend. See." He showed them the poster he pulled off the bulletin board by the bathrooms. "Says that it is their annual apple festival that occurs every third weekend of October."

"Rudi was just telling us about it." Monica sighed. "More people."

"Could we go over there for some food?" Dare inquired. He patted his pocket where some dollar bills were crushed into a ball. "I found a few bucks on the ground by site nine, and no one was there."

"That isn't your money, Dare." Monica gave him a stern look of disapproval. "You should donate it to the ranger station for the park instead."

"But…"

"That is an excellent idea." Vectra agreed.

"An apple festival is going to have food. Delicious, sweet, and scrumptious fair foods. Like that menu at the amusement park." He offered his two traveling companions his best puppy dog eyes, willing them to give in.

"Since the trail we need is in that direction…I suppose a stop off at the food stands would not be too much of an inconvenience. However, as I was warning your sister, we need to keep a low profile among the crowd. The very instant we are beyond eyesight, I will show you how to transform your bikes so that we may reach Martiban's much faster than on foot." Vectra instructed, her face showing a hint of weariness in the lines at her lips. "I have a strange feeling about what is to happen."

"At the apple festival?" Monica did not care for the foreboding sound of Vectra's voice. It was filled with definite uncertainty and she had her fill of running into Taminus. "Or is it something else? You are psychic, aren't you?"

"I am no psychic. And I cannot be sure as to what the feeling means. Every now and then, I get this sense of a warning in the pit of my stomach. It would be far more helpful if I knew what it was telling me, but it is only a feeling." Vectra stood up without wincing for a change and motioned for the kids to grab their bikes. "We will say our goodbyes to Rudi and then be off. On the way to the festival, I will go over a crash course on how to use your Bi-Wheelers."

The Guardian pushed the camper door open to find herself awkwardly in the background of a video conference call with the North Pole. "So…*Vectra* is there. That would explain your aloofness." The other elf commented in dislike. "What does she want this time? Wait till Joy hears about this."

Rudi hastily clicked the pause button on his monitor and waited for the video to minimize out. "She did ask a very valid question. What am I am going to tell her?"

"Joy is your new boss? Did Cookie retire?"

"As a matter of fact…" Rudi's eyes flashed up to the ceiling. "He is in the camper next door snoozing off a five year dose of sleeping dream powder."

"What the…" Vectra saw the sheepish look on her friend's face and shook her head out of disbelief. "You did not! That is why you're being watched so closely."

"It was an accident. Candy opened a bag of her avocado-flavored peppermints right beside me and I sneezed something awful in the powder room. Instead of it landing on me, however, all the powder got shot up through the air vent and landed in Cookie's office."

"Are they going after Candy as well? She should have known better."

"Oh yeah. She got barn duty until Cookie wakes up." The elf glanced at his watch. "Which will be in another three more years." Rudi huffed as he saw Joy on the Caller ID of a red telephone on his desk. Despite the ring tone blasting a cheery rendition of *Jingle Bells* into the air, he was anything but cheery.

Vectra tapped the elf on the shoulder, drawing his attention to the newly made red tassel clipped onto her satchel's strap. "By the way, I said I owed you, remember." It hung down two inches and came with a small holly button sewed on, a charm in the shape of the letter 'R' swaying from the jump ring.

"Wow." Rudi was thoroughly astonished. His words were lost in the presence of the improbable scene taking place. "I never thought I would ever see the day you were indebted to me."

"Use it wisely." Vectra warned. "I do not take kindly to owing someone a favor."

"I hear you." Rudi responded with real care in his words as the monitor blazed to life once more.

"Vectra, are you ready?" Monica called into the camper. "More people are showing up for that festival."

"What is going on there Rudi? Hosting a whole party while you are scheduled to work, are you?" The head elf tapped her shoe against the straw floor of the reindeer stables. "I am in the middle of giving Taffy a yelling when I get interrupted by a pager for a 'so-called' urgent situation. So what could be sooo pressing…" Her nose flared like a rhino's as her face enlarged in the picture frame. "YOU!"

"I was just leaving Joy." Vectra smiled into the web camera. "By the way, it is nice to see that your acne has finally gone away. 357 years was the perfect number, huh?" Watching the now embarrassed elf smack her smartwatch off, a smirk appeared on the Guardian's mouth. "That should get her off your back for the time being."

"She hates it when anyone mentions her acne. How is your talking about it, on a speaker phone conversation, going to smooth things over between her and myself?" Rudi looked scared to return to his computer.

"Because, I told everyone that she was half her real age. She has always enjoyed a little flattery."

"How do you know her true age…never mind. You are

not about to tell me, even if you wanted to, and I am better off in the dark on that." Rudi wished them all the best and then slammed the door shut.

Chapter Thirty-Seven

"I hope they have apple cider donuts." Dare chimed. "They are my favorite." His mouth watered at mentioning the delectable, and very seasonal, treat he rarely ever got to enjoy.

"We can spare fifteen minutes and not a second more." Vectra maintained a stiff upper lip as she spoke, hoping that she could control her emotions upon seeing the old tavern and mill for the first time in decades. "If you want to donate the money you found, Dare, there should be a donation box inside the tavern."

After waiting for one of the rangers to give them the go ahead, the trio walked across the road and along the drive leading further into the park. The ranger station sat opposite the tavern and hosted a meager parking lot for such a large state park, though it did have a substantial number of bike racks. "Good thing we don't need to use the racks. They are jam-packed today." Monica moved to the side when a car came out of the lot. "No wonder they are having everyone park by the lake."

"There is also parking just through those trees." Vectra tilted her head in the direction of a single lane veering off the main drive. She stopped in front of a laminated map pasted onto an old A-frame sign, and pointed to the section labeled 'Food Vendors' by the Milky Way Stream. "Looks as though that is the place to be."

"Hey!" Dare excitedly stared at the old grist mill about two hundred feet from where they stood. "I see some food under a canopy over there." Before anyone else could respond, Monica felt herself being dragged over the curving pavement and stepping upon the stone path marking a trail. Vectra jogged to catch up, watching the other people milling about in their own worlds.

"I think these are only samples." Monica informed her brother. "See the sign they have on the table?" She showed him the laminated printer paper with the words TRY SOME SAMPLES FROM OUR GRIST MILL written in neat hand-writing. "I am surprised to see that the mill is still in oper-ation when it was built before the 1900s."

"Circa 1810, to be precise." Vectra said, transfixed upon the stone and wooden structure as she spoke. To the right, a large seventy-foot wheel spun under the power of water in order to turn the handcrafted gears inside the building. "It was restored in the 1970s by a man who was friends with the family who owned the land. They wished to preserve it and teach others about the traditional methods of creating food staples like flour and cornmeal."

"How do you know all of this?"

"You just need to read the pamphlets they hand out." Vectra brushed away a small tear forming in the corner of her eye, though the siblings were not convinced. "Here." She reached down to pick up two of the apple cider three-ounce cups and offered them to Monica and Dare.

"I'm good." The teen shook her head, holding her hands up to block Vectra from giving her the free sample. "I liked the cider we had at your ship, but I don't drink much of it."

"I can guarantee you that you have not tasted cider like this before."

"Why? Does it have alcohol in it?" Dare happily plucked one of the cups from the Guardian's fingers.

"No. It was made in an old apple press. They should still have one running in the mill if you wish to see it in action." Vectra forced the paper cup into Monica's hands. "You will not regret trying it."

Staring suspiciously at the brown liquid, resembling toffee in hue, Monica brought it up to her bottom lip in order to gently try it out. As the naturally sweet juice slid smoothly down her throat, her tongue picked up on the slight bitterness of the skin in a wonderful pairing. "Wow! You can literally taste the entire apple. Skin and all."

"Yep. The freshest you are going to find anywhere." Vectra called Dare over and escorted the kids to a short wooden bridge, which took them to where the food trucks were parked in a line. Just as the map had shown, the area was marked with picnic tables, trashcans, and a plethora of food options. "Stay close together and try to have a little fun. I will keep an eye out." The Guardian watched the Brownings weave their way through the crowds to see what each place had. Ten minutes later, they came back with a pulled pork sandwich, french fries, and a bottle of water.

"All set and ready to go." Dare announced, with a bag of desserts dangling from his wrist.

"I think it would be better for us to sit and eat what you have. Because once we hit the trail, it is not as though you are going to be able to drive and eat at the same time." Vectra chuckled at the boy's ferocious appetite. "You sure do rival any satyr I have ever known, and they have an enlarged stomach."

"Your world must be so much more interesting." Monica laid out the napkins for her brother on the table and dug into her own meal. "I mean, you certainly have stories that are more fantastical than anyone I have ever met."

"And just how many have you met?" Vectra smiled. "I once heard someone say that if everyone in the world wrote a memoir, few would be boring and even less considered more interesting than the others. See, the more people you meet and talk with, the more you realize that everyone has had bizarre things happen in their lives, and the most soft-spoken of sorts are often times the ones who have the most fascinating of tales to share."

"Like you." Dare said in-between mouthfuls. "You don't talk very much, stay secluded from practically *everyone*, and you have lived a pretty wonderful life."

Vectra smiled. "That is a viewpoint I have not considered in a long while. Thank-you, Derrick." Then her cheerful disposition left. "But it is also a naïve one. There are things about me that would alter your opinion, if you knew them."

"Like what?" Monica sipped down the rest of the lemonade and helped her brother clean up their mess.

"Nice try, Ms. Browning. But we should head into the woods again. Are you going to be alright? The trees will be pretty dense where we are going."

"I'll survive." Monica followed her brother by grabbing onto their bikes and walking along the path marked as Old Firefly Trail.

Chapter Thirty-Eight

"See the old railcar ahead?" Vectra continued to walk beside her bike as people wandered around to the various vendors. "The trail we need is just past it, on the left."

"Okay." Dare could barely be heard as he stuffed his mouth full of the apple cider donuts his sister bought for him. Like Vectra had warned, the simple task was proving to be a rather difficult feat when he also had a bike to balance at the same time. However, the boy didn't mind having a sticky handle grip. "Sounds kind of odd to have an old railcar in the middle of a gravel path, but a lot of this whole trip has been different, to say the least."

At the back, Monica silently observed the families chowing down at the picnic tables and thought about Trevor. She missed his smile, his laugh, and more importantly, his positon of responsibility. It was easier when it was up to someone else to make the tough decisions, and they were blessed with having a legal guardian they could rely upon. But their brother was mainly granted the role due to a promise he made the court of doing better in his own life in order to support his younger siblings. Trevor always had what others deemed a "stroke of bad luck" as his resume consisted of a long list of jobs that didn't work out and credit card debt equivalent to the price of a new car. Until three years ago, things had been looking up for their family and their rocky start was being left in the rearview mirror. *What are we going to do?*

Despite the fact that Vectra told Monica to forget about the police, the teen was finding it rather difficult in letting it go. Since Gaither had stepped back into her family's lives, the past seemed to be echoing itself again and she couldn't help but notice the similarities. It was right after Trevor went to work for Gaither that he became more secretive about his work, and his mood was becoming more volatile as time wore on. His temper grew shorter and he mumbled in his sleep at night about a bridge, the forest, and clearing his conscience. There was also the one Sunday afternoon, when her brother fell asleep on the coach and muttered an almost incoherent sentence about not wanting to find them anymore. The line spooked Monica so much so that day, that she barely slept a wink that same evening, and spent the hours staring blankly at the ceiling of her room. *I just have to believe that it will...*

"LOOK OUT!" A tall boy shouted as his out-of-control bicycle was leading him straight into Dare ahead of his sister. "WHOA!" The boy nearly flipped over his own handlebars just as Dare pulled his bike out of the way and watched the crash unfold before him.

"Are you alright?" Monica saw the tall boy's friends racing down the small slope to join them on the trail.

"I've been worse." The boy shook his head and brought a hand to the back of his skull.

"That sure wasn't fun."

"Yeah, Tommy should have had his bike fixed." A beefier kid stated, causing a number of their friends' heads to nod in agreement. "It wasn't nice for him to bring a busted bike to the festival. He knew the score."

"That's alright. We'll settle with him here shortly." The tall boy smirked at his gang. He was still shaking off the accident when he suddenly caught a glimpse of Dare's wheels.

"Whoa! Nice bike. Haven't seen one like that before. And my dad owns the local shop."

"It was a gift." Dare hesitantly replied and tried to push on through the group until they refused to let him leave.

"A gift you say?" The tall boy's gelled blonde hair was still just as good as it was before he fell, having not allowed a single hair to become out of place. "Well, that is mighty nice of you. Thanks. After you wrecked my old one." He motioned for his friends to surround Dare, deciding that he wanted to have the newer bike instead of the twisted pile near the trashcan.

"I didn't wreck it. You lost control." Dare took a stand as his sister stepped to the side and grabbed a pebble. She threw it at Vectra's back and breathed a sigh of relief when the woman turned around, seeing the developing threat. Within ten seconds, the Guardian was standing right behind the leader of the group.

"I suggest you boys might want to leave while you still can." She firmly ordered.

"Oh yeah? What's it matter to you?" The tall boy went to strike at Vectra, who was shorter than he was, until she stopped his arm cold, preventing him from finishing the blow. "Just wait until my dad hears about this!" He whined. "You'll be sorry!"

"HEY!" A burly man with a gruff voice, and dressed in motorcycle rider gear, approached the group. His steel eyes bore into Vectra as the muscles on his arms flexed. "Get your hands off my boy."

"Would I be correct in assuming that you are this boy's father?" Vectra politely asked.

"That would be a fair assessment." He growled. "Now, get your hands off my son!"

"Very well." Vectra released her grip from the boy. "Dare and Monica, we are leaving. But not until this man's son apologizes for trying to steal the bike."

"What?! I wasn't going to take his bike, Dad. Honest, I wasn't." The tall boy pouted.

"That's not true! He was going to steal it. Him and his hoodlum friends." Dare exclaimed.

"Are you calling my boy a liar?" The boy's agitated father glared at Dare, towering over him by a good four feet.

"You bet I am!" The ten year old stomped his foot on the ground. "He tried to steal my bike and that is the truth."

"WHY YOU…" The burly man was suddenly halted short by Vectra, as she put herself in-between the two.

"Sir, might I suggest that you and your son rejoin the festival as my nephew, niece, and myself, pass on through." She could sense the crowd quickly turning their attention onto the argument and wanted to diffuse the situation as soon as possible.

"Fine." His lips curled into a sinister smile. "That works for me."

Monica and Dare followed Vectra without a word. They glanced up at the boys and the tall one's father, wondering why the Guardian didn't do anything more to the bullies. She gently pushed them along the trail, refusing to look backward, and trying to keep her focus on the path in front.

"You should be grateful that I took it so easy on you, *Grandma!*" The man shouted after them. "Especially with the funny way you dress."

Vectra immediately stopped in her tracks, a smirk

materializing on her face. She turned back to see the gang of friends and the burly man laughing beside the crashed bicycle and handed Monica her Bi-Wheeler. "Hold this for me."

"You bet!" Monica shared a smile with her brother as they watched Vectra steam up her hands to a good 85 degrees Fahrenheit.

"Now, I know you did not mean that." She stated, testing the waters and giving them one last chance to back out.

"Oh…" A toothy grin spread wide under his large nose. "I meant every word."

"I was afraid of that." Vectra looked him directly in the eye. "Go ahead. Make good on your word and fight me."

"Huh?"

"Go ahead. Or are you yellow-bellied?"

"I don't make it a point to hit women." His jaw clenched. "But for you, I think I will make an exception." The burly man balled up his fist and went to strike. To his surprise, his hand landed right into Vectra's hot palms and nearly burned an impression into his skin. "OWWWW!"

"Dad! What's wrong?" The tall boy looked at his father in concern. "Hit her."

"The next time you aim, you will have more than just sores to remember *me* by." Vectra swished her hair over her shoulder and strutted up to Monica and Dare. Their faces showed their disappointment that she didn't blast the man in front of everyone. She retook her ride from the teen, and was about to continue onward, when Monica called out her name as a warning. In a flash, Vectra pulled a .54 caliber Elgin Pistol from a hidden scabbard in her vest coat. The burly man dug his heals into the gravel for a sudden stop, and looked down at the 11 inch attached Bowie Knife that was pointed uncomfortably against his stomach. "You want a bullet in your gut?"

"You….you are no Grandma I ever came across before." He stammered.

"That is because I am no ones' Grandma. And even if I were, I still would not put up with morons such as yourself. NOW BACK UP!" Vectra withdrew the knife as the man sheepishly slunk his way to the festival with the gang of boys in tow.

"What kind of weapon is that?" Monica asked. "And where can I get one?"

"Originally designed in the 1830s, this little terror is called a cutlass pistol. Gears did make a few adjustments, however."

"I bet he did." Dare's eyes lit up. "Where has that been this whole time?"

"I had it delivered with the Bi-Wheelers." Vectra re-hid the weapon before she glanced up to check the crowd once more. "Get on your bikes. NOW!"

Chapter Thirty-Nine

Dare and Monica also saw the two men dressed in black from head to toe, practically announcing to the world that they worked for Gaither. "But we don't know how to ride." The boy mounted with a scared look on his face.

"No time like the present." Vectra instructed them to get on as the men were heading in their direction. "We will have to transform these sooner than anticipated."

"How's that?" Monica held onto the handlebars with unease.

"The brake lever. Pull on it, keeping it down for three seconds. The bikes will change into Skelecarts."

Dare heard a whirling sound coming from the down tube as his bike extended outward in all directions, boxing him into the protective bone work of a traditional four-wheeler. The fork grew longer and the wheels split into two on the front and back. An invisible wind shield formed above the handlebars, being seen only in the small glare of the projected speedometer and navigating compass in the left corner. "This is so awesome! It's like being in a real life video game."

"Punch it!" Vectra called out, pushing down on the

pedal with her right foot to start up the machine. Monica and Dare did likewise to catch up to her, unsure on how to steer it. "Push on the left pedal to decelerate and on the right to increase speed."

"And what about the brakes? Or turning?"

"Simply turn the handlebars in the direction you want to go. As for the brakes, pedal backwards to initiate them." Vectra sped off into the woods, undeterred by any of the trees, rocks, or fallen logs. She soon left them in the wake of her smoke and slowed down to wait for them just over the crest of the hill.

"Don't leave us like that!" Monica demanded.

"I would have come looking for you if you had not arrived." Vectra checked the sky. "We should be able to make it to Martiban's within two hours if we can steer clear of Gaither and his hoard."

"How did they follow us here? They can't be using our cellphones to track us anymore." Monica thought back to when they stayed with the Christmas elf. "Rudi did make a phone call off the clock, when we were all around the campfire."

"That could have been for any number of reasons." Vectra cautioned. "Taminus is working with Gaither, remember? He could have tracked us down from tailing the shipment Gears sent me."

"How much of that theory do you actually believe?" Monica countered, studying Vectra's non-response. "But you are right in the sense that I don't have a lot of proof either way. Still, don't you think it is worth it for us to try and figure out how they keep finding us?"

"Logically speaking, yes. Unfortunately, if we do not end up discovering how they are tracking us, then we will have wasted any chance of getting that much further ahead and be caught like sitting ducks. No, we should continue onto Martiban's camp and go from there."

"Great! Which way is he?" Dare positioned himself better atop the saddle.

"Due West…and then swing a right when you come to Clucky's Chicken Stand."

Chapter Forty

"There! See the floating lanterns?" Vectra pointed to the two cast iron lights suspended in the air, unmoving and unattached to anything. "Enter in the space between, and nowhere else. There is a protective field set up that is immune to animals, but deadly for humans."

"Thanks for the tip." Dare drove through first, followed by his sister and Vectra bringing up the rear. As soon as they all passed the barrier, the Guardian told them to tap on their brake levers twice and the Skelecarts reverted back into their Bi-Wheeler forms. "Do we get to keep these?"

"Depends." Vectra cautiously walked between two boulders, making sure to stay on the trail identified with yellow squares painted on the tree trunks. "We are going to have to make the rest of the journey on foot."

"Again?" Monica was growing tiresome of having to leave their perfectly fine modes of transportation behind and then wishing they had them later. "What if we need a quick getaway?"

"Martiban usually has traps set out in various intervals and it will be too cumbersome to get through the maze with these at our sides. That is why we entered from the south.

272

It is the only way to reach him without getting blown up."

"Then how does he walk around?" Dare asked.

"He has the locations memorized."

"Why is it so hard to reach anyone you know?" Monica complained. "Isn't there just one person, or creature, you are friends with that doesn't have a series of dangerous obstacles to protect them from outsiders?"

"If they did not have some kind of protection activated, I would not wish to be their friend."

"Because it would be easy to visit?"

"No. It means that they are probably working for the wrong side of the fight. That, or worse still…they are for neither." Vectra waved the kids over to where an old bear trap was decomposing. "We can stow the bikes in there."

The seven foot deep and four foot high structure had been handcrafted with the trunks of medium round trees, and a top was created using the method of a log cabin. A cross section above the ceiling was broken from past violent storms, and the sliding door was being consumed by vegetation after being discarded by a hunter years before. "Mind your heads." Vectra pulled a number of branches and dried vines from the surrounding area to cover up the opening and the shining metal of the Bi-Wheelers. "That should keep them hidden from prying eyes."

"When we reach Martiban, will the press be with him?" Monica observed where Vectra was walking and made sure to stay within the same spots.

"No. He only has the key. The press is housed in a place well-guarded from treasure seekers such as Gaither and your brother."

"Trevor is not a part of any of this!" Monica defended. "He was kidnapped and is being held hostage."

"That is what you claim. But try to see it from an outsider's standpoint. It was *his* phone that was being used to track *our* movements."

"Simple explanation. His phone was taken and he was forced to give them his passcode."

"Alright. But tell me this then." Vectra spun on her heels to face the siblings. "Can you not think of *any* reason he might be helping Gaither, and not being held as the victim you say he is? The kidnapping could have been staged."

"Trevor wouldn't do that. He is…" Monica took a pause to think about it. *Still in credit card debt, and his attitude has been different as of late. No, no! What am I doing? I can't possibly be considering this!*

"Well?"

"Our brother would not be in this. Not for greed; If that is what you are implying." Dare stood beside his sister. "Tell her, A!"

Monica glanced at him. "I don't think so, but…she has a point."

"WHAT?!"

"Dare, admit it. Trevor has been moodier recently, mumbling in his sleep, and fighting with himself at times. And he still has a lot of credit card debt."

"Sounds like weak evidence to me."

"But Trevor would be helping them if he believed that it was for a good cause. Gaither might be tricking him by making him think that finding this press would do good in the world. Or if it meant a better life for us. Like when he used to tell us that he was saving up to take us on a world-wide adventure."

Dare didn't sound convinced. "If that is true, then wouldn't the whole 'being snatched up from the sidewalk' thing have proved to him otherwise?"

"Maybe that's why they are after us…for leverage."

"No offense, Monica, but I have a feeling that they are after the journal more than us. Didn't you say it contains a map to the location?" The boy looked over at Vectra.

"Yes. It does."

He tilted his head at his sister. "See. That's why we needed it. For the same reason that they do."

"Which brings me to my next question I have been meaning to ask." Monica folded her hands across her chest. "Why do you *need* the map?" She raised her eyebrows at the Guardian.

"To ensure that no one else had it."

"I'm not buying that." The teenager held her stance. "What is the REAL reason? If you were the one who hid the press, like you claim, then you shouldn't need a map."

Vectra sighed into the cooling air. It was rather embarrassing, what she was about to say, and it took her a lot of courage to own up to it; especially to a fourteen-year-old teenager. "I don't remember certain things about getting there."

"Okay…it's normal to forget. Everyone does that. Why was that so hard to say?"

"Because of why I forgot."

"Go on."

"I brewed up a batch of herbal tea, using *Myosotis Scorpioides*, also known as Forget-Me-Nots or scorpion grass. When the flowers are spun in a counter-clockwise motion, during the steeping process, it unlocks their power to do the opposite of their name-sake. I participated in the drink… just a sip mind you…knowing that my friend would not drink from his cup if I did not from mine. It was meant to wipe his memory clean of helping me to hide the press. But instead, I created the drink with a higher potency than I realized."

"So you erased your own memory?"

"Accidentally. Till this day I do not recall certain things about the place, nor the final step needed to open the room." Her eyes came back to the present after they drifted into a half-remembered moment of time. "Now, are we going to get moving or are we going to keep chatting?" Vectra continued to pass pine trees, old dirt lanes, and a patch of winterberry bushes enjoying the bank of the nearby stream. For more than thirty minutes, only the sounds of the few strangler birds echoed throughout the woods as they walked over the crunchy leaves coating the ground. All directions mirrored the others, in an endless sea of wild lands.

"So what do you think your cousin wants with the press?" Dare asked. "To have your job or to be King of the World?" The boy puffed out his chest and mimicked a mocking bow while pretending to swing an invisible cape behind him.

"Maybe, King Dare. But only he knows what he is truly after. However, there are a few rules to using the press. One cannot simply just stroll in and use it. For starters, that would be highly irresponsible of Clio, the goddess in charge of records and historical accounts. If that was true, havoc would have ensued long ago."

"We are talking about the same gods and goddesses who left all-powerful artifacts behind on Earth to begin with." Dare stated. "That was not very responsible in my opinion."

Vectra held her hands up in surrender. "I do not know everything. No matter how long a person lives, they see with their own eyes only fractions of the entire world at a single time." Returning her gaze to the tree branches overhead, the Guardian searched for old fashioned triangle snares to see if they were getting close.

Monica looked up at the sun sinking lower in the sky.

"So what are the rules?"

"Well, Clio could not be there all the time to record every daily event, so she enlisted a band of helpers. The first journalists with a running newspaper and demanding editor, you might say. So to make certain that everything ran smoothly, she had Hephaestus forge a placard to instill the guidelines into an unbreakable bond.

First, you must have the right materials. Only parchment and animal skin made by the gods, from the sheep of Pan's fields, is to be used on the press. This is for the proper storing of the records; as the ink takes a full year to become permanent from the moment it is created. During the curing time, two changes may be made upon the record. After the year is done, it cannot be altered.

Second, the person to operate the device can only be one of Clio's blood or an oath-bound helper. Since her helpers have all perished long ago, being a relative is the remaining must.

Third, the press follows one timeline. That of old and of Greek making. One that few of your world attempt to understand.

And lastly, if something from the past need be rectified, literally rewriting history, it cannot have happened in the same calendar year. One parchment will be enough to right the deed.

But I must heed a word of caution with this tale, for the operator of the press will be the ONE and ONLY person to remember how things were, and what has changed."

Monica's brows arched inward, skeptical. "One parchment? That doesn't seem like it can literally change history with a single page."

"Oh, no? Life is so interconnected, we barely see it sometimes. How one decision affects the dominos falling during the day. Can you not think of one event, that if altered, could set your life on a whole new course? A page is dangerous enough, and provides ample trouble when used incorrectly. The press takes things literally, and does not do well with the ambiguous interpretations of words. It must be told precisely what to alter. Otherwise, things may go very differently than planned." Vectra looked behind to see a twinkle in the teen's eye light up brighter than a star. She had an inkling as to what the girl would want to make right again, should the opportunity present itself.

"Does that mean…" Dare silenced himself as his sister shushed him with her hand tapping against his arm.

"Yes. The records could be altered so your parents would never come to see me. They could be stopped from leaving you that day altogether." Vectra wondered what false images were running through the young girl's mind; images of how life could have been versus what was, she supposed. *Will she see the entire picture, though?*

"If this press really does all this, why did you not use it to change your past?" Monica curiously asked.

"I am not allowed. Besides, there are far more implications than one realizes when meddling with the past. I knew a thief, once, who was fixated on the press, and…" She stopped in mid-sentence, staring at a patch of overgrown fallen timber in alarm. "What was that?"

Dare and Monica quieted down, searching the rocky terrain with their own eyes. "We didn't hear anything."

"I know I…" Suddenly, a large grey wolf lunged at Vectra with his front claws extended. She barely dodged out of the way in time, feeling the animal's fur brush against her skin. Glancing upward, she was relieved to find the sign she had been waiting for. "RUN! Head for the snare."

Monica and Dare didn't have to be told twice. Both kids

saw the triangular bird trap hanging in the branches, once Vectra pointed it out to them. The Guardian kept the wolf busy, as the siblings raced over the uneven ground until Monica tripped on a twisted root and fell, crying out to her brother for help. When she looked up, the teen couldn't be sure she was seeing things right. "Derrick, am I hallucinating?"

Her brother shook his head, as he took her hand, and hauled her up from the forest floor. "Nope."

They glanced around at the ruins of a castle scattered on nearly 2,000 square feet. Foundation stones were left to rot in haphazard locations, making it dangerous to walk mindlessly about without paying attention to where they were stepping. "Come on!" Dare led his sister down the incline and towards a fire pit encircled by mounds of dirt, compacted against rounded stone walls.

"Great! We're cornered!" Monica frantically glanced up at the smoothed rim, hearing the wolf's snarl reverberating all around. Vectra jumped in after them, holding her cutlass pistol out at the ready, just as someone whistled into the air. The wolf suddenly backed off, obeying the call of the disembodied voice, and gently walked down to the pit.

"What just happened?" Monica whispered. She looked into the fire's orange flames and observed the blue hue among the coals. *It's been burning for some time.*

"Would be like thee to arrive unannounced." A deeper voice came from the entrance of the only surviving structure to their right. It was no larger than a shack, with masonry walls, an open slit on each side, and a sturdy ceiling used for hunting.

"Neither do you." Vectra yelled back. Monica stared into the darkened rectangular hole and watched a man in his late thirties step into the light. He had a beard that reached past his chest and wore clothing more appropriate for a peasant from the times of King Arthur as opposed to someone from the twenty first-century. Chestnut brown was the color of his hair and his bushy eyebrows distracted from his golden irises.

"Doth only comes when it pertains to that which…"

"Martiban, these kids are with me. You can lay off the medieval act."

"As you wish." The hunter's smile was obscured by his mustache. "It appears that you met Winter."

"Yeah," Vectra swallowed and retracted her blade. "Bit of a temper on him." She motioned to the untrimmed hair adorning the man's face. "You don't normally look this rough, Martiban."

"Ah, Vectra. You always were a charmer." The man limped to the fire with a de-feathered goose inserted on a rod and placed it above the heat of the flames.

"What happened to your leg?" Vectra held a note of genuine concern in her voice.

"This? Been like that for ages. A puma escaped from one of my traps and made sure to leave her mark." He cleared his throat. "So, what brings you to my neck of the woods?"

"I need the key."

Chapter Forty-One

Martiban's eyes gave her a sideways glance as he continued to turn his dinner on the rod.

"Do you still have it?"

"Who are they?" He asked, gesturing to the kids.

"Monica and Derrick Browning. They are with me because a man named Gaither stole their older brother and is using him to locate Clio's press."

"Clever story."

"Hey!" Monica leaned forward. "It's no story. We saw it happen with our own eyes."

"Sure you did. Classic cover if I ever heard one."

Vectra pushed Monica back from answering in an attempt to keep the situation neutral. "Martiban, do you have the key?"

"Of course I have it." He retorted. "But are you sure you can trust these kids? It could be a trap. Just like what happened in Würzberg."

Dare did not care for the way the man was accusing them of trickery. "Excuse me! But how do we know that you are on our side?"

"They are *Brownings*, Martiban, not *Brauwnings*."

Vectra vouched for them, recalling a tiff between a family of the later surname and her friend, back in the 1700s. But the man's eyes narrowed in on her.

"You are a fine one to be saying that. You, of all people, know that last names mean little in the verification of character judgement."

"I don't understand this, Martiban. What has gotten into you?" Vectra stood up when he refused to answer her question. "Now, I demand to have the key."

The outdoorsman threw a pair of charred fish to Winter before proceeding to return to his shack and riffle through a box of clutter underneath his bed. He soon reappeared with a wooden piece in the shape of an "L" with a hole drilled where a connector joint should have been. Monica couldn't help but feel as though it looked slightly familiar, however, she couldn't place where she had seen it before, if at all. It was a plain piece of wood that almost resembled a fat boomerang when viewed from a certain angle.

"That is one weird looking key." The boy observed.

"That is because it goes to an old instrument that not many people know about in your world anymore." Martiban handed it to Vectra and stoked the fire with a long, thick branch.

The Guardian was vexed. "I never told you what it was for. How did you figure it out?"

"There is something called the 'internet' nowadays, Vectra. You should give it a try. Libraries even have it for patrons to use for free." Martiban ran his fingers through his beard and grabbed ahold of a rifle that was hidden behind a log he was utilizing as a seat. "If you three wouldn't mind watching my dinner, to ensure it does not become as burnt as Winter's, I have three traps to check on before night falls."

Vectra gave the key to Dare for safekeeping and brought

her teapot out from her satchel as Martiban dashed into his shack for something he forgot. She held the pot in the fading light of day and smiled as the portrait of a man resurfaced in her mind upon opening it. He was tall and commanding, with an unruly beard and pale blue eyes like the ocean. An eagle's talon was strung around his neck as a memento of his first brave dare, a feat he enjoyed over-telling everyone he knew. In her opinion, only a handful of people ever came close to emulating a sliver of his same character. And the shame that once consumed her, hundreds of years ago, filled her regretful heart with a fresh pang of unrelenting guilt.

Her eyes fell to the ground, wondering if it was truly possible for the kettle to be used for anything other than its original, and deceptive, purpose. "Would you two care for some tea?" The image of the man faded away with a single tear she calmly brushed from her cheek. After all the sadness staining the pot's history, it was time for a change. "Since you both appeared to have enjoyed the Dragonwell, I picked up another bag from Catriona before we left. It is not of the same grade, but should be rather delicious none-theless."

"Ah, sure." Monica replaced the drink maker she had pulled out seconds before, curious as to what was so special about the ancient pot Catriona disliked so much. The out-side appeared normal, except for the two handles it notice-ably sported. "Must be a pretty special teapot."

"This is actually a kettle. However, because it is made from cast iron, it can be used as both a teapot and a tea kettle." Vectra poured a pitcher of water into the pot and hooked it onto the stand over the flames, where the bird was slowly cooking. "A soothing, warm drink does good to steady the mind and keep the chill at bay." She nodded to Martiban, who was making his way into the woods as he called Winter to join him.

"I just like to feel the heat in my hands." Monica straightened up her back against the wooden logs behind her, holding her palms out to the pulsating fire in front. She had a number of things swirling around in her head, unsure what to think, do, and say about them.

"You do not need to feebly try concealing your thoughts from me. What is on your mind?"

"How did you bring that ship up from its watery grave in the Bermuda Triangle?" Monica asked.

"Deflecting the question I see."

"You didn't answer mine either."

"That is because the ship is none of your business."

"Fine. Then what happened to the thief? The one from the story you were telling us on the way here."

"The thief was killed." Vectra shifted her boots in the soil surrounding the pit. She locked eyes with Monica and Dare, biting down on her bottom lip for a second. "Promise me one thing…"

The water suddenly almost boiled over, prompting Vectra to insert a custom-made mesh cone into the kettle that was already filled with the tea leaves from a bag written on in Catriona's hand. She pulled out her pocket watch and clicked on a timer for roughly two and a half minutes, not wanting to steep the leaves for too long.

"Promise what?" Dare inquired.

"Never mind. Forget that I even mentioned it. There is no reason for us to have to worry." The Guardian shielded herself behind another tale of an adventure in Africa, fully aware that the kids weren't fooled. It wasn't until she was finished with the story that Dare brought up something unusual about the teapot, diverting the conversation yet again.

"What are those holes on the shorter handle?"

"It is called an assassin's teapot. These two holes are actually separate chambers where the tea gets poured into. Cover the first hole to have the first chamber pour out. To have the second chamber flow instead, cover the second hole. If you wish for them to be combined, then you can pour without covering either of the holes."

"And if you cover both of them?"

"Then nothing will pour out."

"So if you used this pot when you served Bregit, then how was your memory affected?" Monica asked.

"Bregit poured." Vectra filled an aluminum camping cup for each one of them, which came from their bags Gears had thoughtfully packed. "So, how did your brother come to work for Gaither?"

"Not sure exactly. It just happened one day, after he got fired from *another* job. This time it was because he was late three days in a row due to the car having issues, Dare being sick, and the pipes bursting in the basement. His boss let him go the following day. And then…in walked Gaither's job offer. Trevor accepted it immediately, but I think it had more to do with the incoming plumber's bill than what it actually entailed."

"So what is his position?"

"Janitor. Or so he claimed. But that is when he started becoming secretive about work and brought home various sketches in his attaché case. He didn't talk about them, and didn't show us anything." Monica turned her phone on to show Vectra a picture of her brother. With his square-rimmed glasses, short brown hair, and closely trimmed beard, he looked like a young college professor to the Guardian.

"I guess I could see him with an attaché case. But he

reads more like a messenger bag guy to me."

"It was his father's. It was the only thing he really wanted of his." The teen felt the vibrations of all the incoming notifications she missed over the past several days in her hand. Texts from classmates, social media dings, suggestions of movies to watch, and food coupons from various fast food apps all flooded in, one after another. She placed it on the ground to let it finish catching up. *My tracking isn't on, so we should be fine.*

"His father?"

"Trevor is our half-brother. His father died in a car accident when he was five. And Dare is…"

"Adopted." The boy stated. "I'm sure she could tell that by now. I mean, it is not as though we look anything alike."

"I had my suspicions." Vectra showed him a playful smile. "Still, he sounds like a nice brother."

"Which is why even *remotely* considering the idea that he has any hand in this, is absurd." Monica hit the side button of her phone to put it to sleep.

"But…" Vectra sensed that the teen wasn't finished with what she was saying.

"When you asked me to step back from the situation, to view it from an outsider's standpoint, there was something that has been bothering me." Monica paused to take another sip of the tea. "Trevor has been in credit card debt for some time now. He is slowly working it off, but there is a chunk he owes still. And the mumblings in his sleep…they have been really weird with what I think are references to our parents' disappearing."

"Is that it?"

"Well, the really interesting bit is the timing of all of this." Monica looked up from her cup. "Because Trevor was taken two days after our parents were legally declared dead."

"That's not all." Dare chimed in as he was sipping on his tea. "When the plumber came, he told Trevor that the pipes had been tampered with."

"Wait, he did?" Monica didn't remember hearing about that.

"Yep. I think you were outside trying to wring out wet towels when he said it. And the car issue also had a little human help as well."

"Sounds as though Gaither wanted your brother to get fired." A lightbulb went off in Vectra's head. "Can your phone see where Trevor is, just like they used it to track us?"

"I don't know if he has his GPS settings on for that." Monica continued to cradle the cup in her hand and glanced down at her phone, noticing a text from an unrecognized number as they continued to pour in. "You thinking of looking up his location to see where they are?"

"It would be a way to flip the tables on them if we could." Vectra was about to say something else when she saw Monica's focus trained in on her phone instead of what they were talking about. "What's wrong?"

"Here." The girl showed her the screen with a message in a green bubble. "I just saw this, but who knows how long ago it was sent."

Vectra read it aloud so that Dare was also clued in on the message. "To Monica and Dare, if you want to see your brother again, hand over the book at the Clucky's Chicken Stand and come with us quietly. Alert the police…and you can figure the rest out. Oh, and shall we discuss the key?"

"It couldn't have been that long ago. Perhaps those two at the festival told him where we were going?" Dare suggested.

"Something is not computing correctly." Vectra gave the phone back, shaking her head.

"Is there anything else you can tell us about the press?" Monica couldn't help but inquire, if not to satisfy her own curiosity; as she wanted to be a little more prepared to face Gaither when the moment came.

Staring into the girl's pupils, filled with the reflection of the fire, Vectra had an uncertainty beginning to grow in her gut. It was a risk she did not decide lightly to take on, thinking back to what Catriona and Gregon had told her. "Well…there is one more part to the press that I have not told anyone." Vectra leaned in closer to the fire, checking on Martiban's dinner, to buy herself one more moment to think on what she was about to do. "I told you that the press creates records of history, which needs to work on a timeline, a calendar. But much like your modern calendar, which the world now uses, the Ancient Greeks used a system of months and years to keep records by. However, instead of a more uniformed system, each Greek state had their own calendar that went by the phases of the moon and their festivals."

"Which calendar does the press operate by?" A shiver tickled Monica's spine as another thought scratched at her brain. "May I see that key again?"

Dare handed it over to his sister, who studied its odd shape. The teen's eyes widened when she realized that she had seen it before. Her memory flipped through files of long lost images in the deepest bins of her mind. "I've seen this somewhere else. It is a key you play, like on a piano. Isn't it?"

"How do you know that?" Vectra pressed.

"I saw it, briefly, as part of an old schematic of an instrument that looked like an organ, on a parchment Trevor had in his case. When he saw me looking at it, he pushed me out of the way and stashed it from my view."

"No…no…something is really wrong." Vectra's eyes

jumped from left to right and back again. "This cannot be right. The only people who know about it are…"

"What's wrong?" Dare anxiously looked at her, though she ignored his question.

"Even if they returned to the same spot, there is no reason for them to know about…" Her words faded out as she realized that the kids were focused on what she was muttering, though they seemed confused by her spurts of gibberish.

"If they made it where again?" Monica's intuition was that Vectra knew a lot more about the whole thing than she was sharing. And for no particular reason that she could explain, the teenager had the feeling that part of it dealt with what happened to her parents.

"Gaither has knowledge of things he should not. Things that are too impossible to …But…" Vectra suddenly looked up at the fading sun, wondering where her hunting friend had gone. "Martiban should have been back by now." Her shoulders stiffened at the sound of a fox barking at another critter and she slowly stood up, gently resting her teacup on the ground, untouched. "Be prepared to run."

"I'm tired of being chased." Monica whispered. "I'm tired of being shot at and running for our lives." *We came here to find Trevor, and instead, we have been jerked around the forest for almost a week now.*

"A," Dare placed his hand on his sister's wrist. "We're going to be okay."

Monica cleared her throat at the sound of approaching footsteps in the crunching of the leaves. Her heart anxiously sped up in anticipation of having to bolt into the darkening trees in the low light of dusk; waiting for the person to be Taminus, the police, Gaither, or his men. She shoved herself into the wall behind her, gripping tightly onto the cup with one hand, and wrapping her other arm protectively around her younger brother.

Then, Vectra sighed with relief when she saw the person coming closer. "It's just Martiban."

"Who were you expecting? Santa Claus?" His salty words sliced the night air whilst pulling three raccoon skins into his hut.

"Taminus, or worse, as a matter of fact." Monica released her brother and they both retook their seats hesitantly.

"Not sure he would like to hear that you fear something more than himself." The hunter caught a glimpse of the tea kettle as he stomped over for his cooked dinner, now a nice, golden brown with juices dripping into the flames below. "Some things never change."

"What does that mean?" Monica asked, seeing Vectra's hardening eyes.

"Nothing. He is jumping to conclusions that are not there." She hastily warned.

"Let me ask you something, kids." Martiban checked on the bird, got up to grab himself a plate from inside the shack, and leaned against the threshold for a second. "How are you enjoying your tea?" He picked up a fresh towel and wiped his hands clean at the water bowl.

"It was very good. Why?" Dare stared into his cup that was nearly empty.

"Let me explain one fact that is true in the Olde Realm. Everyone is out for themselves in one angle or another. And a cheetah's spots do not change easily." He gestured at their drinks. "If you find yourself spilling your most darkened secrets and feelings, you might want to lay off of the honesty syrup in your tea. At least, that is what Vectra most likely used, based on past experiences." The kids immediately swung around to see what the Guardian had to say for herself.

"No, I did no such thing." Vectra stated. "Trust me, Monica, I did not do that."

"Did you happen to stop by Servius's shop before you left Nectar Hill?" Martiban rejoined them by the fire. He didn't have to hear the answer, as their faces already did that for him. "Sounds pretty conclusive to me."

"I did not put anything in the tea."

"Would not take much, since she is so good at it. A natural, actually. Sleight of hand would be all that was required."

"I did no such thing. Look, I even showed you how this teapot works, and then poured from it. Would I reveal its secret before using it in that manner? Why would I show the cards like that?" Vectra didn't understand what Martiban was doing, but she didn't care for it in the least. He had never been so hostile against her and his behavior unsettled her nerves. *I wonder if he finally found out after all this time.*

"Fine. Then check her bag and prove me wrong." Martiban challenged, going straight for her satchel as Vectra stopped him from touching more than the strap. "I rest my case."

She looked pleadingly at the kids. "Alright, there is a bottle of honesty extract in my bag, but I did not use it on you. I swear." Just then, a sound crunched nearby and a few twigs snapped in half from a forceful weight. "Where is Winter?"

"Right here." Gaither rounded the corner of Martiban's shack, smirking at the group whilst his men fanned out from his sides. One of his henchmen stepped forth with a large cage and an angry wolf growling through the bars.

Monica and Dare went to make a run for it, but they didn't get far when they heard the sound of guns being trained on them from the far side of the fire pit. Gaither clicked his tongue against the roof of this mouth. "I wouldn't try to escape if I were you."

"I presume that you must be Gaither." Vectra's hand gripped onto her other wrist in front of her vest jacket, her fingers stealthily locating the hidden pocket where the cutlass pistol was stored. With the sun setting behind the shorter man, the strong backlighting almost made his features hard to see. His nose was smaller than normal and his chin sported a goatee that was colored darker than the fading hair on his head. He was dressed like an old British soldier, had military-grade boots on his feet, and really captured the persona of a crazed millionaire.

"Correct, my dear lady." Gaither's perfect teeth glistened. "It was fairly easy to capture you, I must say. Taminus made it seem as though you would be as difficult as the wind to snare, but yet, here we are. Considering how much of an admirer of yours I am, this is a great honor to finally meet you face to face." He strode further out from the building with a joy in each step. "We are going to have some catching up to do, I'm sure."

"How did you get past all the traps?" Vectra eyed Martiban suspiciously; who had an equally surprised look on his face.

"Followed up from the south entrance, of course. How else? With the rocky climb over that hill, there was no other way." Gaither quickly ordered one of his men to extinguish the campfire. "We must be diligent with you, I'm afraid. And that includes you too, Martiban. It would be in your best interest if you were to turn off your booby traps so we can exit a little more safely than the way in."

"What are you going to do to my wolf?" Martiban spit through clenched teeth as he tapped on a remote in his pocket.

"Nothing. That is, unless you resist being taken as my prisoners."

"With such an offer, how can we refuse?" Vectra shot Martiban a quick look with her eyes and they both responded in unison. It was the same code phrase they used in Italy when they worked together to save a valuable painting, and she was glad he remembered after ninety-five years.

Monica and Dare instinctively went to the ground to dodge out of the way as Vectra flicked decks of playing cards all over the place and lit them instantly ablaze. A swirling tube of fire ringed itself around them in a shield of sorts as Martiban unloaded a number of rounds into the orange wall. Dare was confused as to why there were no bullets being returned at them, but he didn't care; the lesser the number of flying bullets, the greater the chance of not getting struck by one.

"Take the P.I.!" Vectra tossed an old fashioned compass Monica's way, along with the electrio blade. "It's a person identifier. Use it to find Ailsing. She will help you. Go due North until you see an iridescent birch tree. When you do, press down on the dial's center and it will scan the ground for any footprints within the last forty-eight hours. Once it has locked in on her signature, it will point you in the direction of where you need to go. They must not get the book."

"Got it!" Monica and Dare fled deeper into the trees. A sinking feeling was taking her gut for a horrible ride as she sensed that Vectra would not be meeting up with them later this time. It tore her heart, seeing the Guardian fighting them off as the siblings ran. This should have been the action of a coward by all appearances. But it was, in truth, protecting the very item their pursuers so desperately wanted.

While an escape, unnoticed, would have been ideal, the Brownings were not that fortunate. Gaither's men spotted them just as soon as they rushed past the fiery wall Vectra parted for their exit, stage left. She shouted for the siblings to keep going before planting her feet down and launching herself up from the fire pit. Martiban followed, revealing a retractable spear that was disguised as a small pocket knife. It grew out to nearly fifteen feet in length and came in handy for defending himself against a sword or two.

The bullets sailed right through both of their bodies, as Vectra flicked her leather armguard open and rushed after the kids. She forged a six of hearts into a hard, metal shield and hung it across her back to stop the bullets from possibly hitting one of the Brownings. As she kept pace, Vectra tossed out a whole bunch of small gears on either side, and came to a dead halt in her tracks when she was down to the last one, stuck inside the shallow compartment.

She watched the men advance closer and closer, until they reached the small clearing Monica and Dare had already passed. Vectra waited until they were almost upon her and then gave a determined twist of the remaining gear. A light blinked red in the middle of the bronze object, and a signal was sent out to all its friends recently scattered along the forest floor.

Miniature owl wings sprouted from the gears, rapidly lifting them into the air and propelling them toward Gaither's private army. Like a swarm of locus, they flew straight into their faces and encircled them, picking out their specific targets. The lights changed from red to green, signifying the start of the game as the men ran in all directions to escape the annoying "bugs." Two of them ran for Vectra, guns pointed at her head with their fingers on the triggers. Unflinching, the guardian stood completely still, a smirk spread across her lips. Within seconds, two flying gears released bronze infused nets overtop their chosen targets. They scooped them up before a single bullet could be fired from the chambers and carried their prisoners far past the canopy of the trees.

Vectra could not suppress a few giggles of laughter from seeing the men struggle against the nets, only to be electrically shocked the more they fought back. *I will have to remember to give my report to Gears on how effective his Bounty-Winged Gears are,* she told herself before jumping into the battle once more. Martiban was forced back to where Vectra was disarming a man with a cattle prod-like weapon, and together, they fought side by side like old times. For a short spell, it felt great to be duking it out with the old knight again, and then it all went horribly wrong.

"AAAAAHHHH!" Vectra shrieked into the sky as something cold and hard touched her back. Her hands each flipped a card out to attack, but before she could throw them, they fell to the ground and shriveled into discarded paper balls. She could feel her strength being drained from her unlike anything she had ever known. Martiban glanced over, giving just enough time for one of Gaither's men to hit him on the neck and stun him to the ground. A large man grabbed ahold of Vectra's wrists without any resistance, as she was too weak to counter-attack, and patiently waited for the other henchman to snap on a pair of dazzling handcuffs.

"To be honest, if I can be honest with you, I really didn't know if that was going to work or not. But Taminus did come through after all." Gaither gracefully stepped up to where Martiban and Vectra were being forced to their knees. He tilted his head, studying her paling skin tone and tapped his finger to his lips. "He said it would react just like a suction cup, which apparently is a century's old idea. Rather than sucking water, however, it drains out your power. I just sucked over half of your powers away. How do you feel?"

"What is this?" Vectra had knowledge of only one thing that could immobilize her to such an extent. And the location of that item was sealed solely in her mind.

"The property of the thief, thus stolen from the place of ownership, shall be the downfall of his children and curse them forever more." Gaither held out his hand to show her a large leather-bound book with golden edged pages. He thumbed through the text with a mischievous grin, soaking in the moment of victory. "And this shall be true for one that protects thirteen items of Greek culture from kings and peasants alike. Her soul damned to eternity for a sin committed in the stars above. With a servant for a mother and a thief for a father, only silver can slow her trickery."

Vectra's fear enlarged her eyes and froze her heart. To hear those weighted lines of judgement being spoken again was a punch in the gut, cutting off her airways and stunning her beyond belief. Words failed to describe the anger and retribution she felt coursing through her veins. She was hungry to get even and even more determined to wreak havoc upon the traitor. "That is not a true translation." *They must have melted it down and coated these handcuffs in it. But how did they find it?*

"Well, I had it modernized. Never have been fond for older English texts. Wrapping wording around in a confusing manner and all. One should get to the point and be succinct." Gaither's evil smile made Vectra want to vomit. "Take them back to camp."

"Boss, Tom and Ergon are still going after the kids." A thinner man announced.

"Call them back. We have what we need."

Chapter Forty-Two

"This is insane!" Monica stared at the old compass in her hand, scared out of her wits. The piece appeared to be from the 1700s, functioned perfectly as far as she knew, and was their small hope at staying alive in order to find the woman named Ailsing. Her nerves frayed even more when she looked at the incline the compass's arrow was pointing at, following Vectra's instructions to continue due north. "Up we go."

Dare hurriedly ran alongside, not making a fuss or picking on her for the way she was climbing over the large rocks like he normally would have. He was as quiet as possible, trying not to be the one who goofed up and allowed themselves to be caught. *That way, I will have the ultimate bragging rights*, he told himself. It was a way for him to keep his mind off the fact that Gaither's men were on their trail somewhere behind them, and it helped him reject his urge to desperately scream for help. They were already not the most silent runners over the crunchy leaves, but an outright scream would have alerted the other men as to where they were, without question.

"Do…you…see…the birch…yet?" Dare asked in-between deep breaths of the chilling night air. The natural light was fading fast, and they did not want to have to use a flashlight to continue onward. *Talk about a beacon; we would be a lighthouse to them.*

"There!" Monica almost shouted out of pure excitement, and then remembered what they were doing again and lowered her voice. "Up there, on the top of the hill. See the glow?"

"Yeah, I see it." Dare's legs were hurting from the climb. He suddenly wished he had tried out for the local school sport teams rather than three book clubs at the library. Nothing against reading, but he wondered if maybe he should take up exercising in his neighborhood's park. "Now use the compass thing."

He watched his sister press down on the center tab, resembling a sundial, and watched a nearly invisible purple beam scan the ground for footprints. After three seconds, it was able to pick up on two different tracks of the same human signature. Both of them belonged to Ailsing, going in opposite directions from completing her daily patrols. Monica hoped that the P.I. could identify the correct path they should take, as the sunset had almost diminished completely.

"Do you…" Dare cut himself short when the P.I. dinged. A green light flashed on above the north symbol and its arrow spun to the east. "Great. With the light at our back."

"Maybe they are gone and we can rest here for the night?" Monica suggested, though her brother just glared at her with sarcasm written all over his face whilst an owl hooted into the night, and a raccoon casually walked through the underbrush.

"And perhaps we will wake up tomorrow to find ourselves safe in our beds at home." He retorted. "Come on."

At the sound of the men still in the hunt after them, both Monica and Dare whisked themselves along an old footpath Aisling created from her constant patrolling over the years. It was narrow, filled with overshooting roots and forest impediments, but it was a trail nonetheless and it matched where the P.I. told them to go.

Ten minutes later, Monica slowed down and pulled her brother back as well. "Shhh." She attempted to slow her breathing, trying to listen for their pursuers. "Do you hear anything?"

"No. But I am not taking any chances either." No sooner had Dare responded, than a pop song rang out from a cellphone behind a nearby tree. The kids' hearts pounded against the walls of their chests as one of Gaither's men popped out from where he had been lurking. Monica immediately held the compass up and pressed on the center, shooting the purple beam directly into the man's eyes and blinding him from the powerful light.

"Tom! Get them!" Ergon ordered while ignoring his phone still singing into the night, indicating a phone call from their boss.

Dare ran ahead of his sister, swinging his bag to the front, and managed to barely retrieve the flashlight in time to notice a sharp curve in the path. Clicking the light on, Dare accidentally switched it to OR mode, and the same greenish glow Vectra had on her car emanated from the lightbulb. "What the…" He wasn't quite sure what to make of it since everything along the path was casted in a ghoulish hue, making it appear spookier than before.

"Hit it again!" Monica called out. She watched her brother press on the same switch three more times until the light showed a normal colored beam that extended up to one hundred feet away.

"TOM!" Ergon's ear was pasted to the phone, not believing what he was being instructed to do by Gaither. They were so close to catching the kids, and after all of the complaining they endured from their boss, he was now ordering them to stand down and return to camp. "TOM! Where are you?!"

"I hear water." Monica announced to her brother, unaware of what was going on with the men behind them. They suddenly came upon the same stream they walked alongside on the way to Martiban's camp, just further up the mountain. "Let's go across."

"You know how cold that water is going to be?"

"What other choice do we have?" They plunged into the knee high, extremely cold water and leaned onto one another for support. Their legs moved as fast as the minor current would allow, making it a little difficult to keep splashing sounds at a minimum. Once they reached the other side, the kids collapsed onto the embankment out of exhaustion.

Monica was having a hard time trying to catch her breath. Her lungs heaved in and out uncontrollably while her hand grabbed for her stomach. Dare was not fairing any better to her left. "Do…you…think…" She failed to complete the question, but stared into her brother's eyes instead, as they shared her same ounce of hope that they had lost Gaither's men.

"I…think…he…left." Dare's winded sentence lingered in the air without any other nightly sounds to compete with. His pants were soaked through, and the damp fabric was already helping the cold to eat at his skin and bones. "Where…are…we?"

Monica picked up his flashlight and shined it at the large, thorny bushes that rose approximately five feet above them. Their small and tempting red berries were dotted sporadically among the branches, like confetti. The cheerful pop of color helped to make the dreary, monotone, grass green of their leaves to not seem so frightening. She carefully slid her hand into her back pocket and quickly pulled the compass out, feeling grateful to still have it after the recent chase.

She licked her lips at the sight of the juicy berries as a tantalizing smell indulged her senses. Her fingertips touched the closest patch of three deep red ones, and her stomach growled in eagerness. *They do not look all that dangerous.*

"I would not be doing that, Lass, if I were you." A confident voice broke the unnatural silence where not even bugs dared to sound in the wild fields further upstream. "Those berries be poisonous, and devour your liver."

Monica pointed the flashlight in the direction of the voice, shooting the strong beam right into the face of a slim woman with fiery red hair flowing loose over a white archer's cloak. She wore skinny pants, knee-high boots, and stood defensively against the light, shielding her eyes from becoming blinded. "What's the idea? Huh? Stop pestering me with the shine."

"Sorry." The teen rapidly turned the light's focus onto the ground and waited for her brother to join her. "Who are you?"

"That's supposed to be my line. But I rather we discuss such matters in a more private setting. Through the bushes, my loves."

"Are you mad?" Dare gave their prickly branches a disgusted look. "Our clothing, and skin, will be scratched all over."

"Do you want to take your chances with the fellows

who were after ye? Or perhaps, maybe with the wild animals who prowl the woods at night?" Her pale skin almost glowed under the moon as she moved. "Your decision, but the night will not last forever."

"Are you Ailsing?" Dare ventured.

The woman stared at him, blinking her eyes. "If it's she you're after, then we will speak in private. No negotiating."

"Agreed." Monica grabbed her brother's hand, and they both dove into the threatening greenery, scared and afraid of what was on the other side. Their eyes remained closed as they landed hard on a shadowed section of the ground until Monica risked a peek with one eye. She tapped on Dare's shoulder, signaling that the coast was clear.

"Why were you two out in the woods by yourselves?" The woman stared at them curiously. "My scanners did not pick up on you until you were on my patrol trail, so you are not…"

"From the Olde Realm." Monica finished. "No, we're not. But Vectra sent us." She observed the woman's interest being piqued when she heard the name. "We were about to be captured by a man named Gaither and his men, who are after one of the artifacts Vectra protects."

Dare halted his sister from saying any more. "Are you Ailsing?"

"Aye, my dear boy, that I am. Though I call myself Astrid these days. Every few centuries I like to change it up a bit, as for my real name to not be worn out."

"That is not the craziest thing I have heard this week. Or today, even." The boy nodded at Monica. "Is there anywhere we could sleep for the night?"

"Sure thing. Follow me."

Chapter Forty-Three

Trevor's fingers thumbed over the photocopies of the ancient book Gaither had taken along with him. He secretly hoped that his boss would not damage the hand-designed manuscript any historian would dream of discovering. It broke his heart that it belonged to a man who's idea of valuable artifacts were gold deposits in a remote part of the world. That being said, Gaither ensured pretty tight security on the book and had eyes on it 'round the clock. Whether it be his own, one of his hired help, or that of Trevor's, the book was never further than an arm's reach away from a human being.

Gaither said he had purchased the miraculous find from an archeologist friend of his, even providing a receipt to authenticate the buy. The story sounded plausible, and appeared to have evidence backing his claim, so there was no *real* reason for Trevor to suspect any kind of illegal activity. That was, until his mom and step-dad had been officially declared dead by the court, and he was granted approval to start probating their wills. A slip of paper, adjoined to his mother's will, dictating that he was to take on the responsibility of finishing the task they failed to do.

As part of the note, written in his mother's hand, there was a detailed account referencing this particular book. At least, he believed them to be one and the same.

Being as how he was no expert, Trevor guessed that the book could easily be dated back seven hundred years. Such a treasure should have been in a museum, in his opinion, and not being used as a means to steal from a world he didn't know existed. *I sure wish the boss...why do I still consider him my boss? He kidnapped me for Pete's sake.* Pushing his glasses up the bridge of his nose, the man's mind raced over the same section of text he had been studying for the past three hours. "This has to be the same book." He muttered to himself. "But if it is, where is the next clue?"

Everything fit: the dark leather, the animal skin-based parchment, the drawings depicting various scenes, everything except for the letters VT written on the spine. But those could have worn off, right? *Wait...*Trevor's brain clicked into overdrive as a lightbulb flashed on. *She said sketches, not drawings. This is a completed, illuminated manuscript. Mom would have known the difference and mentioned that. That is why I haven't been able to find out the next part of the map. Though it doesn't explain how this book took us as far as it did.*

Checking his wrist watch, Trevor's worries were mounting when he saw the time ticking uncomfortably close to eleven o'clock. Gaither expected him to have directions as to where the entrance to the cavern was located the minute he returned. "Come on Trevor, think. There has to be something here that I am overlooking. The pages got us this far." He had warned Gaither that he was not his mom and stepdad, with more of a passive interest in historical relics than their amateur exploits. And yet, that did not seem to matter to the company's owner.

When they first went missing, it was a nightmare. Gaither kept showing up with a cookie cutter story of his parents being extremely valuable employees and wanting to check on the family they left behind. The cringe-worthy words didn't sit well for him, and he swore not to walk into the clutches of that man. As time wore on, he tried to make any other job work out, but to no avail. Things were either very against him or they had a little human help along the way. So when the morning came that Gaither offered him a janitorial position, Trevor couldn't refuse. Not only would it help to pay the large plumbing bill coming his way, but it gave him the opportunity to see why this man was so interested in having him be a part of the company.

The job seemed normal in the beginning, however, it slowly evolved into something more as Gaither walked with him to the employee's locker room and chatted with him in the halls as he mopped. Still, it took a year for the truth to finally be revealed, at least part of it. Gaither wanted Trevor's help in locating his missing mom and step-dad. His cover story all hinged on a side project, on a bet, supposedly given to them before they disappeared, and he asked Trevor to find his parents who were probably still alive.

Confused and out-of-his-league, Trevor begged the business owner to explain how a pair of lamp designers got mixed up with an ancient myth they tried to locate on their own. According to Gaither, the reasoning was quite simple. He was walking through the designer offices and overheard Trevor's mom discussing the possibility of time travel with a co-worker. She explained how it would be much easier to study certain design aspects of rare lamps they were attempting to replicate for a high-end client. Then she joked about a mythical press that could re-write history, saying that she was determined to find out if it was true or not.

Gaither, being of money bags and feeling bored that day, decided to make a little wager with Mrs. Browning. If she was able to find the press, then he would give her enough cash to die wealthy or live off of for fifty years; whichever came first.

Trevor pretended to believe Gaither's version of what happened, at least for the sake of Monica and Dare. Since his ex-boss clearly had enough muscle power to go after his siblings, he suddenly found himself in deeper waters than he predicted. There were so many loopholes in the man's story, but no one else could tell him anymore, or wouldn't. All his suspicions were coming to a head when Gaither became very inquisitive about the wills and when the court was to deem them officially dead. And then to be kidnapped from outside his house and transplanted into the woods, was a ride all its on. It seemed to get weirder as they travelled along highways, back roads, down narrow hiking trails, and through an enchanted maze. They survived all of that to be stuck in a valley with a single sentence to guide them onward, relying on his lack of creative thinking to decipher its meaning.

Talking voices, from outside the tent, snapped his attention back to the flap furthest from the desk. He rose frustratingly up from the chair and pumped up his courage to tell Gaither that he just couldn't solve the next clue. His heart beat began to quicken at the sight of lanterns flickering against the fabric walls as the silhouette of the crazed millionaire appeared in the middle of vehicle headlights, shining straight into camp.

A bead of sweat trickled down the back of his neck, as Trevor gulped down his fear while watching the flap being pushed to the side. Gaither strutted in with his favorite buddy, Taminus, not far in tow. They were usually the same two that entered into the General's Quarters, as Gaither liked it being referred to. "So..," a sinister smile spread across the man's face, "how is my favorite janitor doing?"

"I….I…I can't find where the entrance is located. I have looked all over these pages for the entire day now, and the answer just simply isn't there."

"No worries."

Trevor was beyond belief. "You mean it?"

"Yep. Because I have acquired you a little bit of help." Gaither snapped his fingers and smirked as Vectra was thrown into a chair sitting opposite the desk by one of his henchmen. Trevor gripped onto the oak-finished top out of shock, seeing the woman limp with defeat and with barely enough strength to stand. "May I present my new guest, a Ms. Vectra Tillerman. She will be able to guide you by telling us where the entrance resides."

Taminus chuckled in his cousin's face. "You are looking a tad pale, Cousin. Are you feeling alright?"

"Better than your face. However, that is not a real challenge." Vectra spit at the ground, landing on Taminus's recently shined shoes.

The corners of his mouth went up as his lips curled into a snarl. "I like your new look. The helpless, powerless, and completely clueless one. You might want to get used to it."

"I am famished. Taminus, would you care for a bite to eat? A little midnight snack, as it were?" Gaither asked.

"With pleasure." The man stared a heartbeat longer into Vectra's tired eyes and then swiftly left the tent with his boss.

Trever tilted his head, staring at the woman coughing into her arm. "Are you truly Vectra Tillerman?"

"Merely a shade at the moment. Are you truly Trevor Browning?"

"Guilty as charged. What did they do to you?"

Vectra held up the handcuffs adorning her wrists. "They plated these in what you might call my version of Kryptonite."

"The sterling silver chalice that belonged to Dionysus before it was stolen from his temple in the third century B.C., never to have been seen again."

Her fear was solidifying into anger, bearing all its weight into the death glare she cast into the very depths of his soul. "How did you find it?"

"Gaither gave me an encrypted message that was sent to him anonymously. Or so he claims. Once I deciphered it, it revealed the location of where the chalice had been stashed." Trevor shook his head. "You must have been one of the best thieves of Ancient Greece to have kept it hidden all this time."

"You are acting extremely calm to be speaking with a person who has lived for thousands of years."

"I will admit that it's far from being a typical work night for me. But after seeing images of the cup with my own eyes, within the confines of a salt-filled vase buried deep inside the foundation of a mountainside villa…it doesn't surprise me. And let us not go into the whole episode of the enchanted maze with the boar from Hell."

"*You* are the one who found it?"

"Well, actually, no. I was able to crack the code and located the approximate area where it was supposed to have been. However, we were about four years too late. An archeology professor, from a university in Belgium, was given permission to search the land with a grant handed to him by an undisclosed donor. His team of students were the ones who found it and handed it over to a local museum. I went to collect it, with a little inside help."

"So you are also a skilled thief?"

"Nope. Just a guy on the low end of the ladder who didn't appear to be anything more than a nerdy bookworm and was expendable. Someone Gaither could cut loose with a false statement of plausible deniability and could easily sweep my story under the rug."

"Sounds like the same man."

"I was just lucky to have figured out the message. Once I was able to pinpoint which rules it was written by, it was rather easy to decipher. But getting there was the hard part. Puzzles, ancient artifacts, and treasure hunting aren't my thing. I just like to read articles about other explorers and would tell my siblings about them because they enjoyed their stories as well. It was a tradition my mom started with them, and it was one thing I could do to keep some kind of consistency in our lives."

"What did they use? For the cipher, I mean."

"A type of Ceasar Cipher."

"There's nothing special about that code. Simply substitute the letters for another one in the alphabet." Vectra began coughing again, this time, almost heaving up her lungs in the process. Trevor instantly poured her a cup of water from a pitcher and helped her drink it in slow sips.

"I'm really glad you are here now, though. Despite it being under these circumstances. With you here, to lead us to the press, my brother and sister will be safe."

Vectra nearly choked on the last sip. "What are you talking about?"

"My younger sister, Monica, and youngest brother, Derrick, are being held captive by Gaither and his men. I haven't been able to speak to them, but they showed me my brother's backpack. At first, I thought they might have stolen it from our house, until I saw his favorite action figure in the bag. Dare, short for Derrick, wouldn't have left that thing out of his sight. He always packs it along if we go somewhere or if he goes to a friend's house. So they must have them."

"Trevor, your siblings have been with me this whole time. That is, up till the moment Gaither and his men jumped us at Martiban's camp."

"You mean…" His nose flared as his blood ran hot. "Then how did they have Dare's bag, and who is Martiban?"

"An old acquaintance of mine they took to another tent after he tried punching the face of the guard escorting us."

"Like he was planning an escape in the middle of *this* camp?"

"Sometimes he does not know when to quit."

"So, where is the entrance to the cavern?"

The Guardian gave him a faded look of embarrassment. "I do not remember."

"What do you mean? I thought you were the one who hid it in the cavern in the first place?"

"I was, but, it's complicated. Part of my memory was erased. That is why my journal is so important. It has the answers I cannot remember."

"You mean this book?" Trevor showed her the photographed copies of the old book his former boss still had with him.

Her eyes went big, scared for the parts of her life that were never to resurface. "Where did you get these pictures?"

"From the journal Gaither has in his hands." Trevor walked purposefully over the enlarged throw rug and asked a guard on duty to fetch the book from Gaither immediately. "If it is the book you need, you will get it."

"This does not make any sense." Vectra's brain was spinning on autopilot as she studied the images. While the drawings did not look quite the same, the clues and wording were close enough to her own, to pass for government work.

"My book is the only one of its kind, and yet, here is another, almost its twin, in both words and imagery."

"I thought you said your memory was erased?"

"Parts are. But I remember pieces without being able to see the whole picture." Vectra turned to see the guardsman hand the book to Trevor, who eagerly flipped through the pages to find the one matching the photograph she had been looking at.

"I wasn't sure it was the right journal either. I mean, at first it seemed to be genuine, but your initials were not on the spine and this book is an illuminated manuscript, not sketches, as my mom had described in her note she left for me."

Vectra gave him a perplexed gaze until he filled her in on all he knew. "For some reason, our mom wanted me to pick up where they couldn't go. Though she didn't explain much as to why, except to say that it was for Monica's own protection."

"Monica's? I do not understand, unless…" Her eyes widened for the second time in the last five minutes. "Trevor, it is imperative for me to find out who the traitor is amongst my friends. Can you help me?"

"How?"

"Tell me everything you have learned about this book and maybe it will tell us about its writer."

"Oh, um, okay…it is centuries old."

"You don't think I know that?" She placed her hands on the book, feeling a disturbance in her previously reliable skill of remote carbon dating. "I would surmise this was created between 950 A.D. to 1200 A.D., from what I can glean from its age. Normally, I would be able to give you a precise year, if I did not have these infernal things confining my wrists."

"Well…it was made in Germany. At least, it was written in German. I have been using an online translator in order to understand any of it."

Vectra suddenly paused Trevor's flipping of the pages, spotting a rare color pigment in the outfit of a princess and the water of a lake she was standing beside. "That is an ultramarine color created from lapis lazuli."

The eldest Browning brother seemed at a loss for words, not exactly sure as to what that meant. "Is that significant?"

"Very much so, indeed. During that time period, gold's value failed in comparison to what lapis lazuli cost. It was used by scribes for books just like this one, and it was reserved for those of the best skills in drawing. Back then, there was a region in present-day Afghanistan where this particular mineral was mined and shipped along the Silk Road." Vectra did not want to believe herself as she said it aloud. "I would bet every last ounce of strength that this book came from East Francia, in the present-day region of Germany, where a woman by the name of Adalgard resided in what you would call a convent."

Trevor blinked his eyes. "That seems very specific."

"It is. Because Martiban was a knight back then, and his sister, Adalgard, lived at a convent in Germany where she was a female scribe. Her drawings were exquisite, and she would have been granted access to this mineral when her brother dropped off the shipment."

The man's eyes nearly bulged out of their sockets. "W…a…i….wait! Your friend was a knight? Like as 'a knight in shining armor,' and 'swords at the round table?' I thought they were sworn to a code of loyalty and honor?"

"He defied his oath and was stripped of all his prestige." Vectra could feel more of herself draining as the clock ticked on into the wee hours of the morning. She couldn't stay focused as a small discrepancy itched at the back of her mind. Though the detail eluded her, she feared it was dreadfully important to the whole matter at hand and decided to call it a night. "It is getting late, and we should get some rest for tomorrow, or later today as the case may be. Elsewise, we are not going to be at the top of our game when it is needed most."

"Ah, yeah." Trevor hesitantly closed the book and shuffled his papers around on the desk. "But, can I ask you another question?" He waited to see the Guardian nod in the light of the camping lantern swinging from the tent's ceiling. "If all of this is true, what you just said, then that would mean that you discovered America before Christopher Columbus did. Given how old the book is, and for it to have this accurate of information on where the press is hidden, would mean..."

"That is just it. I am not sure how it is possible for *this* book to have all this information. And for his sister to have written out my clues in such a time consuming manner; using their most expensive minerals for pigment, nonetheless, is beyond all reason. She would not have wasted precious supplies on a far-fetched notion that did not pertain to her religious order. Adalgard was not a woman of riddled imagination. Things that were in front of her, plain, obvious, and straight forward, was what she clanged too." Vectra's brain was feeling fuzzier with each passing second. "There is something wrong in the timeline of all of this. But I need to get some sleep, as I presume that you have no idea where the key is for these?" She lifted the handcuffs up as she asked the question.

"Gaither has the key and, unfortunately, he has it on him at all times. But what should we do about this guy, Martiban?"

"Nothing for now." Vectra went to pull herself up from the chair, barely able to raise her butt about five inches off the seat.

"Whoa." Trevor quickly stepped over to her side and helped her to move to where a small pile of blankets, and a pillow, were stowed near a pile of luggage. "You can have the cot if you would like."

"This is fine with me. However, I do appreciate your chivalrous offer." Vectra gave him a weak smile before succumbing to her weariness.

Chapter Forty-Four

Astrid led the kids to a large weeping willow in the middle of a small clearing, whose limp branches swayed in the light breeze that picked up across the field. As they approached, soft dots of light activated under each leaf, providing enough gentle glow to see a downward staircase leading them beneath the tree's roots. "You live under a tree?"

Monica nearly slapped her brother for asking such a rude question, though it didn't seem to bother the nymph at all from the way she chuckled at the boy's curiosity.

"But of course. Nymphs are *literally tied* to their trees. We cannot go far from where it is planted. Not without the proper provisions, that is."

An oversized root arched over the stairs transporting them into the earthy burrow below, screaming of classic cottage core in its atmosphere. Paintings of the Irish countryside were hung next to landscape photographs of the local towns and mountains of where they currently stood. All the walls were well-constructed from the compacted soil, which was perfect with the high component of clay and rock it contained. Accented with the painted color of eggshell white, the whole space created a lighter atmosphere than one would expect from a home of dirt. Another level of coziness was added through the use of staggering wooden bookshelves, going up and down the walls of a reading nook, carved into a section of tangled roots next to the bedroom.

Homemade candles were lined across a repurposed windowsill over the backsplash in a medium-sized kitchen. To the right of the kitchen, complete with an island counter, stood a grand, stone fireplace with two sconces flanking the sides of a pine wreath above the oak mantel. The smell of renewed earth, like that of the ground after a soaking rain, filled the air as pastel mushrooms glowed in different colors throughout the space. Dare looked up at the ceiling, or a lack thereof, above the dining table near a chimenea, where the stars were shining brightly overhead. As though they stepped into a children's book, the whole abode looked akin to that of Peter Rabbit's home.

Monica was a little surprised to see Astrid's unruly curls, much like Vectra's, manage to miss snagging on any number of smaller roots reaching out from the soil. In the better lighting, she could see the Celtic symbol for eternity carved on the front of a bow the nymph had been carrying, and it matched the marks cut into the leather strap of her quiver. "Do you happen to know an annoying little leprechaun by the name of Aidan?"

"It's hard to find one who doesn't." Astrid pressed on a gemstone in the wall and Irish music began to drift soothingly from hidden speakers in surround sound fashion. "Now, my turn for a few questions. What are your names?"

"I'm Dare. And this is my bigger sister, Monica." The boy happily answered, eyeing some food on the kitchen counter. "Did we make it in time for dinner by chance?"

"I might be able to whip up a little something for two hungry kids." Astrid gave them a friendly smile. "And while I am prepping the food, you probably should tell me what kind of trouble Vectra is in."

"You saw what happened?" Dare was skeptical.

"No. But if Vectra sent you alone to find me, then she must be in trouble. She would not have left two kids alone in the woods. That is not her style."

"Are we…are we…" Monica's words stammered out as her mind kept thinking about their flee into the woods and seeing Vectra take on an onslaught of bullets right behind them. Her eyes were glazed over in the consuming fear that finally felt free to surface after her adrenaline started to wear off.

Astrid leaned forward to look the scared teen in the eye, and placed a hand comfortingly upon her arm. "You are safe for tonight. It's alright, Lass. No one is going to hurt you here. I have the place secured."

Monica simply nodded without saying a word, and let Dare tell the nymph all about Gaither's raid on Martiban's camp.

"Ugh, Martiban. That down-trodden sod. He has gone to the dogs, that he has. As old as Methuselah, he is, and as stubborn as he is tall."

"Ah, what now?" Dare's confusion was equally shared with his sister.

"Never mind him for a quick spell. You two are mostly famished, as I reckon. That, and exhausted would be a good word for ye. Have a seat at the table and I won't be but a moment." Astrid pulled three handcrafted ceramic bowls from the cupboards and whipped together a salad in each one, made from homegrown ingredients. She grabbed a bottle of dressing and plopped everything in front of the kids before heading back to the kitchen for the drinks.

"Where did you get these bowls?" Monica recognized them from an online shop she liked to look over in the wee hours of the morning when she couldn't sleep.

Astrid gestured toward a pottery wheel in the far corner. "I make all of my own dishes, plus a few more. I sometimes go to local festivals to sell my pieces." A beaming smile crossed her face. "Even have me own website to sell online." She pulled a laptop out from a small nearby shelf and popped it open. "Was working on uploading a few more images when you two showed up on my radar."

She flipped the laptop around to show Monica, who about jumped out of her seat. "You own CelticMud?!! I follow that shop…YOUR shop. I knew I recognized these bowls."

"You are too kind. I have had a number of years to perfect my craft, as it were. Though, that does not mean I don't still make mistakes. Perfection is *highly* overrated."

"That is really neat." Dare wouldn't normally have dove into a salad mercilessly, but he was too hungry to care and drastic measures were called for in a crisis such as this. "But what were you going to tell us about Martiban?" He shoved a dandelion into his mouth, unsure as to how it was going to taste.

"He continues to live in eternal hope for that wretched woman."

"Come again?"

"That is why he was camping out where he was. Every year, he returns to the ruins of Gardnee Hall in search for the woman that captured his heart, soul and mind. Any good part of that man was stolen by her for a greed she never could fill. She even took away the one part of his job he enjoyed when he was still a member of the knighthood.

The ruins, of course, were transported here from Europe, countless moons ago."

A piece of lettuce spewed out of Monica's mouth, dropping back into the bowl it had just been forked from. "Are you saying that Martiban used to be a knight? From the medieval ages?"

Astrid scooped a large helping of tomato chunks and darker leaves. "Yes, my dear Lass. He used to travel on the Silk Road to ensure that certain shipments made it to their destinations without any disruptions."

"No wonder he was dressed like a peasant." Dare whispered to his sister.

"I am surprised Vectra did not tell you about that. Then again, she has been closed off from many of us since…" She paused, looking at the two kids and trying to decipher who they really were. "What is your last name?"

"Browning." Dare absentmindedly replied, more focused on a patch of flax seeds, with an uncanny resemblance to crawling bugs atop sliced grapes in his salad. Shaved carrots acted like large sprinkles mixed in with chopped radishes strewn throughout the weird mixture. "This all looks and tastes as though it was freshly picked."

The nymph pointed her fork in the direction of the island counter where a bin of the red vegetable, or fruit, sat. "Those tomatoes were just picked today. My plants were blossoming a little further past their usual season this year. So I have extra, if you would care for more. I want to use up as much as possible before recycling the overripe ones into fertilizer for the next growing season."

"Thank you, but no. I'm good." Dare gave her a toothy grin with mini green pieces stuck on their semi-white surface.

"Martiban would be the perfect example of love being

blind. Josephine was able to take an honorable knight and transform him into her personal assassin, corrupted by her greedy desire for power. Oh, she did well to keep him no closer than arm's length, only interested in using him as a puppet to do her evil bidding. We could see straight through her cloud of manipulation, building them castles in the sky she was. But sadly, Martiban could not see past his nose. When he went as far as to kill one of his brothers in arms, we knew something had to be done."

"Did Vectra have anything to do with Josephine's death?" Monica moved a tomato slice around in her bowl, watching the red juice smear over the greenery like a battlefield in the aftermath.

"I swore never to tell another soul. That promise is a permanent bond that I cannot break."

"She did, then. Didn't she?"

"Why do you care?"

"Martiban was acting sort of hostile to us, more towards Vectra in particular. I mean, he did allow us to stay by the fire, though, and watch over his dinner, so I wouldn't think he didn't trust her. If I suspected someone of being untrustworthy, I certainly would not leave them near my food unattended." Monica sipped on the water gratefully. It felt good on her throat, running down into her stomach. "Is it possible that he found out after all?"

"There were only four of us who remember the event, and each of us swore an oath of silence, punishable by years of duty being a servant to the Debt Collector if we were to ever break that vow."

"You have to pay taxes in the Olde Realm?!" The boy's jaw about fell off.

"No. In our world, currency is not as straight forward, or as universal, as government issued cash money is. We still function on the bartering system for various trades, and one of the strongest currencies we have is debts owed." She showed them two short tassels with a letter initial dangling from a split ring just like the one Vectra had gained after their visit with Rudi. "They have no expiration date and are to be redeemed by the person they are owed to in any manner they see fit."

Dare looked over at his sister. "You mean that you could be forced to marry someone because you owe them a debt?"

"Marriage and other such favors of the sort are prohibited. Besides, if that was the case, I would take my chances with the Debt Collector, and that man is no harmless, annoying leprechaun. His is the Grim Reaper's younger brother, you know." Astrid retook her seat as Monica noticed one tassel being hidden behind the other two. The letter "L" dangled over the top of its blackened thread.

"I do not see Vectra's letter in your collection of debt."

"That is because I would do her a favor without the requirement of a debt being owed." Astrid motioned to the tree above them. "You see this place? This land? Vectra purchased it when a housing development company was about to buy it, and allows me to live here rent free."

"Where does she get all this money?" Dare ate the last seed of his salad.

"That is her business, and hers alone. Vectra does not like to be asked a number of questions, as she is more of a quiet and reserved person, than that of a churchbell."

Monica finished the last of her water and left the tomatoes in the bottom of the bowl. She felt like a mixed-up ball of emotions herself, or a lost bird who didn't know east from west. Here they were, another night away from their brother and the press still seemingly a world's length out of reach. But she was beginning to think that it was all for the better. "May I ask you…Astrid…would you want to go back home? To Ireland?"

The nymph hesitated, allowing a suspenseful silence to fall between them. Only the crackling fire in the belly of the chimenea pot could be heard. Her hands rubbed themselves together as though they would spark from the friction, before she placed them on her seat, on either side of her legs. "Monica, that is something I have pondered for what seems like eons; would I go back and change what happened that day I was banished? Change my fate? And truth being, however absolute, it just isn't possible."

Monica's shyness could be seen on her cheeks. "But what if it was possible?"

"Yeah. Vectra told us that the press can rewrite history." Her brother interjected.

"Oh, Lass. That is a grand idea at that, it is. But I am from an age so long since past, when Great Auks were abundant and the legends of today were still unfolding. Changing my life, back when I was a woman unattached to any tree, would unleash an unknown ripple within the fabric of time itself. Various stories would be altered, creating a wide amount of unforeseen affects." Astrid swallowed the last of her salad. "No, that would be too much on the old books. And while your thinking is well and good natured, Ireland is far different from that of whence I lived. I would be a stranger in my own homeland, as though I have never stepped foot upon its soil ever before. Sure, the stones may have survived, and the heritage has been passed in song and tradition, but the trees have been uprooted, the animals faded, and the buildings modernized within city limits."

"It is ranked as one of the top most unspoiled landscapes in the world." The boy helpfully added.

Astrid's eyebrows raised at him. "This place is my home

now."

Monica handed the woman her bowl as their hostess cleaned up the table. "How else can we repay you for your kindness?"

"I already told ye, I would help Vectra regardless." She returned to the kitchen, giving the kids a full view of her art studio area.

Suddenly, Monica jumped up from the table after noticing something sitting by the clay wheel. "Where did you find that case?"

"What case?"

"That attaché case!" The teenager raced over to where a brown briefcase was sitting on the floor, partially obscured by a draped drop cloth. "That belongs to Trevor, our brother."

"Are you sure?"

"I am certain of it. Look at the wear mark here. And here. And the marker lines I accidentally drew on it." Monica whipped around to face the nymph, ready to interrogate her if need be. "Where did you get it?"

"I found it discarded, where my land borders alongside World's End. It was left opened, with nothing inside except for pine needles and small chunks of wood."

"Can you take us there?" A surge of new-founded energy coursed in her veins. Here was a promising lead that meant they were on the right track, and getting closer to finding their brother.

"Calm down there, Jumping Bean. How about you two get a good night's rest and we will head there in the morning?"

"But…"

"Monica, you may be working on adrenaline right now. However, it is not going to last you forever and you will fade out at the wrong time, come tomorrow. Help me set up two cots for you and your brother." Astrid pulled the glaze-spotted cloth further over the case, and led the teen back to the table.

"She's right, Sis." Dare yawned, glancing up at the clear sky above the forest. "Who knows when we will get to sleep next."

But Monica did not want to sleep, nor did she feel at all tired for the moment. Still, she could not go into the woods alone and had to ultimately surrender to the judgement of the other two. "Fine!"

Chapter Forty-Five

Monica tossed and turned in the soft glow of the fireplace. She tried laying on her side, changing which end she rested her head upon, and how much of the thick blanket she had covering her on the cot. Even counting the stars she could see, through an invisible ceiling, did not help to convince her mind it was time to sleep. And trying to read over Vectra's journal was a waste of time.

She gazed down at the handwritten book between her fingers, and the initials decorating the spine: VT. Monica felt rotten to the core, mindlessly flipping through the pages in a funk over the Guardian's sacrifice. The image of Vectra, running as bullets shot straight through her body, would not leave her thoughts in peace. Instead, the Guardian's face kept waking her up and was decidedly not going away.

Slamming the book shut, Monica picked herself up from the cot and strolled over to the kitchen. Her rumbling stomach was begging for a midnight snack more filling than what the salad had done for her at dinner, and she fumbled her hand around in the unfamiliar set-up, searching for the faucet. As she looked, a scrub brush fell into the sink with a small clink and she winced from the noise it made. "Sounds as though someone cannot sleep."

The startled teen turned to see Astrid rock forward in her wooden chair, bringing her face next to two mushroom lights so Monica could identify her in their red and green glow.

"Do you normally go to bed in a rocking chair?"

"No. But I do when there are houseguests under my roof who are being hunted down."

"I thought you said that this place was safe?"

"It is." The nymph lifted her nose slightly higher into the air, sizing the teen up. "Perhaps it is because I do not fully trust ye either. Ye may be friends of Vectra, but she is a slippery fish to catch, so that leaves me with a few unanswered questions. With that on me brain, sleeping was not a logical option."

Monica kept her mouth shut, understanding the woman's insinuations, and not wishing to discuss the matter any further. She pried the refrigerator door open to find the carafe of milk, front and center. "There is also some leftover chicken on the third shelf." The nymph offered. "Or are you not a cannibal?"

"What is THAT supposed to MEAN?!" Monica was raging mad from the blatant accusation. She didn't care if she woke her brother up at this rate, considering it was his idea to stay the night there anyways.

"How did Vectra get captured? If I am going to help ye, I need to know who I am dealing with, as well as whose side you're on."

Monica let out a large sigh, sinking her head in towards her chest as her gaze fell to the ground. "Vectra sacrificed herself so that we could escape with her journal. She told us to run and to not let them get their hands on it. I…I…" A tear formed in the corner of her eye, threatening to spill off her lashes. "I can't help but feel as though I could have done something more to stop it from happening."

Astrid moved swiftly across the room, light as a feather and just as quiet. She placed a hand on each of the teen's shoulders and looked her square in the face. "If Vectra told you to run, then you did the right thing. That book holds a great deal of information in it…if that is what I suspect it to be."

"It's Vectra's journal. I tried reading through some of it, to find out the answers everyone is searching for, but I can't understand it because it's in Greek."

"That, I can be of some assistance, my dear Lass." Astrid aided her in gathering together a meatier snack, and walked her back to the cot in the warmed corner. She sat down next to Monica and began to scan over some pages the teen had bookmarked for passages that might be promising.

"How long have you known Vectra?"

Astrid chuckled, interrupting the still air. "Too long, by many accounts."

"Do you know about the scar she carries from a back-stabbing friend?" Monica patiently waited as the nymph finished mouthing her lips as she read over an underlined section.

"That scar has lived in her skin far longer than anyone knows, and it had nothing to do with your parents, if that is what you were wondering."

"I wasn't thinking that. Vectra said it occurred from someone she considered to be her sister. And she would not have considered my mom as that, seeing as how she didn't know Vectra before heading after the press." Monica took another bite of the meat in her hands. "I was wondering why she cut you out of her life, is all."

"That is something only she can tell you. And when

she does, you might want to let me in on the secret as well." Astrid glanced over at the girl. "And yes, that is smoked paprika I sprinkled on the chicken."

"How did you…"

"I suggest you stay away from poker, or any betting game at that." The nymph smiled, easing the unspoken tension in the room about the upcoming morning. "Your face is a book, my dear, and one easily read."

"Well, I do believe she has you pegged." Dare groggily answered.

"I thought *you* were fast asleep." Monica sassed. "Eavesdropping on our conversation is more like it."

"Well, I was sleeping until I heard the call of the chicken."

"The call of the chicken?"

"Yes. It said 'eat me, Dare, come eat me.' It would be rude of me not to answer the call, don't you agree?"

Monica tossed her pillow at his head. "You are unbelievable, you realize that?"

"And proud of it." Her brother smiled in a joking manner.

"Alright you two, that is enough. Monica, fetch him some chicken so that we all may be able to get some rest this evening." Astrid continued to read over the pages rather hurriedly, and stopped when she came upon a handwritten sheet of music. "It appears as though there is a back route we can use to cut off Gaither before he reaches the press." As she turned to the next page, a few pressed flowers skidded out of the crook of the spine, falling into her hand as gently as feathers. Their telltale baby blue color allowed her to identify them immediately, and she offered them to Monica with the same amount of kindness.

"That's great!" Dare thanked his sister for the food and didn't hesitate to begin devouring it. "Please tell me that the back way is off a highway exit ramp and not in the middle of nowhere."

"What if we just destroyed the book?" Monica asked.

"Why would we want to do that?"

"Because without the book, no one can get into the press, and without those pages, there is nothing to be searching for." The teen snatched the book from Astrid's hands, tearing her away from the map she was deciphering.

"What are you doing?" The nymph stared after the book, clearly concerned over it.

"I'm going to get rid of the problem." Monica's hand went backward with the journal, ready to throw it into its fiery grave in the fireplace.

"STOP!" Astrid rushed over and yanked the book from the teen's clutches right before Monica was about to let go. "This map will take us to the press so we can stop your brother's boss from using it. Don't you understand the importance of this?"

"So? Vectra explained the rules to us on how it operates, which is impossible to use unless you are one of Clio's helpers or a relative of them." Monica eyed their hostess suspiciously. "Or perhaps there is something you haven't told us?"

Astrid's widened eyes switched between the siblings, who were both staring at her, waiting for an answer. "Vectra used to work for Clio."

Chapter Forty-Six

"My ears must be filled with wax." Monica tossed the journal onto the cot and put her hands to her hips. "She said that all of the helpers were dead."

"Vectra is forbidden from using it herself, given her Guardian role. But she did help Clio for two months before the Romans invaded her state. Her ranking was the lowest of the low, however, she took the oath that granted her permission to operate the press right before she had to resign." Astrid paused, making sure that she still had their attentions. "Gaither won't care, and he will force her to use the press regardless."

"And what will happen to her, should he force her to operate it?"

"Nothing short of eternal punishment by those fate playing gods on Mount Olympus."

"Well, we all know how forgiving that lot can be." Dare sarcastically added to the conversation.

"Astrid, what about the thief who used the press a long time ago?"

She gave Monica a confused look. "What thief?"

"Vectra told us that a thief used it before and died from

it."

"I have no idea, Lass. None 'tall. She didn't really speak much to me about her time working with Clio. Although, she did tell me that her uncle would never go near it, no matter the power it wielded." Astrid glanced up at the clear sky. "Now, rush on back to bed before the sun is glistening high overhead. We have a long trek to make."

✷✷✷✷✷✷✷✷✷✷✷✷✷✷✷✷✷✷✷✷✷

Morning shined bright and cheerful onto the Brownings' faces. Its strong rays were relentless, beating against their closed eyelids until they had no other choice but to wake up. Monica yawned her worn out jaw and blindly smacked her brother in the side to get him moving. "Dare, it's time to get ready."

"Five more minutes." He flipped onto his other side and instantly fell back to sleep.

Astrid shook her head in dismay at the sorry sight and began cooking up eggs and bacon in the skillet. As she expected, Dare's nose started to twitch, causing his head to lift off the pillow and slowly lead the rest of his body to the source of the mouthwatering aroma. "That smells delicious." The boy licked his lips for the full effect.

Monica complimented the nymph on her creative thinking and used the bathroom to freshen up a bit. Upon returning, she gladly accepted her plate of food, padding a zippered pocket of her jacket to ensure that the flowers were where she put them the night before. "This tastes great."

"Why, thank you." Astrid motioned to the filled packs she had prepped near the foot of the staircase. "Whenever you two are ready to leave, we can go."

Dare splashed a handful of water on his cheeks and

rushed out to catch up to the others. He climbed the stairs after his sister, taking notice of the white Victorian archer's cape Astrid was wearing at the front of the line. "You are going to wear *that*? Aren't you afraid of it getting dirty or something?"

"This old thing? I've had it for over two hundred years and I am not about to change it now."

"I really wish we could go back and get our Bi-Wheelers." Monica blinked her eyes, coming out of the burrow and seeing the daylight in all its glory.

"Who said anything about us walking there?" Astrid's brow rose up. "You think I walk my entire boundary every day?" She stepped onto the grassy meadow, and whistled a tune of Celtic origins. Within thirty seconds, a large elk strutted out from behind the curtain of the forest. Its massive antlers were spread out like an eagle's wings, spanning ten feet in width. His broad shoulders sported a darker brown coat than that of his torso and legs, but continued in a streak along his back. Seeing the eyes of a proud and powerful animal, Monica and Dare felt like ants in comparison to his enormous stature. "May I introduce Eachan. He is an Irish Elk. Long thought extinct for the past 7,000 years, Vectra asked me to watch over them in exchange for staying here rent free."

She reached out her hand, scratching under his chin, and whispered to her ancient friend, telling him where they needed to go and why. Eachan dipped his head at Astrid's guests and knelt down for them to climb aboard his back. Monica clumsily got on, helping her brother next as Astrid brought up the rear. "What about his antlers? Don't they get caught up in the trees?"

"There are certain paths I keep open for such reasons. Though, they know how to make do in a pinch."

"How many are there?" Dare stared out at the strange view from sitting high atop the elk.

"About one hundred. Not all of them live here at once. There is a cavern that transports them to another sanctuary, so they can come and go as they please. But Eachan is my favorite, isn't that right, Boy?" Astrid petted his side. "He sticks by me throughout the year. His brother, though, has the largest set of antlers I have ever seen, measuring an eleven foot span. He protects the herd in Harpeon."

Through the aid of his long strides, it did not take them more than thirty minutes for the Irish Elk to come upon the boundary line with World's End, a park and area named for its high cliffsides and the dangerous roads people used to drive on. "This is where I found the case." Astrid tapped on Eachan's hind quarters, and he knelt down for them to disembark. "It was halfway under that bush, like they did not care if it was found or not."

"Monica!" Dare called. "Look. It's Trevor's glasses." He pointed out the reflecting lenses peeking out from between twigs with orange pine needles still attached.

"That's his back up pair. See the red rim?" Monica's heart sank an inch deeper. "Maybe he put up a struggle here. With the debris, it is hard to tell."

"We had very high winds the other night." Astrid observed the scene that had drastically changed since the day she discovered the attaché case. "A lot of these tree branches must have fallen during it, because this path was cleared when I discovered your brother's case."

"But doesn't this mean that Gaither and his men are close by?" Dare took the risk to peek over the edge of the cliff they were standing atop of. His stomach fell into his foot at the sheer drop before him. "Wow! Talk about watching your step."

"It just means that they passed this way at some point. We don't even know how long it was before Astrid found the case."

"That much, I can vouch for." Astrid answered. "It was not here when I did my morning patrol on Tuesday, but it was there in my evening round."

Monica stomped on the grass. "Tuesday! This is Friday. Great! They are probably miles ahead of us by now."

"Wait, how do *they* know the way?" Dare looked up from the daunting drop-off to see his sister's angry face. "If Vectra's book has the map, and all the information needed to find the press, then how are they that much farther ahead than us?"

"I don't know anymore, Dare." Monica's brain was going to implode on itself. "It's like, whenever we think we are *finally* getting somewhere, we are actually moving two steps back."

Astrid stroked Eachan's shoulder and neck area as the siblings talked. "If they took the North Trail, it gets pretty narrow in certain areas, so they would have to walk it. At that pace…" Suddenly, a branch cracked from behind a thick patch of pine trees and vines. Eachan's muscles tensed as he sniffed the air and slowly turned in the direction of the sound. With a simple tap on his fur, Astrid signaled for him to leave whilst stringing her bow and kneeling to the ground as he obeyed. She sliced her arrow through the trees, cutting into the undergrowth, and heard a man cry out in pain. "Follow the path!"

Monica and Dare raced down the sloping trail marked by small patches of blue paint sprayed onto the trees. As Astrid had warned, the width of the ledge was steadily decreasing and soon enough, it was no wider than a single person could travel at a time. Thankfully, the bottom of the gorge was in sight and the kids easily jumped atop a soft pile of moss to reach the ground. "Where's Astrid?" Within a few minutes, the nymph had rejoined them and called out for them to keep running.

"I needed to make sure that they were Gaither's men after you, and not a pair of hunters after Eachan."

As a bullet struck a tree on their right, Dare took a quick glance over his shoulder. "I don't think they are after Eachan."

"We have to keep going. Stay close to me, but don't stand directly in my line up."

"I have no idea what you are talking about." Dare fell in step with his sister, and side by side, they followed the nymph along the gorge's floor. Dodging trees, rocks, criss-crossing timber, even hopping over a frog or two, the group was keeping a good pace until one of the henchmen popped up on their left. Astrid halted to a stop, holding the kids back with her hands and stared the taller man down. He aimed his weapon straight at her head and didn't hesitate to pull the trigger.

To the kids' astonishment, including Gaither's man, the bullet went through Astrid's head like water, and she remained standing there for all to see. Using his split-second of being stunned, she pulled a knife from her belt and stabbed him in the eye. "Come on!" She pulled the kids in the direction of a cliffside where a large over-cropping rock jutted out far above them.

"Okay, I understand now." Dare puffed out between breaths. "But we are going to talk about the whole bullet-through-your-head thing, right?"

"The same thing happened with Vectra." Monica noted aloud, thinking back to when they escaped Martiban's camp, and she placed a shield on her back to keep the bullets from penetrating the Brownings in front of her.

"New weapons cannot harm us. Only the ones from the ancient world." Astrid took a sharp turn just as an arrow sailed by her head.

"Someone else got the message too." Dare gulped.

"We are almost there." Astrid promised, making another sharp turn in the opposite direction. They were now racing almost directly underneath the ledge now, and the terrain was becoming harder to run through.

Monica's foot tripped on a few strands of old rope and she landed on the other side of a rock pile, where the grass was thankfully soft and wispy. As she reopened her eyes, the sudden feeling of something bony fell across her arm. Through the surrounding bushes, Monica was horrified to find a skeleton's hand laying on her wrist. Unlike in the movies, however, she had no real inclination to scream out, but found herself mesmerized by its presence instead. When she looked upward, she caught sight of a few scraps of wooden boards still clinging to pieces of cut rope, which were dangling from the rocky outcrop. It was the meager evidence of a broken bridge, whose rope matched the one she had unfortunately collided with, and her mind began to whirl.

The skull sat merely three feet away from her own, where it's empty sockets blankly stared out at her. A cracked bullet hole was where the temple would have been, telling of the skeleton's untimely demise.

"Monica, are you alright?" Astrid rushed up to her side, unfazed by the skeletal remains practically laying on top of the girl. "Are you hurt at all?" She grabbed the teen's arm and helped her up. "Monica!" The nymph tried to get through to her.

"I'm…I'm…fine." The teenager looked over her shoulder to see one of the henchmen taking aim with another arrow, her eyes widening in panic. Astrid also saw the man, and stepped in front of her as the arrow was released; pushing the girl to the ground again as Dare helplessly watched on from the safety of a boulder.

Astrid stood her ground and waited until the right moment, "i bhfolach."

Monica flashed her eyes up just in time to see the archer's cape turn invisible and allowed the arrow to pass through her body like the bullets. A second later, the cape materialized once again and she turned to face the teenager. "WE NEED TO GO!" With a silent nod of agreement, the group was back on the run, though Monica's head was not focused.

"Was that…"

"No, it's not. That one died of a bullet wound." Astrid hurriedly pointed out. "NOW MOVE IT! See the tree with the three rings in its bark?"

"THERE!" One of their pursuers called into the forest. "I SEE THEM!"

"How many men did this guy hire? A whole private army?" Dare looked behind himself in time to hear another bullet whizzing by his ear, slicing through the leaves inches from his head.

"YOU IDIOT!!" Another man's demanding voice rang clear. "We need the kids alive! If you want to kill anyone, take care of the woman!"

"But we've tried!" The other pleaded.

Monica could feel her power and strength being sapped from her body at an alarming rate. She wasn't sure what was wrong; all her limbs still seemed attached, and she saw no blood oozing from any cuts. Then it dawned on her that she hadn't had any water since breakfast, and even that hadn't been much. "I need…to…stop." Her brain felt lightheaded as she tried reaching out to touch Astrid.

Ignoring her request, the nymph plowed on and disappeared from view in a matter of seconds. Monica's heartbeat was racing, her lungs were worn out, and her feet felt dead. She made the turn into a semi-hidden passage and collapsed onto a fallen log, gazing around at her surroundings for the first time after discovering the skeleton.

The passageway was a branch off from the main gorge, both narrower in width and height. Above the top of the trees, the deep blue sky smiled upon the grass growing thin and tall, swaying at her thighs from a small amount of wind. A pain began to fester under the right side of her rib cage as a cramp formed, causing her to hunch over.

"Astrid?" Monica dared not to make a sound louder than her regular voice. "Where are you?" Her hand gripped hard onto the cramp in a vain attempt to apply pressure to her sore side. "Where did you go?" She quickly piped down, as the noise of the two henchmen came from the passage's entrance. *Oh come on!* The teen winced up from the log, and pressed on at a slower pace than before, continuing to make her way around shrubs and trees, with no sign of the nymph anywhere.

She was beginning to think that Astrid and her brother, had abandoned her; especially when she reached a dead end in the shape of a solid rock wall. "Now I know they vanished." Monica stood still, fighting off a panic attack that threatened to consume her. Closing her eyes in a desperate attempt to find even a shred of inner peace, Monica was starting to feel hopeless. *I am so sick and tired of...*

"Monica?" Dare's voice surged her with a new sense of strength, flashing her eyes open.

"Derrick? Where are you?" She searched the wall wildly,

trying to find her brother. "Where are you? Please tell me I did not imagine your voice."

"Back here. Remember, things are the opposite as what they appear in the Olde Realm. Trust me."

Monica's fingers hastily tapped against the rocks. *What am I looking for? A secret door? A trap door? An obvious door? Not a door at all?* She proceeded to knock her knuckles against the cold and dampened rocks instead. "I don't see it."

"See what?"

"The door."

"There is no door. Just walk on through. Between the fourth and fifth rock on your left."

"You can do it, Monica." Astrid encouraged her. "Walk on through."

"Okay." Monica reached for the fourth rock, clutching onto it with all her might, and swung her body around onto the other side of the false wall. Her brother helped to haul her away from the opening, allowing Astrid to seal it shut with a fortuitous rockslide and a well-aimed arrow.

Covering their faces against the billowing dust, they silently watched the rocks tumble into the gap like a giant set of children's building blocks. "You could have told me that it was a false wall instead of giving me those riddles."

"If you hadn't swung in when you did, my next move was to just grab you myself." Dare hugged his sister, grateful to see her alive. "If you tell anyone about this, I will deny it fully."

"Duly noted." Monica smiled. Returning his embrace, she remembered the skeleton in the bushes and a haunting feeling returned. She went to speak, but was cut off instead by the nymph.

"You will find a clearing on the other side of that tree

line up there." Astrid pointed to a row of maple trees growing in the midst of evergreens and spruce trees. She danced around muddy puddles, slippery rocks, and gnarled tree roots without a glance back at the siblings in tow, sensing the oncoming confrontation that Monica wanted to give her. It was not hard to feel the coal hot fire of anger being cast at her back from the girl's penetrating glare.

"Whoa!" Dare's mouth dropped. His eyes surveyed the spectacle spread out before them: a vast clearing, which lead into a sprawling valley, and a view so beautiful any realtor would beg to list it for sale. Calling out in the sky above, a bald eagle soared along a stream of air, lifting his wings higher into the sky whilst clouds began to roll into the area. Indeed, the scene was tranquil, and would have captured Monica's attention for ages, had it not been preoccupied with the undiscussed matter at hand.

"Before you get excited…" Astrid tried to gently ease her way into the conversation.

"How on Earth did you know that my parents weren't killed by a bullet?!" Monica was not about to play that game.

"What is going on?" Dare was all confused, having not been privy to what was not discussed earlier.

"I fell into a skeleton near that collapsed bridge hanging off the cliffside, and when I asked Astrid about who it was, she informed me that it could not be one of our parents because that person was KILLED BY A BULLET!" Her blood was boiling over now.

"There is something I think you should know…"

"You better believe it!" Monica fumed. "We are supposed to tell you, and Vectra, and all of the others, everything we know. We are supposed to trust you, with nothing less than our *very lives*, regardless of whether or not we have known you for more than a total of five minutes! And yet, we have been kept in the dark for…" She stopped when her brother tapped her arm.

"Let's hear her out."

Astrid looked gratefully at the boy, and then patiently explained. "Vectra does know what happened to your parents. And so do I."

"I KNEW IT!" Monica huffed. "Did she kill them to protect her precious press?"

The nymph was horrified at what the teen had said. "How foolish can you be, child?! Vectra is a woman of honor and…"

"A thief!"

Astrid sighed. "I think it is time you were shown something. Though, I warn ye, that discovering the truth is but the start to healing from even deeper wounds. They are not to be blamed on Vectra. That, I am certain of."

The nymph led them to a shaded section of the land, where the unlimited meadow melted into the sprouting forest of the hillside. Astrid squatted by a patch of tall weeds and gently parted them to reveal a gravestone marker. Carved into the dark stone was a bas-relief of her parents' faces, with their full names and dates listed below. Monica's hand instantly clasped over her mouth as she almost pushed Astrid out of the way. Her knees knelt overtop the decayed remains of a flowering plant, whilst her brother stood close behind her for moral support. "I found Vectra out here, digging their graves, seven years ago. She carried their bodies up from the ravine where you found the other skeleton. Every year, Vectra plants Forget-Me-Nots in the spring like clockwork. She has never forgotten what happened that day."

All of a sudden, the feelings of the past resurfaced for Monica. Time stood still as the inescapable nightmare she endured for the fourteen months following their disappearance, flooded back. It was the same one that drowned all reason and shocked her senses beyond comprehension. A pit of darkness opened once more inside her soul, siphoning the goodness hiding in the far reaches of her heart. It had been an everyday vacuum she lived through for what seemed like forever, until one day, years later, when the pain slowly began to ebb away. And now, she finally had the answer she had wished to know for so long.

Seeing their headstone was surreal for the teenager. All the times she spent wondering what happened, being angry at them for leaving her and Dare behind, and the entire roller coaster of turmoil they caused, felt wasted on possibilities that never were. "They have been gone, all these years?" She could see and understand what this meant, but processing it was another matter entirely. Tears were about to pour down her cheeks as she turned to look up at Astrid. "Why didn't she help them?"

The nymph hesitated, observing the raw emotions written on the girl's face.

"Why?" Monica could feel the tears begin to fall as an overwhelming sense of disdain for Vectra blazed in her eyes. "How could she have been so callous, and cruel, when they came to her for help in stopping Gaither?"

"She did what she believed to be right on that day." Astrid stated, defending her friend's name.

"WHAT WAS RIGHT?!" Steam billowed from Monica's ears as her blood pressure mounted. "Was it right for the newspapers to badger us for a story they wanted, *only* so they could sell their articles? Was it right for the kids in my school to call me names, and bully me as the kid whose parents didn't want her? Was it right for us to be dumped on Trevor's shoulders when we barely knew him? Was it right for…"

"And is it *right* for you to be blaming the woman who told your parents to go back home, to you and your brother, for a choice that was theirs alone to make?" Astrid countered, forcing Monica to stop her rant and to listen to what she had to say. "You can shove the blame in any direction you like, Lass, but that piece fits but one way in this jigsaw puzzle. It was *your parents* who decided to leave, *your parents* who went to Vectra for help, and it was *your parents* who chose to continue onward, instead of going back home. I can't imagine how hard this is for you to hear, but Vectra is not the one you should be angry with…and…" She paused to ease into the next line, "it is something you have probably known this whole time."

Monica opened her mouth to come back at her, but then closed it shut again. Astrid couldn't be more right, and she hated that. She wished for nothing more than to curl into a ball and cry herself to sleep under that tree, away from the world and everything in it. Dare quietly moved closer to his big sister and gave her the most heartfelt hug he could muster.

"Are you going to be okay?" He asked.

"I think so. Just, not at the moment." Her lungs gasped for air from the pressure caving in on her chest. "They aren't coming back, Dare. They're never coming back." *Why doesn't having closure feel better than what it does?*

Astrid remained in a deafening silence out of respect for the girl's pain. In the middle of a sob, Monica's hands balled into fists, and the wind brushed her hair away from the back of her neck. "Who did kill them?"

The nymph let out a short gasp before recomposing herself. "I don't know, honestly, I do not. But Vectra does. And if you want to find out, then we better get to her before

Gaither reaches that press."

Chapter Forty-Seven

Vectra flipped onto her other side, feeling a rock under her left thigh. She was nearly fast asleep again when she heard footprints coming up to the wall of the tent and the voices they belonged too.

"Why didn't you tell me that we needed the kids LAST NIGHT!" Gaither angrily scolded at Taminus.

"I tried to, but you would not listen to me as you, and I quote, 'wanted to get an ounce of sleep before the sun rose.'"

"So why can't we just have Vectra operate the press, again?"

"Because she is forbidden to work any of the artifacts she protects. We must have the kids. That much I know."

"Which one?"

"Must I do all of your work for you?" Taminus snorted in disgust.

Gaither pointed a threatening finger at the man. "Just remember who you work for. Because without my help, you won't be able to find what you want."

"A misfortune, I am painfully aware of." Taminus briskly walked away as Gaither followed him across the camp. Their voices grew more faint and distant the further they moved away, until she could no longer hear them at all. Vectra was about to say something to Trevor, in the hopes of discovering what her cousin was after, but the sound of the tent's flap being pushed open stopped her from moving an inch.

A loud thud rang out as Martiban was tossed onto the ground by one of Gaither's hired help. "Have fun with your little party!" The man attempted a bad example of an evil laugh and then proceeded on his way to breakfast, leaving the threesome alone in the General's Quarters.

Vectra pretended to wake up for the first time, shifting slowly around and blinking her eyes blearily open. "Martiban?"

"Sorry I've joined the party a little late." His beard quivered as he coughed. "Apparently, Attila the Hun, did not take too kindly to me calling him a cumberworld."

"And he knew what that meant?"

"After he searched it up on his phone." A mischievous smile was almost visible below his bushy mustache. "Sometimes it pays to be older."

Not even thirty seconds later brought the boss man himself upon their tent, boasting his puffed out chest as he held court over his prisoners. "Ah, I see that my favorite trio of treasure hunters is already up this fine morning." He smugly stared at them all in turn, making a mental note of how weary they all appeared, instead of being refreshed from the chilly night. "What's with the long faces? Surely, with Vectra's help, we have the location of the entrance by now."

"There is a little hiccup in your plan…" Trevor gulped, regrettably awake now, and gave the Guardian a sideways look of fear.

Gaither clenched his teeth, displeased to hear that there was yet, another issue, this close to finding his coveted treasure. "And that is?"

"She doesn't…"

"I do not remember all the details about where and how the press is hidden." Vectra answered for herself. She saw no reason for Trevor to be getting into trouble on her behalf.

"Well," Gaither straightened his collar. "I must say that I expected better from you. Being the Guardian of all those powerful artifacts, one would think you could come up with a more convincing excuse."

"It is the truth." Vectra confirmed. "I really do not recall as though it was stashed away two months ago. Centuries have come and gone since then."

"Yes, yes, but it is not like this is much different from the first time our paths have crossed." Gaither looked directly at her, his face devoid of any emotion. "You will take us to the entrance by sundown, or else," he whipped out his finger to point at Martiban, "you can say your farewells now."

"I could not do that, even if I wanted too." Vectra answered, keeping up the false pretense that she had no suspicion about Martiban being a part of their ultimate plan.

"And why, per tell, not?"

"Because the way through the valley can be seen only during a clear sky at night."

"Then, for your sakes, tonight's sky better be crystal clear." Turning on his heels to leave, Gaither stopped short of exiting the tent, thinking about saying one last remark before deciding against it, and exiting altogether.

As soon as the flap reclosed, Trevor let out the breath of air he had been holding in and looked at Vectra with a questioning look as to Martiban's presence. She quickly gave him a short shake of her head, indicating for him to remain mute on the subject. "Did you get any sleep?"

"Not much." Martiban introduced himself to the

Browning sibling, recognizing the name and connecting him to his younger brother and sister. "They are pretty brave kids."

"That is what Vectra was telling me." A half-smile showed on his face. "Anyways, welcome to the study! Where we slowly lose our brain cells over where to find the next clue hidden within German text and centuries old illustrations."

"German?" Martiban painfully hauled himself up from the floor and shuffled his feet across the ground until he reached the paper strewn desk, overfilled with notes, doodles, and print-offs of translations. "You do not think…" He cast Vectra a concerned glance she couldn't be sure was genuine or not. "That Adalgard penned this?"

"Did you tell her about the press?"

"Well…I may have said a few things, but I would not have dreamt she would write it in a book with such elaborate care." A smirk appeared under his mustache. "Though, she was a perfectionist. That is why she was entrusted with their highest quality of pigments." From the corner of his eye, a small tear began to form as he touched the book's pages with the tips of his fingers. *No matter what happens next, please forgive me my dear sister*, he silently spoke inside his mind. He pulled himself away from the well-bound text, unable to keep a few sniffles from escaping. "We have to get out of these handcuffs."

Vectra studied the hunter's movements, watching his left hand shaking slightly. "Trevor said that Gaither is the sole owner of the key."

"We can try picking them, like in the movies." Trevor rummaged underneath a pile of papers in search of a pen or a letter opener. "So...do we have a plan? Since there is no one coming and we are on our own."

"You do not think much of your sister and brother." The Guardian stated, curious as to how Martiban would react.

"Monica and Dare?" Trevor's voice sounded skeptical. "They are just kids, and are not big on the forest."

"They traveled with me this entire way."

"We can't be talking about the same Monica Browning then. My sister doesn't go near the woods after…well," He seemed a tad distracted from his words as his fingers managed to locate the pen he knew was on the desk. "She wouldn't consider entering the woods, let alone go camping."

Vectra had a sudden hunch, seeing a touch of unease in the man's eyes as he talked about his sister's issue with the trees. "Are you ever going to tell her that it was you who induced her fear of the forest?"

Trevor nearly cleared the table off, being startled at hearing her question aloud. "How…how…how did…did she tell you that? I mean, does she know?"

"No. She did not have too. Dare told me that you refuse to speak of it, and Monica has no recollection as to why she is so scared of the woods. Just a fear, that most likely occurred when she was too young to remember. But the terror of what she experienced still haunts her."

Trevor shook his head while Martiban just stared on in confusion. "Don't…don't say it like that. I feel guilty enough as it is."

"What did you do to her?" Vectra could feel herself becoming protective of the girl who wasn't even in the room. Her hunch had sadly been right, and she was determined to find out why. Not just to know if he was truly the brother his siblings had been describing, but also to see whether or not he could be a person she could trust. At the moment, that list was growing smaller as the minutes passed.

"It was foolish, alright? And stupid too. I am twice her age, so as you can imagine, I was the typical brat of a teenager, who went a little too far on a practical joke." He wanted to leave his explanation there, but the Guardian demanded him to go further into detail. "When she was five, I told her that we could play hide and seek while on a family vacation. Out of the corner of my eye, I saw where she hid and instead of looking for her, I went to take a nap. It was nearly dark by the time I woke up and my mother was furious. She thought I was taking care of my sister, and not leaving her alone in the middle of the woods. Monica was crying when we found her, scared out of her wits and afraid to enter a forest ever since. That is when I went off to live with my Uncle, after I told my mom that Monica would never be my real sister."

Vectra and Martiban remained silent, unsure what to say.

"But I have been trying my best to make it up to her, and Dare. When my mother and step-father were planning on leaving to find the press, they sent me a letter, explaining that they needed someone to watch over my siblings for a little while, and that they were willing to pay me for the first few days to help sweeten the offer. I wasn't going to accept in the beginning, but my Uncle thought it would be a good way to patch things up. So I accepted, and honestly, I don't regret it in the least."

Martiban coughed into his hand. "Then why are you out here, Trevor?"

"For a couple reasons, actually. Gaither had told me that he believed there was a chance my mom and step-father were still alive. And while I do enjoy Monica and Dare's company, I am not our mother, or their father. So, years ago, I made a solemn promise, to myself, that if there was a sliver of a chance at finding them alive, then I would risk it for the sakes of my sister and brother. They need their parents more than a rambling idiot who doesn't seem to be able to hold down a job."

Chapter Forty-Eight

Astrid walked behind Monica and Dare as they traveled alongside the stony brook depicted on the map. Rising and falling with the natural landscape, the trek was unreal in the unapologetic forest. Majestic trees, reaching toward the sky, stood strong and proud of the woodlands they called their home. Roots, gnarled and thick, dove deep underground to keep themselves thriving, and nourished, by the plentiful soil below their feet. In the cheerfulness of the sunlight, Monica felt the weight of her childhood fears slowly fading away ever since they stepped foot in Leonard Brimy State Park, back when Vectra showed them her floating ship-wreck.

She stared down at the drawings in the Guardian's journal, trying to keep their group from veering off course. A jagged rock, about to come up on her left, was the last noted landmark before reaching the star symbol located at an opening amongst a sketch of dense trees. *Okay, this hasn't been too bad so far. Maybe it will be a little easier from now on.*

Gentle whispers brushed through the barren branches and passed their ears in a foreboding manner as Astrid maintained a short distance at the back of the line. The nymph continued to sip on a flask of sorts, and kept the small bottle in a pocket when not touching it to her lips. *So the nymph is an alcoholic,* was the first thought that went racing through Monica's mind. But, that would have been from their world and not of the Olde Realm's many possibilities. Deciding that it was a matter best left alone, Monica refocused her priorities onto making it to the marked spot without getting a twisted ankle amongst the numerous roots.

"This is like playing that floor game, you know, the one with the spinner and the colored dots you have to move around people to find." Dare almost tripped on the top of a walnut tree's large octopus-looking arm. "Except, that one was a little more fun to play." He lowered his head to go under a short branch leaning toward the ground. "What maze is this?"

"We're here." Monica stopped in the middle of the path, to see a section of well-packed evergreens and a singular entrance directly in front of them. Her eyes panned the expansive wall of pine needles extending from east to west. "I think the maze hasn't begun yet."

"Come again?" Dare stared into the darkened hole where no light seemed to be penetrating. "Oh." He waited for Astrid to walk ahead of them, stopping at the star-marked stone, which sat out like a welcome mat to the non-existent door. "Who wants to step into the darkness first?"

Astrid rested her hand against a vine covered tree trunk, gazing into the hole without any visible emotion. Again, she sipped on the small bottle she had dangling beside her, and his time, Monica decided to ask. "What are you drinking?"

"Sap from my tree." Astrid suddenly closed the flask, rather protectively, and slid it away from her view. "As a nymph, I have to stay close to my tree, or at least drink its sap to keep alive. So, what does the map say now?"

"Nothing much. There is a star, here, to indicate the star-shaped rock on the ground. And it appears that there is some tiny writing just underneath the tree line." Monica squinted her eyes in order to better see the inscription, and became flustered with herself. "Why do I continue to try reading a language I don't understand?"

Astrid glanced over the wording, slurping up a stray drop of sap that was threatening to fall off her chin. "Listen to the sound of the flute."

"What flute? All I hear is the rustling of the leaves from the breeze passing through." Dare looked up at the dancing branches, as if they were going to point the way at any moment.

"But of course." Spoke an airy voice from within the darkened entrance. "This is the most enchanted maze in all of the Western hemisphere, fading only in comparison to King Midas's in the Eastern, guarded by the minotaur. So many wonderful traps, deadly perils, and glamorous surprises lurk in these trees."

"Okay, who or what is that?" Dare quickly backed-up as a nearly transparent figure materialized in the passageway.

"Yingzalti, at your service. And do not inquire as to how I obtained his post in the Mirrored Woods. It is a woeful tale I wish not to dwell upon."

"Um, okay…" Monica looked to Astrid for guidance. "What are we supposed to do?"

"Listen for a flute. That is apparently silent right now." The nymph closed her eyes and tried connecting with the evergreen's essence.

"That will do you no good. These woods are unlike that of the common variety. For they act like one and are resistant to all outsider influence." The transparent being stated as a short smirk appeared on his face. "Guess you will have to go through the hard way. Just like the others did."

Monica shared a worried look with her brother. "What others?"

"The others of the most gruffness of manners. A man in a British uniform, with the most envious of perfect teeth, came strolling up to this entrance and demanded that I guide them through. Obviously, I declined such a rude invitation, as it is against my vows in the first place." Yingzalti's form waved slightly in the breeze. "Well, you better get hurrying along if you want to beat the storms that are headed this way."

"Storms?" Monica had completely forgotten about the impending thunderstorms Vectra had predicted from Rudi's radar. She hastily gazed into the sky above, where the clouds were steadily increasing in volume and darkness.

"Yep, and they are bound to have some awesome displays of lightning this time." A wide expression of excitement was painted across the ghost's face. "Addictions die hard, my friends. Or in my case, they do not die at all." Yingzalti pointed upward, showing a few toasty fingers in the process. Dare tried hard to suppress his laughter as his sister remained silent as the grave.

"Then, we shall get moving…" Astrid was about to step into the maze when an odd sound rang into the air. The kids looked over to see the nymph staring at a handheld device much like an older gaming system. A perimeter line was drawn in a gridded section of land, as a red dot flashed to alert her about an intruder close to her willow tree. "I have to leave immediately. Someone is near my home and…well…I think you have the idea. Fair well, Brownings. Remember, Vectra and the world is counting on you."

"No pressure." Monica whispered into her brother's ear while waving goodbye to the nymph.

Dare turned to face the ghost again, hands at his hips, and raised himself taller than what he truly was. "So, are you going to help us or not?"

"Let me think about this…" Yingzalti contemplated the notion, squinting his eyes and holding his thumb just below his chin. After a dramatic show of thought, he inhaled deeply and gave a resounding "no" before a smug smile spread on his lips. "I merely watch and report what happens in the likely case that you die. That, and I protect this maze from intruders."

"Well, you did not do a very good job at preventing the others from going through."

"But they had the same clue you did. That clue, is the passkey to entering. For only those with knowledge of how to leave, may enter. No one can say that we do not give someone a fair shot."

"Some shot." Monica bravely stepped into the maze, keeping her eyes locked onto the ghostly being, out of suspicion that he might try to pull a fast trick on them. Dare followed next, trying to gather up his fleeing courage at seeing the all-consuming darkness swallow them whole during midday.

"May the wind ever be in your favor, my friends. Do not fear, for I shall return your bodies to your family for a proper burial. We may be callous, be we are hardly ever cruel." With an almost evil laugh, the ghost vanished from view; his voice echoing strangely around them, seeming to reach deep into their minds as well.

Dare latched onto his sister's hand. "I sure hope you have a plan, Monica."

"Don't be ridiculous, Dare. Of course I do." Her words

may have sounded confident, however, her voice faltered slightly on the last line. *Of course I do? And what exactly is your plan, Monica?*

Chapter Forty-Nine

Vectra and Trevor looked up at the sky, seeing the oncoming clouds darkening in tone. "We might not have a clear night after all," the eldest Browning commented, holding a plate in both hands that was filled with food. He helped the Guardian in taking hers back to the tent, something she regrettably agreed too.

Upon her own request, Vectra opted to walk to the camp's smaller version of a Mess Hall, in order to assess her current condition. She was worse off than she first believed, and knew that the cuffs had to be removed if she was to have any decent chance at fighting back. "It may move through the area faster than you think."

"Because of Taminus?"

"No. Our powers are to serve our purpose, and not that of changing the planet's natural eco-system. It may sound confusing, but think of it like this; I can create a column of fire to defend myself, or others, from an imminent attack, but if a tornado rips up the country side and starts a fire, then I can merely change its course to protect people, but I cannot extinguish it. Gaea will always be more powerful than either of us."

"So, you can use your power to either run into battle or to cook food, however, you cannot use it to take out another country without provocation?"

"Precisely. It is our rules of engagement, as your military would call them. Helps to minimize the death toll."

The guard who walked them back to the General's Quarters, opened the flap and allowed them to enter, just as Martiban stepped out to use the restroom. Vectra waited for them to be out of hearing range before she told Trevor what she recently remembered. "This afternoon, it came to me why there is such an issue in the authenticity of that book. I did not hide the press here until 350 years ago. So there is no possible way for Martiban's sister to have penned those pages. It should have been so obvious to me last night, but my brain feels as clouded as this sky."

"That means that Martiban most likely created this?" He gestured at the book, sitting peacefully atop the desk.

"It would appear as such. For what reason? I am not sure just yet, though I have a sinking feeling that he may have found out the truth about something in the past. If he did, the strength of its sting will make him truly unpredictable." She looked at the meat sitting limply on the disposable plate beside her hand. "Our best bet is to go along with their plan of locating the press, and see what happens."

Trevor nearly spit out the food in his mouth. "WHAT?! Are you insane? Your brain is definitely not thinking straight." He refilled his fork with herb and buttered baby potatoes, and added a few corn kernels to the mix. "We can't help them. What if they reach the press and we are still not able to stop them? Then they have accomplished their goal and I have failed my mother yet again."

"And what do you propose we do then?" Vectra challenged. "I have no powers, hardly enough strength to walk fifty feet, and my mind is stalled in a slumber haze. You probably haven't even tried boxing for the fun of it, and you expect us to go up against at least ten guardsmen and a wealthy mad man. All of whom, have more weapons than we do."

"What about your knight friend? Think you could swing him back onto our side?"

"Not a chance without knowing his ulterior motive. If it is what I fear it to be, then we will be lucky if he doesn't kill me as soon as we find the press. Which is another reason why these cuffs must be removed." Vectra gazed upon the metal pieces in disdain, for the cursed coating they were drenched in. She suddenly felt all alone in the world, unable to trust a single soul, as she helplessly watched her deepest secrets float to the top, one by one.

"Okay." Trevor nodded in reassurance, causing her head to rise. "We do it your way. I just hope that we aren't making a big mistake."

"So do I, Trevor. So do I."

Chapter Fifty

"Ow!" Monica smacked her brother. "Dare, keep the flashlight aimed at the ground and not in my eyes."

"I thought I saw something above your head. Sorry." The boy flipped the green beam back to the floor of the maze, his grip on the light shaking from his unsettled nerves. It was his sister's idea to use the green beam, as Vectra had done on her car, and while it was supposed to alert them to the presence of Olde Realm creatures, the added eeriness of the glow did not make their situation any less scary. "Are you sure we have to use this beam?"

"Yes."

"What…what about the other colors it shines out? The orange and purple? Either of them are not as spooky as this one."

"I'm not sure what those others do. And we don't know enough about the dangers in this maze as it is. Vectra told us that the green light seeks out Olde Realm creatures, and that is what we go with." Monica retook the lead away from her younger brother as the path grew narrower ahead and fog blocked their sight from seeing anything. "Dare, hold onto my hand so we don't lose one another."

"Okay." Dare grabbed onto his sister's cold hand and continued to point his light into the waterfall of fog pouring in from the left wall of the maze. "You think we can walk through the wall? I mean, they are just plants, right?"

"I'm not sure we should try. You never know what things are living inside those dense bushes." She looked up at the tall evergreens, taking note that they appeared to mark where intersections were located, right before the fog consumed all air in sight. "There has to be one seriously large fog machine nearby."

"Or maybe something else is creating the fog?" Dare bumped into his sister's back, not able to see more than two inches in front of his face. "Now what do we do?"

"*How should I know?*" Was what Monica really wanted to say to her brother, but she couldn't. There was no one to guide them any longer, and she now had to be the decision maker once again. Straightening her back, in order to stand taller, though no one could really see her, Monica marched forward determinedly. "This way. The faster we get out of the fog, the faster we will be able to get our bearings." *I hope.*

For what seemed to last over an hour to the siblings, took place in actually thirty minutes, as the fog's density began to lighten and their flashlight beams were reaching further ahead with every step. "We are almost out, Dare." Monica called, feeling excitement building in her chest. "We are almost there."

As she walked into a cleared patch of the maze, the teen took a second to enjoy the small victory with a short jump up and down. "Yes." She whispered to herself. "At least, we can see again. You know, I wonder what terrors are hidden in here? The ones, that ghost, was talking about. Because, if they are anything like that fog, they are probably not as bad as…" It suddenly dawned on her that Dare hadn't spoken one word since they entered the clear air, despite him still holding onto her hand. She gulped her fear, turned her head slowly around, and looked down to see a smiling gnome staring back at her. Her hand immediately let go as she scrambled to remove herself from the garden ornament. "Who…who are you?"

"Orville." The gnome blinked, without saying anything else. His red hat, pointy shoes, and blue vest, all gave him a cartoonish appearance, though his plastered smile let off a creepier vibe. "Thanks for getting me out of there."

"What are you talking about? And where is my brother?"

"So that's what happened." Orville shook the shock off his face, flexing his cheeks until their movement returned. "Hey," his eyes squinted at Monica, trying to get a good look at her beyond the flashlight that was aimed directly at him. "Are you a human?"

"Why do you want to know?" After observing how the Olde Realm operated, she was not about to give an answer without being informed as to what the implications would be. Unfortunately, for her, she unknowingly already had.

The gnome's eyebrows pinched inward. "So you are!"

"I didn't say that."

"You didn't have to. The mere fact that you obviously have no idea about what I am, speaks for you."

"But…I…" Monica wondered if it was okay to begin panicking now. "Where is my brother?" She shoved the beam harder into his face like an interrogator on television. "Tell me where he is RIGHT THIS MINUTE!"

Orville talked behind his hands, shielding her light from his sensitive eyes. "Your brother is with my kin, fighting our Boar War."

"Boar War?"

"At least, that is what is should be called." Orville peeked out over his index finger. "We are still in the midst of it, so it technically doesn't have a name yet. Though, I feel like that name has already been taken. Or maybe, it hasn't? History isn't my strongest suit, you see."

"No, I don't 'see.' There is no war going on around here. Elsewise, I would hear screams, swords clashing, guns being fired, or something like that. But…" Monica gestured with her arms spread wide at the vast emptiness on either side of the path. Not even a cricket was sounding off, providing an absolute quietness to shiver the bones.

"Wow, you must be a human." Orville coughed. "For starters, we do not 'scream.' Secondly, the battle isn't up here. It's underground." He pointed to the grass covered forest floor. "My kind live beneath the soil. Have so for as long as I can remember. We drive the boars insane by popping out and stealing their food after Yingzalti feeds them. It is tradition."

"Great. So take me to my brother and we will be out of your way."

Orville swung his hands in the air, cancelling the suggestion. "No can do. The only reason I am not going to eat you is because you led me out of the fog, and saved me from one of the boars."

"EAT ME?!" Monica raised her flashlight up like a club, ready to strike at will.

"NO, NO, WAIT!" The gnome replied. "Ugh. All because of our cousins. Listen, I am not a garden gnome. My ancestors are from Switzerland, where we are known for…it doesn't matter. The point is, once my mates discover your brother, he might be in a deadly situation. I say 'might,' because it will depend on whether or not fighting for their lives will be more important than feeding themselves."

"Then, you are going to help me save him!" The teenager demanded of the short tunnel-dweller.

"Hold on there, sister!" Orville stomped his foot for emphasis. "Look, the only way to reach your brother is to stop the battle. If he fell through the same trapdoor that I escaped through, then he is stuck behind our third flank. That is where the fighting is one of the most fierce, and the only way to reach him is if we can stop the battle."

"And how are we supposed to do that?"

"By freeing the Erymanthian Boar. You know, the one that used to live in the sacred hunting grounds of Artemis, and devoured everything in its path? She is their leader and is the whole reason behind them attacking us on our turf. They think we captured her, imprisoning that monstrous pig in a cage with an impossible lock."

"Did you?"

"Me? I should say not!"

"Then how do you know all these details?" Monica cast him a glare, watching the proclaimed "non-garden" gnome squirm under her hardened eyes.

"Perhaps...I saw what happened before they attacked."

She took a pause, studying his face. "That settles it. You are going to lead me to where the Elaminus...Earthma..."

"Erymanthian."

"Erymanthian Boar is, and we are going to set her free."

Orville pulled his hands away from his eyes. "You are the most human person I have ever met."

"So? Time is wasting. Which way?"

He pointed straight down the path they were on, watching Monica's longer strides outrun his own, and shouted after her. "Because you are the most stupid one I have ever met."

Chapter Fifty-One

Rain soon soaked the ground Monica and Orville were racing across, whilst the gnome led her to where the caged beast was hidden. Thunder boomed overhead, alerting everyone to the impeding rage coming their way, just as Monica nearly slipped right pass the corner Orville had rounded. She quickly regained her footing and caught up to him. "Has this maze ever flooded?"

"A few times." He called back against the wind. "When it does, we have to open a runoff tunnel we built into our system underground." Orville skidded to a halt when a camouflaged trapdoor suddenly flipped open from the momentum of a boar's head hitting it from below.

In the brief moment it was up, Monica was able to capture a glimpse into the hole before the gnome slammed it closed. Exactly as he had described, gnomes and boars were attacking one another in an all-out-battle that consumed a complex network of underground tunnels. It was a fascinating concept; to think that there were two mazes in one. "You weren't joking."

"Why would I?" Orville asked, continuing on his way in great haste.

Only a few more turns later, Monica's feet stopped on a dime when she found herself face to face with the Eryman- thian Boar, barely three inches separating her nose from the barred enclosure. An enlarged snout was pressed into the steel rods, breathing heavily on each side of the teen- ager. Darkened eyes almost blended into the blackened coat covering the creature's entire body, until the boar's pupils lit up with an intensified blue. "What the…" Monica slowly backed away to provide a little separation, and stared down at the gnome who was more scared than she was. "What's the big idea, Orville?"

"Hey, don't look at me. She wasn't there the last time I saw her. She must have moved the cage somehow." The gnome failed to hide his fear as he madly dove behind the nearest bushy wall, sprinting as fast as he could.

"Orville!" Monica raced after him, reaching him in almost no time. "You have to help me free her and end your war."

"That's alright. She can stay right there where she looks happy and content."

"Who are you trying to kid? That boar doesn't look happy. You are not running out on me now…" The teen grabbed ahold of the gnome's arm, ensuring that he couldn't escape. "We are freeing that animal."

"Our deal was for me to take you to her. I upheld my end!" Orville's eyes began glowing red. "Let me go!" Razor sharp teeth sprouted from his mouth, prompting Monica to release him and watch him take off down the path.

"HOW DID YOU CAPTURE HER?" Monica's question faded into the drenched night as the gnome vanished from view.

As soon as he felt safe enough, Orville's pace slowed, his breathing labored from running and the panic induced by seeing the boar recognize him. He had thought his hiding spot had been concealed from her sights, though, clearly, it had not when the cage was set. His hands still contained the scars from when the boar was first captured, physically healed but reddened in guilt nonetheless. The war began under his decision making, and the weight of his friends' deaths was heavier than anything he could have imagined possible. *Why couldn't I have left things alone?! But when I saw those men being chased, and the weapons they had at their disposal, I...why didn't it work out like I planned? Ugh. I'm just so tired of living like vermin under the ground.*

Lost in his own mind, and shame-riddled flashbacks, Monica was able to sneak up on the gnome, who did not hear her approach. "You did help Gaither and his men to capture the boar, didn't you?" Orville stayed mute, not wanting to listen to a human, of all beings, utter the painful truth aloud. "I am not as stupid as you think. I saw that boar's eyes light up when she zoned in on you. My guess is, that since you know where the cage should have been, that you also helped them capture her. The question is why? So that you can live above ground for a change?"

"Pineapples." Orville turned around to look at her with a shade of embarrassment adding a pinkish color to his cheeks. "Pineapples are her favorite. By planting a pile of pineapples in the middle of the trap, covered by a cloak of vegetation, the cage was sprung on all sides of her as she ate."

"And the whole concept of a possible retaliation never occurred to you?"

"Our traps can only be opened from below. Why would I even consider that the boars could find a way to breach our stronghold?" Orville looked up at her with a saddened gaze. "So…do you have a plan, human? Because once that thing gets loose, then there is no stopping her from wanting to kill us both."

CRACK! A fierce bolt of lightning abruptly struck a tree at the end of the path, splitting it into two, and giving Monica an idea. "Perhaps I do." She reached into her pack and pulled out the electrio blade, which was merely a hilt at the moment with three small switches on the butt end. A sudden hesitation came over her when she realized there were no symbols or wording to indicate which settings she needed to charge the weapon, but she didn't want the gnome to see her lack of confidence. *It is up to me now. There is no one else here to save Dare.*

"Do you know how to use that thing?" Orville cautioned. "Not that I have any notion as to what it rightfully does, but you might unleash a hurricane…or something, if you hit the wrong button."

"Don't be ridiculous." Monica laughed off his warning. "This attracts lightning, not the wind. Besides, there aren't buttons to pick from, Smart One. They're called switches."

"That makes me feel a whole lot better." He sarcastically replied. "Buttons. Switches. Who cares? You still don't have a clue how to use it."

"Well, if I created the device, I would have the controls in order of operation. To charge would be first," The teen switched the first toggle, finding herself wrong as thin rods jutted outward from the hilt and sprang into a "v" formation on both sides. "Looks like a stand?"

"Good going, Genius."

Monica ignored the gnome's sour-noted sarcasm, and went about her business figuring out the next switch in the lineup. While nothing visually happened, a clicking sound started emanating from the handle, as an indication of the battery being primed for a charge, and the last toggle caused a lightning rod to shoot out of where a metal sword should have been. Since the teen didn't want to end up being fried in the process, she hastily placed the handle in the middle of the path, pushing the legs into the ground for stability, and pulled Orville away with her. From a safe distance, they watched and waited.

One would have thought that capturing lightning, during a highly active thunderstorm, would be relatively easy. However, it took longer than twenty minutes to get all three blasts required to fill the battery to capacity. When the mechanism registered it was fully charged, the rod automatically retracted, along with the stand, leaving the hilt behind, once again, in the grass.

"I have to admit, that was pretty awesome." Orville stated as he gazed upon the powerful weapon being held in the teenager's hands.

"Yeah, it was." Monica studied the handle, trying to decipher how to produce the blade Vectra said it created. She remembered the Guardian telling her that it offered up to three blades by personal choice of the one who wields it, but she couldn't see how. There were no other switches, or buttons, or anything else, that appeared to operate the unit. It was then that the circular gear on the hilt, where the rod had recently came from, triggered something in her mind. It was the same one used on the mobile drink maker. "I wonder…"

Monica clicked the gear one notch, unleashing a pulsating blade fashioned from no physical material. Instead, it breathed like a living lightning bolt, molded into the rounded edge of a Spartan sword, with a straightened back of deadly precision. Adjusting the gear again, caused the singular blade to split into two, and then into three as she moved the gear into the final position. With a flick of her wrist, the three blades merged and elongated themselves into a sword of shocking proportions. She could feel the power coursing from the weapon, a level of strength that was both alluring, and scary, at the same time.

"Electricity and water are not friends." Orville tried wringing out his vest in the midst of the ensuing storm, though it did little good. "So you have a weapon now. But we still have to unlock the cage and *somehow* convince the boar not to eat us."

"You said she has a favorite fruit. But does she have a least favorite?"

"She despises cabbage."

Ugh, don't we all. Monica had secretly hoped for the boar to disdain apples or grapes or a food item with a sweet smell that she could deal with. *But, cabbage it must be.* She unzipped her pack again, located the portable drink maker with ease, and prepped it for the right settings. "Okay, Orville. I think we are ready now."

Chapter Fifty-Two

Monica sneaked her way back up to the boar, rain pouring into her face as she kept blinking her eyelashes, in an attempt to clear her vision. Coming upon the turn, she hunkered close to the ground and slid across the opening where the cage was still standing tall. The Erymanthian boar remained motionless, feeling defeated after trying to reach her kin, in vain, for what seemed like weeks.

Glancing along the side of the cage, Monica spotted a padlock of sorts and slowly inched her way up to it. The lock looked old fashioned from the outside, but it contained six numbered tumblers that required the right combination to unlock it. *Great.* Thinking back on the little bits of information Trevor shared with her about Gaither, a few possibilities came to mind: the day he took the business over from his father, the day he swore he saw Bigfoot racing up a mountainside, and the number of a winning lottery ticket he purchased years ago. *He does have a fascination for legends and myths. And if that is the case, then the combination could be anything! What does he hold in the highest of regards, above all else?*

The answer suddenly came to her. *The company!* She

knew that Gaither loved his family's business more than anything else in the whole wide world. He constantly reveled in telling people about how his great-great-grandfather started out working in the railroad yards, before pursuing his dream of starting up a business making lanterns and household lamps. His ancestors accumulated a small fortune that grew exponentially when his great grandfather diversified their interests into other markets. From there, their company continued to increase in size and power. There wasn't anything he wouldn't do for W.K. Lowell and Sons.

"What was the date? August 24, 1872." Monica remembered those dates the most because 08.24.72 was stamped on every lamp in their house. When her parents went to work in the design department, their house soon became filled with retro lamps, replicated and re-imagined from every era dreamt possible. It was even a running joke that the International Space Station would see their house from outer space if they had every lamp plugged in.

"Please be it, please be it." Her fingers turned the final tumbler, hearing the releasing click with glee, before her joy sunk into the waterlogged grass below. While she did have the right number combination, the front of the lock had been a smoke screen for the actual keyhole residing behind the façade. Without any of Vectra's picks to override the mechanism, Monica was starting to feel the pressure get to her.

Another flash of lightning crackled in the sky above, prompting her to move a little faster as she turned the electrio blade on and jammed its tip into the keyhole, melting the entire padlock off the cage. Monica raced back the way she came, as the Erymanthian boar roared to life in the wake of her impending freedom. Orville waited around the corner, as instructed, and turned to run as soon as he saw the teenager make the bend. The ground pounded from the beast's mighty hooves, sounding into the sky with a rage equaling that of the storm. Its focus narrowed in on the gnome, kicking up chunks of grass and dirt behind her, as she made quick work of the shortening distance between them.

"She's gaining on us!" Orville warned. Monica skidded herself to a sloppy stop, and clicked the blade into trio mode. She whipped around to face the mad creature with the reflection of the powerful weapon pulsing in her eyes.

"I WAS THE ONE WHO SET YOU FREE, SO LEAVE US ALONE!"

The gigantic boar paid no heed to the teenager's demands, and swung her tusks at the blade in her hands. Monica was able to move the sword out of the way, in the nick of time, and did an upper thrust into the underside of the animal's chin. Blood seeped from the wound as Monica clicked all the blades off, and picked Orville up, before running down another leg in the maze. Left, right, right, left, she listened to the gnome's instructions on how to return to where the fog was thickest.

"We're almost there." The gnome frantically glanced over his small shoulders, seeing the beast steadily make her way toward them. "Boar, at twelve o'clock."

"I hear her."

"Time for another one of your great ideas."

"I thought you said I was stupid?" Monica slipped on a pile of wet leaves, causing both of them to go tumbling onto the ground.

"You were saying?" Orville looked up at the boar still bearing down upon them, his face covered in mud. No sooner had he wiped the dripping, brown goo from his eyebrows and cheeks, when a waterfall of green juice cascaded throughout his hair and onto his clothing. "What the…?"

"Purified cabbage. She is after you, not me." Monica abandoned the green-coated gnome to face the music without her, diving to the side in order to watch the plan unfold. She recapped the drink maker to keep the rain out, and held her breath in suspense. *I hope this works.*

"Monica…" Orville closed his eyes shut, preparing for the sheer force of the collision to squash him like a bug. He stood perfectly still, his breathing shallowed, and waited for the payback that was to come. When it didn't happen, he cautiously opened his eyes to see the boar sniffing him with a disgusted look in her eyes. With a final sniff of the revolting pureed cabbage, the massive beast lifted her head into the air, smelling the breeze for any sign of her family, and dripped blood on top of Orville, before running off in another direction.

"You can thank me by giving me back my brother." Monica firmly stated, smiling at the gnome, who was returning back to normal by the rain's good grace.

"I…I…don't know what to say."

"Orville. My brother?"

"Right, right. On it." The gnome shook off the green liquid from his hands and proceeded to run into the fog, dropping globs as he went along.

About thirty seconds later, Monica's eyes lit up at the sight of her brother walking towards her. He was dazed, and a little wobbly on his feet, but otherwise, very much alive, and still in one piece. "DARE!" She wrapped him up in a huge hug. "I'm so glad to see you're alright."

"Am I going insane?" Her brother rubbed the back of his head, where he felt a small bump under his hair. "I fell down a hole and hit my head. When I came to, I found myself lying behind a barricade that was in the middle of enormous gopher tunnels. And…I thought I saw a bunch of garden gnomes fighting off an attack from wild boars.”

“They aren’t garden gnomes, but I can explain everything later. For now, we have to focus on finding our way through this maze. And to listen for the sound of the flute.”

The boy glanced down and took note of the water puddling around his feet. “How long has it been raining like this?”

“A bit. Come on. This way.” She motioned for him to follow her down the path where she had met Orville, and turned left, rather than right, this time around. “I haven’t tried this way yet.”

“I must’ve been out for a little while.” Dare’s head moved side to side, as if shaking off his daze was that simple. “Where…” A sudden burst of rage from the Erymanthian boar made his eyes enlarge. “What was THAT?”

“That is one very angry, and ancient, mythical boar.” Monica darted down the passageway, leaving her brother hustling to catch up. “We need to get out of here. And fast!”

“This place is a literally a maze! With so many different paths to take, it could take us a month to figure this out.”

“We don’t have a month.” Monica took another turn.

“Too bad the P.I. can only identify tracks made within the last forty-eight hours.”

“DARE! That’s a great idea!” The teen brought the compass into the rain, studying it to make sure it was still working properly before aiming it at the ground.

“But Astrid told us that the group must have walked through her area on Tuesday. That’s more than forty-eight hours.”

“Yes, but Gaither and his men took Vectra and Martiban last night. Yingzalti said that the group had already been through here, which means that they must have made it past the maze and are in need of the next clue to the press. There is no easy way to circumnavigate around this place, so that would mean…" Monica smiled out of joy when Gaither's footprints, along with his men, Vectra and Martiban's, all were picked up by the fantastical device, "that they came this way."

"But their footprints do not show up behind us. Only in front." Her brother pointed out. "How can they just show up in the middle of the maze?"

"Maybe they were on a vehicle of some kind when they entered." She gestured her hand to the sandpit they avoided stepping into. "And it got swallowed up by the sand. Could be sinking sand for all we know. This place sure is weird enough to have them."

"Look out!" Dare pushed his sister out of the way as a wild boar charged at them. He was about to be trampled on when a jungle man's call cried out from the side, and a gnome with a razor sharp spear came flying in to the rescue. He kicked the boar's head with all the momentum he could muster, knocking the poor animal off its course, and sailing it into the dense maze wall, where it was quickly pulled in by pointy bird claws. "Whoa."

"The flute will play when you reach the owl statue with a battle helmet upon its head. Its eyes are the sensor that sets it off." Orville promised, smirking at the Brownings and giving them a nod of his head. "If you tell anyone, I will deny helping a human escape."

"Deal. Thanks." Monica and Dare fled as fast as their feet could go, following the compass as they wove their way through the rest of the maze with alert eyes and a rekindled sense of hope.

Chapter Fifty-Three

Monica walked along the rocky side of a muddy trail, as they continued following the map in Vectra's journal. After successfully exiting the maze over an hour ago, the siblings' next landmark was a lake on the other side of a distant hill. "Dare, who do you think is leaking information to Gaither?"

"I don't know." The boy was still trying to process the fact that he had been almost eaten, by carnivorous gnomes, after his sister briefed him on what occurred while he was stuck underground in their tunnels.

"If you think about it, everyone we've met, so far, could be the traitor Vectra is searching for." Monica protectively placed the journal inside her backpack, seeing the upcoming hill to climb, and tightened the straps over her shoulders. "For instance, Catriona Locksmith knew that Vectra's water friend…"

"Bregit?"

"Bregit. Had his memory erased, in order to keep him safe from being able to tell anyone about how to access the press. So, she could have told Taminus that we were at her house. Especially with the way she dislikes Vectra's teapot."

"But she didn't leave our sights the entire time, remember?"

"That may be true. However, Vectra was very cautious with her cup of tea when we were there, having not taken even a sip of it when we cleared the table. Perhaps she was duped before by the old tea seller, and all Catriona had to do, was push a hidden button to alert him, just like the one she used to defend her home against him."

"What about Martiban?" Dare rolled his eyes, thinking about how smug looking the millionaire's smile beamed when his men surrounded their camp. "For someone who had a lot of traps everywhere on his land, Gaither sure showed up pretty easily."

"And Astrid did tell us about the wicked love of his life, and her murderous ending. Perhaps he discovered the truth about what happened, and who killed her, after all this time. Though, that pact sounded like it was sealed shut, with the threat of the Grim Ripper's little brother to hunt them down, nonetheless."

"Yeah. But his attitude toward Vectra was not heartwarming."

"No, it wasn't." Monica took a small break, sitting on the grass and taking in the sun that was sinking lower in the sky. Soon after, her brother did the same. "Don't forget that Taminus knows who Vectra's friends are, and probably keeps a tab on them. Like when those two caught sight of us at the apple festival? We were right across from Rudi's campsite. And I still don't care for the way he left to make a phone call that night."

"Well, what about Astrid? Did you take note of her red hair? The same colored hair as the person you remember dropping Vectra's journal off to Mom and Dad on Halloween."

"She doesn't seem to harbor any resentment toward Vectra, quite the opposite in fact. But, one might say that she protests too much on how she would do *anything* for her. Though, she is also the one who helped us get here, and even took us to where our…" Monica's heartbreak was still too raw to discuss their parent's graves, so she quickly moved away from the subject altogether. "If she is in league with Gaither and Taminus, then why help us? Astrid could have kept us at her tree, or killed us herself."

"That is true." Dare tried removing a piece of dirt that had flown into his eye, rapidly blinking his eyelashes and picking at it with his fingers, whilst his sister remained deep in thought.

Monica ignored her brother's minor issue, and continued on speculating. "What bothers me is when she let out that short gasp, as the wind brushed my hair away from the back of my neck."

"She saw your birthmark?"

"Maybe. Though, I am not sure how that has anything to do with Clio's press."

"Search me. Oh, and don't forget about Gaither." Her brother suggested, glad to have finally retrieved the dirt from his eye.

"Gaither isn't of the Olde Realm."

"Isn't he? We have no idea who is, and who isn't, at this rate. As Vectra already explained to us, 'nothing is like it seems in this world.' Although, we could flash him with the green light on our flashlights and see if it picks up on anything…creepy." Dare chuckled, causing his sister's face to crack a smile in return.

"I also have a few ideas on Gregon as well. Vectra's journal was stolen while it was in his care, and he didn't tell her about the robbery until we showed up. When we talked about it, he acted very strange, and he also had ample amount of time to read its secrets before it was stolen."

Dare counted on his fingers, whispering each of the possible names aloud as he went around his hands. "You haven't eliminated anyone."

"I know. That's what scares me." Monica picked herself off the ground and made her way up to the crest of the hill, inhaling a deep breath of the beautiful view, while her brother came up beside her.

"Monica, there is something else that is bothering me."

"More than the fact that you have gone almost half a day without eating anything?" The teenager joked as her brother slapped her in the arm.

"Don't remind me! Seriously, though, whoever the traitor is, they must have a great deal of information on Vectra and the press. Enough to be able to lead Gaither here, down the trails at World's End, and through Yingzalti's magical maze of horrors. Because isn't this supposed to be the back way in? A shortcut that is not known to anyone else?"

"That is a good point, Dare. I don't foresee Vectra revealing all the answers to any *one* person, no matter how much she trusted them." Monica decided to sit on top of the closest rock she could find, and drink in the fading light while she still could. She cast her eyes onto the reflective water of the lake, seeing the ripples on the surface spread from one end to the other undisturbed. "But Catriona didn't need all the information to know that water must be an important enough clue for Vectra to have done what she did." *There's something we're still not seeing.*

"I don't think any of them have a good enough motive to betray her. But, then again, they have been around for centuries. That's plenty of time to gain a grudge, and for them to let it fester over the years." Dare rested his weary feet on a hollowed log and began looking for any hidden snacks in his bag, irritated at his sister for even mentioning the word "food" to his empty stomach. "We could go on and on about possible suspects, but where is the evidence?"

As they sat there, admiring the natural beauty of the landscape, Monica's eyes suddenly lit up when a parting in the clouds allowed for a few rays of sunlight to shine through. The water shimmered almost white in certain areas, reminding her of one very important clue they over-looked. "I got it! One of them practically told us that it was them and we missed it. And you were right, Dare."

"I am? I was? Which part?"

"We are going to need to be extremely careful with how we play our cards if we want to prove it, and not have Vectra turn against us."

"What? Who are we talking about?"

"We need to be sure though, before we tell Vectra." She turned to her brother. "We have to get to her before they reach the press. If we're right, then she may be in more danger than she knows."

Chapter Fifty-Four

"When are you going to tell me?" Dare begged his sister. "This is not a murder mystery show, where the detective waits until the end for the *big reveal*."

"I have to be certain that I'm right before I expose the person. There is a slim chance I'm wrong."

Dare couldn't resist it. "Slim?" Monica punched him in the side, hearing a satisfying "oof" coming from him, as they hiked to the other side of the lake. His stomach growled in the need of nourishment, having not found even a trace of any snacks in either of their bags. "I'm so hungry that I could go for a rotten apple."

"If you find one of those, you better leave it where it is because I know who is going to have to deal with you when that apple makes you sick." The teen plowed on ahead, glancing up at the storm clouds rushing past them in the upper levels of the atmosphere. "At least the rain is holding off, but the daylight sure is fading fast. We don't have much time before it is going to be hard to see anything with this cloud coverage."

"How much farther do you think it is to Gaither's camp?"

"Like I'm supposed to know?" His sister huffed. "The next marker on the map indicates a clearing up near the base of the mountain range over…." She pointed toward the rock formations resembling a sleeping dog. "There."

"I hope they have food." Dare licked his lips at the thought of a juicy cheeseburger topped with spinach, tomatoes, and two strips of premium bacon. *A side order of french fries, with a small packet of ketchup and a condiment cup of fresh coleslaw would pair nicely with…*

"Dare! Stop drooling!"

The boy jolted himself back to the task at hand, only to find that they were already coming upon the outside edges of Gaither's camp. Monica pulled him down behind a bush with half its leaves still intact, and gave him an unnecessary sign to keep his mouth shut.

Both Brownings observed the tightly compacted camping city that Gaither had instructed his men to build. It was well-protected, through the use of large rocks stationed every so often, and armed guards posted in-between them with guns. Taminus's face oozed with boredom at watching the others go about their business as they dried off their equipment, from the recent deluge of rain, and leaned against a tree extending its branches over the tents. Next to a warming fire, Vectra and Martiban sat opposite one another, staring into the blaze under Taminus's care. The tents, and off-road vehicles, reflected the flames against their smooth surfaces, while Gaither was spitting out angry commands from inside a mobile headquarters.

Monica looked over at her brother with an expression of pure dread, weighing out the options in her mind.

"What are we going to do?" Dare asked. "I mean, there are at least ten of them, and only two of us."

"Ye must have faith, my little friends." Gregon's voice

suddenly whispered in their ears as he popped up alongside the boy, scaring the wits out of the two kids.

"Where the heck did you come from?" Monica suspiciously stared at the Kurzian, who handed her brother a beef stick to munch on.

"From the field on the over side of that mountain range." His larger hand pointed to the mountains on the far side of the valley. "There is a nice selection of maple trees where the acorns have an especially wonderful flavor, making them perfect for grinding into flour."

"How did you know to come here?" Dare shuffled himself closer to his sister, looking pleadingly for her approval that he could eat the meat. She nodded, having secretly cleared the dwarf of most of her doubts, though she reserved her full judgement for a later time.

"Rudi phoned. He figured Vectra could use a hand after she showed up on his doorstep, an inch from meeting Hades." Gregon smiled at the boy when he noticed that the beef stick had been already devoured, and happily handed him another. "He knew I was in the area because I visited him the day before you arrived. The black walnuts were coming down and he had a whole bag waiting for me to pick up." His eyebrows moved up and down, excited for the thought of being able to cook up one of his favorite meals at home. "Appears as though I have missed quite the action, however. When you and your brother went driving a bumper car on the main road!" A slight chuckle escaped his lips. "Heard about it on the radio, and also how the police are after you. You two are quite 'hot,' as it were."

Monica and Dare just looked at each other, not wishing to think about that at the moment.

"So," Gregon sat down on a large root sticking out of the soil. "What's the plan?"

"For us to save Vectra, the press, and the world, naturally." Dare smiled. He was about to continue on when they all hunkered lower to the ground as one of Gaither's men stopped to listen merely five feet away. They all paused, waiting for him to move on, and sighed in unison when he finally decided that the coast was clear.

"That much, I gathered. I am talking about the immediate plan on how we are going to save Vectra."

"We surrender ourselves."

"What?" Dare and Gregon flipped their heads to face Monica, who gave them a neutral look in return. Her brother nearly had a stroke when she suggested it.

"Just what I said."

"Have you gone looney?" The boy couldn't believe what his sister was saying. "We have done all we can to stay away from their clutches, and you want us to give ourselves up freely?"

"No, not freely. At least, not to make it look as though we are giving ourselves up." Dare looked confused, vexed even. So Monica continued to explain her plan to them. "We have to make it appear like we are coming to rescue Vectra, and then let them capture us in the act."

"With you two, that should not be that difficult." Gregon jabbed, receiving glaring stares from both the siblings.

"At least we do not have bright white archer capes like Astrid does." Dare retorted.

"That is called a Destruction Cloak, or a De-materialization Cloak, I'll have you know. When any object is thrown at her, she says a certain word and the cloak allows the object to go right through her body. Hence, the name. It deconstructs her physical makeup and then realigns after the object is on the other side." He beamed a set of semi-crooked teeth at the kids, who just blinked at him.

Monica brought the conversation back on topic, worried that they were wasting too much time as it was. "It is the only way to verify my theory, and to be of the most help. You said so yourself, Dare. There are too many of them and they're all armed. Even if we did rush them in some far-fetched, half-brained scheme, we would still be caught."

"What if we tried beating them to the press and surprising them there?"

Monica showed her brother a few of the pages within Vectra's journal. "I don't see how we can. There are various puzzles to solve, and we don't know what all protective measures she has in place."

"But all the answers are right there!" He slapped his hand against the book.

"Do you read Ancient Greek?"

Dare blinked his eyes at her. "Ooh."

"I can." The Kurzian replied.

"That is a very nice gesture, Gregon. But we need to have someone on the outside, who can get us help if things go sour."

"So, what do you want me to do?" Gregon looked at the teen with an eager face. "Haven't had this much fun in countless years."

"Stay hidden." Monica handed him the journal, pushing it into his chest with an emphasis on what she expected him to do. "Keep the book with you and stay along the edge, within sight of the camp, just in case we need to call you in as the cavalry." She tossed him the P.I. as a backup, in the off chance he would lose track of them.

"Got it." Gregon wished them well, and caught Monica right before she was going to head into the underbrush. "Make sure they do not get their hands on Vectra's necklace. The one with the green stone encased inside the wrapped metal. You understand me?"

"Sure. I guess."

"You *have* to promise me this, Monica. Because if anyone of those hoodlums gets their hands on her necklace, then it is game over; no matter what."

"What is so important about an artistic necklace? Does it contain acid or something?"

"It is her soul." Gregon stated with dead seriousness in his face. "Her soul is literally trapped within its hardened edges."

"You are not joking." Monica felt like she was stating the obvious, but the reality of it all was hard to hear.

"Whoever has control of that necklace, has control over Vectra. It was part of her being sentenced here to protect the artifacts, and it used to be in the hands of a goddess, though I forget which one, until she stole it back from them. But she has not been able to set it free from its prison as of yet."

Monica stared him straight in the eyes, with a heavy sense of duty. "I promise, Gregon."

Chapter Fifty-Five

"How are we going to make this look like an accident? Us, being captured by those guards, I mean. Oww." Dare pulled his hand away from a thorny bush.

"Not sure yet. But, continuing to talk would be one option." Monica leaned over the large trunk of a fallen tree, where she had a clearer view of where Vectra was sitting by the fire. "I don't see any sign of Trevor." She whispered to her brother.

"Maybe he is inside one of the neighboring tents?"

They both quickly hushed up, as another guard walked by, blocking the campfire from their current position while three additional guards were acting like they were on a coffee break. Their game of poker appeared to have been started long ago, as many chips were in the center pot, favoring the men on the left with a decent streak of luck. Over the new winner's joyous laughter, the kids could hear the sound of Gaither shouting at another shadowy figure within the largest tent. Though the words were muffled and barely audible, the argument was not casual by any means.

"We need to wait until the guards come this way again, and then make enough noise to get their attention." Monica instructed.

"Rodger." Her brother replied, pretending to speak into an invisible walkie-talkie. "We are about to head into the Delta Point, over and out." He smiled, trying to alleviate his worsening fears of going straight into the lion's den with a little joke.

Monica pleaded with her eyes for him to stop. She knew it was his coping mechanism, but they needed to make this look real enough to fool the guards. Otherwise, they would suspect something was amiss, if they willingly walked into the camp.

A few seconds later, the teen moved stealthily behind one of the boulders marking the perimeter, and motioned to her brother to follow. "That guard with the blonde hair, he is about to turn back, and when he does…"

"You be joining us for a cozy fireside chat." A gravelly voice finished her statement from above. Monica and Dare froze; allowing goosebumps to crawl up their necks as they slowly looked up to see two large hands grabbing them.

Vectra's eyes widened as soon as she saw the Browning siblings being thrown to the ground near the fire, by a man named Weston. "Found a few urchins sneaking about in the woods. Didn't keep their yappers shut." He spit next to Monica's hand, smirking at the scowl painted on her face. For the first time in over an hour, Taminus moved away from the tree and alerted the bossman about Weston's catch.

"Monica, Dare, where is…" Vectra suddenly silenced her own question, catching a sign of caution shining in the teen's eyes. "Are you two alright?"

"Soaked to the bone, but other than that…" Dare picked a few stones out of the skin on the palm of his hand, "right as rain."

With the flapping of fabric in the distance, everyone

turned their heads to see Gaither exiting the tent and making his way over to the newcomers. "Ah, how nice of you to have dropped in at the most perfect of timing. We are about to embark on the final leg of our journey to find the press, and would have sorely missed not having you there to see it in all its glory." He cast a look of smugness at Taminus, flashing his straight teeth that were whitened beyond natural ability. "I told you, didn't I? Go for the leader, and the rest shall fall into place."

"So you did." Taminus bit back his tongue of disdain for the boastful man that crawled under his skin. "You are so smart." He sassed back, drawing himself up another three inches by just stiffening his back.

"Now that the gang is altogether, we must continue preparing to leave as soon as the clouds have dissipated. Weston, see to it at once. We hike the very moment the stars are visible."

"I'll take those." Weston stole the backpacks off of Monica's and Dare's shoulders, shoving the kids closer to the fire. "Here. So you can dry yourselves out."

"Nicholas, you stand charge of them as I take a rest in my tent." Taminus ordered. "It appears as though there is going to be a long night ahead of us." The guard with the blonde hair stepped forth, tipping his head in response to Vectra's cousin, and stood with a rifle at the ready.

Monica shuffled herself over to the Guardian, seeing the handcuffs upon her wrists and wondering why she was not attacking with a source of fire right in front of her. "I'd thought Taminus wouldn't want you out of his sights?"

"He has assured faith in these." She brought her wrists up slightly in order to demonstrate her point. "They suppress my powers because of what they are plated with; the stolen chalice of Dionysus, the god of wine. My father stole it during one of his festivals." Vectra actually cracked a smile for a brief minute. "The look on Dionysus's face was price-less."

"We have to get you freed then."

"It is no use." Vectra shot a quick look at Martiban, who nodded in agreement. "You want to tell her?"

"Gaither has the key, but we don't know where he keeps it on his person. Your brother…"

Monica and Dare nearly jumped up from their seats. "Trevor? You've seen our brother? Is he alright?"

"Yeah, he's fine. But he tried picking the handcuffs apart unsuccessfully. Apparently these are both magically enabled."

"He isn't exactly pickpocket material either." Monica smiled, before she turned her attention back onto Vectra. "I think I know who the traitor is."

"Oh, you do?" She glimpsed over at Martiban, who shuffled his feet in the mud, digging his heels down in. "And just who do you believe it is?"

"Someone with red hair, like the woman from my memory. Someone who knows a lot about you and the jour-nal. And someone who can read Ancient Greek."

"There is more than one person that fits that descrip-tion. One of whom you know nothing about, so presum-ably…"

"Then try the other one."

"Aisling?"

"Yes, but she calls herself 'Astrid' now."

"That is hardly conclusive. For starters, many of the people I know can read Ancient Greek, and red hair does not catch her red-handed. Where is your proof?"

"I don't mean to butt in on the conversation, but Aisling has known us for centuries. The idea that she is against us is absurd." Martiban stroked his beard. "What would she have to gain?"

"That part, I am a little weak on at the moment."

"Then I suggest you have something more than a theory, the next time you go accusing one of my old friends of betraying me." Vectra huffed, trying to make it look good.

"I thought you told us that you didn't have any friends?" Dare jabbed.

Martiban rose from his log and asked Nicholas if he could get a drink of water. As the two of them walked off, another guard stepped over to fill in, and was more interested in his lack of cell service than in watching the prisoners.

Monica and Dare immediately leaned into Vectra to let her in on Monica's real suspect.

"We actually think it's Martiban. And before you get irritated with us, allow me to explain." Monica paused to gather her thoughts. "When Gaither surrounded us at Martiban's camp, the sun was setting behind him, and yet, he told us that he had to enter from the south, because the high hills prevented entry from any other way."

Dare was lost. "Then why did you say it was Astrid a moment ago?"

"I wanted him to think that we didn't suspect him, to make him feel safe."

Vectra winked at the teenage girl. "That was good thinking, Monica. Because he might alert them that his cover is blown otherwise."

Monica sensed another meaning behind the Guardian's eyes, though. "You knew. Didn't you?"

"I had a hunch based on something completely different than what you deduced. That is why I did not try to stop you from talking. I figured you were smarter than to accuse him like that. It truly was a great catch though. Where is my journal?"

"Safe." Monica exhaled a huge weight off her shoulders, now that they at least warned Vectra. However, that didn't mean that they were finished telling her the bad news.

Dare was a little slow to pick up on it too, but when he did, he was a tad embarrassed to not have understood his sister's clue earlier. "Because the sun sets in the East."

"Bingo!" His sister patted him on the back.

"Monica, we are going to need my book. They do not have all the clues to get us there and for us to make it out alive, we are going to have to play along for the time being."

"We can manage that. But Vectra, have you thought about the possibility that Martiban might know more than you think?

"What do you mean?"

"He was most likely there when you shared your tea with Bregit, to have known how to get this far. Surely you figured that out by now. With the way Gaither took you here through the maze. It is the back route you wrote about in your journal, and not the longer trek one would have normally taken."

"I am ashamed to say that these cuffs do not just affect my powers, but they also drain me of any strength and cloud my mind as well. You are right, Monica. I should have caught onto that sooner."

"Where is the key?"

"With Gaither. But we do not know where. That part, Martiban did speak the truth on."

Monica absentmindedly placed her hand inside the pocket of her coat, hearing a crunching sound as her fingers rediscovered the dried petals she stuffed in there earlier. "Does he like tea?"

Chapter Fifty-Six

"Come in." Gaither called from inside his private tent, more focused on numbers then who was actually outside his door. Monica stepped forth, forced more or less by Nicholas so he could return to watching the others by the campfire, and took a quick glance around at all of the operations being housed within the heavy, fabricated walls. It was a mobile command headquarters of epic Fortune 500 Company proportions. Laptops filled one unit of collapsible bookshelves while paper reports littered two 6ft long tables in the middle of the space. Lanterns hung from the ceiling with various ropes attached, making the entire room appear like a misplaced conference center. Everything, short of a grand foyer entrance, was there, including the underappreciated assistant running from table to table in great haste.

"Ah, Ms. Monica Browning. What can I do for you?" Gaither pointed to an image of an ornately designed piece of furniture, shaking his head with frustration, and ordering around the frazzled woman who needed a vacation. "No. No. No! I specifically told Abigail to recreate a chair from the 1750s, and not from post 1820s."

"Sorry, Mr. Lowell. I will see to correcting it right now."

His assistant straightened out her black pencil skirt, and shuffled her way around the tables, to an office corner where a side table and a computer had been jammed beside boxes marked as canned food.

"I…uh…" Monica paused, collecting her courage, and restarted what she was going to say. "I've come here to negotiate the freedom of my family."

"And what makes you think that I would let you go before I find the press?"

"You have Vectra. She is the one you need. Not Trevor, nor Dare nor myself. If you let us go, we promise not to talk to anyone about it."

"Well, while I do admire your noble gesture, surely you do not expect me to believe you. Especially since the police have been looking for you and your brothers. Your faces are plastered all over the media outlets back home, not to mention the newspapers having a good ol' time with their headlines."

"But that was not our fault."

"Doesn't matter at this stage of the game, Kiddo." He walked closer to her with smiling eyes and a creepy grin. "Monica, I think it would be good for us to have a little chat, in private." His clammy hand reached around her back, guiding her over to where a small kitchenette had been set up to serve the boss his own special food. As they walked past the mountain of paperwork, and into the marked off space, Monica noticed Vectra's satchel perched on the table and her tea kettle resting atop a portable burner. Steam was beginning to billow from the spout, promising a glimmer of hope in the midst of the small clouds.

"If you could have anything in the whole world, what would it be?"

The teenager shifted her focus onto the table where

Gaither was offering her a seat, across from another chair. "I guess it would be for my family to be safe."

"But you don't have your whole family with you, do you?" Gaither placed his elbows on the table's shiny surface. "Your mother and father aren't here. Not physically anyways." He sighed into the air, making a sympathizing face at the young girl. "And you probably know what happened to them by now."

"You killed them." She steadied her glare at the man taking the other seat, and watched him pick up a mostly full bottle of water in his hands.

"No, Monica. I didn't. See, I came to find them after I discovered that both your parents quit, without giving any prior notice. They were good employees, Monica. Two of my very best. They may have been amateur historians, but their designed replicas were the best in the business and I had a hunch that something was wrong. So, after talking with their coworkers, and riffling through some notes in their mostly cleared desks, I came searching for them. And do you know what I found?" The teen shook her head, not sure where this was leading to, and whether or not she wanted to hear it. "I found them out here, in the thickest part of the woods. They were trying to search for something beyond their capabilities, and I offered to help, but…"

"Excuse me, Mr. Lowell." His assistant interrupted, prompting the man to crush in the sides of the plastic water bottle he had been sipping throughout the day. "I have the bank on line one and the lady insists that she cannot be put on hold indefinitely again."

"Alright!" Gaither grumbled, and stomped his way over to where his assistant held out a cell phone for him to talk on. Monica took her chance and reached into Vectra's bag, quickly locating the vile of honesty extract and pouring a smidge into the crumpled plastic bottle in front of her. She then turned to see how far along the kettle was at making the water boil, and used a hot pad to remove the top lid. Unzipping her jacket's pocket, Monica dumped the pressed flowers into the water, and stirred their petals counterclockwise with a wooden spoon, watching them begin to steep. "WHAT DO YOU MEAN HE SAID NO?!"

The teen jumped at the sound of the company's owner shouting at the top of his lungs, and driving a fist into the nearest table with all of his caged-in anger. Undeterred, she continued to stir the petals around in the water as Gaither raged over his agonizing phone call. She counted down the seconds by "Mississippis," trying to keep the flowers from steeping too long, as Vectra had warned her.

Monica was in the process of removing the first of the flowers, after about a minute for the right amount of forgetfulness, when she heard his temper being redirected at his assistant. Just as she was retrieving the last one from the kettle, Gaither slammed the phone's screen with his thumb, and threw it against the wall, sailing it above his assistant's head as she ducked out of its way.

The action drew Monica's attention for a mere moment, but it was long enough for her to lose the flower from the spoon, and back into the pot it fell. She jerked the utensil out of the water, and gently placed it on the counter where it had rested before, scolding herself for making such a clumsy mistake. Out of time, she hurriedly went to retake her seat, and desperately hoped that he wouldn't find the last flower still floating in the kettle's water.

"There is no talking with those heartless cows!" Gaither stormed up to the kitchenette, pulling out an expensive blend of silver needles to steep in the kettle that was still boiling hot. He was so blinded by his recent blowout with the woman from the bank, that he failed to inspect the water inside. "All they see is a bottom line and not the heart of the people who built the businesses up from the bottom, with their own calloused hands!"

"Is that why you want the press?" Monica asked, frantically watching his every move. "To take over the banks?"

"That is none of your concern." Gaither pulled a timer from the drawer below, and set it to the precise minute needed for his tea to be ready. He returned to his chair, and grabbed the water bottle with the strength of a bulldog, crinkling its thin walls as he took a sip from the now tainted liquid. "I am more powerful than all of the banks put together."

"Well, if you are so powerful, then why do you have to keep Vectra and Martiban in cuffs? Seems to me that if you were smart enough to capture them, you can outwit them again if you had too."

"You know, you're right. I was pretty smart in the way I captured them. Although, if I am being honest, Taminus had a big part in helping to sway that old knight to our side."

Monica held back a triumphant smile, seeing how fast the extract truly did work. "Besides, no one knows where the key is hidden. You would be showing your power over them by presenting the key to their freedom. The ultimate symbol of status."

"What? You mean this key?" Gaither pulled it from his breast pocket, allowing it to glisten in the light of a camping lantern. "Amazing…isn't it? How such a small trinket, a trifle really, could open up passageways into greatness or an eternal spiral of suffering and defeat." He slapped the metal item onto the table and left it there to check on his tea.

"Sir?" Gaither's assistant bravely reapproached her boss. "There is a buyer on the phone for you."

"I do not wish to be disturbed, Collette. Is that not what I said?"

"Ah, yes, Sir. You did say that. But this particular buyer is the one with the hotels in Italy."

Gaither swatted at her, apparently motioning for the cell phone he chucked at the tent wall earlier, and prepared himself to talk with a happier tone in his voice, as though nothing was wrong. Without leaving the kitchenette this time around, everyone listened to him trying to reassure the buyer, that the bounced check of refunded money, was a technical error, and was being looked into as they spoke.

Monica's breathing quickened as she stared at the key, deciding whether or not to take it in that dire moment. His back was turned away, and she could reach over in a split second. However, he was still on the truth serum and would have noticed it not being on the table when he sat back down. It would be obvious as to what happened until he drank the tea, which would be steeping for a few more minutes. *Or is the timer about to go off?* The view of the counter was blocked by Gaither's body, so she couldn't see how much time was left.

Ring. Ring. *Too late.*

Gaither finished up his conversation with the wealthy hotel owner, and tried to calm his nerves down as he went to fix himself a cup of tea. "What the…? Something is blocking the spout and only a trickle is actually making its way into the cup. Ugh. This is why I normally have servants do this."

Monica froze. Panic was rising in her stomach. *Stay calm, stay calm.* She tested the sturdiness of the table, feeling a wobble in the one leg, and smiled with a newly hatched idea in mind. *There is hope yet.* "Here. Allow me to get it out."

"No. You will probably put something in my tea that

will most likely kill me." He laughed. "Just like in a fairytale, huh?"

"In a fairytale, they like to use poisoned apples." Monica pulled on her sleeves, making a lighthearted joke as though it was the beginning of a magic trick. "Nothing up my sleeves. I was also just taught by an old expert in the craft. Allow me."

"Very well. It is not as though you have anything to hide. Though Taminus feels differently." Gaither sat back down in his seat, and played with the water bottle as Monica went about removing the blockage in the spout.

"Why does he think that?"

"He says that Vectra is forbidden from using the press, and we need you kids in order to operate it. Something about bloodlines."

"Bloodlines?" Monica flashed back to the moment when Astrid had gasped at seeing her birthmark, located at the base of her neck.

"Yeah. Don't ask me what he is referring too. He is only along because I promised to tell him where something is hidden. Something that was lost at sea, and I am not allowed to say anything more on the matter. Apparently, it is supposed to be quite secretive."

"Is that right?" Monica poured the first cup, sitting it off to the side and then proceeded to pour another two, full of the tainted liquid. "And why are you in this?"

"To save my family's company, and their legacy." Gaither played with the label peeling from the plastic of his bottle. "You know, my father died unexpectedly, and left me the company in a sorry financial state. He invested some of our capital in a doomed venture called Bark to Talk. It was supposed to a revolutionary communication device so that people could understand what their dogs were saying. I can still see it in his face, all excited to be branching the company into the retail market, with a product that was for the average pet owner. The day after he closed the deal, he died in his office, and those fraudulent inventors made off quite handsomely. And while I have been managing to keep us afloat, it has only been bandages over the larger problem."

"Oh. I'm sorry to hear that."

Gaither coughed into his hand. "I miss him though. Much like how you must miss your parents." He paused, looking up to see the girl about to bring him his tea. "The press could bring them back, you know. It has the ability to re-write history, and to change it."

Monica placed the kettle back onto the burner and turned to face the man she had grown to hate. "I suppose."

"It's no bedtime story, Monica. This press is real, and so is the possibility of getting to see your parents again, alive and well."

The teen stared into the drinks she was holding, hesitating on giving them to him, and thought about what he was saying. She could hear Astrid's words rolling through her mind, filling her with a peaceful sense of understanding. "That would be nice. It really would be."

Monica went to walk forward, and pretended to trip, causing the table to be knocked over and tea spilling everywhere. "I am so, so sorry."

"You clutz!" Gaither looked down to see the spilt drink running down the front of his shirt. "This shirt costs $340!"

"I said I was sorry. Here, have my cup instead." Monica handed it to him, watching the man gulp down the mixture without coming up for air. She bent over to find the key on the ground, silently celebrating, when her fingers located the metal object. As she glanced up at the mad and broke millionaire, Gaither pulled the cup from his lips, and blinked at the table lying on its side.

"What happened?"

"Ah, I accidentally tripped and knocked into the table. You managed to save your tea in the nick of time." Monica forced a smile. "And I think I will be heading back to the other prisoners now. Before my clumsy feet bump over anything else of yours."

"And you were here because?"

"You summoned me here, remember?" Monica acted perplexed, though wondered if she had accidentally steeped the tea for too long. Taminus would be onto them in a heartbeat, if Gaither's memory loss was too extensive. "You were talking to me about the press and asking if Vectra had an update on the next clue as to its whereabouts."

"Ah, yes. And is there any?"

"Boss!" Weston speed-walked into the tent, blinking in confusion at the sight of Monica standing opposite of Gaither. "The sky is clear. We should move out."

Chapter Fifty-Seven

Nicholas rushed Monica back to rejoin the others, having been called to ensure the vehicles had enough gasoline in all their tanks. When she arrived, Trevor distracted Martiban long enough for his sister to bring Vectra up to date on everything she had learned from Gaither.

"Very good, Monica. Are you sure you do not want to be a spy when you grow up?" The Guardian joked.

"Ha-ha. Anyways, here's the key." Monica placed it in the palm of Vectra's hand, and looked over at her younger brother. "Did he get your paper airplane?"

"I believe so. Hey…" Dare felt the ground being pushed up from underneath his feet, and moved backward so that the gnome could poke his head above the surface.

The teenager blinked. "Orville?"

"At your service." The gnome tossed Vectra's journal out of the hole and winked at the young girl. "For the record, I am doing this for Gregon and not for you. He is like a brother from another mother."

"Gregon? What is he doing…" Vectra was suddenly cut off by the unexpected presence of Weston, making his way into the tent. Monica quickly stepped to the right, in order to block his potential view of the vole-digging gnome.

"Vectra and Trevor are to travel up front. The rest of you will be guarded near the back. We move out in two minutes." He tapped on his gun, giving the group a surveying glance. "No funny business. Got it?" They responded vocally, to please the big oaf, and went back to cleaning up Trevor's notes from the desk as Orville's hole closed up like it had never existed.

✻✻✻✻✻✻✻✻✻✻✻✻✻✻✻✻✻✻✻✻

Thirty minutes later, their convoy was hiking alongside a swelled stream; stepping over rocks and roots too numerous to count, with their flashlights trained on the gnarled ground to prevent them from twisting any ankles. "Are we there yet?" One of the guards called out, clearly not a night person and missing his sleep.

"Halt." Vectra instructed the group, pausing in front of a small circle of charred firewood. The blackened chunks were wet from the recent rains, but that did not stop it from self-igniting upon sensing the people standing nearby. They all watched, as a strong gust of wind blew in from the east. It swirled around the blaze, tinged with blue, and carried it to the top of the tree canopy, in what almost looked like a forest fire about to commence. As it whipped upward, the fire rose higher into the sky, taking on the shape of a winged horse, before it disappeared into the night.

"Were we supposed to follow him?" Trevor asked as the horse vanished.

"No." Vectra raised her hands to point at the tree tops. "The path is hidden in a river of stars. The fire only tells you which constellation to keep as our heading, since the stars change throughout the year. Currently, we are to use the

405

constellation of Pegasus as our guide." She motioned for them to keep moving, shifting her gaze around in the darkened woods. "It's not visible during the day because the gaps in the tree canopies move and the fire is only seen at night. Once the flames are awakened, and the signal released, the path will reveal itself." *Let us just hope that a part of my memory comes back when we reach the cliffside.*

Trevor and Vectra took a pause to look ahead in the journal, and reviewed the troubling sight of ripped pages at a crucial part of the journey. They maintained silent on the situation, not wishing to alarm any of the others until they reached the fateful spot. It was also supposed to give the Guardian time to remember, but the closer they were to reaching the next marker, the more doubtful she was becoming.

"This better not take all night!" Gaither spat out. "I am tired of waiting!" He crushed a broken twig under his foot, as the group continued onward for another twenty minutes or so. They soon reached the base of the mountain, where a "VT" had been burned into a tree trunk, next to a path taking them up the cliffside.

Monica and Dare watched their footing as they hiked the narrowing ledge, and desperately wished they were back home. While in front, and behind, Gaither's men inched their way along, with Vectra and Trevor leading them to a small outcropping, and a dead end on the side of the mountain. Gaither looked madly around, only seeing vines and dying vegetation coating a large sheet of rocks, as a sheer drop met them on the other side. "Well, where is it?" He seethed through a clenched jaw. "This had better not be some kind of trick!"

"If you merely look at the surface, then you will miss all of the beauty within." Vectra reached over and pulled the vines away from the rock face, revealing the cut out of a square, with a singular shape stuck near the middle. Upon hearing her voice, speaking in her native tongue, a carved border lit up around the larger square. Pieces of rock, broken into various sized triangles, one quadrilateral and one trapezoid, fell from the border. With skilled ease, Vectra caught them in her hands, not allowing a single one to miss and possibly shatter against the ground. No sooner had the last piece touched her fingers, then a grinding sound erupted from the outcrop, where it merged into the cliff wall.

Rising up from a patch of thick ferns, was a podium carved into the classic image of an Ionic column, boasting an old hourglass on the top for everyone to see. Dare gulped as he watched the brownish grains begin to slide down, marking the passage of time in a foreboding way. "What does…" Monica looked up at Vectra, not remembering anything about the old time piece in the journal's notes.

"I would think it would be set for five minutes." Vectra scattered the puzzle pieces along the ground, instructing Trevor to hand them to her from largest to smallest in size. "It is the oldest known puzzle, designed by Archimedes himself. Some call it the Archimedes box, and this may take a little bit to solve."

"You don't know the answer?!" Gaither skeptically asked.

Vectra whipped her head around and stared directly at him. "There are over 500 distinctive ways to solve this puzzle, not to mention the thousands of other options that are mirrored versions or simply altered variants." She pointed to the fixated piece already on the wall. "This shape purposefully narrows down the possible solutions, so we cannot just freely solve it."

"And there is no answer to this puzzle in the book?" Taminus inquired, sharing in the same skepticism his boss was showing.

"That page was ripped out." Trevor showed him, indicating the torn edge near the spine with his index finger. "We have no idea where it is."

Furiously, Vectra worked at arranging the pieces as fast as she could with the sand's dire warning constantly in the back of her mind. It had been decades since she completed the puzzle, and even then, it was when all fourteen pieces could be used at will. With the handcuffs still on, her brain fog was keeping her thoughts in a lagged slumber. *I will have to use the key once we are inside, where there will be more light to see, without it being so noticeable as to what I am doing.*

Monica and Dare worriedly watched around Gaither's back, silently pleading for her to hurry up. But as time ticked on, Vectra kept moving the pieces around and around, frustratingly coming to no real solution. Each try resulted in one or two pieces being left off the puzzle's board, as the others were being held securely in place through a natural magnetic attraction. Gaither stomped his foot impatiently after her fifteenth attempt, anxious to be in the cavern before the moon was to sink any lower in the sky. He moved his flashlight away from where they worked, aiming it straight at the hourglass of doom. "Enough already! Blast it!"

One of his men stepped up to Vectra and Trevor, armed with a few bricks of C4 explosives and a detonator.

"STOP!" The Guardian yelled, shouting in the larger man's face with a small blaze in her eyes. "If you do that, we are all dead." She pointed to a barely visible wire leading away from the sand timer to where it disappeared into the rock bed beneath their feet. "You destroy that hourglass, and we will be splattered on the bottom of this valley in nothing more than indescribable goo."

"Perhaps we should release one of her hands, to help the process go a touch faster?" Taminus reasoned. It was not as though he sided with his cousin, but he did feel like surviving, in order to see the morning light crest the horizon again.

Monica and Dare sealed their paranoid mouths shut. There was no telling how Gaither was going to react when he discovered that the key had been taken, and they anxiously waited to see what was about to unfold.

"Maybe I can help." Martiban pushed his way forward, standing with Vectra and Trevor in front of the challenging puzzle. "I still do the crossword puzzles in the newspapers, so my brain might work better than you two lunkheads."

"Fine. Then you three had better solve it before that timer runs out." Gaither warned. "Or else, I am going to kill you myself, just to make sure you go down with me." He aimed the gun at Vectra's forehead, calm and with purpose. "Now, move it."

The Guardian rolled her eyes. *When will these guys ever learn?*

Martiban turned with the other two, appearing to help before he abruptly yanked his hands free of his handcuffs, and pulled Vectra toward him. With the point of a small blade sitting against the skin of her neck, the old knight threw his cuffs to the ground and positioned his hostage between Gaither and himself. "If you want the solution to the puzzle, then drop your weapons and give me the diamond."

"Martiban, what are you doing?" Vectra whispered.

Taminus took a step in their direction. "You know the deal, Martiban. You can have the stone *after* we reach the press."

"No. I'm not falling for that. Maybe an old dog doesn't learn new tricks very well, but he can certainly sniff out a bad agreement when he sees one." Martiban jammed the blade further against her skin, slightly breaking the surface and causing a few drops of blood to emerge. "The stone, now!" He gestured to the mostly-empty top half of the hourglass. "And it would be best to make your decision rather quickly."

"This is your mess, Taminus. You clean it up!" Gaither shoved the man closer into the fray of the situation, and backed up to join his men.

"Martiban, the stone can be found only after the press is located. That is why I do not *have* it to give you. Believe me. If I had it right now, I would hand it over without another thought."

"Why would you take his word?" Vectra tried not saying anything that would drive the blade further into her muscles as she spoke. The whole thing was falling into place now, as Seraphine's Diamond was the one artifact that could bring his Josephine back to life.

Forged from the ashes of the Underworld's fires, the tears of ultimate sorrow, and a drop of Aphrodite's blood, it contained the power to reverse the flow of death itself, by allowing one soul to travel into the living from Hades's domain. For that very reason, the diamond was harbored in the safe confines of Harpeon, far away from the world where most of the Olde Realm resided. "Listen to me, Martiban, there is no way he can access Seraphine's Diamond."

The old knight tightened his grip on the Guardian, staring down her cousin. "You promised to give it to me if I delivered the goods. And no one backs out on a deal with me."

"I understand. I really do, Martiban." Taminus treated his words with great care. "This means a lot to you, but you aren't the only one who lost something precious to a cruel twist of fate. Let me help you. Just, put the knife down."

"Taminus does not know where it is, Martiban. Please listen to me." Her eyes panned over to where the sand was unsettlingly low. "Stop this, Old Friend."

"Old Friend? What sort of old friend kills the one you love?!" He could sense her surprise and visible shame, despite not being able to see her actual face. "Oh, yes. I know. After all these years, centuries even, I finally know what really happened that day, and why I cannot find any trace of her in the ruins of Gardnee Hall. And don't pretend that you did not already figure it out, that I was the one who created the book."

"And she will pay for what she did. Just let her go and solve the puzzle." Taminus also eyed the diminishing seconds with bated breath. He refused to take in any more air until the old knight threw Vectra at her cousin, and hurriedly placed the puzzle pieces in the exact pattern he had memorized, from the journal's ripped pages.

The last triangle fit perfectly in the cut out just as the final bits of sand were about to fall into the bottom half of the hourglass. A collective sigh filled the quietness of the night, as Martiban pushed in on the fixated shape to open the hidden door. "If you want to make it through alive, then you WILL not double-cross me. Is that understood?" He slowly turned around, dramatically pausing to make sure his point was not lost on the group. "And I mean it."

"Fine." Gaither waved his hand dismissively in the air. "Taminus is the one you made the deal with anyways." He went to step into the entrance, when Martiban's foot slammed down to block his path.

"You sent him, remember? Any deal he made with me, goes for you too."

The business owner bore a hardened stare into the taller man's eyes, looking passed the wild beard and untrimmed mustache. "Weston. Keep Vectra at the front with Trevor. Leave this old knight at the back of the pack, with a watchful eye."

"Yes, Sir." A snap of the fingers signaled for the others to obey, and they escorted Martiban toward the end of the line once more.

"Now, we press onward." Gaither demanded.

Chapter Fifty-Eight

Monica looked up at Gaither's six, tall helpers, after four were left at the entrance to keep anyone from escaping. They did a good job at keeping the hostages separated between them, on another narrow passageway, as they proceeded down the next length of a darkened tunnel. Unlike the first segment, which contained a flashing blue light, this glow was purple in hue, and pulsated in waves similar to that of a heartbeat. The edges were coated in a fine, powdery dust, patiently waiting for someone to misstep into its slippery clutches. And on either side, spiky rocks, sharpened stalagmites, and prickly cacti sat there in the hopes of having a fresh victim very shortly.

In the faint light, nothing was presenting itself as a means to escape, or anything to fight Gaither's men off with. The guards were over twice Monica's height, and much stronger than she was. *We could do with a little element of surprise right about now.* It was then, that Vectra's words sparked her imagination. *Nothing is what it seems in the Olde Realm.* She looked about at their present surroundings, and saw the dangerously sharp rocks staring back. An idea began to form in her mind, just as soon as the line stopped dead in front of her, and she rear-ended the guard named Nicholas.

"You better not be pulling any tricks on me!" Gaither's voice echoed ahead in the tunnel.

"I am not. Monica and Dare, both, need to be brought up to me, in order for us to continue on."

The teen's heartrate quickened at hearing Vectra mention her name. *Could it be that she already has a plan to take them over? Of course she does. This is Vectra we are talking about.*

"Very well." Gaither ordered the Browning siblings to come up and meet Vectra at the lead of the group. He watched the foursome with studious eyes, ensuring they did not advance too far from the rest of the group.

"Don't think it." Vectra warned.

"Think what?" Monica couldn't be sure if the Guardian had telepathic powers or not. Could she have sensed that the teen was trying to scheme their way out of this mess?

"There are always exceptions to the rule, and the sides to this tunnel are it."

"How…"

"You remind me of myself in many ways. But do not forget why I picked this place and stay close to me."

Dare gripped onto his sister's arm, not caring what the others thought about his lack of bravery. He peered around Vectra's side hesitantly, expecting some horrifyingly deep hole of death to be right around the corner. What he saw, instead, baffled him more than anything.

A large, and sturdy, vault door blocked the entrance. Dare waited for Vectra to begin spewing out an old riddle they would have to decipher, or for Trevor to start analyzing the bas relief sculpture it contained. Instead, however, the Guardian stood perfectly still with her back to Gaither and his men. As the lighting was the brightest here, she tried to finish picking the lock on her cuffs, feeling as though she almost had it.

"What's the holdup?" Gaither waved on impatiently. He gripped hard onto Dare's arm and yanked the boy backward where his gun was at the ready. "Open the door. NOW!"

Vectra's ears picked up on the boy's soft gulp, and she wasted no time in giving the ship's wheel a crank to the left, conceding to the handcuffs, and hearing the unmistakable clink of the key falling to the ground. One groaning notch, and the watery battle scene rose upward, dust falling from its aching parts and causing a resounding cough to fill the air.

"What is this place?" Weston picked Monica up from the dirty floor, who had appeared to stub the toe of her shoe on the rocky terrain.

"One filled with great riches!" Gaither surmised, gazing about the large room being revealed before them.

A dazzling spectacle of an enormous geode created the walls of the spacious area the group was walking into. Purple tints, tones and shades alternated back and forth, based on the angle from which the crystals were viewed. Akin to stalagmites and stalactites, the rock hard substance dripped down from the ceiling, and reached for the roof in an artistic display. Dare refused to blink, as if closing his eyes for a split second would make the amethyst vanish. "Where are we?"

"This place is part of a fault line that runs under the mountain range. Think of it like the blood system of a human being. The tunnel we just walked through is like the branching veins, and this section marks the adjoining end of a major artery, so to speak." Vectra caught the boy trying to take a step forward, and instantly blocked him with an outstretched hand. "We must be extremely quiet and careful in here. The slightest sound over our normal voice level will trigger the crystals above us to fall, and there is no shelter until we reach that opening across the bridge." She motioned toward the carved entrance on the other side of the chasm, located in-between two massive pillars, and on a ledge mirroring the one they were standing upon.

"Is that all the bigger the path is?" Gaither waved his gun at the narrowed walkway no wider than two people at a time.

"Yes. We will have to move in a single-file line in order to continue."

"I'm standing right behind you, Cousin." Taminus bolted up from the back, sneering at her as he approached. "To ensure no tricks are up your sleeves."

"I do not wear sleeves, Taminus." Vectra's eyes began to glow when he grabbed ahold of her arm. "Whatever he promised you, dear Cousin, it is worth to you, no more than mud, and as sturdy as sinking sand."

"I suggest you start walking." He growled behind clenched teeth, tightening his grip on her until he could feel her heartbeat through the skin. "You always did like to talk about things you knew nothing about."

Vectra gave the kids a nod of encouragement before she started to cross the dangerous canyon below the walkway. Keeping her focus glued to the opposite side, she wondered if setting off the ceiling was such a bad idea. With the kids at the front with her, the back half of the group would be vulnerable. Her mind wandered slightly when she looked into the flat cut of a large amethyst nearby, and her hope was instantly dashed. Trevor had been shuffled to the back of the line, where her cousin's place had previously been. *I must say, they sure do like their insurance policies.*

Further and further, they silently marched to the opening ahead, staring at the natural beauty encapsulated within the mountain. Vectra waited for the rest of the group to reach the wider ledge, before proceeding up the winding staircase. The longer their trek became, the hotter the air, it seemed.

"How many stairs are there?" Monica asked, after her brother's count surpassed fifty, and received no response. Twisting round and round, the group traveled up three more flights of stairs, created from knotted tree roots and dehydrated vines. When they made it to the top, a single door blocked their path, inscribed with one word; ἔρχομαι (enter). Vectra spoke it aloud, and the door swung inward on patinaed hinges without a sound.

Monica pushed Dare into the room ahead of her, as Gaither shoved his way up to the front of the line. Trevor and Martiban were left at the back, stepping into the desert dry atmosphere behind even the hired help. Once they were all cozily inside the dried-up space, a soft motion of the door closing could be heard. To their horror, it shut them in under its own power, as the last guard frantically tried to reopen it in vain. "You cannot exit a door marked only for entry." Vectra called to him in the looming dark.

"Then give us some light that we can see with." Gaither ordered, swinging his flashlight wildly around in fear of what he couldn't see.

"You have barred me from my powers."

"Taminus!" Barked Gaither. "Handle this."

"Where is the key?"

Monica hastily bumped into a few of the guards, and tossed the key on the ground, just as Gaither was nearly shoved into the wall whilst searching in his pocket. "WATCH IT!" He shouted, dropping his flashlight's aim onto the floor, and seeing the familiar object next to his foot. "You made me drop the key!"

Taminus took it from the millionaire's hands, and unlocked the cuffs around his cousin's wrists. He gave her a threatening promise to kill the Brownings if she were to try anything, then took a step back from where she stood in the center of the room. Vectra rubbed her irritated skin where the metal had rested, and felt the draining sensation beginning to subside immediately. Her mind was clearing up and her energy was slowly being restored.

"We are going to have to be careful once I start a fire, due to the extreme dryness of the room." The Guardian flicked out a deuce of hearts, and it sparked instantly. She licked the decorative side of the playing card, and pushed it into the wall to stick like glue. Repeating the same action four more times, Vectra tacked each one in the same method, so that the flames acted as though they were old torches around a bountiful treasure.

"Look at that!" Trevor pointed to the camouflaged furniture hiding in the farthest corner. It was a cobwebbed instrument, plagued by dust and dried out dirt, and standing idle for all to see. The piece had been built into the room with a series of extinct micro-streams leading underneath the strange base it sat upon. Frozen keys gave Dare the feeling that it was a precursor to the piano, but the various pipes extending upward from the instrument looked more akin to that of an organ.

"How do we get through the door?" Weston asked, using his flashlight to illuminate a sealed entranceway made from petrified wood. A carving of a satyr in a mythical forest, playing on pan pipes, adorned the solid construction.

"It's called a Harmonia Lock." Vectra explained. "It can only be opened when the right song is played in the right tone.”

“That hydraulis is what opens it.” Martiban gestured toward the forgotten instrument to the door’s right, noticing the missing key it required to have a fully operational set. Taminus inserted the L shaped piece of wood he had collected from Vectra’s satchel, and watched a layer of dust fall from its muted structure. They all waited in baited breath, for something more to happen, but nothing did.

“Well?” Gaither studied the musical device, a foreign thing to his business-sense of a mind. “Why is no one going to play the song on it?”

“Do you feel the heat coming from the cracks along the walls?” Taminus complained. “There is no water to be found anywhere in here. The ground is dry enough to be considered sand and the trickles from our water bottles will not be nearly close enough to what is required to work the hydraulis.”

“You said you could do it.”

“In a regular environment. This is dried beyond comprehension.” He scoffed at the ground, kicking up dust with his foot. “Nothing here is even giving me the faintest presence of water. I…” The ancient warrior stopped himself when he caught sight of one of Gaither’s men having a bloody nose. Seeing the red liquid run onto the man’s top lip gave him an evil idea.

“What?” Gaither asked, desperately wanting to know what the man had seen.

Taminus gently placed his hand on the ground and the rocks began to rumble above their heads. Gaither and his men drew their weapons out of fright, and glanced around worriedly, as the small room began to shake. Suddenly, four large boulders crashed upward from the rocky floor and killed the same number of men.

"We had a deal, Taminus." Gaither shot a warning round into the ceiling, aiming the next bullet straight at Taminus's forehead. "In exchange for the press…"

"And we still keep it." Placing his index finger in the barrel of the gun, Taminus calmly stared down the shorter man. "Help me move their bodies over to the hydraulis and I will show you." He saw the skepticism in Gaither's face. "Or maybe you are ready to quit."

Gaither waved at Vectra and the Brownings to move the bodies, enforced by the remaining two guards behind him, Weston and Nicholas. Without delay, the dead men were placed atop the old water streams, and their blood dripped into the dried up routes. Taminus closed his eyes and focused on the men, his hand extended in the air. Slowly, he pulled the water out from the wrinkling skin of the guards until shriveled husks were left to rot.

Before long, water filled the instrument's reservoir and the hydraulis gratefully shuddered to life. It was time for the song to be played.

Chapter Fifty-Nine

Vectra stood in front of the hydraulis, squinting at the notes on the makeshift music sheet she had created in her journal. *At least it is a lot easier to document it in this format, than how we used to write songs down in Ancient Greece.* Her fingers began to play, while Monica and Dare pumped the side cylinders to keep a consistent amount of air pressure in the chambers. She pressed the mini-levers up and down to emit the song in the hyperiastian mode, forcing everyone to drown out the overbearing loudness with their hands over their ears. As she continued through the notes, utilizing all three rows of pan pipes, a clicking sound could be heard from behind the door, signaling that the lock was about to release. But it wasn't until the final note was struck, that the mechanism did unlatch, and the door swung wide open.

The press sat in the middle of an inch deep water puddle that consumed the entire floor of the cavern, leaking from the instrument in the first room after the door partially damaged it. A large boulder was propped against one wall, standing out as a sore thumb in comparison to the hand-painted murals of books, writings, and Clio with children.

No stray rocks were scattered on the ground, nor rough patches found on the floor, giving them the treacherous feeling of a slippery surface. A single torch lit at the back of the room, the very second Vectra stepped over the threshold, illuminating the space with enough light to power an entire house.

Everyone was speechless, except for Vectra, that is, who silently wrestled with the anxiety of seeing the hunk of trouble again. She wished for it to disappear, or for permission to burn it to ash, beyond all recognition. "Here. You found it. Now, let us go and be content with your power trip." The Guardian headed straight for the boulder, wanting to leave its sight for good, before she was stopped by one of Weston's hands.

"Oh, no. Not so fast." Gaither stated. "If what I have heard from Taminus is to be believed, then there is more to this than you are letting on. And after all we have gone through in order to get here, I would not put it past you to have another trap on the press itself."

Vectra flipped around, hot tempered and irritated by even standing in the same room as the vile thing. "I did not need too. Clio did that pretty much herself. And even if I had, and I told you, why would you think that any of it was true? I could lie to your face about it." She grabbed his gun, and shot a bullet straight through her body. "Why should I care what you threaten me with?"

"Because you do not want another three tick marks added to the body count on your conscious." Gaither smiled, showing his annoyingly perfect teeth in a masterfully evil grin. "Especially after you killed their parents."

"What?" Trevor glanced over at his siblings in confusion.

"No. YOU were the one to kill them." Monica countered. "We know the truth."

"Oh, do you?" Gaither laughed, along with his fellow henchmen who remained alive. "And who did nothing when they asked for help in locating the press? Who was the one who might as well have shot them herself, as they fell from the bridge? Who was the one, who neglected to do her duty in protecting the press, and refused to listen to their plea of help?"

Dare turned to his older brother, matching his stare with that of his own. "Don't listen to him, Trevor! We saw our parent's graves. They are buried on a hillside where Vectra gave them a proper burial. She is not the monster he is making her out to be."

Vectra's gaze fell to the floor, not being able to look at the kids she had grown fond of.

"Aww, how touching." Gaither mocked. "To see them coming to your defense; even when you haven't told them the whole story." He moved about the room, looking for the special parchment only the press could mark, and smugly explained. "See, I had Weston keep an eye on your parents when they arrived in Nectar Hill. They approached her with a plea of desperation, to save their kids' lives from a fate of ultimate ruin. A prophecy, foretold by an oracle, which said that one of their children was destined to rewrite history into tyrannical devastation."

Monica and Dare didn't know what to say, especially when the madman yielded the floor to Taminus, who smacked the back of his cousin's head and popped out the contact lens of her left eye. The siblings tried to withhold their gasps at the sight of an Eclipse Eye, the exact same as the fox/coyote creature Rae's was; a large, rust orange-colored circle, with a sliver of silver tinged on the outer edge and illuminated like a full moon.

Gaither shook his head. "You two are truly naive. She wouldn't help your parents protect their own children's lives, your lives in point of fact, and you believe that she is going to save you now? When will you finally recognize that she is only out for herself and to save her job?"

Monica squeezed her younger brother's hand in reassurance. He was right in the sense that they did not actually know Vectra all that well, nor of her elongated past. But they had seen her character, the way she treated them, and the sacrifices she had gone through to save them from Gaither's clutches. That *had* to mean something.

"It certainly does rock us to the core, when we suddenly realize that we have put our trust in the wrong person." Gaither tapped the Guardian on the shoulder, just as she broke her arm free from her cousin's grip.

"My secrets outnumber your years, Gaither. Do not make it your mission to peel them all back tonight." She seethed in his face.

"Then tell me which one of the kids has the power to operate the press!"

"Neither of them do. It is impossible to use it anymore. Did Taminus forget to mention that to you?" Vectra sassed, prompting her cousin to throw her to the ground. As she fell, her hat went too, and the sound of a smaller object plopped into the water. To her dismay, it was the green stone necklace that spilled out from underneath her vest, and when she went to retrieve it, Taminus snatched the pendent from her hands. He yanked it clean off her neck, leaving a stinging red mark on her skin, and closed his fist around the twisted prison.

Gregon's warning came flooding back to Monica's mind and she could see their glimmer of hope dwindling to a mere flicker. *If he has any idea as to what that is...but her cousin is certain to know.*

"Which one?" He allowed the necklace's chain to swing like a broken pendulum in a grandfather clock, reinforcing the grave situation the Guardian was now in. "Or else, you do not get your precious necklace back. Which, if I am not mistaken, dear Cousin, is the one containing your very soul."

Vectra gave the Brownings a shameful gaze, when Monica suddenly winked at her in return. The Guardian blinked, seeing her make the same gesture again, and decided to hand the reigns over to the teenager.

"Tick-tock. What's it going to be? Your freedom is dependent upon this." Gaither reiterated.

"Monica. She is the one you want." Vectra hesitantly replied.

"No!" Monica called out. "You bitch! You're just another traitor! You did the same thing you did to our parents!"

"You leave my sister out of this!" Trevor shouted, ready to pummel his former boss as Weston held him back with great ease. "She has nothing to do with any of this."

"Oh, but she does." Gaither held his palm out for the necklace to be given to him. He flashed his fingers out again when Taminus was reluctant to hand over such a wondrous prize he had been chasing after for centuries. Still, he ultimately did concede with visible disdain. "How does she activate her power?"

"You need to prick her finger, and have a drop of her blood touch the birthmark at the back of her neck." Vectra solemnly answered.

"Good." Gaither tossed her the necklace, and ordered Weston to do as the Guardian instructed, ignoring the look of betrayal on Taminus's face.

"You said…"

"The deal was for me to tell you the location of what you were searching for, and that her necklace was a possible bonus, if the matter would be beneficial to my cause." The millionaire blatantly restated. "But I needed her information more."

"How could you?" Monica glared at Vectra, as Weston pricked her index finger with the sharp tip of a pocket knife. A drop of the blood, landed on the bottom groove of the birthmark on her neck, and quickly filled in the lines to showcase Clio's name. At the same instance that the goddess's name was revealed, a thin ring of red lit up around Monica's pupils, even though she didn't feel any different.

Dare struggled against Nicholas's restraints. "What are you doing to my sister?"

"There are only two kinds of people who can operate Clio's press: a child of hers, which none exist, or someone of descent from one of Clio's helpers." Gaither drug his finger down the side of the press, giving himself a splinter that penetrated deep. "Oww."

"Then take me instead." Trevor offered. "And leave my sister out of this."

"You don't seem to understand, you pathetic excuse for a man! Taminus, explain it to him."

"Your mother was only half a descendent, and so was your stepfather. So she is the one who can operate it." He begrudgingly answered, becoming more frustrated with the way the millionaire treated him like a pet.

"And, if you want your brothers to see the light of day, you will do as I tell you to." Gaither snapped his fingers for Weston and Nicholas to hold their knives up to each of her siblings' throats. "Now, go over to the press and make it work."

"I've never used a traditional press before."

"Then Vectra will help you."

"I don't want the likes of her helping me." Monica snapped.

"I don't care what you *like*." Gaither thrust a paper at her, with printed words on its white surface. "Set up the type, and have it print this out, EXACTLY as it is written."

Monica laid the paper upon the top platen, and gave the tiles of Greek letters a nervous glance. To her surprise, the letters shifted into their English translations for her, and she easily could understand them as though it was her native language.

"Do what you are told, Monica, and press *your* words." Vectra stared directly at the teenager as she spoke, hoping that the message rang through loud and clear.

Chapter Sixty

Gaither impatiently paced back and forth along the south wall, having watched Monica and Vectra sort through the jumbled letters scattered about in an old wooden box for what seemed like forever. Like a metronome, they moved back and forth between the paper Gaither had printed off and the lower platen where the metal type was being placed; a single letter, comma, period, and space at a time.

Monica could feel the void of any hope for anyone in Gaither's new world. It was filled with an earthy existence remembered only by fragmented skeletons of what once had been, and nothing of the democracy the current world boasted. While Gaither did wish to save his family's company, the darker truth of wanting to hold a monopoly, on both the retail and interior design market, was also being written. Every person was to feature at least fifty percent of their household belongings from his brands, and he would wield the power as the executive board member of a large banking empire, merged into an institution rivaling that of the United States Government.

Going through the list her brother's former boss had created, Monica began noticing the underlying theme of not just money, but also of power. That was the ultimate goal for Gaither; a hidden power that resided in the shadows. He didn't want to be President, he wanted to be the man pulling the strings in the background, without having to bear the public face of scrutiny. Dates, times and specific details, were all lined out in a systematic order, as the teen followed the words to the exact letter. She could hear the sound of coffin nails in her mind, fearing for the tyrannical ambitions of this madman.

As she worked, Monica tried to focus on something else, and pictured the campfire Vectra had helped the kids build at the shipwreck. They were sitting around the warming flames and looking up at the stars above, where the specks of light appeared free and smiling with kindness upon them. *Well, at least for Dare and myself,* she remembered. Her flashback accidentally caused her to knock the lower platen to the ground, resulting in the already assembled text to float in different directions, and setting them back by an hour at least. A unanimous sigh resonated around the cavern in agony.

"You are not serious right now!" Gaither fired a shot into the wall behind Monica. "Get this done or else." He quickly aimed for Trevor's leg and fired again as the bullet ripped a hole in her brother's pants, merely scrapping his skin. "I will not miss on purpose next time."

"Alright, alright. I'm sorry." Monica held her hands in surrender. "It was an accident."

"This is not like texting a friend." Vectra added. "So I suggest you all get rather comfortable while we work." She bent over to help the girl clean up all of the scattered letters and scooped them up like fish.

"Very well. But we haven't got all night and day to be doing this." Gaither anxiously peered down at a watch he wore under the sleeves of his shirt and jacket. His one hand twitched around the clock's face, holding the fabric back so he could read the time. "We have to get this up and running before ten o'clock in the morning."

All of a sudden, an idea came to Monica. She felt stupid at first, but that soon passed as she realized the golden opportunity she had at the tips of her fingers. *The letters are still in Ancient Greek! So Gaither can't read them.* Monica's mind was on autopilot, whispering to Vectra to follow her lead, and began placing type at a blazing new speed. It was not something she could explain, but in that moment, she knew exactly what she had to write, and in the correct order. Her hands moved at twice what they had before, and within half the time, the press was set and ready to be used.

Gaither's sneer oozed in an essence of evil. "That was more like it. Finally." He raised his arms, spread wider than a vulture's span, and commanded her to crank the press. Monica gave Vectra one final look, seeing her nod in encouragement, as the teenager gently put her hands in the same divots on the wooden handle, that had been used thousands of years prior to that night. Closing her eyes, she could picture the goddess Clio standing in her place, the crank obeying a single thrust from the skilled operator.

Using all her might, Monica felt a burning sensation on her neck as the crank went down, searing her birthmark in the lower right corner of the parchment. Her strength faded for a split second, as the press tattooed the piece of lambskin they found in a nearby stand. As a shimmery light, golden in hue, seeped from in-between the platens, a strong pulse reverberated throughout the small space, and a large tree-splitting sound erupted from the old machine. Everyone gripped onto the walls for better stability, and stepped away from an expanding crack traveling along the floor of the room.

The water instantly drained into the fresh gap, and once the shaking subsided, Gaither gave Vectra a cautionary glare. "What's next? Did it work right?"

"We have to pull it and see." She motioned at Monica to lift the top platen, carefully watching the rest of the onlookers, just as the parchment's edges were becoming visible. It was the moment of truth, to see what the teen had really printed.

Monica could not keep a joyous smile from appearing on her lips, when the parchment was finally released from between the two platens. The paper rose into the air by itself, and magically folded into a predetermined form that stunned all of the unsuspecting faces in the room. Gently picking the newly created item up, Monica presented Vectra with a small pair of origami wings. Printed text could be seen on both sides, with various words such as truth, light, strength, valor, and kindness having prime spots for all to see. Vectra's eyes were stunned, not sure what to say at the amazing sight before her. She had no idea what the young girl had in mind when she placed the letters in such a meaningful order.

"What are those?" Gaither's temper was boiling mad. "That is not what I asked for. And why are we still sitting around in this room? It clearly didn't work!" He instantly grabbed onto the teen's arm, forcing her toward him with the gun aimed at her left temple.

"πέτομαι." Monica said aloud, meaning "to fly," and threw the wings at the Guardian, who scooped them up with great ease. She covered her ears as Vectra flung a small explosive four of hearts at Taminus, as he wielded a number of rocks into a defensive wall to counter her attack. Heading for the only exit from the room, Vectra swung a supercharged seven of hearts at the large boulder, blowing the rock backward, and ran through the hole to bring the fight outside.

With the entranceway unblocked, the small space was inundated with the morning light of the rising sun, causing them all to have temporary blindness. "GET HER!" Gaither demanded, holding his hands up to shield himself from the intense bright, light. He could hear his remaining two men stumbling up to the smoldering rocks surrounding the hole, as he forged that way on his own.

Trevor and Dare followed suit, leaving their sister behind, who hid underneath the press until everyone had run out of the room. As the dust began settling upon the debris coated floor, Monica crawled into the open and gazed around at the mess she had created. Part of her wanted to destroy the press past the point of no return: to remove some of the burden felt on Vectra's shoulders. Her thoughts went racing back and forth, fighting an inner voice that stood fast against the crazed notion. Even a single spark from the remnants of a playing card sat temptingly nearby, begging for her to pick it up and touch the dried wood of Clio's press.

Still, for no good reason, she could not bring herself to do it. "I would not do that, if I were you." Gregon's voice brought her face up from the floor, in order to see his silhouette against the strong backlight of the sun. "I see you wishing to, but you cannot. Because if you do, she will be the one punished."

"Despite it not being done by her own hand?"

"She is the Guardian. She is the protector of these artifacts. For you to light it ablaze, would mean that she failed in her job. And that will bring judgement down upon her." Gregon warned, stepping into the room from the hole his friend blasted in the wall. "Your intentions are good, though this cannot be."

"I wish that was the real motive for my hesitation." Monica cast him a slightly embarrassed look.

"You are a descendent of Clio, and therefore, you cannot destroy it without harming yourself in the process." Gregon suddenly looked down at her wrist, where a small word materialized in her skin, stamped in the same ink that the press used. "For what it's worth, you are a very brave girl to have done what you did."

Chapter Sixty-One

Vectra clambered up the mountain side, and reached the peak before opening her hand to see the wings still in her palm, without even a small scar. "ανοίγω." Upon command, the folded paper flapped itself open, spreading outward into large eagle-like wings that whisked into the air and fell neatly into place right behind her shoulder blades. Her latest addition had barely enough time to fully adhere to her clothing, when the first arrow whistled past her ear. The rocks trembled under her feet, making it a do or die moment for her to try the wings out for the first time.

She flashed around to see Taminus coming within striking distance, and willed the wings to carry her away from the mountain. They awkwardly transported her above the trees and over the steep gorge far below, in a frighteningly new experience for the seasoned warrior. The sheer drop spread out dangerously beneath her dangling feet, but instead of giving her mounting fear, an invigorating feeling coursed through her veins with a profound sense of freedom she hadn't felt in eons. No god or goddess could tear her down, nor rip the inner peace from her very soul, no matter how hard they tried. In that moment, Vectra Tillerman was invincible.

Another arrow slashed into the air near her head, reminding the Guardian of the real life dangers still looming at the present. She gathered herself together and slowly worked on using the updrafts to propel her toward the mountainside once more, as rocks were being thrown in her direction. Taminus growled through clenched teeth, missing his cousin by mere inches time and time again. He started to call up larger rocks and boulders, utilizing his energy at a faster pace, and launching them at her in clumsy attempts.

"Why, dear Cousin, one would think you smarter than that by now." Vectra smirked, dipping to one side and riding the breeze until she was directly behind him. She eased the wings into a gentle landing, sensing his watchful eye from over his shoulder. He was too smart to turn around, knowing fully well that she would not waste her energy on him, whilst his back was to her. It was the older code, and one many of the Olde Realm still abided by.

"So, what do we do now? At a bit of a stalemate, as it were." Taminus's chest heaved, his breath trying to catch up after chucking half of the mountain side at her.

"Call this a draw?" Vectra hopefully offered. "Perhaps you will have better luck next time?"

Taminus chuckled. "In your dreams." He smashed his palms together and expanded them to reveal a tumbling ball of water he extracted from now wilted plants.

Vectra flicked four playing cards at him, landing in a perfect square around his feet. She clapped her hands the instant he aimed the high powered water at her face, causing fire forged bars of steel to eject into the air and form a cage around him. Taminus slammed his fist into the ground and disappeared below the Earth's raised surface through a drilled hole, leading him back into the room with the press unexpectedly. Cautiously, Vectra leaned forward, inspecting the empty cage where her cousin had been standing moments ago. The billowing dust got sucked into her lungs, though she could still hear Dare's distress call through her coughing.

"Let me go!" The boy kicked Martiban in the leg; about ready to bite the old knight's fingers as a last resort. "I said let me go!"

"Taminus might not be able to kill you, but I sure can." He stared long and hard at the woman he had deemed to be a close friend, for more than twenty-five generations worth of battles and adventures. "But I can also kill the boy in a flash."

"This is not who you are, Martiban." Vectra pleaded, wishing desperately to be seeing the man she used to know in front of her, rather than the darkened shade she currently was talking to. "Josephine was using you to do her biding. Killing all those people only inflated her ego and wealth, while dissolving the man you truly were. A Knight in the Order of…"

"DO NOT SPEAK OF IT!" He bellowed, clutching onto Dare with even a fiercer hold. "Do not speak of that wretched name."

"You were proud to be a part of them. Greenfield was proud of you too." Vectra was uncertain how he would react to hearing the name of his fellow knight, a brother in arms, and the one he had slain under Josephine's orders. "She wanted him killed because he was her *only* competition for your attention, and he was starting to show you what her manipulation was doing to your soul."

"You were jealous of her. That is what you were. Jealous. Envious that I paid more attention to her, instead of our friends."

"That is not true, Martiban. And you know that. Deep down, you always knew that."

The old knight seemed confused for a brief second, shaking his head, and clearing it of a long buried memory he refused to listen too. "Where is the stone, Vectra? Where is Seraphine's Diamond?"

"I told you, it is on Harpeon. Artenian and I…"

"She's lying, Martiban." Taminus reemerged with a hostage of his own, Monica, who struggled against his grip. "I can give it to you, *after* you help me get the press working to settle my deal with Gaither."

"Well, it is nice to see that we haven't arrived too late to the party." The boss man, himself, walked into the small clearing with Trevor in tow, being shuffled forward by one of his men. "Seems like your feeble plan at separating did not succeed." He pretended to pout before shooting his weapon into Trevor's right arm. "The next one goes into his foot. Now, we're all going to reassemble back in the press room, and get this done right. Got it?!"

"Okay, okay!" Monica answered, seeing the pain riddled on her brother's face. "We will use the press again."

"Excellent." Gaither went to leave, flashing a victorious smile at Vectra. But as Monica went to step forward, Taminus yanked her back and pushed the tip of his short sword into the soft flesh of her neck.

"I believe we had a deal." Taminus spit at the ground. "You had your chance at the press, now, you have to tell me where it is."

Monica's heartbeat raced, feeling the sharp point of the obsidian blade, threateningly close to her jugular vein. She tried to focus on her breathing as Gaither turned to look at the ancient warrior, obviously irritated by yet another interruption.

"Of course. After she uses the press to give me what I want, you will have your information in return."

"No. I want the location now. Where is it?" His temper was mounting. "WHERE IS IT?!"

Gaither snapped his fingers, instructing his two men to leave Trevor's side and to walk in the troublesome man's direction. With a simple gesture, the knife began to break Monica's skin, allowing droplets of blood to drip from the fresh cut.

"Your men take one more step, and she is dead." Taminus summoned the rocks under his feet, rumbling the ground like the warning of an oncoming avalanche. "I mean every word I say. Unlike some."

Vectra watched on in silence, studying the situation playing out, and trying to calculate the best response to what was happening. There was no good way for her to attack without someone being able to hurt any of the Brownings. No possible move could be concealed in the open space of the clearing, since the trees outlined the furthest edges. It was a standoff of unbalanced proportions, and one that she had to accept as being out of her control. *At least, for now.*

"Taminus, do you really think I would back step on our deal?" Gaither's slimy smile was an insult added to injury. His word was as good as an eel is on land, and just as reliable.

"Without hesitation." Vectra's cousin replied, with his voice as steady as the rocks he commanded. "Now, give me the coordinates to what I am searching for, and you get the girl to use the press as you see fit." He kept an eye on the old knight, chilling in the corner with his own piece of leverage. "Martiban, relieve these men of their weapons."

"Not without the diamond."

"You will have your bloody diamond." Anger seethed through clenched teeth as Taminus was feeling the building frustration raising his blood pressure. Water boiled up from the ground, being drained out of plants and soil alike, as his powers were reflecting his volatile mood. "Just get their darn weapons!"

Suddenly, Weston dodged to the right for a distraction whilst his partner threw a powdery rope over the ancient warrior. The ensuing dust cloud created a near smokescreen effect, aiding Monica in her escape from the man's grasp, as Trevor searched the blanketed air for a sign of his sister, holding his arm as the blood seeped from the bullet wound.

"WHAT THE HELL?!" Taminus ushered in a washing wave of water to allow himself to breath.

"You don't think I would be as stupid as to make a deal with a powerful ancient being, without having a little insurance on hand, did you?" Gaither laughed in a pathetic attempt at an evil cackle. "After you told Weston what your father stole, we had it located in the Alps, exactly where you said it would be."

Vectra's brows moved inward, wondering why her cousin would have been so clumsy in telling someone such a devastating secret as that. It simply was not like him to slip up in a careless way. *And how could he grind down Hermes's favorite winged hat? That thing was created by Zeus, himself.*

Taminus gazed upon the ropes now wrapped around his body, covering his clothing in a fine powder of white chalk. At first, he pretended to be beaten, portraying a fake fainting spell before breaking his playact into a deep laugh of his own, mocking their epic failure. "Do you honestly believe that I was so gullible? Having Weston get me drunk before asking all sorts of questions?" His mouth smiled smugly. "I saw that cliché coming from the other side of the horizon."

Gaither was the one who now appeared confused, unsure as to what the man was finding so funny about being captured. "My father did not steal something as trite as King Midas's seashells!" Taminus sneered, shrugging the ropes off with minimal effort. He raised his hands over the trembling stones, and raised them up like daggers. Needing no time to aim, Vectra's cousin willed them through the air at the annoying shorter man.

Weston and his partner were ripped to shreds, lying limp on the ground as Taminus's barrage merely slashed up Gaither's arms. Martiban released Dare, uncertain as to what value his hostage now held. And as the boy ran over to meet up with his older brother, he caught sight of a familiar toy in Taminus's hidden pockets.

His eyes lit up with an idea, quickly shooting a glance at Vectra, who felt his gaze and matched it. "Like in Clover Land!" Dare announced.

Vectra paused a moment to think, wondering what this boy had up his sleeve, but nodded anyway, and prepared to ignite a ring of fire around the clearing, trapping Martiban out from the scene unfolding from within. Taminus easily deflected the sparks spraying off the main flames racing along the tree line, while still keeping his hands latched onto Gaither's squirming form. He squeezed the man's neck between strong fingers, dealing him a taste of his own forceful medicine. "YOU DO NOT BETRAY ME! AND YOU DO NOT TREAT ME LIKE A WORTHLESS SLAVE!"

Dare ran to the outside, nearing the wall of the ensuing fire so close that his clothing had become singed in multiple sections. Taminus blindly struck out at him, fully aware of the running child behind his back, as he kept his focus pinned on the struggling millionaire in his grasp. The boy leaned forward and back, avoiding the high powered rocks coming his way as he weaved up to the warrior's side.

Vectra collapsed her wings into her body, keeping them against her back as slim as possible, so as not to get them burnt, and attacked from the right flank to give Dare time to do whatever he had planned. Playing cards were shuffled as numerous as mosquitos at her cousin, who wielded a shield of water from his own body, along with that of the air, weakening his power. The stronghold of a defense managed to keep Vectra's blows at bay, as he demanded for the boss man to give him the coordinates to what he was searching for, in desperation. "Tell me this instant, or you *will* die."

Dare slid up to Taminus's left side and reached for his stolen action figure. It wasn't the easiest to grab, diving in and out between blows, but he finally was able to snatch it out of the man's pocket. He double-checked that the battery was still charged, and moved the arms of the robotic character into position.

"What…" Taminus didn't have a chance to say anything more as a large electrical zap coursed through his soaked body, magnifying its charge in the water shield, before re-electrifying him once more. His arms shook from the surge, dropping his hold on Gaither, who was barely affected from the blast. As the millionaire fell away from Taminus's stiffening form, he was headed straight toward the fiery wall of Vectra's own doing.

"No!" Vectra lunged forward and used three skillfully placed cards to change the man's trajectory, landing him safely on the ground with inches to spare. She breathed a sigh of relief when his head hit the grass, untouched from the fringes of the burning flames. When she looked over to where Dare was still standing, she saw the young boy staring at her with an overloaded action figure in his hands. He was smiling, proudly holding his burnt robot, where the hidden stun gun was partially exposed. "Step away from him, Dare. He is not dead."

As she ordered, Dare walked backward, not risking the chance to turn his back on the fallen ancient warrior. He gripped tightly onto his deadly toy, waiting for Vectra to give the sign that everything was alright, while the flaming wall continued to encircle them. As the crackling of the fire, and the heat raised the temperature of the air, the Guardian stepped up to her cousin with a card at the ready. She watched for the movement of his chest, seeing his faint breathing, and was about to snap a coma inducing strike, when an arrow came from beyond the fiery wall, piercing through Vectra's hand.

Dare whipped around to see nothing in the flames, only his elongated shadow cast upon the section nearest to him. In that heartbeat of a second, Taminus opened his eyes with a mischievous twinkle in their pupils. With one strained motion of an outstretched reach, his dehydrated hand forced the ground to roll Gaither into the flames, where his body was instantly disintegrated.

Vectra's face fell to the grass as her heart felt an immediate twinge, causing her to clutch at the necklace where her imprisoned soul was still resting under her vest. She quickly grasped the pendent as the green gem dulled for one pulse, before its shine returned to full strength. Anger fueled her temper, igniting a final wrist throw of an eight of hearts. The card encased her cousin in a tomb of molten lava rock, hardening beyond all penetrable weapons of Dare's world, just after she retrieved her short sword from his side.

The fire faded out, feeling the pang of fear consuming Vectra's heart as she watched the unmarred earth of where

Gaither used to be. Dare hugged his brother, Trevor, who was at a loss of words for his younger sibling's blackened toy. "That is why your father said you weren't to have it until you were seven, right?"

Dare smiled. "Yep. In the letter that it was wrapped with, Dad told me about his souped up powers, and to not tell you. Because you would most likely either take it away or use it yourself."

If Trevor had not been in pain, he would have laughed, though none of it covered up the fact that one of the Brownings was still missing. "Where's Monica?"

Begrudgingly, Vectra raced past the two brothers and down the mountain side on the path she was sure Martiban had taken. She had a bad feeling she knew where he had gone, and needed to save herself, now that the threat of Gaither and Taminus had been squashed. A silent tear of ultimate sorrow woke up in her heart, realizing that she was going to have to stare him down like the rest of the ramble who went after the press before. All their history together, their friendship and battle-born trust, would not be allowed to sway her stance. It was the exact issue she dreaded to face, but her heart also knew that this moment had been inevitable for a long time coming.

Her eyes stayed alert, keeping watch along the tree tops, bushes, and underbrush lining the path, in case he had any traps planted anywhere on the route. *He was most likely on the hunt, rather than being worried about me.* A throbbing ache resounded from the arrow she yanked out of the wound, reminding her of the night Josephine had been killed all those centuries ago. Memories flooded her mind from the night they slit that siren's throat, and threw her body off a cliff, into the waves of the ocean far below. That night, Martiban had been used as the bait, and then forced to commit a task they made him forget. *And now, the tables have been turned.*

The closer she came upon the blown out entrance to where the press resided, her pace slowed even more, and she listened to the voices speaking from inside the well-lit room. Martiban's voice sounded agitated and demanding, compared to Monica's frightened and hurried tone, as he was shouting at her to rewrite his own history. It was like the Guardian had feared, and there was no other way to stop his madness from winning.

Vectra inhaled a deep breath of the fresh pine and crisp morning air the woods had to offer. She straightened her posture, and confidently stepped in front of the opening, breaking the light beam that was pouring in. "Martiban, it's over."

The old knight paid her no mind, watching Monica set the type as fast as she could. He fed her the words as she moved along, ensuring that they were to be pressed the same way he wanted them to be. There was no room for error, like Gaither had done, and he continued to tell her the words like Vectra wasn't even present. "She did not leave the castle that night, but instead…"

"I said, it's over." Vectra announced again. "Martiban, leave the girl alone."

"No." He rose his head up to stare her in the eyes. "It's not over. It was *never* over. Not for me, anyway."

"Leave Monica go, Martiban. And then, we can sit down and discuss what happened that night."

"I KNOW WHAT HAPPENED!"

Monica shuddered at the decibel his voice had grown too, shaking her to the core. Her scared face pleaded with Vectra to help her, fearing for her life too many times already that day.

"I know what you, Aisling, and the others did." Martiban studied the knife in his hand and the way it reflected the natural light cascading around Vectra's silhouette. "You, my so-called *friends*, forced me to kill Josephine. With this very blade, I slit the throat of the love of my life, by your deceptive plan. And for what?!"

"We did it to help you. Martiban. We did it to save you from her control." Vectra tried to reason with him, still wanting ever so much to reach through to the noble knight she hoped was alive yet. "She was a wicked siren. The only way for you to be released from her spell, was to have you kill her by your own hand."

"TO SAVE WHO?! Vectra, the knight I was, died when the last breath of Greenfield left his limp body. There was nothing else to save! All I had to cling onto was Josephine. As she died, so did any honor and valor to my name. I was marked a traitor, sentenced to death for my crime, and all I had…the woman I went to see for the very last time, was taken away because of your trickery!" Martiban ran his finger along the sharp edge of the sword. "And when we *all* shared in a drink together, you offered me a mockery of insult. A toast to me, as it were. Where you said that I would be missed beyond all measure, and thought of often when the wind would blow."

Vectra hesitated, taking a pause in order to come up with the right words to say. She remembered that drink, and the toast. It was fake, of course, as he obviously stood there for her to see. And like the memory gaps that she sustained, partaking in tea with Bregit after hiding the press, he had also become a victim of the dainty flower's potency. *But there are no words for what I am about to explain. None that will make the sting any easier to bear.* "Yes, we had you forget all about it and told you an alternative story to believe. Because…"

"I discovered what you did. So, instead of facing me, and owning up to what you three had done, you resorted to tainting tea, like the cowards that you are!"

"No…Martiban. You had not suspected a thing, believing our lies that she escaped in the dead of night, fleeing across the border under a darkened moon in hast. It worked so well, in fact, that your pain grew worse with each day that passed, since we spared your life from prison. Her hold over you never ceased, and she consumed your mind more than ever before. You searched endlessly for her, to the point of near ruin. That is when we…"

"Tried erasing her completely from my memory." He placed the tip of the blade in the small of Monica's back, eyes searing into Vectra's. "You take one more step toward her, and she will join my Josephine."

"I cannot allow you to do this, Old Friend."

"Do not…do not continue to mock me. That person is gone. That life was drowned into despair and an agony nothing could fulfill."

Vectra quietly nodded, a tear on the verge of falling down her cheek. "Yes. It was. It was also something I was too blinded to see, until now. Then, you know what I must do."

Monica arched her back away from the blade, just as the old knight shoved it further against. "And I as well."

Vectra held the palms of her hands outward and closed her eyes for a second. When she reopened them, fire illuminated her irises as cards extended outward like strands of rope. Martiban instinctively ran to the front of the press and stabbed his knife deep into the rocky ground. Turning the red ruby counter-clockwise, on the hilt, he dragged it across the room. A chasm opened up where his blade pierced, separating the floor into two halves that started to migrate away from one another. Monica hugged the press with every fiber of her being, as the split's edge became dangerously close to the ancient machine's left corner.

Although, stones and chunks of dry dirt broke in sections, disappearing into the darkened depths below, Vectra did not appear phased by the abrupt change in landscape, and continued to release her onslaught of cards. Her hands gripped onto a pair of nine of hearts, and swung them up from the abyss they were draped into. Martiban whipped out a fishing net from the lining of his coat, extending it out till a thin handle was resting comfortably in the palm of his left hand.

A calm stillness enveloped the air for a brief moment, surrendering to the fight that was about to commence. Vectra whirled the rope of cards, on her right, into a horizontal tornado of sorts, slowly igniting each card as she generated a powerful cone of suction Martiban deflected with his net. His massive bug-zapping contraction was no joking matter, having the ability to capture one's strength to draw them in.

Using the other rope as well, the Guardian securely wrapped its band around Monica's waist and pulled her to safety on her side of the enlarging chasm. She ran out of the cavern, and met up with her brothers, who were waiting around the corner, as a little friend was watching from a distance. With a wink of his eye, Gregon slid past the teenager to toss the electrio blade near Vectra's feet. Its soft thud alerted her to its presence and she gladly scooped it up.

Martiban rushed up to the press and slashed a part of the wood from its sturdy frame. "I will take us both down."

"Go ahead. I have learned to live with my mistakes. My only regret, was trying to save you from yours." Vectra pushed herself up from the ground in a single shove with her right foot, sending herself up in a spiral as her wings spread out to beat the air around her. Cards shot off in all directions, littering the room in a sea of white and red. Her hand clicked the dial to three, switched the electrio blade on, and used the final charge to connect every single card. The shock generated a thundering boom of an explosion, tearing apart the cavern and almost everything in it.

Monica, Dare, and Trevor, slowly peeked into the newly exposed area, wondering if Martiban was dead yet. What they saw, silenced any victory chant they felt like sharing.

Vectra stood over her fallen comrade, his hands unfolded upon the ground and his beard smoking from the powerful charge that took his life. She felt torn to pieces, unable to feel much more than an incurable brokenness shrouding her heart. The feeling of ultimate betrayal, the one thing she never wished to pass onto others, had finally caught up with her. There was an eerie silence that followed the explosion, as if the birds were unsure as to what just happened, and shared in her grief.

Chapter Sixty-Two

The sun was hanging high in the sky by the time the last rock had been gently placed atop Martiban's recently dug grave. Vectra stared at the freshly carved stone she adorned with his family's crest, thanking the Brownings for helping her to bury the old knight with the dignity he didn't deserve. She lifted a camping cup up in the air, giving him a sendoff for the second time.

"You will be missed, Martiban. Missed beyond…what words can express. And I will think of you…when…" The words got caught in her throat, unable to say the lines that caused Martiban so much pain during his lifetime. "I will think of you when the night is darkened to pitch black, with no hope in sight. Because that was when you used to tell me, 'we have the best chance of survival, for to have nothing to lose makes us the most unpredictable. And the most alive.'" She looked into the cup, filled with Martiban's drink of choice, and saw her own reflection upon its shiny surface. "My mother once said to me, that there is a sunset, or sunrise, meant for each person, becoming a mirror of their character and the beauty of their soul. Tonight shall be your sunset, Martiban."

Monica and Dare raised up their own cups, helping Trevor with his, and nodded to Gregon in a mutual sign of respect for a tortured man, now at peace. "To Martiban," the Kurzian added, "he was a man of failed ambitions, however, he was as loyal as they come. And that, is a virtue slowly fading from this world."

They each sipped on their drinks, taking in a moment of silence in the quiet acknowledgement of their victory. Vectra had successfully moved the press to the clearing, waiting for a new home to hide the troublesome artifact of the Olde Realm. Surprisingly, it had sustained very little damage, considering what it could have been, and she sent a request to Gears for assistance in relocating it.

As they sat there, resting from the sleepless night, Gregon proceeded to tend to Trevor's bleeding arm, while Dare worked as a nurse, helping to extract the bullet and wrap the wound up. Monica decided to seek out the Guardian, rather than staying to watch the "operation," and ended up finding the woman on a ledge, under a large outcropping of rocks. The shadowed area was cooler than that of the clearing, since the sun was striking the other side of the mountain at that time of day. She wasn't sure what to say, as Vectra sat there peacefully, her feet dangling over the cliff face. "Are you alright?"

Vectra quickly wiped away her tears, continuing to study the electrio blade, now depleted of all charge and only an empty hilt in her hands. Her face stared at the vast landscape sprawled out before her, taking in the odd tranquility she felt after the battle had sapped most of her energy. "He was right, you know. About there being another reason for us wanting him to kill Josephine. Not for what he believed it to be, but there was one, nonetheless." Monica didn't say a word as she sat beside her on the ledge, allowing the woman to tell her the story at her own pace.

"There was a rumor going around that Josephine was going to have us hunted down: Aisling, myself, and another one of our group. We had been stealing from her, like in the legend of Robin Hood; using the unsuspecting Martiban to learn information about where to strike next. So, we decided to take care of her first."

"No, Vectra, don't blame yourself for Martiban's choices." Monica tried comforting the Guardian. "He picked his fate, and was fully aware of what he had done. You gave him more chances, and was more of a loyal friend, than he ever deserved."

"Those words are kinder than what I have earned."

"You would not have been able to use those wings, if that was not true." The teen gazed at the dense fog gently covering the treetops, seeing an eagle flying majestically in the far off distance. "I have it written that only one of truth, valor, and honor, can wear the wings of strength more powerful than the blade, and as impenetrable as their intent." She cast a glance to the word imprinted in her skin like a tattoo.

"That was a very brave thing you did." Vectra slid the hilt into a pocket of her vest jacket. "Using the press to create something that was for the present, took a toll, did it not?"

"Yeah, Gregon explained that one to me." A smile formed on the teenager's lips. "I don't regret it one bit, though. And actually, I don't know how I just knew, but I had an idea of what I was doing when I made the decision."

"Did you feel it, then? When Gaither was evaporated in the flames?"

"Yeah, I did. It was a faint twinge of pain, almost like an ache from a past memory." Monica rubbed her fingers over the inked word, stamped in greek, realizing that she was now tethered to the press for as long as she lived. "Writer. How appropriate. Will I always be able to read and understand Ancient Greek?"

"Only when you are close to the press. Once it is moved to its new location, it will be as if nothing had ever happened." Vectra patted her on the shoulder. "For awhile, I was not sure whether you were going to do it or not. Change history so you could bring your parents back."

"Well, I thought about it. I would be lying if I didn't admit to that." Monica kicked her feet into the air. "But, I also thought about what Rudi told me, as well as what you had, and realized that without their passing, Trevor would not have come back like he did, and I would have been the only one to know what was. All the things we have done over the last seven years, would be like an alternate reality and I would feel like an alien within my own family."

"This may sound strange, Monica, but your parents would be proud of you, and your decision. Not many people realize what they have until it is too late."

The teen cast her a semi-smile, pondering whether or not she wanted to ask the woman a question that had been on the forefront of her mind. "Vectra, what really happened to my parents?"

"I had just reached the gorge, when I saw them on Charlie's Bridge, suspended between the trails on either side of a narrow section. As I looked up to where they were standing, Gaither was blocking their path on the southern end, while some of his men blocked off the northern end. They were given a choice, to either help him in finding the press, or he would kill you and your brother. Your father was already bleeding, having a deep gash in his leg." Vectra matched Monica's gaze as a deep pause consumed the space between them. "After looking toward one another, they wove their hands together, and your mother cut the ropes supporting the bridge, taking two of his men with them."

Monica felt tears coming to her eyes, picturing the scene as Vectra told it. "My parents knew that in order to save us, they had to die." She took in a deep breath. "Because, with them dead, we were Gaither's only lead to any clues they left behind."

Vectra gave the girl a slow nod of her head. "Every few years, I have to endure saving those piles of junk, from greedy pigs who want their powers for themselves, like Gaither. And over the years, I have lost good people who came in search of my aid to stop such evil. People I came to care for, people who share a part of their lives with me, and who they were inside. Each death was a fresh arrow piercing my heart; again, and again, and again. Until one day, I didn't feel anything when I stared into the face of another grave to dig. That scared me, Monica. More than I ever felt possible. Scared me into making the decision not to continue my job and risk my very soul to keep good people like your parents from making the same mistake."

"They left little kids alone, in a house by themselves, so I won't go giving them sainthood." Monica chuckled, in an attempt to lighten the mood.

"No, but I suspect that your parents had an inkling about the power you possessed." Vectra brushed the teen's hair back from her neck, exposing the birthmark for all to see. "And she didn't leave you alone." Monica looked up to see the rest of their group descending the mountainside trail to join them on the ledge. "I could not risk being caught by Gaither to help them, even if I had showed up earlier."

"I can see that now. So…is that why you didn't want Gregon to come along?"

"He is one of the last friends I have left. If his death was on my hands, I could not live with myself." Vectra clasped her fingers together, completely covering her palms, and then opened them up to reveal the origami wings Monica created with the press. "I believe that these are yours, My Lady."

But Monica kindly refused her offer. "They're for you. I have a feeling you will have more of a use for them in your world, than that of mine. Although, you never know with the way traffic is on the highway nowadays." They both had a laugh, hugging one another in a sisterly embrace. "What you said, around the campfire, back at your shipwreck of a home, is what inspired me to create those wings."

"I did?"

"Yeah, when you said 'If imagination gives you wings, my cynical nature is not where you want to fly,' it gave me the idea to use my imagination as it were."

"Thank you, Monica." Vectra whispered in her ear right before Dare, Trevor, and Gregon stepped up to them.

"Are you two finished gabbing yet?" Dare teased, poking his sister in the back and quickly jumping away from her returning blow.

"You had impeccable timing with throwing me the electrio blade, Gregon." Vectra's eyebrows raised, squinting at the Kurzian.

"Yeah, well, you know me. I like to wait to the last minute when it comes to helping. It is not as exciting the other way around." A small grin stretched across his face, as he tapped her on the shoulder with a playful fist. "You survived to fight another day, kid."

"Well, I would say that we should be getting back, but Dare tells me that the police are looking for us at home?" Trevor had an obvious reason to be concerned. "How are we going to explain any of this?"

"I think we can make something work out." Gregon winked at Vectra, who's mischievous look made the silent agreement.

"This *one* time, we can."

"Ah Vectra," Monica's voice was suddenly shyer and quieter than usual. "About the fact that I didn't change history…I might have tweaked it."

The Guardian's eyes nearly bugged out of her skull. "WHAT?!"

"It was nothing bad, and nothing that would have affected much." She quickly clarified. "All I did was go back to make sure that I caught sight of the face of the woman with the red hair, who gave the book to my mother on Halloween night."

"What if the woman has now seen you, Monica?" Vectra speculated. "You could be in grave danger."

"I took care of that, and made it so that she didn't. I wrote it so that I peered out from behind my mother's leg, and that she did not look down at me." Monica described. "I was precise with the wording, and I did nothing more than see her face."

"Then, dare I ask, who was she? Was she Ailsing?"

"Ailsing?" Gregon questioned, being hushed by Vectra's hand in the air.

Monica shook her head. "No. I never met this woman before. But I could identify her, if I ever saw her again."

"Well, thank you for trying, Monica." Vectra cast her a sincere smile.

"Will they be mad at you?" The teen's eyes shot up to the heavens, and then back to the Guardian in front of her. "The gods and goddesses, I mean?"

"Why would they be mad? She saved Clio's press, with our help I might add." Dare puffed out his chest and raised his head in a grand manner.

"Because Gaither had a splinter of the press in his finger when he was killed." Monica reminded.

"Vaporized, would be more like it." Trevor contributed. "And they would really care about a sliver, while the main unit is still intact? And working?"

"Like they have anything better to do?" Vectra shook her head. "Who knows. It is not as though I am one of their star pupils."

"That is an understatement." A female voice spoke up from the depths of a darkened wall, covered in green vines. They all flashed around to see Artenian step into the open as if there was a hidden passage behind the flourishing plants.

"You do not show up for years, and now, all of a sudden, I hear your name and receive an in-person visit from you in a matter of a fortnight. That is not ominous, is it?" Vectra sassed at the ghostly figure, looking as real as she did when Monica had dreamt about her.

"I can see that your hostility toward me has not softened any."

"Good guess." Vectra sprung up, not wishing for the old warrioress to see how weak she truly felt. "What do you want?"

"I came to check on how things had turned out."

"Oh, am I on some sort of probation?"

"Not yet." Artenian surveyed the group. "It appears as though things are well in hand. Hi, Gregon."

The Kurzian gave a small hello in return as Vectra stepped into the fellow warrior's space, their noses barely two finger widths apart. "I do not need your supervision. We both know how well that worked out the last time."

"That was not my doing. You knew the score, and still allowed yourself to be swayed. Though, I am pleased to find that you stood tall on this one. I am sorry that it came to this, between you and Martiban. I remember how many times you two fought side by side over the years."

"Thank you." Vectra's voice was hardened with skepticism and self-protection. "Anything else?"

"No. I must be going anyhow. The time is soon upon us to train another batch of Zodiac Warriors. Until we meet again, Vectra." Artenian returned to the curtain of vines and disappeared like a summer breeze at morning daybreak, leaving them nothing more than a quiet minute in her wake.

"Well, let us get out of the shadows and warm up while the sun is still in the sky." Gregon ushered the Browning siblings up the trail. "We must get camp set up before dark soon takes over."

The sound of their feet petered out the further they moved up the stony path, back to the clearing where Gears was supposed to arrive with help at dawn. Vectra did not join them, but rather stood there, listening for the sound of another's voice she sensed to be close by.

"Did you get it?" A Greek woman materialized on the same ledge of the cliffside, coming out from behind a strong oak tree instead of the vines like Artenian. Her red hair was woven in a singular braid, running down the back of her shortened toga, and ending at the top of her gladiator sandals. It was a weapon in its own right, and held a deadly secret within its leafy adornments.

Vectra turned to see the woman impatiently waiting for a response. "Here." She presented her with a strand of hair that was barely visible in the light sinking behind the outcropping rocks. "I figured you would be arriving shortly after she did, Onesta."

"Be careful with that hair." The woman gently plucked it from her grasp and placed it in a vile, sealing it under a water-tight lid. She then slid the precious bottle into a hidden pocket of her skirt, and lovingly patted it with her hand. "You did good. Keep this up, and you will be free very soon."

Vectra seethed with anger, throwing her a warning pair of deuces that boomed louder than she had predicted. "Do not DARE talk to me as if I were a child or a pet."

"You and your cousin! Watch your temper, Vectra." Onesta warned. "You might catch the attention of the Brownings, and I will feel obligated to tell them how Gaither found where their parents had gone." She took in great delight seeing the Guardian wriggle in her own skin. "Then I really would enjoy watching you try to explain to them how you fell into one of your own traps. Besides, now that I have what I need from Artenian, I do not have to hold up my end of the bargain with you. It is by my good graces, that I see it worthy of my time to deliver."

The Guardian was surprised by her statement. "Hmm. To be willing to break an Alethia Oath, in the house of Apollo, must be more valuable than your very soul." She studied the stoic face of her counterpart. "Whatever it is, I would wager that Artenian and the Celestial Warriors would not be too pleased to hear about it."

"You know nothing, and it would be better for you, and your new friends, if we kept it that way." Her words oozed with contempt and bristled in promise.

"Yes, it would. But hear me, Onesta. You are going to deliver me my freedom, elsewise, I tell the truth of what you did to become the leader of Artemis's Hunters."

The old warrior, whose age was deceptive behind young skin, did not take kindly to her promise, stepping forward in one large and threatening stride. "Who told you?"

"Never mind who. That is irrelevant, though the bottom

fact remains that I know. And if you wish to keep me silent on the matter, then you *will find* a way to free me from this fate."

"All in good time, my friend." Onesta swished her long braid to one side.

"We are not friends."

"That is right…you do not have any friends, correct? Do not waste your spitefulness on me, Vectra Tillerman. You knew what you were signing up for, the minute we spoke our agreement into existence." She turned to walk away, feeling no returning threat from Vectra, and gracefully stepped into the shadows of the tree, disappearing from view altogether. "We will be in contact."

"Vectra?" The ancient warrior frantically looked over her shoulder to see Dare rushing down the path in her direction. "We heard the explosion. Is everything alright?"

"It is fine." Vectra faked him a smile. "I was just blowing off some steam."

"You sure?"

The Guardian simply nodded. "Tell me, what does Gregon have for us to eat? Hopefully not some of his horrible mushrooms he goes foraging for."

Dare laughed. "You might want to skip dinner then." He took her hand, and led her up to the others, as storm clouds rolled over the mountain range with water-colored tones and a majestic presence across the vastness of the sky. For none of them, not even Martiban himself, had ever discovered that he shared the ancestral blood of King Arthur.

Epilogue

Darkening clouds loomed over the weeping willow, as Astrid cautiously approached her home. Her strength had been fading fast for the last half mile, as the remaining drop of her tree's sap touched her lips. Squirrels raced up the pine tree to her left, abnormally scared, when her presence would usually attract their attention and pull them close to her instead. *That is quite odd.*

An eerie feeling suddenly creeped up the nymph's spine, causing her to reach into the quiver on her back for an arrow, and string her bow at the ready. She crouched behind the large bush line near the stream's edge and tried to calm her unsettled nerves. Astrid took a deep breath, forcing her mind to focus, and popped up like a jackrabbit, poised to make her last stand.

"About time you showed up. I was worried that you had died from being so far from your tree for too long." A tall and thin man casually strolled in front of the arrow's tip, unconcerned with its lethal danger and the person behind its sharpened point. "Thought maybe I was going to have to come looking for you."

"Am I not in your debt enough as it is?" Astrid dropped

her shoulders and marched up the embankment. "I should have known it was you, Leander. Very few pass this way in the Summer, and no one comes at this time of the year. And that is without your trademarked haunting chill that is your cologne."

"Only one debt remains after that last little chore. We did work splendidly together that day; a wonderful performance that would have made the audiences cheer back home. Such a theatrical marvel at the fair. Though you almost gave us away with that final piece of information you let slip, *Mrs. Browning.*" Leander's deep voice gave Astrid a crawling sensation on her neck. "I think I must have picked up a few side effects from that job. Been seeing two faces in the mirror ever since we shared a cup of tea with them."

"And you almost started a fight with a street vendor, as I recall." She thought to herself for a fleeting moment. "Over a spittoon from the Midwestern United States, was it not? One good fist blow to your face, and the trick would have been ruined. All that work at assuming their identities…"

"Remind me, which one of your elk friends do you like the best?" His evil tease left a slimy residue in the air.

"Tell me what you want and then be on your way."

"I have come to claim my final debt owed to me."

The Celtic nymph flashed herself around and studied his eyes. She knew exactly what it meant when he looked to the left as he spoke. "No. I will not do it."

"Do what?"

"I am not going to kill anyone for you."

"How did you know I am going to ask for that?"

The nymph remained silent, her lips drawn in a line and her back tensed up. Leander's mouth broke into a sinister smile. "Ah, I would have bet my life that I made the right choice, and you have just confirmed it. She has taught you well."

"I have no idea as to what you are referring to." Astrid pushed him away and started for the stairs that led down into her underground house. "I am not a hired assassin."

"You will do this." Leander followed her, grabbing ahold of the nymph's arm and swinging her around to look at him once again. "It would be a shame if I had to call the Debt Collector, and report to him that you are reluctant to pay your dues." He snickered.

Astrid's face went cold as ice. "Who is the target?"

The older man smirked, removing the few wrinkles his cheeks carried. "I want you to kill my niece, Vectra Tillerman. Do that, and you are free of me...forever."

The End

Vectra Tillerman will be back in...
The Fall of Time

1. Were Giant Irish Elk real?

Yes, they were. The descriptions, including the span of their massive antlers, I have in this book, come from the estimated appearances for what they are believed to have looked like. I state it like this, because while their antlers have survived, only skeletal remains have been excavated in Ireland, as they have been deemed extinct for thousands of years.

2. Is there a difference between gnomes in mythology?

Depending on which culture you dive into, gnomes can be good or evil. The modern-day garden gnomes can be associated with the folklore of Ancient Greek or European origin, where they are seen as good protectors of plants and closely relate to the elements of nature. While in Swiss folklore, they like to wreak havoc. However, living underground and having magical powers are a common characteristic they share across tales.

3. Was Adalgard, Martiban's sister, a real person?

While her character is fictional, the basis of her background is quite real. Female monasteries did exist in the East Francia region of present day Germany, where a female skull had been discovered with Lapis Lazuli embedded in its teeth. During her time period, this material was used by highly skilled illustrators during the process of creating illuminated manuscripts. Its source was most likely Afghanistan, a known stop along the Silk Road, which was the place to go for such an invaluable pigment, whose worth outweighed that of gold.

For book discussion questions, more behind-the-scenes research, and art/book-ish news, please visit my website.

Did you like this story? Be sure to spread the word and tell your friends. And don't be afraid to post a review! Thanks in advance.

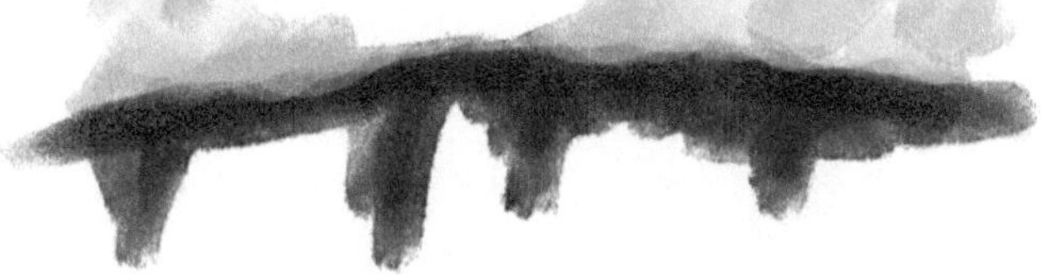

ABOUT THE AUTHOR:

Sarah Ickes has her Associates Degree in Arts and Design. She has always held a passion for writing since her first publication of a poem in fifth grade. Not only does she persue writing, but she also creates artwork that is available for purchasing, such as the illustrations and book cover of this story. Historical references and topics are a favorite of hers, since she loves learning about history. Please visit her website for more details or follow her on social media.

www.SarahIckesArt.com

Thank you for reading my novel and I hope you enjoyed it.